Alice Wandesford Thornton, Charles Jackson

The autobiography of Mrs. Alice Thornton of East Newton

Alice Wandesford Thornton, Charles Jackson

The autobiography of Mrs. Alice Thornton of East Newton

ISBN/EAN: 9783337118761

Printed in Europe, USA, Canada, Australia, Japan

Cover: Foto ©Raphael Reischuk / pixelio.de

More available books at **www.hansebooks.com**

THE

PUBLICATIONS

OF THE

SURTEES SOCIETY.

ESTABLISHED IN THE YEAR

M.DCCC.XXXIV.

VOL. LXII.

FOR THE YEAR M.DCCC.LXXIII.

THE
AUTOBIOGRAPHY

OF

MRS. ALICE THORNTON,

OF

EAST NEWTON, CO. YORK.

Alice Thornton;

Published for the Society

BY ANDREWS AND CO., DURHAM;

WHITTAKER AND CO., 13 AVE MARIA LANE;
BERNARD QUARITCH, 15 PICCADILLY;
BLACKWOOD AND SONS, EDINBURGH.

1875.

At a Meeting of the Surtees Society, held in Durham Castle, on Tuesday, June 2nd, 1874, Mr. Robinson in the Chair,

It was Ordered, "That the Autobiography of Mrs. Thornton of East Newton should be edited for the Society by Mr. Charles Jackson."

JAMES RAINE,

Secretary.

Mitchell and Hughes, Printers, 24 Wardour Street, London, W.

THE PREFACE.

The autobiography which is now for the first time given to the world through the medium of the Surtees Society, is a specimen of a kind of family history which lies hid, we believe, among the archives of many of our ancient houses ; concealed there, partly because it touches upon matters of domestic concern, and partly because, in the opinion of its owner, the trivial subjects or the devotional aspirations which such volumes generally record ought not to be brought out into the full glare of day. We can appreciate this feeling, although we cannot concur with it. Works like the present, from their intrinsic merit, have a right to be considered *publici* as well as *privati juris.* Do to them as Archbishop Matthew wrote on the title of one of his favourite tomes, as a hint to its future possessor, *Lege, Relege, Perlege.*

Alice Wandesford (afterwards Thornton), the author of this volume, was born at Kirklington in the southern part of Richmondshire, in February, 1626–7.* The village of Kirklington lies a few miles to the north of Ripon, in a beautifully undulating country, somewhat low, indeed, as in a basin, but surrounded by rich pastures and woodlands. An ancient church, built in the fourteenth century, is an ornament to the village ; and there is a hall, erected in the time of Henry VII., which, although somewhat in decay, has evidently been the residence of a family of distinction and substance. Thither came in the fourteenth century, through an alliance with the heiress of Musters, the

* Page 2.

race of Wandesford, which enriched itself still farther in the days of Henry VIII. by a double marriage into the house of Fulthorpe. This gave them many additional acres, and a new mansion at Hipswell, on the southern bank of the Swale, between Catterick and Richmond. A fragment of the old hall, decorated with the armorial bearings of the Fulthorpes, may still be seen.

Christopher Wandesford, Mrs. Thornton's father, was a person of no ordinary character and ability. The filial piety of his daughter drew up a memorial of his life, which seems, unhappily, to have disappeared; not, however, before one of his descendants drew from it a few graphic pictures which make us regret the more the loss of the remainder.* Mr. Wandesford's portrait, which is still extant, represents a fair, oval-faced man, with a sanguine complexion and auburn hair; a face in contour somewhat resembling that of the unfortunate Charles, and such as Vandyke loved to perpetuate on his canvass. We see a noble gentleman of a very comely presence and bearing, and this Mr. Wandesford undoubtedly was. He had a good estate in spite of his father's extravagance, and this he considerably augmented without being in any sense penurious. In his domestic virtues he was a model for all. He was a man of strict religious principle and honour, with the keenest sense of what duty and his position demanded. But, more than this; he proved himself a statesman of repute, in an age when statesmen were numerous. The great Earl of Strafford was his cousin, and drew his kinsman, who had been his intimate companion, into that world of politics of which he was so fond. Wandesford accompanied his friend and patron to Ireland, where he became Lord Deputy,

---

* Written by the Rev. Thomas Comber, and alluded to before. Dr. Whitaker, in his History of Richmondshire, gives a very admirable sketch of Mr. Wandesford's life and character.

acquiring a noble position and estate. Had his life been prolonged, he would in all probability have been rewarded with a peerage, to which his grandson was raised. He died at an early age, killed, it was believed, by hard work, and grief at Strafford's misfortunes and the evil condition of the realm.

Mr. Wandesford's wife was Alice, daughter of Sir Hewett Osborne, whose father, through a romantic adventure,* became one of the wealthiest citizens of London. Sir Hewett was a valiant soldier. He increased his estate by marrying a Fleetwood, by whom he was the sire of Sir Edward Osborne, vice-president of the Council in the North, a gentleman of singular intelligence and wisdom. Sir Edward's sister became Mr. Wandesford's wife. To say that she was worthy of her husband is but slight praise. On his decease she brought her children from Ireland into Yorkshire, not without adventures by the way. For a while they resided at Kirklington; afterwards at Hipswell, the dowager-house of the family. The home education of the children had been of the strictest and most exemplary kind. Father and mother had combined to devote themselves to their good, and few households, probably, even in those days of parental care, were so thoroughly imbued with the principles and practice of religion. Thrice in each day, at six, ten, and nine o'clock in the evening, the family met together for devotion. The mother assembled her children every morning before breakfast, hearing them pray, and read or repeat Psalms and chapters of the Bible, and then they knelt for her blessing. The tenderness with which her daughter speaks of her† in after days shews how deeply seated in her heart was the recollection of her happy childhood. The good father observed them all

---

* Collins's Peerage of England, 1812 ed., 253. Hunter's South Yorkshire, i., 142.

† Pp. 100—122.

with the keenest and most affectionate solicitude. For the
guidance of his eldest son he wrote down a series of instructions for his conduct,* which shew that their author was not
only a man of shrewd, worldly wisdom, but a person of the
highest religious excellence as well. The child for whose wel-
fare Mr. Wandesford was so anxious did not live long enough
to carry these exhortations into practice; but the rules which
he laid down for his guidance have always been cherished by
the members of his family as one of their most precious heirlooms. The example that the father set was not in vain, when
it produced such fruits as the home virtues of his daughters
and the pious munificence of his grandchild, Mary Wandesford
of York.†

The father died, but the mother lived on to carry out his
wishes and continue his affection to their children. It was at
Hipswell that she chiefly resided, and there, for the most part,
Mrs. Thornton grew up to womanhood. She tells us in her
book some of the incidents and adventures of her youth, among
which the death of her eldest brother is most pathetically described.‡   Her matrimonial projects and perils are also related.
They terminated in 1651, in a marriage with William Thornton
of East Newton in Ryedale.§   With this portion of Mrs. Thornton's life we are principally concerned.

For more than three centuries the family of Thornton had
occupied a fair position among the minor gentry of the North
Riding of Yorkshire. In the reign of Edward II. a member of
it married an heiress who brought with her the name and estate
of East Newton. West Newton, an old property of the Cholmleys, with its ancient chapel and manor-house, lies at a little
distance, in the parish of Oswaldkirk. East Newton is situated

* P. 187.   † See her will, p. 323.
‡ P. 57.   § Pp. 75—82.

a little under the ridge which divides the vale of Mowbray from Ryedale. Ascend a few hundred yards, and you see Oswaldkirk and Stonegrave beneath you, with the noble woods and castle of Gilling, backed by the round hill of Brandesby with its tuft of trees, on the other side across the deep hollow below you; whilst the eye passes on to Hovingham and the beautiful villages which nestle under the opposite bank. Turn around, and go a short distance towards the north, and you are on the verge of a softer and more widely spreading landscape. You see the Rye winding amid woods and pasture-land, and beyond it are Helmsley and Kirkby Moorside, with half a score of hamlets lying between you and the heather-clad hills in the distance. You are on the edge of a magnificent basin, ornamented by Nature's most lavish hand. On this edge East Newton lies, itself on undulating ground, terminating in rounded hills to the east and south, and sloping gently northwards. The hamlet consists of a few houses clustering around the remnant of an ancient hall. In this many a generation of Thorntons was reared. The most conspicuous person in the family is the collector and transcriber of a number of English romances and verses, preserved in the library of Lincoln cathedral,* of which in modern times great use has been made. Until the beginning of the seventeenth century the family seems to have clung to the Roman Catholic faith. What induced them to desert it we do not at present know; probably it was the persecution to which the Romanists were subjected. We may be sure that the Thorntons would be closely watched, as they were allied by marriage with the Wrights of Plowland in Holderness, who had

* Some notes on the fly-leaves connect this volume with the family of East Newton. I do not think with Mr. Perry that Robert Thornton, archdeacon of Lincoln, had anything to do with it. From the fact that Dean Comber, in his MS. pedigree of the Thorntons, mentions one of the notes on a fly-leaf, I am disposed to think that the MS. was in his time preserved at East Newton.

a share in the Gunpowder plot. There was a chapel also at East Newton, dedicated to St. Peter,* which it was the great ambition of Mrs. Thornton to restore. Saturated as she was with the religious principle, it would have been a delight to her to have a shrine so near in which she could daily worship. Her husband in this respect would not enter into her feelings. The revulsion from Roman-catholicism made him a moderate Presbyterian, a belief which his brother-in-law, Mr. Denton, would encourage, and Mr. Comber check. Had he lived, Mr. Thornton would have become a devoted Churchman.

Soon after the youthful couple came into Ryedale they began to make great alterations in their house.† Hitherto it seems to have consisted of a block standing north and south ; to the east of this they erected a similar building, joined to the other by passages above ground and below. In the new work were several handsome rooms. To the older part they made additions, throwing out windows, and altering the exterior as well as the inside. The whole must have formed a very comfortable home for a Yorkshire gentleman. At the present day that part of the house which Mr. Thornton built is given up to the purposes of the farm. The other is the residence of the tenant. Long passages, a noble kitchen chimney, several nicely wainscotted rooms, and a large four-post bed with fading hangings of yellow, carry you back to the days of the Thorntons. On the outside is the chapel-croft, the site of a building which has disappeared, the remains of an avenue, and a garden. At the entrance into the grounds stands what is called a summer-house, of brick, somewhat resembling a tower, in which, as tradition

---

* 5 February, 1397-8. Robertus Thorneton de Neuton licentiam habet celebrandi missas in capella in villa de Neuton, durante sedis vacatione (Reg. Dec. et Capit. Ebor. sede vacante).

† Pp. 131, 134.

asserts, Dean Comber wrote his *Companion to the Temple*. Here, surrounded by his books, he could enjoy a hermit's privacy, whilst outside there were the bracing air and the charming scenery of Ryedale to bring back the colour into his pale, consumptive cheeks.

In this quiet retreat, in the midst of green fields, a mile from any village or house of equal repute, Mrs. Thornton ended her days. Her wedded life was only of short duration. Her husband, who had long been in infirm health, died in 1668.* He was a weak, improvident man, but his widow always looked back to him with affectionate regret. Many a lady in her situation would have fixed her residence in some neighbouring town, but Mrs. Thornton's straitened circumstances, as well as her own love for solitude, made her cling more keenly to her husband's home. She came to East Newton in 1662,† and never left it until she was carried to her grave in Stonegrave church in the winter of 1706-7. Solitude this was in one sense, yet the good lady was not without visitors of her own rank and condition. By the neighbouring clergy and the poor, " Madam Thornton," as she was called, was consulted and honoured. She had always the care of her children and dependents; and, better than all, she had resources within, more used then than at present, for which, even in those days of religious exercises and discipline, she seems to have been distinguished. As far as we know, Mrs. Thornton moved but little from her home. Retirement suited her disposition, and brought her into closer contact with the past, in which she delighted to dwell. The short and happy days of her youth came back to her, followed by the misfortunes which began with her marriage and ended only with her death—the loss of her children, the carelessness

* P. 175.   † P. 134.

of her husband, her many pecuniary embarrassments, and the unkindness of relatives and friends—the constant presence of all these trials in memory or reality sobered and saddened her life. The book itself which she wrote must tell part of her mournful story. To give even a summary of its contents would take away from the pathos which runs through it.

The cause of writing this autobiography was no doubt one personal to Mrs. Thornton herself. It was chiefly to rebut slander and vindicate her own good name. Like many a lady of good birth and fortune, Mrs. Thornton must have experienced some disappointment in the means and position of her husband. They were scarcely answerable to her expectations, and she was, besides, unfortunate enough to be deprived of the greater part of her own inheritance. Thus for more than fifty years she had a struggle with poverty. Her affairs too were occasionally mismanaged, and she was anxious to clear herself from reproach. She had also to contend with one or two cruel slanderers; and to shew to her descendants that she had neither tarnished an honourable name, nor wasted her means by improvidence, she committed to paper the record of her earlier life.

The book is that of a true daughter, wife, and mother. Affection and piety pervade it. The memory and the example of her parents were always uppermost in her thoughts. She never forgets that she is a lady by birth, but it is the inheritance of virtue that she is mainly anxious to commend and perpetuate. It is plain to see how devoted she was to her husband, although by his carelessness and weakness he might at times have been censured with justice. But the true woman shines out when she speaks of her children. Their little ailments, and acts, and words, detailed every now and then with a minuteness which may provoke a smile, were to the affectionate mother the main incidents in her life. She was so bound up with their troubles and joys that she carries the reader along with her, and every one must regret that a life so sensitive and loving should have had so large a share of suffering and death. Still she knew from Whom everything came, and submits herself to every dispensation of Providence with true Christian resignation.

Mrs. Thornton's autobiography ends with the year 1669; it is from the diary and letters* of Dean Comber, her son-in-law, that we gain some information about the long remnant of her life. Three of her children, two daughters and a son, grew up to maturity. The son, a child of many hopes and prayers, went to the University, and took Holy Orders, but he got into debt, and died in early middle age under his sister's roof at Durham,† to the unspeakable grief of his mother in Yorkshire. He was the last male heir of his line. The inheritance that should have been his devolved upon his two sisters, the elder of whom, the wife of Dean Comber, was her mother's chief comfort and stay; the younger by an ill-assorted marriage on two occasions brought debt and misery on her family at home. In 1700 Dean Comber died, and was laid in the grave at Stonegrave,‡ of which parish he had continued to be the rector. In 1703 his son William followed him. It seemed as if Mrs. Thornton was to survive every relative that she possessed. She lived on in her husband's house at East Newton, surrounded by worn-out and yet familiar furniture, dispensing her charities out of her scanty estate, and preparing herself for the great change that was to come. She died in 1707, and was buried beside her husband in their aisle at Stonegrave. The monument which she set

---

* A selection from these papers, which are of considerable interest, is being prepared for publication by the Surtees Society.

† See pp. 303 *n.*, 344.   ‡ See his will, p. 330.

up in his memory, in the shape of a hatchment, with an inscription painted on canvass,* hangs still against the wall. Over her own grave, on the floor, was a stone with nothing upon it save ALICE THORNTON, 1706.

Mrs. Thornton's last will and testament, from which large extracts have been given, is a faithful picture of her principles and character. An early draft of it is in existence, shewing that the document had been long brooded over, and changed and amended. It is probable that the scantiness of the good lady's means made it impossible for her executors to carry out her wishes to the full. The domestic chapel at East Newton was never rebuilt. It was only within the last twenty years that the Thornton aisle at Stonegrave was properly restored and arranged. It was then almost distinct from the church with which it is now incorporated, and at a much higher level than the floor of the nave. Some of the fittings and ornaments which Mrs. Thornton bequeathed to the use of the church are still remembered.

Mr. Comber has in his possession a portrait of his ancestress, Mrs. Thornton. The picture is not a striking one. It represents a middle-aged lady, clad in widow's weeds, which she probably wore to the end of her days after the decease of her husband. In mediæval times she would have been a vowess.

The manuscript, from which this volume is drawn, is in the possession of the lineal descendant of Dean Comber and one of Mrs. Thornton's daughters, the Rev. Henry George Wandesford Comber, M.A., Rector of Oswaldkirk. Mr. Comber has placed it at the disposal of the Surtees Society in the kindest and most unrestricted manner. It consists of three small

* P. 342.

volumes bound in brown leather, closely written in a small hand, which it is not always easy to decypher. In size, the two first volumes are five inches by three, containing respectively 303 and 291 pages; the third is seven inches by five, containing 216 pages. These three are amplifications of a more tiny book, which has been kindly lent to the Editor by Mr. Thomas Comber, of Newton-le-Willows, another descendant of the Dean.

All these volumes are in Mrs. Thornton's handwriting, but it is evident from the very numerous repetitions which they contain, that they were written at different periods. These repetitions are so considerable, that it has been found necessary not only to make omissions, but to transpose passages here and there, to preserve to a certain extent the chronological sequence of events. Everything, however, has been inserted that is of any interest and value, and the Editor has taken every care to do justice in this respect to the manuscript, and to assist the reader who peruses the work. The plan which he has adopted is the same that was made use of by the Rev. Charles Best Norcliffe, who made a transcript of the Autobiography many years ago, which he has very kindly placed at the Editor's disposal. For this and other assistance, freely and generously rendered, the Editor tenders to Mr. Norcliffe his sincere thanks. He desires also to express his obligations to the Secretary of the Society for his very kind assistance; and to the Rev. Augustus White Wetherall, rector of Stonegrave, for much valuable information derived from the Registers of his parish.

C. J.

July 26th, 1875.

AUTOBIOGRAPHY

OF

MRS. ALICE THORNTON.

A PREFACE TO THE BOOKE.

For as much as it is the dutie of every true Christian to remember and take notice of Allmighty God our Heavenly Father's gracious acts of Providence over them, and mercifull dealings with them, even from the wombe, untill the grave burie them in silence, as also to keepe perticuler remembrances of His favours, both spirituall and temporall, together with His remarkable deliverances of theire soules and bodies, with a true and unfeined gratitude to His glorious Majestie for them all : I therefore, His creature and unworthy handmaide, who have not tasted (only) of the droppings of His dew, but has bin showred plentifully upon my head with the contineued streames of goodness, doe most humbly desire to furnish my heart with the deepe thoughts and apprehensions and sincere meditations of and thankefullnesse for His free grace, love, mercys, and inconceavable goodness to me His poore creature, even from my first beginning ; and, with a most cordiall and sincere heart, thankefully doe returne Him the glory of all; first—

For my birth and baptizme in the name of the most Holy Trinitye; my strict education in the true faith of the Lord Jesus Christ by my deare and pieous parents, through whoes caire and precepts I had the principles of grace and religion instill'd into me with my milke. Therefore shall I begin with the first mention of my deliverances that presents itselfe under the notion of my first knowledge and remembrance which are most worthy of perpetuall memmorie, and which I hope shall not end with this life, but spring up in my soule to an eternity of haleluias of praise and thankesgiveings to the Blessed Trinitie for ever. Amen. Amen.

Alice Wandesford, the fifth childe of Christopher Wandesforde, Esq., late Lord Deputy of Ireland, was borne at Kirklington in the county of Yorke the thirteenth day of February, beeing on a Munday, about two of the clock in the afternoone, in the yeare 1626; baptized the next day. The wittnesses were Mr. Lassells,* minister of Kirklington, Mrs. Anne Norton, and Mrs. Best (i., 5).

* Roger Lassells was rector of Kirklington from May 19, 1590, until he died. In the parish-register of Kirklington there is this entry about him—

"Mr. Roger Lascells, person of Kirklington, aged 73 yeares compleate, and having continued a most relligious and faithfull pastor ther the space of 40 yeares, departed this life Julye the 21st, and was interred the 22nd.

  In perpetuam ejusdem memoriam epitaphium.
  Scripta Sacrata probant, æterna memoria justi est.
  Vives ore hominum vivus in arce Dei.
    Anglice.
  The just's remembrance lasts for aye, so saith the worde,
  Then live with men thou ever, whoe livest with the Lorde.
    Dixit Radulphus Cotesius.

Mrs. Anne Norton was Anne Wandesford, wife of Mauger Norton of Clowbeck and St. Nicholas, near Richmond.

Mrs. Best was probably, Olive Mallory, wife of Thomas Best of Middleton Quernhow, M.P. for Ripon 1615.

KIRKLINGTON, 1629.*

*Uppon my deliverance from death by a fall when I was three
years old, when I cutt a great wound in my forehead of
above an inch long.*

My father and mother liveing at Kirklington† where I was
borne, and my brother Christopher‡ allso, the same maide-
servant attended uppon him, and was his day nurse (Sara
Tomlinson), which kept me affter I was weaned, beeing likewise
both nurrsed by one wett nurse (though uppon haveinge a fresh
milke, she had a childe betwixt the nurrsing my brother and
myselfe; and haveing bin very good and cairefull of the first
child, my parents saw it fitt she should nurrse the second child,
too, discharging that duty soe well to me). I heard it observed
that I was both a strong and healthfull childe all a long, never
haveing had either the ricketts or any other disease, for which
I most humbly and heartily give thankes to the God of my
salvation, which still had His gracious eye of Providence over
me both at my birth, when my deare mother§ brought me
forth in great perrill of her life, she beeing weake uppon the
birth of all her children, haveing had seaven in all, four sons
and three daughters. Yett the Lord gave me a sound healthfull
body, streight limbes, and of a resonable understanding, praised
be His glorious name for ever! Yett has His goodness bin
more extended to me in this and all other preservations that I
might not forgett His mercys for ever; and that hath manny
ways of the extent of His favours to young infants in there
deliverances from death and destruction in this world, besides
that of sickenesses and weakness of body, for if His Divine

---

* ' A recollection of memmorable accidents and passages forgotten to be entred
into my booke. This must be placed in the first place.' (Vol. i., 286).

† A parish in the Union of Bedale, North Riding of Yorkshire. See account
of it, with pedigree of the Wandesfords in *Whitaker's History of Richmondshire.*
(Vol. ii., pp. 139—164.

‡ A notice of the family of Mrs. Thornton will be found in the Preface or
Appendix.

§ Alice, daughter of Sir Hewett Osborne, of Kiveton, co. York, knight.

Providence did not send His angeles to keepe and guard little children, they could not continue nor be preserved from all evill accidents and casualtys incident to that feble and weake estate of infants and childchoods. For although there innocency be not capable of offending others, yett that innocency and harmlessness is not able to defend them from injurious dealings from evill persons, neglects and brutishness of nurrses, and cairelesness of others, not to mention those infinitt hazards of overlaying, and badness of there food and evil milk ; added to the dreadfull malice of Satan, who doth by all meines endeavour to destroy mankinde, setts on worke all his engines against us by more designes then we can see or be capable to understand. Therefore am I for ever bound to blesse the etternall name of God, who hath sent His guardian angell to watch over me and mine for my good preservation ever since I was borne. The number of His miraculous deliverances are past finding out, yett will I call to mind what I can, that He might receave the glory of all.

There was now a most great preservation to me when I was but a little childe, and was following my maide, Sara Tomlinson, who caired my brother Christopher in her armes, and I tooke hold of her cote. My weake hand, beeing but about three yers old, could not goe soe fast affter her, but I stumbled against the thrachhold and fell uppon the corner-stone of the harth in the chamber called the passage chamber, which leads to my deare mother's bed-chamber. At which time I broke the scull of my forehead in the very top against the said rowbe so greivously about an inch long, in soe much that the skin of the braine was scene, and in great danger of death, beeing like to have bleed to death, it beeing soe desperate a wound. But by the Providence of God, and my deare mother's skill and caire of me, she did make a perfect cure, only a great scarre still remaines, and will never be gon, to putt me in fresh mind of my great obligations to and deliverance of Almighty God for my life. How hath my forgettfull soule lett this mercy slip out of mind, and not remembred to give the Lord His praises due to His name ! Butt now, O my soule, returne thy

solemne thankes and praises to this great and gracious God,
Who hath had mercy and compassion both on thee when thou
wast a poore weake infant, and brought thee to these yeares
through infinitt more dangers. To the Lord my God, therefore,
doe I poure out my soule in humble gratitude for this great
preservation in the beginning of my daies, beseeching Him to
accept of me now His hand-maide both to serve Him and praise
Him for ever; and with all my might doe I sing praises to His
glorious name, Who hath had the same pitty and compassion,
both as a tender and deare parent and gardian. O lett Thy
Providence still goe along with me all my daies, and that Thy
angell gardians may defend me with Thy sheild to preserve me
from precipic or falls or dislocation incident to this life, who
now growes in my later age even almost a child in strength.
Leave me not nor forsake me, who has non to depend on but
Thee the Lord of mercys, Who hath made and upholden me
ever since I was borne. Bring me into that state of innocency
of soule, by a conversion truly into that state of grace, that I
may freely beare Thy trialls and beleive Thy promises, that
through them I may at the last be conducted into the land of
etternal rest, there to sing and praise Thy holy glorious name
and holy Trinity for ever and ever. Amen and Amen.

Another Deliverance (i., 8).

The second deliverance of that kinde was in the yeare 1630,
when I was left at Richmond under the caire and deare love of
my beloved aunt Norton,* uppon my father and mother's
goeing to London. It pleased God to bring me into a very
dangerous weakenesse and sicknesse, uppon an accident of a
surfitt, by eating some beefe which was not well boiled; this

---

* Anne, wife of Mauger Norton, of Clowbeck, and St. Nicholas, near Richmond, co. York, Esq., sister of her father. At the time of the Visitation in 1665,
Mr. Norton was residing at the latter place, which is a picturesque old house
perched on the hill to the north-east of the town of Richmond. It is doubtful
whether he was even the tenant of it in 1630.

causeing an extreame vomitting, whoes violence drove me into
great feauer, and that into the meassellss, and both brought me
so low and weake that my aunt and Sarah Tomlinson (our
maide) allmost dispaired of my life. But it pleased the Lord
my God in great mercy to heare the hearty praiers and requests
of my aunt for me, that I was spaired from death at that time,
and by His blessing uppon the use of good meanes was
recovered of my health perfectly againe. Oh, that I may grow
in grace, and in the knowledge of Jesus Christ our Lord,
beeing a comfort to my deare parents and relations. And that
I may dedicate my childehood, youth, middle and old age (if
He shall spaire me so long) to His service and praise, yea, even
to my live's end, and that for my Saviour's sake alone, the
Alpha and Omega. Amen. I was about five yeares old then.

A Preservation in the Smale-Pox, 1631 (i., 9).

Beeing removed to London by my father's order, with my
brother Christopher, I fell into the smale pox, haveing taken
them of him. Both of us was sent into Kent, where we lodged
at one Mr. Baxter's, beeing kindly usd with much caire in
that house ; and by the blessing of God I recovered very soone,
nor was I very ill at that time. I therefore will praise the
Lord our God for my preservation, that did not suffer that
dissease to rage or indanger my life, but raised me soone
again. O set forth His goodnesse for ever. Amen.

The first dawning of God's Spirit in my heart, London, 1631
(i., 10).

After this it pleased God to come into my soule by some
beames of His mercy, in putting good thoughts into my mind,
to consider His great and miraculous power in the creation of
the heavens, the earth, and all the hosts of them. I was
moved to this meditation upon the reading of the dailie
psalmes for the months, happening that day to be Psalm cxlvii.

v. 4th :—" He counteth the starres and calleth them all by theire names." From whence there came into my heart a forceable consideration of the incomprehencable power and infinite majestie of Allmighty God, Who by His wisdome made all things in heaven and earth, bceing above all His creatures in the world; knoweing what is in man, and searching all theire waies ; seeing my heart and thoughts, and knew allso that I was but a childe both in age and understanding, and not able to doe any thing that was good, which strooke me into a deepe feare and great awe of His glorious majestie, least I should offend Him at any time by sin against Him or my parents, and He would punish all sinnes, were they never so manny as the starres ; yet He was as well able to keepe an account and punish for them as to tell the starres and give them names. This, with other the like meditations of His omnipotency and greatness, and that He out of His love made man, did so move my heart that it caused in me a sincere love to Him for His goodnesse to me, His poore creature, whom my Creator had made to serve Him heere, and to take us up to heaven when we die, and crowne us with glory. Giveing Him my hearty thankes for His great and perticuler love and favour to me, a little childe, in giveing understanding and reason to know there is a God that ruleth in heaven and earth, and doeth whatever He will, and to reward them that serves Him truly with joy in heaven that should never end. Amen.

A Deliverance from a Fire in London, 1631 (i., 11).

There was a great fire in the next house to ours in St. Martin's Lane in London, which burned a part of our house, bceing neare to have burnt it downe, but through the caire of our servants it was prevented. This was don at night, when my father and mother was att Court; but wee were preserved that time of fright at my Lady Levestone's house, being caried by Sara, our maide. This fire seemed to me as if the day of judgment was come, causeing much feare and trembling ; yet

we were all delivered from perishing, though my father had
much losse.   But blessed be the Lord my God, Who gave us
not over to perish by this fire, but preserved our persons from
evill at that time.

My Mother's goeing into Ireland, 1632 (i., 12).

It pleased God to give my deare mother, my two younger
brothers, and myselfe a safe passage into Ireland about the
yeare 1632, my father being there a yeare before, and my
eldest brother George.   In which place I injoyed great eassie-
nesse and comfort dureing my honoured father's life, haveing
the fortunate opportunity in that time, and affter when I staied
there, of the best education that kingdome could afford,
haueing the advantage of societie in the sweet and chaste
company of the Earle of Strafford's daughter, the most virtuous
Lady Anne,* and the Lady Arbella Wentworth,† learning those
qualities with them which my father ordered, namlie,—the
French language, to write and speake the same; singing;
danceing; plaieing on the lute and theorboe; learning such
other accomplishments of working silkes, gummework, sweet-
meats, and other sutable huswifery, as, by my mother's vertuous
provision and caire, she brought me up in what was fitt for her
qualitie and my father's childe.   But above all things, I
accounted it my cheifest happinesse wherein I was trained in
those pieous, holy, and religious instructions, examples, admonitions, teachings, reproofes, and godly education, tending to
the welfaire and eternall happinesse and salvation of my poore
soule, which I receaved from both my honoured father and
mother, with the examples of theire chast and sober, wise and
prudent conversations in all things of this world.   For which

* Lady Anne Wentworth, born Oct., 1627; m. 24 Nov., 1654, to Edward
Watson, 2nd Baron Rockingham, grandfather of Thomas, Marquess of Rockingham.

† Lady Arabella Wentworth, born Oct., 1630; m. Justin Macarty, son of
Donagh, Earl of Clancarty, and died s. p.

things, and infinitly more opportunitys of good to my well-beeing than I can expresse, I render my uttmost capacity, etc. Therefore doe I most humbly and heartily acknowledg my bounden duty of thankes and praise to the great God of heaven and earth, from whence comes every good and perfect gift, Who is the author and finisher of our faith, that He has put such good things into my honoured parents' hearts to bring us up in the feare of the Lord. Next, I humbly acknowledge my faithfull thankes and gratitude to my deare and honoured parents for theire love, caire, affection, and sedulity over me from my birth till this present, and for theire good performances towards my education in all things. Begging of God to give me the grace of the meanes, as well as the meanes of His grace afforded me, that so I may walke in all holie and strict obedience, in Thy lawes and theire precepts, according to all the goodnesses of God and theires, performing my cordiall duty to them in all godlynesse and honnesty, obeying my parents in the Lord to the end of my life. Amen.

A great Deliverance from Drowning in Ireland by a Fall out of the Coach as my Mother and us Children was going to Killdare, riding by the Coach, October 6th, 1636 (i., 288).

As my deare mother (my honoured father rideing by the coach), myselfe, and brothers George, Christopher, and John was goeing in the coach to see Kildare, after my father bought it, there was a narrow place we were to passe, by a river side. Joseph Browning beeing the coachman—a very cairefull man—yett could not avoy that way, being none other to take; but for seeing the apparent danger of falling, by Providence he rather chose to throw the coach on the right hand towards the dry land, uppon a banke side, which did hurt some of us, than to fall on the left hand, there beeing a great river close by the coach, which, if we had gon down on that side, it had bin impossible we could have bin saved, any of us, but all in the coach and horses had bin utterly lost and perished in that deepe river. My father did ride on horsebacke, but by reason of the narrow way could not make any assistance, nor his men, to helpe us in that danger, but was much affreyed att the sudaine accident. But when he saw the coach fell from the river did much rejoyce, and glorified God with us for all preservations.

A great deliverance from a Second Fall att Sir Robert Meridethe, in Dublin, in Ireland, 1637 (i., 290).

My Lady Anne Wentworth and Lady Arbella, with cozen Anne Hutton,* Mrs. Anne Loftus,† and my selfe, beeing invited to dinner to Sir Robert Meridethe to dine, the ladies ussing the costome to swing by the armes for recreation, and being good to exercize the body of children in growing, it was ordered by my Lady Straford they should doe it moderately, and found good in it, soe that they used to swing each other gently to that purpose. They would make me, beeing a young girle, doe the same with them ; and I did soe, and could hold very well by the armes as they did, and had never gott noe hurt by it, I blesse God, but found it did me good. But att this time, very unfortunately, some of the young ladies bid one of the pages (calld Don de Lan), a French boy, that he should swing me, being stronger than they, and they weary with play. But I cryed out, desireing them not to bid him, but could not gett off soe soone from him, and deliver my selfe from danger, before he had came to me. He immediately pushed me soe violently from him with all his force, as I was swinging by my armes, that I was not able to hold my hands on the swing, soe that he throwed me downe upon the chamber bords. I fell downe upon my face, fell to the grownd, and light with such a violent force with all my weight on my chinn-bone uppward,

* One of the family of Hutton, of Marske, who was connected with Mrs. Thornton through the Bowes's.

† Probably a daughter of Sir Adam Loftus, Lord Chancellor of Ireland, 1619, created Viscount Ely, 1622.

that both the chinn and chapp-bones was almost brok in sunder,
and putt the bone out of its place, and did raise a great lumpe
as bigg as an egge under my chinn and throte, which sudainly
astonished me, and tooke away my breath in soe much as I was
nigh death; thcy thought I had bin dead for a good space of
time, till by the great mercy and power of my gratious God, I
came to my selfe againe uppon the use of good meanes. The
whole house was conserned for my distresse and this sad
accident, butt much more my deare Lady Anne, that her page
should doe soe greatt a mischefe to me. At length it pleased
God I came to my selfe again, but a long time ere I knew any
body, beeing in great paine and extreamity, beeing kept there
till night before I could be able to goe home. But comming
home to my deare mother she was surprized to see that sad
misfortune befallen to me, though (blesse God Almighty) she
applied such good means as did recrute me after a long time,
beeing soe bad. But, oh! what great cause have I to cast my
selfe downe att the feete of the great and dreadful Lord God,
who am but dust and ashes, made by His power, and preserved
by His Providence ever since I was borne, and has delivered
me this time soe wonderfully from a sudaine and violent death,
eaven when I was in a childish sport or play, or what ever it
was then, O Lord my God, which did deliver me both now and
att all times of my life; therefore will I give all thanks and
praise for ever with my soule and body and speritt for ever.
Although I was not willing to swing at this time, yet did Thou
deliver me. Lord, make me thankfull for ever, and that I may
never forgett this mercy to glorify Thy great name, and that I
may still be preserved to live to Thy glory in life and conversation for Jesus Christ his sake, to whom be praise for ever
more. Amen and Amen.

A dreadfull fire in the Castle of Dublin, 1638 (i., 292).

About three yeares before my noble Lord of Straford his
death, there happned a great and dreadful fire in the castell of

Dublin, which did goe nigh to have burned it downe, and destroyed it to the ground, had it not bin prevented by Providence, there being some up in the other part of the court where Sir George Ratclif's * lodgings was, which saw it, and cryed out for helpe; bceing at the dead time of the night it was very terrible to behold. It began upon the account of a maide-servant setting a dust-baskett of charcole embers taken out of the chapell chamber, and cairlessly sett under the stair that went up to the store-house, that night, which kindled of itselfe, burned downe staires, and that roome called the chapell chamber above the chapell, which was most richly furnished with blacke velvett, imbroidered with flowrs of silke worke in ten stich; all fruit trees and flowers, and slips imbroidered with gold twist; and it burned the statly chapell built by my lord and my laidies lodging with the young laidies. But by the great mercys of God prevented there destruction, and was awakned by the flams apeard on the other side of the court, and great helpe was made with speed to preserve my lady, and the rest which was brought out of bed in blankets. Blessed be the great God of Heaven for there delivery, and all His glorious Providence to this family, and all the kingdom in them, and to my father and his family. Amen. Amen.

A deliverance from a fire, and other remarkables (i., 14).

While we were in Dublin there was a fire in our house, but by the providence of God it was soone discover'd, and soe quenched without much harm don, blessed be the name of our

---

* Sir George Radcliffe, or Ratcliffe (for he appears to have written his name both ways), was the son of Nicholas Radcliffe, of Overthorpe, in the parish of Thornhill, in the West Riding of Yorkshire, who was a younger son of Charles Radcliffe, of Todmorden, Esq., by Margaret his wife, daughter of Thomas Savile, Esq., of Ecclesey. He was baptized at Thornhill, April 21, 1593. He was principal Secretary (an office regarded as equivalent to Prime Minister), to Thomas Earl of Strafford, when Lord Deputy of Ireland. Died at Sluyce, 25 May, 1657. See *Life and Original Correspondence* of him, by T. D. Whitaker, LL.D., 1810.

good God.   About the time I was twelve yeares old, in the yeare 1638, I was readeing of the great wisdome of our Saviour in the gospell of St. Luke, 2d chapt. 49 v., where He was disputing with the doctors with so much power that He put them to silence. In the reading of which passage I beeing that day twelve yeres old, I fell into a serious and deepe meditation of the thoughts of Christ's majestie, divinity, and wisdome, who was able to confound the learned doctors and confute theire wisdom, who was aged, He beeing so young Himselfe, but then twelve years of age.   And then I considered my owne folly and childish ignorance that I could not scarse understand meane and low things, without a great deale of teacheing and instruction ; and although I daily read the word of God, yet was of a weake capacity to know the way to salvation; and, therefore, in my heart begged of my deare Saviour to give me knowledge, wisedom, and understanding, to guide me all my daies.   Amen.

1639.

A deliverance from shiprack in a passage into Ireland with my mother, brother, and two nephewes, Thomas and Christopher Danby, in the yeare 1639 (i., 15).*

Haveing come over into England, when my mother came for her cure of the disease of the stone to the bathes and Bristoll water, St. Vincent's well (uppon which rock hanging over it is gott the Bristow diamonds), in her returne backe into Ireland, she carried my sister Danbie's two elddest sons, for theire better education.   When we came to Nesston, at the seaside, we staied for a winde a weeke ; and in that time there was a great storme on the sea, insoemuch as there was five ships cast away upon the shore before our eyes, so nigh were some of

---

* Sir Thomas Danby, of Farnley, Thorp Perow, and Masham, Knt., born 1610, married Catherine, eldest daughter of Christopher Wandesford, Esq., of Kirklington, and sister of Mrs. Thornton.   Thomas was the eldest son, and Christopher the fourth son.   They both married and left issue.   See pedigree in *Whitaker's Richmondshire*, p. 98.   *Fisher's Hist. Masham*, etc.

them, that the mainemast did allmost touch the window of that house where we laid. Yet the night proveing calme, and winde faire, we tooke ship for Ireland in one of the king's ships, new built, upon the 22nd of August, 1639; within one houer's saile a most terrible storme and tempest arose soe fiercely that we were drove on lee allnight, and within lesse than ten houers we were twelve miles beyond Dublin, lieing at hull and anchor all day. And but for a fisher-botte, sent from Mr. Hubert, to assist the king's ship in distresse, wee had undoubtedly perished, beeing drove by the force of tempest backe in to the crosse seas, and ten houers were at anchor, beaten on the sandes before that fishermen could come neare to help us. At the last, about eight o'clocke at night, we gott safe to harbour through the infinitt mercys of our great and powerfull Lord God. We landed safely at the shore of the Skirries, where the same Hubert, with all his familie and friends, mett us with great joy, entertaining my mother and all hers with abundante affection and kindenesse, which he did uppon the account of obligation, to shew his gratitude for an emminent piece of justice don him from my father, whoe had decided a grand controversie in law suites, which was depending twenty yeares, almost to his utter ruine, his adversary being so potent that he could not gett his cause heard till that time, when through the uprightnesse of the judge, and honnesty of the man, his cause rightly determined, and he preserved. This providence was the more remarkable that God soe ordered our ship to this shore, where my mother found all manner of reliefe for us, all which we wanted. And on the next day came my father from Dublin, in the company of many noble friends in coatches, to carrie us home to Dublin, where my deare mother was receaved with all joy and gladnesse, liveing in much peace and happinesse till the death of my honoured father. When about a yeare affter his death she was forced to flie into England, uppon the rebellion which brake out in Ireland. But I must not forgett a second preservation of my owne selfe from drowneing out of that ship, at that time, when a cable from the bote that came to carrie us to land, and beeing tied to our ship, by its force had like to have pulld me out of the ship in to the sea, which it had don, but that by God's providence a shipman comming at that minuite from under the decke pulled me backe, and saved me from falling into that tempestious sea, when I was halfe over borde. This great and wonderfull mercy, and my single deliverance, must not be forgotten, but had in a perpetuall remembrance of me for ever, and therefore will I humblie sett forth the mercys of the Lord to me.*

Observations uppon Severall Accidents happening in Ireland uppon the Earle of Strafford, etc., in the yeares 1640, 1641, *and on his fatall Murder, May* 12, 1641 (i., 20).

After my mother's returne from the Bathes and Bristoll, where she found much good as to the cure of the stone, the Earle of Strafford† was sent for by the king in to England

---

* Mrs. Thornton here inserts a thanksgiving on her escape, which it is unnecessary to print.

† Thomas Wentworth, eldest son of Sir William Wentworth, of Wentworth-Woodhouse, baronet, by Anne, eldest dau. and coh. of Robert Atkinson of Stawell, co. Gloucester, Esq.. was born 13th April, 1593; succeeded his father in 1614; married 1st, 22nd Oct., 1611, Lady Margaret Clifford, dau. of Francis, Earl of Cumberland, who died 1622; 2ndly, Lady Arabella Holles, dau. of John, Earl of Clare, who died in 1632; and 3rdly, in 1632, Elizabeth, dau. of Sir Godfrey Rodes, of Great Houghton, who died 9th April, 1688. Elected Knight of the Shire for the County of York, 1620; M.P. for Pontefract, 1624, and again for the County of York, 1628. On the 22nd July, in the latter year, created Baron Wentworth, of Wentworth-Woodhouse; on the 10th December following, Viscount Wentworth, and soon after made a Member of the Privy Council, Lord-Lieutenant of the County of York, and finally Lord-President of the North. In 1633 he was appointed Lord-Lieutenant of Ireland, from whence, in 1640, he returned, when he was created Baron Raby, of Raby Castle, and also Earl of Strafford, and K.G. He was beheaded, 12th May, 1641, and buried at Wentworth. See *The Earl of Strafforde's Letters and Despatches, with an Essay towards his Life, by Sir George Radcliffe; Whitaker's Life of Sir George Radcliffe,* p. 175, *et seq.; Strafford's Letters,* 2 vols., *by Dr. Knowler; Hunter's South Yorkshire,* vol. ii., p. 84; *Life of Thomas Wentworth, Earl of Strafford, by Elizabeth Cooper,* 2 vols., 1874, etc.

Mrs. Thornton has written here in the margin, "My Lord Straford tooke ship for England with my Lord Raby his son, on Good Friday, the yeare 1640; gave my father the sword then."

uppon the complaints of some factious spirritts, weary of a lawfull and peaceable government, both in England, Scottland, and Ireland, whoes spirritts and ambitions could not indure a subjection to theire most pieous and good king nor his lieutenant, which ruled them in Ireland with a wise and prudentiall government, to the preservation of his majestie's crowne and dignities; the settlement of the church and state uppon the right foundations of truth and peace, which these people had noe such intentions, as was too apparent in the following rebellions, both in England and Ireland, the Irish being heard to say that theire religeiou would not prosper as long as Strafford's head stood on his shouldiers, which saying strongly proved that this noble earle was noe pattron of the Romish Church, allthough falsely accused so by his seditious enemies, and his owne innocency was cleared uppon the scaffold in his speeche made then. But all the discontented parties too well agreed in this one point, to strike the roote of the foundations, the king being aimed at, to succeed in this tradegie, as God knows to sadly followed. The Earle of Strafforde haveing farre different designes then those secrett plotters of rapine and ruine, could not longer be endured, because he stood in the way to hinder and prevent by his wise councell; so that, till he was removed, they could not prevaille, either in Ireland or England, to compass theire ends; nor could there be found a better expedient for theire purpose then to make a cloake of religion, that under such a populer specious pretence theire horrible practices might not be found out. The Irish, thirsting affter the blood and lives of the English, pretended oppression to be made subject to the laws of England, and the other of that nation could not be subject to our church government and orders, but affected a loose libertineissme to their owne pernicious waies, joyned with the Irish in theire complaints against this wise and noble person, whom, indeed, they were not worthy of, under whoes jurisdiction that kingdome had enjoyed seven yeares of peace and plenty; all his endeavours ever tending for theire good, the true establishment of his king and religion, the honor, peace, and wellfaire of the English nation, and the due ordering of that

barbarous people, and theire civilizeing them to our good lawes
and government; but this was against all theire intrests of
rebellions and close couched treacheris which lay hatched
under soe specious pretensions that he would subvert the church
and state; theires was for the establishment of heresies, popery
and destruction of church and state, to advance horrible paricides
and murders, breaking forth, first in Ireland, to the destruction
of millions of the poore protestants Christians who suffered
martyredom for theire God and his religion; and in England
many thousand suffered by the sword both with theire king and
for him, and the truth of religion there established and for the
lawes. But, to returne to my lord-lieutenant, while the
pretences of religion so filled the eares of the parliament of
England then sitting in the yeare 40, and false suggestions of
oppressions against this noble earle, he was called before them
to give answer to such articles as his enemies of all factions had
unjustly laid to his charge. The whole transaction of this
businesse was prosecuted with soe much malice and rigour of
his enemies side, and so much wisdome, prudence and galantrie
on the earle's, that all the world (save his enemies thirsting
[for] his blood) did admire his incomparable wisdome and
abilities in his cleare and brave defence he made for himselfe,
notwithstanding they gave fresh charges each day, which he
had never heard of, nor had he any time spaired to give in his
answer, but was set upon with new blood-hounds, as theire
fancies pleased; neither was he allowed the benifitt of his
wittnesses, only theire was that in his triall don, which was
never heard of before, for want of full evidence against him
(which was servd to the hight too), an invention forged of
accumulative treason, and a perticuler act made in that parliament to confirme the same till they had gott his life; and
then annother following act affter his death, to abrogate and
disannull the other for ever, that it might never be in force
against any other person. The world may by this judge the
truth and legallity of these proceedings against this brave
person; but the truth is, he had soe much of wrong and
injustice don in all the prosecution, as noe man but of infinitt

abilities, which God had wonderfully given him, could have withstood those mastives and blood-hounds, in the quicke retorts and vindication of his innocent actions, returning theire malice on theire owne fallse suggestions; soe that least these articles and other artifices in the house should not prevaile with the king, whoe did cleare him in his owne judgment, there was the invention of abundance of lies and callumnies cast about and instill'd into the eares and hearts of the vulger meaner peopple, such as had ignorance and pride to be theire leaders, which, beeing tould a fallschood, that the lord-leuctenant did councill the king to subvert the lawes and bring in popery, gathered together in infinitt numbers of prenticies of London, and head-strong seperates and schismaticks; the great numbers meeting at the Parliament House daily clamoured and cried out against my lord and the king did soe increase, that the tumults had nigh to have pulled his sacred majestie in pieces, as he removed from White Hall to the parliament, still crying out for justice against Strafford. Soe that to sattisfie their cruell malice, and to give them all content, theire was noe other expedient would doe but this innocent earle's life to be taken from him. This the most pyous king could very hardly be drawne to, being pressed to signe the bill, he still declaring his innocency in his conscience he was not worthy of death. But the king, being constrained for the savegard of his owne life, passed that fatall bill, with two others that day, which proved as destructive to him and the churche and kingdome as this of Strafford's,—that of excluding the bishops out of the house of parliament, and the other of triennial parliaments, which were preludiums of this most excelent king's owne destruction, when the commons had got the reines of power by this in to theire owne hand, and the better capacitated to fight against theire lawfull soveraine, albeit they pulled upon themselves and the kingdome a fatall ruine within a few yeares affter, but principally agansst our sacred majestic, which was the marke with the crowne which they aymed at. But this galant earle soe much desiring the peace and happinesse of his majestic and kingdome, did acquitt

the king, constrained and cheerfully submitted to that sentance
with so much serenity and tranquility of thoughts as is
immaginable, only did justifie his innocency to the death, as
may be seene in his papers and last speech. He forgave his
adversaries, and wished, as he was the first that had laid downe
his life in this way, for the preservation of the king and
church, so that he might be the last innocent bloodshed, but
he much feared it. He put up praiers for the king and the
whole kingdoms, as it may be seene in his triall, written by an
eye and eare wittnesse, and uppon the 12th of May, 1641, he
suffered martiredome, being beheaded on Tower hill. The fall
of this brave man was an infinitt losse to the church of God,
his king, and the three kingdomes, who through his wise
counsell (the same) had bin fortunate to the preservation of
peace and truth for severall yeares; but now the Scottish
faction began to breake out againe that had apeared in the
yeare 39. And our sins, contracted in so long a peace, was
ripe for judgements. God's sword was drawne out against us
to fight His quarrell, till by our punishments He humbled the
pride of our hearts. When the just and wise men faile and
are taken away, the cittye will be left in darknesse and distruction.

*A Relation conserning my honoured father, the Lord Deputy
Wandesforde, and of his death, December 3rd, 1640 (i., 27).*

Uppon my lord lieuetennant's of Irland's goeing for
England, the king was graciously pleased to send his commission, under the great seale of England, to my father, to succeed
my Lord of Strafford in that weighty place of deputie-ship,
in which he acted with so much pietie, loyalty, candor, and
justice, that his memmory is blessed to many generations. In
his time there were many causes determined and decided of
great concernment betweene parties, which had depended, some
ten, twenty, thirty yeares; and the cause of the widdowes and
oppressed, strangers and the fatherlesse, was rightly adjudged

and determined, which through the imbecility of the parties, the power of the adversaries, or corruption of the under officers, had bin till then neglected ; but to the comfort of the injured was rightly settled, and allso to the sattisfaction of the other parties, who being convinced by the paines, and Christian advices, and wise, just mannagercy of his government, they confessed the equity of his determinations to be just, legall, and right. Yea, such was the sweete affability and prudence of his carriage in general, that none which went from England gained soe much uppon affections of that nation, and all whome he lived amongst. His life was given for a publicke good to that kingdome, as well as to be a blessing in his owne familie, who was exceeding happie in such a father and head. His deare and beloved wife, most blessed in such a comfort, support, and husband as the world could not paralell in all chaste, pieous, deare love, and conjugall affection, with temperance, meekenesse, and sobriety. They both injoying many yeares of happinesse together in that holy bond of a loyall wedlocke, even to the admiration of all, for theire godly and righteous conversation. All his children infinitely happy, and blessed in such a father and guide in theire youths. His relations, freinds, and tennants were all blessed in him, doeing them what good he could. Lett his raire and excelent booke* of advice to his sonne George speake his great endowments, his pietie, parts, knowledge in divinity and religion, his wisdome and paternall caire and prudence, tender and deare love to his whole family and generation. A grand patron of the church, and incourager of all ingenious schollars of what age or degree soever. An incouragement and exemplear of learning, sobriety, temperance, chastety, holinesse, patience, humility, charity, justice, and clemency, was thys heroick soule replenished withall. Rich in good workes, lovely and desirable in his life, a deare and loving brother to his brothers and sisters, takeing caire for theire advantage in education and preferment, as branches from the same stocke with himselfe. He had a wise

* This book was published by the Rev. Thomas Comber from a MS. copy which is still preserved at Oswaldkirk.

and prudentiall love towards all his children for theire picous
and religious education, with faire and noble provissions for
them in his last will and testament. His life was spent in
great sedulity and watchfullnesse, to discharge a good conscience towards all : towards God and man. A true labourer in
God's vineyard, in which he plaied the good husbandman, and
God att last gave him his wages, even the crowne of glory for
ever. And guiding his waies with discretion, God gave him a
foresight of those changes was comming uppon church and
state. And offt in my hearing would he say to my deare
mother, in his health, that whoesoe should live to see it should
see great changes and evills, both uppon the church and state.
Such was the sinnes and pride of those daies, that there hung
a cloud over thes kingdomes ; he praied God to divert the same,
and establish the same uppon those excelent foundations on
which it was built.

It pleased God to vissitt my deare father with a feaver, at
the latter end of November, which kept him about a wecke or
ten daies in the house, but finding him selfe somewhat better,
went to church, beeing attended home by the Earle of Ormond,*
the Lord Dillon, Sir George Ratclife, and many other persons
of quality, as the usuall custome was to waite on the deputy
to dinner. When he came into the dining roome, and perceived
himselfe not well, craved leave of the company to rest himselfe
a little in his bedchamber, intending to have satt att dinner
with them, but still he grew worse, and sent word he found
himselfe soe ill that hee went to bed, and desired the pardon of
that noble company. And affter dinner, the company parted.
Calling to minde the sermon, my father tould my mother, that
he had that day heard the best sermon that ever he had heard
in all his life, and blessed God for it, saing it was as if it should
be the last. He knew not what it might prove, but, if he lived,

* James Butler, 12th Earl of Ormonde, K.G., created Marquess of
Ormonde 1642, and, on the restoration of Charles II., advanced, in reward of
his unshaken loyalty to that King and his father, to the dignity of Duke of
Ormonde in Ireland, and created Baron Butler, of Llanthony, and Earl of
Brecknock in England ; died 21st July, 1688.

he would reward that minister plentifully, and he should not want the best preferment he could helpe him to. The feaver, still increasing, seized on him strongly, but he, full of patience and Christian magnanimity, was prepared for the Lord's dealing with him in His Providence, either for life or death. About Tuesday, the 29th of November, 1640, he called for his 'will; commanding my cozen Wandesforde,* one of his executors to the said will, to reade it, it being signed, sealed, and finished a good while before. He had it then all read over to him in the presence of divers persons of qualitie, as my Lord Bishop of Derrey† (an executor), theEarle of Ormond, the Lord Dillon, and severall others, before whome he ratified and confirmed the same, declairing it publickly to be his last will and testament, commanding his executors to see it ·fulfiled and performed to my mother and all his children, and that all his just debtes, whether by bill or bond, and justly proved, should be paid; againe charged them to be cairefull of his wife and children.‡

* William Wandesford, his half brother, to whom he left £30 a year. See notes of Will afterwards.

† John Bramhall, a native of Pontefract, where he was born about the year 1503, and ultimately, through Wandesford's influence, Bishop of Derry. "At the restoration he was deservedly promoted to the primacy of a church which by his activity and judgment he had raised from a state of almost utter destitution to that condition of dignity and opulence in which it has ever since continued." *Whitaker's Hist. Richmondshire*, 1823, vol. ii., p. 152. Bramhall was ordained deacon at York 24th Dec., 1615, and priest 22nd Dec., 1616, being then curate of St. Martin's in Micklegate (Reg. Matthew). When ordained deacon he is said to be of Emmanuel College, Cambridge, but he was really of Sidney Sussex College, being admitted there 21st Feb., 1608-9. and graduating B.A. 1612, M.A. 1616, B.D. 1623, D.D. 1630. (Ward's *Fasti Riponenses*, MS.) He held several benefices in Yorkshire before he went to Ireland. See Surtees' Soc. Pub., Vol. LV., p. 33, note by Rev. G. Ornsby, editor.

‡ Mrs. Thornton in the course of these volumes sometimes described the same incident, etc., more than once. It has been thought the best plan to give these renewed descriptions, when the language is different, in the form of notes. "Next to the blessing of my father's book and preserving it to our posterity, we did allso receave a great mercy by the right ordering of my father's temporall consernes, by the making and ordering of his last will and testament in a perfect and just and upright manner, settleing and disposing of his estate so as all conserned in it was rightly provided for; either his widdow, children, friends, and

About Wednesday, my mother desired the phisicians to give her a true state of his condittion, whom she perceaved grew weaker, but they would not deale truly, nor acknowledge his desperate case, albeit they found by his blood that it was corrupted, and most fatall signes. That night pigeons cut* was laid to his soles of the feete; when my father saw it, he smiled, and said, " Are you come to the last remidie? but I shall prevent your skill," for all along this sickness he expected his change, althoughe he would not acquaint my mother for increaseing her greife. All the time of his sicknesse, till the last period, hee had the perfect use of reason and cleare understanding as in all his life, which was an infinitt mercy afforded him; most quick and acqute in all facculties, as in perfect health. The entertainement in his sicknesse was full of divine medittations, ejaculations, and praires, with praises to his God, and preparations for death. He gave many instructions to his son George to be diligent in the service of God, obedient to His commandment, obedient and dutifull to his deare mother, who had bin a faithfull, tender, loving wife to him and his children; he commanded him to love, honor, obey her in all things all his daies, due to her for her wisdome and vertue, and doeing this God would blesse him the better; charged him to suffer his will to be performed, which was just and equall, there beeing right don to him and all persons else, ending with many good advices to feare and love that dreadfull Lord God, and He

creaditors, by which justice, equity, and charity was rightly disposed for, and noe person injured. This soe wise and bountifull disposall of that estate which God had graciously given him uppon his honnest industry and indeavours, who had paid all his grandfather's debts. God had increased his store to six fould of what my grandfather had left to him. Soe as he had gotten and increased his estate soe much by his honnest waies and payment of his father's debts, now he as wisely leaves it to his children and family with a blessing, and settled it by deed and will to preserve every branch thereof by noble and paternall devissions." (Vol. ii., p. 106.)

* In the olden times, when the treatment of the sick was not so rational as in later years, remedies of this character were not unusual. The idea seems to have been that a living or recently killed creature, applied to the patient, communicated some of its vitality to him. A moribund person has been wrapped in the skin of a sheep fresh from the animal.

would blesse him and provide for him as He had don to him-selfe. When he laid slumbring, still would he be as if dis-courseing in judicature, that he would doe uprightly to all in his power; if the poore man's cause be right, he should not suffer for his poverty, nor the rich gaine for being soe, if his cause were bad. Neither could he respect the persons of the rich or poore, but doe uprightly according to the lawes of God and man. Many such like expressions I have heard him my selfe. Then would he call on me to his bedside, and stediely lookeing on me, would sighe and say, " Ah ! poore childe, what must thou see and thine eyes beholde ! " and praing for me turned away with a great grone. Which expressions strucke soe deepe that I never forgate them, but has sadly experienced those miseries which he prophetically foresaw. The Bishop of Derrey being called on Thursday at night, who tould him he perceaved he grew weaker in bodie, that he would do well to declaire in publicke his faith and hope in God, not that he questioned the same, he beeing fully sattisfied, but that it was usuall in those cases, for the comfort and instruction of the companie. Immediately my deare father raised up himselfe with all his force, and stedfastly fixed his eyes to heaven, then made (before many persons of qualitie, with my mother), a most heavenly and patheticall confession of his faith, hope, and confidence in God, and that his heart did fully relie upon the all saveing merritts of Jesus Christ his Redeemer, in Him alone hoped for pardon and remission of all his sinnes, and for salvation through His Blood which was shed for him, and that in Him he hoped for eternall glorie, of His owne free grace and mercy. He desired the Lord to forgive all his sinnes, as he freely forgave all the world, and declaring that he died in the faith which was professed in the Church of England at that time, beeing most pure and holie, and agreeing with Christ's institution, praing to God to continue it flourishing. Many other praires for himselfe and his wife and children, desireing to be accepted of the Lord in mercy, according to the sincerity of his heart. After devout praires for him by the Bishop and the solemne pronunciation of absolution, in order to the

Churchis' command, this deare and sweete saint freely yielded up his precious soule to God, with these words, "Into Thy hands, oh Lord, I commend my soule : Lord Jesus, receive my spirritt. Amen," with which he fell asleepe ; which blessed end of his life, beeing a happie close of his holie life, has, I hope, receaved a full reward of joy in the kingdome of heaven, and strooke a most deepe impression upon all that knew him. I pray the Lord continue his memory fresh in my heart to imitate his virtues, graces, and pietie. He departed this life on Thursday, the 3rd of December, 1640, at his owne house in Dammaske Streete, in Dublin, beeing in Ireland. His bodie beeing imbowelled was affterwards imballmed, and all the noble parts was very sound and perfect, saving the heart, which was decaied of one side. It was thought this proceeded from much study and bussinesse which his weighty and great imployments called him to, great watchfulnesse and paines in the faithfull discharge in his offices. He was the maister of the rowles in Ireland seven yeares, one of his majestie's privey councell, a judge in the king's bench, once lord cheif justice of that nation, and lastly, he died the lord deputy of that kingdome of Ireland, beeing the only man in that place (as was observed) which died untouched or peaceably in theire beds. He was found faithfull, and soe beloved of his prince and countrey. A most generally lamented person in that kingdome, who had found the swetenesse of his government in much meekenesse and clemmency. He was also the last deputy for many yeares, beeing the last in King Charles the First's time, the warres following affter his death. The next lawfull governer theire was the Earle of Ormond, in King Charles the Second's time of restoration into England. The corpes of my honored father was carried from the Castle of Dublin in a stately manner, according to his dignitie and place, beeing interred in the cheife church, Christ's Church, under a faire marble before the deputies' seate of estate, on the 10th day of December, 1640. The Bishop of Derrey preacht his funerall sermon. [Text, Matt. xxi. 8.] And I am sure amongst the multitude of people there was not many drie eyes. Such was the love that God had given to the worthy person, that the Irish did sett up their lamentable hone, as they call it, for him in the church, which was never knowne before for any Englishman don. His funerall's charges did amount to above £1,300, dieing in that capacitie of a deputy, which soe increased the debts upon his estate as proved very heavy in the times of trouble succeeding. The king did give order that this should have bin discharged out of his treasury, as allso that my brother George's wardship was given him by his gracious majestie, both in regard of my father's faithfull service in that place and his dieing deputie. But the parliament seising uppon the king's treasury and power, these charges fell sad uppon all my father's estate and his children, beeing charged for the wardship by the parliament with the summe of £2,500, which never came to the king. This was the begining of troubles in our familie, affter which followed the breaking out of the Rebellion of Ireland, beeing about nine months affter my father died, in October 23rd, 1641.

Meditations and Praier uppon the death of my honored father, the Lord Deputie Wandesforde (i., 38-48).

Isaiah lvii. v. 1, 2.   " The righteous perisheth, and no man laieth it to heart, and the mercifull men are taken away, none considering that the righteous is taken away from the evill to come."   *   *   *   *   Well might this be applied to our very case, in my deare father's deliverance.   For his eyes did not see those great and terrible evills, which we did that survived him, even bitter ones, that fell uppon the whole English and Irish nations, such as was never heard of the like; such horrid treasons, tretcheries, bloodsheds, burnings, fammins, desolattions, and distructions, which fell so heavily uppon our holy, good, and pieous king, whom the world was not worthy of; and that excelent, pure, and glorious church then established, for soundness in faith and doctrine none could parrellel since the Apostles' time.   And surely these things was foreseene severall yeares before by him; he laid out his endevors to prevent the falling of them uppon us, by his frequent admonishments and reproofs for theire vanities, his zealous praiers and deepe humiliation of his person, and daily intercessions att the throne of grace for these thre kingdomes. But our sinnes crieing soe loud in generall for vengeance that the Lord would not spaire those which offended with soe high a hand against the sweete mercys and forbearance of our gracious God. Yet, notwithstanding all those calamities and distractious of those times, I must ever acknowledge and sett forth the loveing kindnesse, mercys, and goodness of the Lord of Hosts to us in our deliverances in all these troubles, He makeing places of refuge for my father's wife and children, soe that not a haire of our heads perished in the generall destructions either by the Irish or English rebellions. In Ireland were we miraculosly preserved in Dublin, for severall weeks affter the rebellion was broken out in the countrey. And though in much frights by alarums from the enimies, yet were we delivered from those evills, till by a safe passage into England with all my mother's familie and goods with her at Dublin, we got quit of Ireland and got to the beerehouse at Nestton.* Thus was there a sanctuary from those perills for this righteous man's familie, when a thousand was swallowed up in the common calamities of that kingdome by the Irish papists. And soe alsoe thus did the Lord deliver my deare father in this way, the best way of all, most certainely it was, for there the weary be at rest and the wicked cease from troubling. He died, and was gathered to his fathers in a quiet and peaceable time. As he lived in peace, soe he departed in peace, and to peace, giveing him rest in his sleepe, the sweete sleepe of death to him, though sad to us hee left behind him.† * * *

---

* Great Neston, a market-town and parish in the union of Wirrall, southern division of the county of Chester, eleven miles N.W. from Chester, and situated on the south-west side of a peninsula formed by the estuaries of the rivers Dee and Mersey.

† After this there follow in the MS. *A Praier uppon my father's death ;* and *A Praier to be said before wee receive, made by my father before he went into Ireland,* 1628, which need not be printed.

My mother's preservation from the Irish rebellion, Oct. 23d,
1641 : a thankesgiving for our great deliveration (i., 62.)

Many and great was the sorrowes and sufferings of my
deare and honored mother, with her whole familie, uppon the
sad change by the death of my honored father. And she continued in her house in Dublin, maintaining the great household
in the same condittion as it was, at her owne charges, for the
honor of the same; to her owne disadvantage many waies, for
she by this meanes tarried in Ireland discharging those servants and paieng many debts which should have bin don by the
executors, longer then she could well doe; in regard of her
joynture beeing in England she wanted suplies. Thus she
contincued till about the October affter, when, on the 23rd day
in the yeare 1641, that horrid rebellion and massacre of the
poore English protestants began to breake out in the countery,
which was by the all-seeing providence of God prevented in the
citie of Dublin, where we weare. In the vacancy of a wise and
prudent governor after my father's death and my Lord of
Strafford's imprisonment by the parliament in England, that
nation was under the authority of justices, the Lord Parsons and
Lord Burlacey. These two old gentlemen, havein lived in
Ireland many peaceable yeares, could not be made sensable
that the Irish had an ill design against the English, and therefore did not take notice of theire frequent numerous meeting in
a strange insulting manner; but, when they were informed by
some judicious men, neglected the searching into that businesse,
till through theire remisseness the faction had gott deepe roote,
and headed there designes to a full maturity, which undoubtedly had overwhelmed the whole bodie of the English
there as well in Dublin as the countery, had there not bin a
most miraculous discovery of the plot made in Dublin, by
which, as the meanes our gracious God appointed, we weare
delivered from perishing in those flames intended for us. The
Lord Mackmaughan and Mackguire, two of the ringleaders of
this wickedness, was desined to sease upon the castle of Dublin,
which at that time was richly stored with all ammunition,

armes, ordenances, and other artillery for the defence of the castle and kingdomes, by the Lord Lieutenant Strafford, well knowing that the Irish must be ride with a curb. But this place of the English strength was then cairlessly at that time deserted, none being sett to guard the bridge and gates, but four weake old men that could make no resistance. That night, being Satterday, before Mackguire should have taken possession of the castle, he beeing desined the governor thereof by the rebbells, and should have seised on it on the Sunday morning, Mackmaughan, willing to save a kinsman of his owne name that lived then as a servant with Sir John Clottworthy, an English man, writt his cosen a letter to Dublin to meete him in great haste about a bussinesse of great consernment. His cosen imediatly tooke horse and ride into the country, but finding him gone to Dublin, followed, and discovered where he and Magguire was sett drinking in a blind alehouse,* at which dore they had sett men to guard it. Now this had bin converted a protestant about a yeare before, and married to an English woman, but they knew not that he was turnd. He observed a long time by there waies and impious expressions that they used towards the English soe much as he feared some bad designe in hand, and therefore was the more diligent in foll[owing] them to discovery. When they were mett they fell to drinke much, they causing him take more, that he might be drunk; but he desired them to tell him what they sent to him for. Mackmaughan clapt him on the backe and tould him that there was the galantest designe which was ploted, and to take effect shortly, against the English doggs, that could be, to cut there throats; and to-morrow by six a clocke in the morning, said he, my Lord Mackguire will be master of Dublin Castle, and they would batter downe the towne over the hereticke dogs' eares and not spaire one of them. After which speach his cosen the protestant started and cried out, "What shall I

---

* "Found the said Lord Mackmahoone and other two rebells, the heads of them, Lord Macguire and Sir Filoman O'Neale, all in a blind ale house drinking." (Vol. ii., p. 118.)

doe for my wife?" They said, "Hang her, for she was but an English dogge, he might gett better of his owne country;" soe he considering himselfe to be in theire hand, whoe would murder him if he resisted, complied for that time, till he found an opportunity to gett away, which they began to suspect, and gave warning to the guard to kill him if he went out. Soe they dranke on, till the protestant was forced to require leave to goe into the next roome, for they durst not trust him farther; and he, withdrawing thither, broake downe the window, and leaped out of an upper roome, and over a wall, before he could make an escape, to acquaint the lord justices. But this man had allso the river to swim att that time of night, which was twelve a'clocke, before he came to the first justice, which was Sir William Persons. Being come to the gate, he was forced to threaten hard before he was admitted, and then he tould him, "My lord, I am sent to you by the providence of God to save your life and all the English. I am bound in conscience to deliver my owne soule in there preservation from the Irish, whoe intends to destroy them all;" and tould him all the fore-goeing circumstances, telling him withall that he must not looke on him as an idle drunken fellow, but as one which had allmost lost his owne life to preserve his, and that if he did not take caire to prevent this mischeife, all the innocent blood of the English would be required att his hand, with many such like expressions. Affter which there was search made for the two rebells, but non was found till the same man which discovered the plott found them himselfe, hid in the top of the house within a trap dore; soe they were taken and secured, and we all poore sheepe destinated to destruction was thus wonderfully preserved and delivered in Dublin. Whereas the rebellion began that Sunday in the country, with sword, fire, and mur-dering all before them, not spairing infant of daies, nor old age; all was made havocke of,* and so continued till they had notice

* "Above forty thousand protestants were butchered with almost every con-ceivable circumstance of cruelty" (Anderson's *Puritan Women*, vol. ii., p. 110). "When millions was cutt of and destroyed there by murders, by fire, by drown-ing, and by all the wicked and unheard of crueltyes of the bloody Irish papists

that it was discovred in Dublin, and were prevented by our
forces which defended the cittie. Yett cannot it be immagined
but we had our shair in Dublin when we were forced upon the
alarum to leave our house and fly into the castle that night
with all my mother's familie and what goods she could.* From
thence we were forced into the cittie, contineing for fourteen
daies and nights in great feares, frights, and hideous distractions and disturbances from the alarums and outcries given in
Dublin each night by the rebells, and with these frights,
fastings, and paines about packing the goods, and wanting
sleepe, times of eating, or refreshment, wrought so much upon
my young bodie, that I fell into a desperate flux, called the
Irish disscas, beeing nigh unto death, while I staied in Dublin,
as allso in the ship comeing for England. But my deare
mother's caire was exceeding great for my two brothers,
Christopher and John, with Tom Danby and Kitt, my sister's
two eldest sons, and myselfe, in providing a ship to transport
us all together with her goods, plate,· and household stuffe in
Dublin, which she affterwards delivered to my uncle William
Wandesforde affter she came to Weschester.† But it pleased
God to give us all a safe and quiett passage out of Ireland into
England, landing att the beerehouse neare Neston, where we
tarried severall weeks by reason of my distemper, brought out
of Ireland when we fled from the rebells. This, I say, brought
me exceeding weake, so that I had a doctor from Chester for
my cure, affter which, with the great caire and love of my deare
mother, God was pleased att that time to restore my life and
strengthen my great weakeuesse, inabling me to goe to Chester
in a coach. Thus did the great God of heaven and earth preserve us most miraculously in all our dangers and extreamities,
bringing us safe all to our owne native countrey. Blessed be

against our innocent soules of the protestant religion, it beeing the designe of
hell and Satan to have extirpated us of the true faith for ever out of the world."
(Vol. ii.)

   * "O this is a night worthy to be observed in all our generations affter us,
October 23, 1641, when the Lord did bring us (as He had don to the children to
Israell) out of the land of Egipt." (Vol. ii.)

   † An old name of Chester.

the most high God, possesser of heaven and earth, Which preserved our lives from all manner of destruction.*

Uppon my mother's comming to Weschester from Ireland, and of my haveing the smale pox, in Feb. 20, 1642 (i., 69).

After our comming to Weschester from the beerehouse, neare Neston, when wee fled out of the Irish rebellion, it pleased God to move the gentry of the cittie to be exceeding courteous and civill to my deare mother and my selfe, assisting her with what necessaries she wanted in a strange place, and such pittie and favour we found that she wanted nothing in that place which our neighbours procured not for us; in which number was Dr. Manwaring and his wife, Sir Thomas Smith and his lady and familie, all beeing very deare friends to us, my Lord Cholmeley and his lady, with many other persons of qualitie, severall of which would have furnished her with moneyes, but she was unwilling to trouble any, still expecting returnes out of Yorkeshire; but the warres falling out hott at the time [July 17, 1643], beeing wee were beleagured in Chester by Sir William Brewerton's† forces for the parliment, there happened a strainge accident which raised that seige, July 19th, 1643. As I was informed, there was three granadoes shott in to the towne, but, through Providence, hurt noe bodie. The first, beeing shott into the sconce of our souldiers within, two men of the Captaine Manwaring, but having an oxe's hide ready, clapt it thereon, and it smothering away in shells did not spread but went out. The second light short of the cittie, in a ditch within a pasture amongst a company of women milking, but was quenched without doeing them harm at all, praised be the Lord our God. The last fell amongst theire owne horrse, short of the towne, slaing many of them, and by that

* After this there comes in the MS. *A Thanksgiving for preservation from the Rebellion in Ireland*, Oct. 23, 1641.

† Sir William Brereton, of Handford in Cheshire, a well-known parliamentary general, and the author of a volume of travels, which has been published by the Chetham Society.

meanes the seige was raised. Thus was we freed from great evills to befall that towne, while wee staid theire, that succeeded affter we came into Yorkeshire, which still the Lord's hand was streached out for our preservation. In each place we came to it was a sanctuary to us, blessed be the Lord most high for all His goodnesse towards us. But I had in this time of the seige a grand deliverance, standing in a tirritt in my mother's house, haveing bin at praier in the first morning, we weare besett in the towne; and not hearing of it before, as I looked out at a window towards St. Marie's Church, a cannon bullett flew soe nigh the place where I stood that the window sudainly shutt with such a force the whole tirritt shooke; and it pleased God I escaped without more harme, save that the wafte tooke my breath from me for that present, and caused a great feare and trembling, not knowing from whence it came. I blesse and praise the Lord our God for this my perticuler preservation at that time. Allso my brother, John Wandesforde, was preserved from death in the smale pox, he haveing taken them of one of my cozen William Wandesford's sonns, liveing then at Chester. Greate was my mother's feare for him, and caire and paines she tooke about him, and at last hee, through mercy, was recovered, although he was very much disfigured, haveing bin a very beautifull child, and of a sweete complection. In the time of his sicknesse I was forbiden to come to him least I should gett the smale pox and indanger my owne life, and so observed my mother's command in that, but my love for him could not containe itselfe from sending in letters to him, by a way found out of my foolish invention, tieing them about a little dog's neck, which, beeing taken into his bed, brought the infection of the dissease upon my selfe, as allso the sight of him affter his recovery; beeing strooke with feare seeing him so sadly used and all over very read, I immediately fell very ill, and from that time grew worse till I grew so dangerously ill and inwardly sicke, that I was in much perill of my life, by theire not comeing well out but kept att my heart; notwithstanding all the meanes of phisicians or others, that my deare mother cost and caire she used for me, yet I was well nigh death, but blessed be the most gracious God and Lord of mercy Which pleased to heare our pettions for my life and to spare me in much mercy, and caused them to come well forth, and so, by degrees, the malignity of that disease abated when there was many in that place died of it.

There was in our house a little boy that my father had taken for charitie. This Frank Kelly falling sicke on Good Friday (and I on the next day) was most sadly used in great extreamity of paine and sicknesse, and miserablcy sore and could not swallow; his sight was eaten out and his mouth very sore, notwithstanding all the great caire and industrie of my deare mother, two wattchers, and the same helpes of a doctor and meadicens which we both had, and great was my mother's love and charitie for him, so that my deare mother she did sit up many nights with this poore boy, and drest his sores, with all offices, as diligently as if he had bin her owne childe, notwithstanding his loathsome dissease. All the time of this boy's sickenesse he was so full of sweete expressions and heavenly minded, with much acts of religion, that it was a great comfort to my mother, and all about him, with abundance of patience and gratitude to God and my mother for all they had don for him. Every one being astonished to heare his wonderfull hope, repentance for his sinnes against God in the time of his ignorance, before he was converted from popery, and since; his severall confessions, with sorow and bitternesse of heart for them, and praing them to intreat God for him. Then would he, beyond expressions, stedfastly diclaire his faith, hope, and beleife in the mercys of God, through his Redeemer Jesus Christ alone for salvation of him, and commending his soule to God in much praiers and meditations, both aloud and offten in his slumbring, to theire great admiration, that the goodnesse of God should condescend to make Himselfe knowne to a poore childe, in uttering forth infinittly more then allmost any could expresse; and was an abundant sattisfaction to my deare mother to see an improvement of grace and religieon in his heart, since he was brought into her house, it beeing not two yeares, at which time he was a papist affter his owne poore parents' religieon; but affter he came into my father's house in Ireland, and brought into England by my mother, he was through all good instructions, and teatchings as to read, and his cattechisme, and it pleased God to open the eyes of his soule, and he became a true convert, and a patterne of much goodnesse and vertue, that I never saw the like in many yeares above his, being about nine yeares old. This poore boy, al along his sickenesse, still praied for me; when he heard I was in danger of death, desired with teares that God would be pleased to spaire my life, and to blesse me, that I might live to doe much good to others, as to him, and that he might rather be taken away and I spaired; and he lived till I was well againe, and would have gon to seen him, but he by noe means would suffer me, least his extreamity should doe me harme; but I standing where I could heare his voice, and he mine, he blessed God heartily, and rejoyced to hear I was delivered, and hoped God had heard his praier, and that you, said hee, might live to the glory of God. And it did please our Gracious Father to releive him out of his missery by death, about fourteen daies affter. This good childe, whom He had fitted for Himselfe, died uttering many gracious speeches out of the Scripture, and abundance of pathaticall praiers and pittitions to God for himselfe, and mother, and us all; with hearty thanks offten to God, Who had taken him out of that wicked way, as he called it, wherein he undoubtedly had bin damnd, bring him to beleive aright in God for his salvation; with many hopefull and religious expressions, more then could be expected from such a childe, he freely and willingly gave up his soule into the hands of his Redeemer, with "Come, Lord Jesus, and receave my soule," and so died.

I had great reason to take especiall notice of the great goodnesse of God to us in giveing us opportunity to bring this poor soule out of the darkenesse and ignorance of his sinfull education in which he was, and it was this good providence of God so to order it. Thus the accident was. As my father was upon the Greene one day bowling, seeing a poore naked boy in rags, yet pretty and nimble, was very officious in gathering up his bowles, he tooke notice of him with intentions of charity towards the boy. Askeing him severall questions, and hearing his witty answers; seeing him an Irish orphan, had compassion on him, and tould him if he would be willing to forsake all his old waies that he was bred up in, his papist friends, he would bring him up in the true feare of God, and he would take caire of him, and provide for him that he should never want all his daies. At which the boy was very glad, and said he thanked his lordship, and that he would be willing to learne what he should put to him, and would pray for him all his daies; so from that he tooke him home, clothing and nourishing him till hee died, and then my mother contineued the same in her house, where he receaved such instruction, etc., as that I hope the Lord had glory thereby, and that poore soule now reapes the benefitt of such charity.*

A discourse of passages and deliverances of my mother and us three children affter her removall from Chester to Snape, and till we came to Kirklington, 1643 (i., 78).

[Aug. 28, 1643.] From Weschester my deare mother removed, with her three younger children, Alice, Christopher, and John Wandesforde (she having sent her two grandsons home from Chester before the seige). With these and severall servants and tennants, though with much difficulty, by reason of the interchange of the king's armies and the parliament's, she was brought into the towne of Warrington towards coming into Yorkeshire: she finding more favour by reason of the captain's civility, and by a passe from Coll. Shittleworth† then usuall. Seeing nothing but a weake company for her person, and haveing lost all in Ireland, only two trunks of wearing

* After this follows *a Thankesgiveing affter my recovery from the small-pox in Weschester,* 1642. *Receaving the first Sacrament.*

† Richard Shuttleworth of Gawthorpe Hall, born 1587, and died 1669. He was M.P. for Preston in 1640, and a Colonel in the service of the Parliament. (A Discourse of the War in Lancashire, ed. Chetham Soc. 101).

linning, they gave her leave to passe, and about ten a clock at night we came weary into the towne of Warrington. After a while we were entertained with alarums, as was pretended, from the king's party in Chester; this was but to awaken theire diligency the more, but there was noe cause, for the poore towne had worke enough to defend itselfe from its enimies. From Warrington we went to Wiggen * the next day, beeing a towne zealous for theire king and church; wee found it sorely demolished, and all the windowes broaken; many sad complaints of the poore inhabitants, beeing at our first comeing was scarred, least we should have bin of the parliament party. Theire cries weare the greater in respect they weare inforced to see the burning of five hundred of theire owne bibles publickly at the Crosse by the soldiers, which they plundered under pretence of beeing popery in theire service-books, and reviling them with the name of papists' dogs. But this town had bin preserved from such fallse doctrine or herisie, and would have died for the true proffession of the prottestant religion. The memory of Dr. Fleetwood was so famous at that time with them, which was a most pieous godlie minister, liveing about thirty yeares since with them, and by his life and doctrine had sett such good order amongst them, that they still retained the true religion he taught. They hearing that my mother was his neece,† flocked abundantly to see her, using all the civilities and kindnesses imaginable to her for his sake, and notwithstanding that theire bibles and bookes were burnt, never neglected the praiers at six a clocke in the morning, and four in the affternoone. The next day we passed from thence towards Yorkeshire, with many praiers from this people, and when we came to the borders of Lancashire, at a place called Downham,‡ we were not permitted to passe, but with harsh language and

---

* Wigan was taken by storm on April 1st, 1643, and the town was plundered by the soldiers. (Discourse of the War in Lancashire, 36).

† That is, his great niece. Dr. Fleetwood's sister, Joyce Fleetwood, married Sir Hewett Osborne, father of Mrs. Wandesford, the mother of Mrs. Thornton, the journalist.

‡ In the parish of Whalley, co. Lancaster, three miles from Clitheroe.

abusis by a parliament corporall and his gang; they would not beleive our passe, but tooke us downe, swearing and threatning we should be striped; so my deare mother and all of us was forced to come into a pittifull house for shelter, and lie there all night, with heavy hearts, least we should have bin used barbarously, as they contineued in threatning against my father's widdow and children; but, loe! our gracious Lord God, Who sees all wrongs and indignities offered to His servants, in His due time rights them, did bring us safe out of all our feares and dangers, blessed be His holy name for ever, and turned shame upon those cruell men that did abuse us. That night two of themselves, with my mother's servant, went to Coll. Shittleworth, ten miles off, who, upon the sight of his owne passe, did declaire his grand displeasure for theire rudenesses to my mother and children, causeing his nephew,* Captaine John Ashton, to punish those vilaines, and convey her safe as farre as his quarters laid, wishing her a good jorney. Thus did the Lord of Hostes deliver us all, and makeing our enimies our friends. O praised be the Lord God of our salvation, delivering us from bonds, imprisonments, and plundering, feares, and frights! O that we might live to His praise and glory of His name!

[Sept. 2, 1643.] My mother was minded to goe to Snape,† where my sister Danby ‡ was, and beeing invited by her she went thither to live till she could better dispose of herselfe and us in those troublesome times. For it beeing in the heate of the warres, she could not live at Hipswell,§ her joynture,

---

* Not nephew, but son-in-law, Captain John Ashton, of Ouerdale, having married Anne, Colonel Shuttleworth's eldest daughter. (Dugdale's Visitation of Lancashire, i., 10).

† A township in the parish of Well, three miles from Bedale, in the north riding of co. York. Here was a castle built by the Nevilles Lords Latimer, temp. H. VII. When the Cecil family became owners they transformed the castle into a quadrangular house, *circa* 1587. This is now partially in ruins. (See Whitaker's Hist. Richmondshire, vol. ii., p. 90).

‡ Catherine Wandesford, wife of Sir Thomas Danby, Knt., about whom more afterwards.

§ Hipswell lies a few miles to the south of Richmond. The estate came to

which was molested sometimes with the parliament's, and then the king's forces amongst them, soe that for a whole yeare we lived with great comfort and safety with my sweete sister Danby at Snape, where she was delivered of a galant son.* Even in the midest of troubles God gave her comfort, and my brother would have him called Charles, because of his ingagement for the king's service.

[Sept. 15, 1643.] About the yeare 1643 we went to see my Aunt Norton at Richmond, and to live a while with her till Hipswell was fitted, and there itt pleased God to preserve me from death, which I was nigh unto by eating a little peice of lobster: that day I had taken phisick, for it turned on my first sleepe when I wakned into an exceeding terrible vomitting and purging, and so followed with such violence that they could not make me any helpe, nor could I have soe much respitt or ease till I could take any thing: and this contineued all that night and the next day till night, butt by the gracious blessing of God upon some respitt and things given by Mr. Matrum, with my deare mother's caire, I escaped that desperate fitt, and by degrees was cured, only it brought me very weake and faint.

[To Snape from Richmond, October 11, 1643.] Now, while we lived at Snape, my brother Christopher Wandesford was exceedingly tormented with the fitts of the spleene,† haveing taken them uppon the death of my father, with greife in the

the Wandesfords through an intermarriage with an heiress of Fulthorpe. There are still at Hipswell some remains of the old manor-house, with some coats of arms on its front.

* 1643, June 6. Charles, son of Sir Thomas Danby, Bart., bapt. (Well Parish Register). He was a lawyer, a member of Gray's Inn, and died in 1672. (Fisher's Masham, 277).

† Dec. 10, 1640. My brother, Christopher Wandesforde, beeing in the church called Christ Church, in Dublin, hearing the great and dreadfull cry that the Irish made att my deare father's funerall, was soe frighted that he fell into the most greivous fitts of the splen, which much tormented him for many yeares affter, and had like to have taken his life away; butt, blessed be the gracious God, by my deare mother's excelent caire, cost, and paines, he was cured, and became a very strong man, and lived to be the father of that family of which he was descended, and was my beloved brother, living to the age of sixty-one yeares, and died at London, Feb. 23, 1686. Buried at Kirklington by his antienters (i., 293).

church at his funerall seiseing then upon him; they contineued sore notwithstanding all good meanes used, laboures and endeavours of my mother and us all, with all meanes, meadicens, and advices of phisicians for him. I am wittnesse, and many more, that not anything was wanting which might conduce to his recovery. At the last she sending him to Dr. Batthurst,* at Yorke, where, by God's blessing, he was perfectly cured of this distemper. This was, indeed, a great deliverance of him from this distemper, wherein many that has seen him has begged of the Lord to take him out of those torments, and at length, through great mercy, he was delivered.

[Brother Jack to Bedale scoole, Nov. 16, 1643. Christopher to scoole, Nov. 23, 1643.] It was advised that my mother should goe from Snape and live at Yorke, for the better education of my two brothers Christopher and John.† As for my eldest brother George, being then in France,‡ was happie under the tuition of one Mr. George Anderson, a Scotchman, but a most sober, wise, discreet person, a great scholer, and excelent qualified man, and of grand abilities, a zealous devine for the Church of England, as indeed a most excelent good Christian for his life and conversation. Under the conduct of this good man was my deare brother George happiely placed for his education in all good and commendable qualities, in France, during the heate warre in part, allthough he § was compelled to returne into England for lacke of supplies, when his rents was seized on by the parliament, through which he indured a great deale of hardship. But to return to my mother, whoe prepared for Yorke with her children and goods, intending to live there.‖ But it pleased God we was prevented from goeing

---

* John Bathurst, M.D., a famous physician, afterwards of Clints, near Richmond. (See Canon Raine's account of "Marske," in *Archæologia Æliana*, vol. iv., 1860. Munk's *Roll of the Royal College of Physicians*, p. 206.

† The chief school in York at this time was that in the Horsefair, in the patronage of the Dean and Chapter.

‡ "Being sent into France by his guardian for education, as most of our English gentry was." (iii., 38.)

§ "And Mr. Anderson, his tutor." (iii., 38.)

‖ "In order to the better education of my brothers, Christopher and John

further then a place in the halfe way, when we were mett with a freind, Mr. Danby, of Cave, who gave expresse notice to my mother that as she loved her life not to goe to Yorke, for the parliament forces had mett with the king's, and they were all betrayed, and so was forced to retreat, and that towne would be beseiged ; and soe this councell came seasonably and happicly to hinder our greater troubles and sorowes uppon that towne's surprisall. Praised be the Lord our God which did prevent those evills, and preserved us in our way, when we were nigh to danger, and knew it not, for this poore gentleman, Mr. Danby, was soone affter killed on the Moore for the king, when the king's forces was allmost all destroyed and cutt downe by the Scotts and the parliament army. Affter this, my mother and family returned, and came to Kirklington, where she staied at Mr. Daggett's,* the minister, beeing most kindly entertained and received till the hall was made fitt to dwell in. In that time, affter she came thither, in the yeare 1643, was the battle of Heasome,† and the taking of Yorke, and she was much con-

Wandesford, at scoole there, and not knowing anything of the ingagement of the armies, was gott as farre towards Yorke as a place called Ten Miles Hill from Kirklington ; when, just as we were goeing on our journey, there came a messenger in great hast to my deare mother, from Mr. Thomas Danby, of Cave, who was then ingaged in the fight at the time, who, out of the caire he had to preserve her and her family, had sent that man on purpose to prevent her goeing to Yorke ; and tould her that he feared the king would lose the day, and beged she would save herselfe and returne backe to Kirklington ; which she did doe immediatly, and returned backe that night to Kirklington, and soe saved us all. But all as we heard the sad newes of the king's losse of that day, with thousands poore soules being slaine of all parties, but most of our deare king's faithfull servants ; and most trouble to us was that poore gentleman was shot to death with a cannon bullett, and cutt off by the midest of his body, he being locked in his sadle that very day, while we by this providence of his sending that very day prevented our ruine, and I alive this day to sett forth the glory of our God, and praise His holy name." Ps. ciii. 2, 3 (iii.)

* Robert Daggett, B.D., instituted to rectory of Kirklington, 30th April, 1639. Died 19th, and bur. 20th August, 1649. (Kirklington Par. Register.) He was, no doubt, one of the Daggetts of How.

† Hessay, in the parish of Moor-Monkton, 5¾ miles from Yorke. The Moor was enclosed in 1830. The village is situated a little to the west of the road from York to Knaresborough.

serncd for my brother Christofer Wandesforde, beeing then at Yorke for cure and att scoole. Butt it pleased God in providence soe to order it unexpectedly, my brother George was newly come out of France, beeing at my uncle Osborne's, at Keveton, and wanting supplies in the warre's time was forced to come toward his estate about Richmond, att that time when the armies was in battaille, and was surrounded in his passage to Yorke; but, when he perceaved that the day was lost from the king, he rid to fettch my brother Kitt from thence, where, as he happiely mett him riding out of the towne to see the fight,* he took him up behind him, and brought him safe to Kirklington that night, butt was pursued by a party of horrse of Scotts; and at a eleven or twelve a clocke att night we receaved both my brothers home safely † out of those great dangers of beeing murdered. Blessed be God our Saviour, and high deffence to the poore desolate widow and her children in these horrid distractions and feares of our and the churche's enemies. Thus did we receave them home againe with great joy. But my poore brother George Wandesforde durst not stay at Kirklington the next day, by reason that a party of horrse was dispatched to seise on him, suposing him a commander in armes for the king, but he was forced to fly for his life, and secure himselfe where he could, the Lord still preserving him from his unjust enimies, being an innocent person, and never ingaged in either party, and who was but newly returned in to his country; and this was his first salutattion and welcome into it.

Affter this when the Scotts had helped to overthrow the king's army at Yorke, for which designe they were called into England, and to destroy the regall power of his majestie, waiting upon the parliament's motions to fullfil the intent of the Scottish covenant in rooting out the prelaticall party, and the establishment of their Scottish presbitery in the ruine of the king and episcopacy, these Scottch rebells quartered them-

---

* "Riding towards the moore with other boys, which was goeing in their simplicity to see the bataile." (iii.)

† "Coming to the gate att twelve a clocke att night by a backe way, and not through the towne, by which they were preserved, blessed be God!" (iii.)

selves all over the countery, especially in and about Richmond, forcing all people to take the covenant, how contrary soever it was to theire duty of aleagance or conscience, and those who would not, weare forced to flie, or was imprisoned and ruined, soe that my poore brother George was upon this account compelled to live obscured from all people, in regard that he would not be compelled to this treason, nor was willing to be imprisoned by them.

Affter I was recruted in strength, my mother went to live at Hipswell, her joynture, with my brother George, myselfe, and George Lightfoot,* and Dafeny Carrell, and my brother George Wandesforde his man. And there she was troubled with the Scotts one while, and the parliament forces another while tormented us, gitting all our provissions of meate and drink, lett us want all nesscessaries, that there dominiereing and insulting voluptuousnesse must be supplied, and my mother was charged for eighteen or twenty months together with £25 a month in monnys to the soldiers, besides the quartring of a troope of Scotts on free quarter, which was trible the valeue of her estate, and at that time she borrowed monnyes to maintaine all her four children, which she paid afterwards. My brother Christopher and John were at Beedall scoole from Nov. the 16, 1643, many yeares. Albeit we had a perticuler maintenance to have bin paid out of Kirklington, and for the heires part out of Hudswell.† Yett even in these times most sad and lamentable did the Lord most high preserve us from ruine utterly, and made us have a place of safety under His wings of protection, all those evill times of feares and distractions, blessed and praised be the God of our salvation. Amen.

* George Lightfoot afterwards married Daphne Carrall.
† In the parish of Catterick, near Richmond.

A gratefull remembrance of my beeing preserved from the fury of the warres in the time of the Scotts being over the poore country in there madnes against us when I was att Hipswell, with my deare mother in 1643–1644.

In this time, affter the battaile of Hessom Moore, when the blessed King Charles had by treachery lost the field, and his two generalls, Prince Rupert and Lord of Newcastle, exposed all the brave white cots foote that stood the last man till they were murthred and destroyed,* and that my poore brother George Wandesforde was forced to fly to hide himselfe att Kirklington, and brought my brother Christopher behind him; affter which time we gott to Hipswell, and lived as quietly as we could, for the madnes of the Scotts who quartred all the country over, and insulted over the poore country and English. My deare mother was much greived to be abusd by them in quartring them at her owne house, yett could not possibly excuse herselfe totally from the men and horses, tho' she paid duble pay, and was at 1*s.* 6*d.* a pt.† when others at ninepence only in a month. She kept of the quarting captains and commanders, and would never yeald to have them. Att length there came one Capt. Innis, which was over that troope we had in towne, and he comming on a surprize into the house, I could not hide myselfe from them as I used to doe; but comming boldly into my mother's chamber, where I was with her, he began to be much more ernest and violent to have staid in the house, and said he would stay in his quarters, but we so ordered the matter that we gott him out by all the fair means could be

---

* " When that fatall battaile was fought, and his majestie's armye was betrayed to the Scotch and Cromwell, who was assistant against theire lawfull king, and by the cowardice of some, and treatchery of others, that noble army was over-throne, many thousands valiant, brave, stout men, killed and inhumainly buttchered; and soe overcame the loyall party, forcing them to fly for releife and refuge to save them where they could. In the yeare 96 is 52 yeares, called Long Marston Moore by the parliament. Of Scotts army in all twenty thousand." (iii.)

† *Sic orig.* apparently; probably intended for a contraction for *apiece.*

to gett quitt of him, who was soe vild a bloody looked man, that I trembld all the time he was in the house; I calling to mind with dread that he was soe infinit like in person my Lord Macguire, the great rebell in Ireland, was in a great constrnation for feare of him. Affter which time this man impudantly tould my aunt Norton that he would give all he was worth if she could procuere me to be his wife, and offered three or four thousand pounds, and Lord Adare* shold come and speake for him. She said it was all in veine; he must not presume to looke that way, for I was not to be obtained. And she was sure he might not have any incoragement, for I was resolvd not to marry, and put him of the 'best she could; but writt me private word that my Lord of Adare and he would come to speake to me and my mother about it, and wishd me to get outt of his way. It was not to further that desire in me, who did perfectly hate him and them all like a todd † in such a kind; and imeadiatly acquanted my deare mother, which was surprised and troubled, for she feard they would burne her house and destroy all; wishd me to goe whither I would to secure myselfe; and I did soe forthwith, ran into the toune, and hid myselfe privatly in great feare and a fright with a good old woman of her tenants, where, I bles God, I continud safely till the vissitt was over, and at night came home. We was all joyful to escape soe, for my deare mother was forcd to give them the best treat she could, and said, indeed, she did not know where I was, and sent out [servants?] a little to seeke me, but I was safe from them. Affter which time this villaine captaine did study to be revenged of my dear mother, and threatnd cruelly what he would doe to her because she hid me, tho' that was not true, for I hid myself; and about the time that the Scotts was to march into Scottland, beeing too long here on us, when my mother paid offten £25 and £30 a month to them, this Scott in a bosting manner sent for his pay, and she sent all she ought to him, which he would not take from her, but demanded duble money, which she would nor could not do; soe on Sunday

* Adair.   † A fox.

morning he brought the company, and threatned to breake the house and dores, and was most vile and crewell in his oaths and swearing against her and me; and went to drive all her goods in her grownd, haveing this delecate cattell of her owne breed. I went up to the leades to see whether he did drive them away, and he looked up and thought it had bin my deare mother, cursed me bitterly, and wished the deale blaw me blind and into the ayre, and I had bin a thorne in his heele, but he would be a thorne in my side, and drived the cattell a way to Richmond, where Generall Leccley * was. So my deare mother was forcd to take the pay he was to have, and carried it to the generall that laid at my Aunt Norton's, and acquainted him how that captaine had abused her and wronged her; which, by mercy of God to her, this Generall Lecely did take notice of, and tooke her mony, and bid her not trouble herselfe, for he would make him take it, or punish him for his rudness. He said more, did Innis, that if ever any of his countrymen came into England, they would burne her and me and all she had ; butt yett she servd that God which did delever us out of the Irish rebellion, and all this blood shed in England till this time, and did now delever her and myselfe and all we had from him. This was a great deliverance at last, and joyned with my owne single deliverance from this beast, from being destroyed and defloired by him, for which I have reason to praise the great and mighty God of mercy to me. There was one of his men that I had cured of his hand, beeing cutt of it, and lame ; soe that fellow did me a signall returne of gratitude for it. Thus it was some times a refreshment to me affter I had sett up much with my deare weake mother in her illness, or writing of letters for her, that she did bid me walke out to Lowes with her maides to rest myselfe, soe I used this some times. Butt this captane man who I curd, came to me one day, saing " Dere mistress, I pray do not thinke much if I desire you, for

---

* General Leslie. Jane Yorke, half-sister to Mrs. Norton's son-in-law, Sir John Yorke, became the wife of David Lesley, afterward Lord Newark, in Scotland, and her sister Elizabeth married Sir James Lesley, Lord Lindores, in Scotland. See *Dugdale's Visit. Ebor.*, p. 92.

God sake, not to goe out with the maides to Lowes." I said,
"Why?" He said againe, "he was bound to tell me that his
captaine did currs and sweare that we would watch for me, and
that very night he had designed with a great many of his com-
rades to catch me at Lowes, and force me on horsebacke away
with them, and God knowes what end he would make of me."
I said, "I hopd God would deliver me from all such wickednesse:" and soe I gave the man many thankes, who was soe
honest to preserve me from these plots, rewarding him for his
paines, and did never goe abroad out of the house againe, but
forcd to keepe like a prisoner while they was here. Blessing
the great God of heaven, who did not suffer me to fall into the
hands of those wicked men, nor into the hand of Sir Jeremy
Smithson,* who could never prevaile by noe meanes to obteine
me for his wife, and I was then delivered allso from such a force
by the discovery of Tom Binkes.† Lord make me truly thankfull for preservation of me, thy poore handmaid, and make me
live to Thy glory. Amen.

---

* A turbulent person. (See Depositions from York Castle, 131.) He was the
son and the father of a Sir Hugh Smithson. 1689 "Anthony Smithson, of
Armin, esquire, was buried in the tombe besids Sir Hugh Smithson, his father,
knight and baronet, the 18th of January. Jerimie Smithson, knight and baronet,
was buried in the foresaid tombe, the 18th day of February." (Par. Register of
Stanwick, N.R.Y., from duplicates at Richmond, 1553.) The uncle was probably
Francis Smithson, of Richmond, merchant, who made his will Aug. 9th, 1670,
proved there 13th June, 1671.

"A great deliverance from the violence of a rape from Jerimy Smithson, Sir
Heugh's son, who had sollicited me in marriage by his father and uncle Smithson,
who would have setled on him £200 a yeare if I would have married him; but
I would not, but avoyded his company, because he was debauched. And he hired
some of his owne company to have stolen me away from Lowes, but Tom Binks
discovered it, I bles God." (i., 299.)

† "Tom Binkes" was a connection of the Smithsons.

*My deliverance from drowning in the river att Midlam, when I
went to be a wittness to my sister Danby's first Francis,
borne att Midlam Castle, in the yeare 1644 (i., 298.)*

At that time Sir Thomas Danby was forced with my sister
and children to be in safty from the parliament forces, he beeing
for King Charles the First, to Midlam Castle,* a garison under
my Lord Lofftus. There she was delivered of her first† son
Francis Danby, my sister having gott my Lord Lofftus and
myselfe with cozen L. Branlon‡ for wittnesses. I was forced to
goe over the river neare Midlam, caulled Swaile, which had some
stoops sett up for guides, and if one had missed the caucy they
had bin errecoverably lost. At that time I was very hearty and
strong, and did venture to ride the same, or ellse might have
gone backe, and rather then she should be disapoynted did
venture over affter my mother's servant, who led the way. But
it happened the river proved deeper than we expected it, and I
kept up my horrse as well as I could from standing, and soe
bore up a long time. Butt when we were gon soe farre that I
could not turne backe, the river proved past riding, and the
bottom could not be come to by the poore maire, which was an
excelent maire of my poore brother G. Wandesford's, soe I saw
myselfe in such aparant danger, and beged of God to assist me
and the poore beast I rid on, and to be mercifull to me and
deliver me out of that death, for Jesus Christ his sake. And
the poore maire drew up her fore feete, and I perceived she did
swime I gave her the reines, and tooke of the short reines of
the breech, and gave her the head with all the helpe I could,

* Middleham, ten miles from Richmond. About 1190 a splendid castle was
built here by Robert Fitz Ranulph. Edward IV. was confined here by the Earl
of Warwick. King Edward, whose son Edward, afterwards Prince of Wales,
was born here, gave the castle to his brother, Richard Duke of Gloucester. The
remains of the fabric stand upon an eminence near the town. (See Whitaker's
Hist. Richmondshire (i., 330–349.)
† *i.e.* her first son of that name.
‡ This is not very clear in the MS.

and clasped my hands about her maine, did freely comit myselfe to my God to do what He pleased with me. And she did by mercy beare up her head and swimd out above halfe a quarter of a mile crosse that dreadfull river, and by God's great mercy brought me over that river in safety : which deliverance soe great and dreadfull I cannott forgett to praise the God, and my great and gracious Lord God, Who had pitty on me at this time, to spare me from this death and destruction. Oh! what shall I render to the great God of heaven Who has delivered me from perishing by the water, and caused this poore creature to bring me out safe. All glory be to my gracious God of heaven by all the powers of men and angels for ever. O lett me live to Thy glory, and serve Thy Majesty for ever ! Amen.

A remembrance of a great deliverance I had from drowning as I was going over the river Swaile to St. Nicholas, to my aunt Norton's, when a flood came downe on me, and Ralph Ianson, in the yeare 1646.

The death of my sister Danby, Sept. 30, 1645, *att her house at Thorpe* (i., 86.)

About this yeare, my deare and only sister, the Lady Danby, drew neare her time for delivery of her sixteenth child. Ten whereof had bin baptized, the other six were stillborne, when she was above halfe gon with them, she haveing miscarried of them all uppon frights by fire in her chamber, falls, and such like accidents happening. All her children were sons, saveing my two neeces, Katherine and Alice Danby, and most sweete, beautifull, and comely were they all. The troubles and distractions of those sad times did much afflict and grieve her, who was of a tender and sweete disposition, wanting the company of her husband, Sir Thomas, to manage his estate and other conscrnes. But he, beeing ingaged in his king's service, was not permitted to leave it, nor come to Thorpe but seldom, till she fell sicke. These things, added to the horrid rudnesse of the soldiers and Scotts quartered then amongst them, which

vexssing and troubling her much with frights, caused her to
fall into travill sooner then she expected, nor could she gett her
old midwife, beeing then in Richmond, which was then shutt
up, for the plague was exceeding great there, soe that all the
inhabitants that could gett out fled, saveing those had the
sicknesse in their houses. At this time did my deare mother
and whole family receave grand preservation from the Devine
Providence in delivering us from the arrow that flieth by day,
when as hundreds died so neare us, and thousands fell at noone
day; nay, all that towne was allmost depopulated. How did
our good and great Lord preserve all us at Hipswell, so that
noe infection seised upon any one that belonged us, allthough
the malice of the beggers was great to have don harme by
raggs, notwithstanding all her charitable releife daily with much
meate and monny. Blessed be the great and ever mercifull
Father, Who did not deliver us up to this heavy judgment of
the Lord, but did rebuke the destroying angell, and at last
stayed this plague in Richmond.

But to returne to my poore sister, whoes extreamitie called
her friends to her assistance. She had bin very ill long time
before her delivery, and much altered in the heate of her bodie,
beeing feavorish. Affter exceeding sore travill she was delivered
of a goodly son about August 3d, by one dame Sworre. This
boy was named Francis, affter another of that name, a sweete
childe that died that sommer of the smale-pox. This childe
came double into the world, with such extreamity that she was
exceedingly tormented with paines, so that she was deprived of
the benefitt of sleepe for fourteen daies, except a few frightfull
slumbers; neither could she eate any thing for her nourish-
ment as usuall. Yett still did she spend her time in discourse
of goodnesse excelently pieous, godly, and religeous, instructing
her children and servants, and prepairing her soule for her
deare Redeemer, as it was her saing she should not be long
from Him. That weeke when I was left with her, affter my
lady Armitage,* and my aunt Norton was gon, though she

* Lady Armitage, Sir Thomas Danby's sister, married Sir Francis Armitage,
of Kirk Lees, Bart.

could not gett rest, yet all her discourse was very good and
profitable to the hearers, whoe might learne piety, chastiety,
holinesse, patience, humilitie, and all how to entertaine the
pleasure of God with contentednesse, makeing soe excelent a
confession of faith and other Christian virtues and graces that
Mr. Siddall exceedingly admired her partes and pietie, giveing
her as high a carracter as could be. She did intreat Sir Thomas,
her husband, to send for Mr. Farrer, and to joyne with her in
the receaveing the Holy Sacrament, but he would not give
leave, which was to my knowledge a great greife and trouble to
her thoughts. That night she poured out her soule in praier
with such comprehensive and good expressions that could be
for her owne soule, for pardon and remission of her sinns, for
grace and sanctification from the Spiritt, faith, and assurance;
and then for her husband, children, mother, and all her other
relations and myselfe; for the restoration of the king, the
church, and the kingdom's peace; with such patheticall and
zelous expressions that all did glorifie God for [the] things He
had don for her. Affter which, she did in a manner prophesie
that God would humble the kingdome by afflictions for there
sin and security; but affter that when we were humbled and
reformed, whosoever should live to see it (for she should not)
should injoy happie daies for church and state. Thus, she
contineued, and with praiers for our enimies, and for they
stood in need of our praiers for the forgivenesse of all their
evills, she called her children, exhorted them abundantly to
feare God, serve Him, and love one another, be obedient to
theire father, with admonishing them and her familie. She
was kinde and dearly affectionate to her husband, to whome,
under God, she left the caire of her seven young children.
Sometimes she did expresse abundant joy in God, and would
sweetely, with a melodious voice, sing aloud His praise and
glory in anthems and psallmes proper for her condition, with
many sweete verces praising Him for all things; nor was she
in the least conserned to part with her husband or children,
nor any thing in this world, haveing her hopes and desires
fixed upon God, leaveing her children freely to the providence

of her God, Who had releived her soule out of all her distresse, Who had promised to be a father to the fatherlesse. All her words weere full of sweetenesse and affection, giveing me manny hearty thankes for all my paines and caire I tooke with her, and watching a whole weeke together; if she lived she would requite my love; with an abundant of affectionate expressions to this purpose. My greife and sorrow was soe great for her, that I had brought myselfe into a very weake condition, in so much as my mother came to Thorpe with Dafeny Lightfoote, a cairefull servant, to helpe with my sister, and sent mee home who was allmost spent in that time. Att which time I tooke my last leave of my dearest and only sister, never could gett to see her for my owne illnesse afiterwards. But she, waiting her Lord's time to be called, was fitting her soule and heart for Him. As the dissease increased of the feaver, notwithstanding what could be don for her in that condittion, it did to her as many others in such extreamity, deprive her (for want of sleepe and food, which she could not take by reason of a sore throat) of part of the use of understanding for a little while when its fury lasted. But Dafeny was alwaies with her, who she had a great love for, and as she grew weaker afiter a mouth's time of her delivery, holding her head on her breast, said to her in a faint, weake voyce, "I am goeing to God, my God, now." Then said Dafeny, "Nay, maddam, I hope God will please to spaire your life to live amongst your sweete children, and bring them up." "How can that be?" answered my sister, "for I find my heart and vittalls all decaid and gon. Noe; I desire to be desolved and to be with Christ, which is best of all. I have made my peace with God." And immeadiately she said with as strong a voyce as she could, "Lord Jesus, receive my spirritt;" then, giveing a little breathing sigh, deliverred up her soule in to the hands of her Saviour, sweetely falling asleepe in the Lord. And thus ended that sweete saint her weary pilgrimage, haveing her life interwoven with mainy caires and afflictions. Although she was married to a good estate, yet did she injoy not much comfort, and I know she receaved her change with much sattisfaction, beeing, she hoped, to be freed,

as she said, from a wicked world, and all the evills therein.
Thus departed that good soule, haveing bin young called to
walke in the waies of God, and had made His service her contineuall practise. The Lord sanctifie this sad losse of this
virtuous sister of ours to the whole familie, and that, as she
lived the waies of godlinesse from her youth, soe she may be a
godly example to all her children. She was a most obedient
childe to her parents, loving and loiall, affectionate and obser-
vant to her husband, a tender and prudent mother to her
children, bringing them up in the severities of Christian duties,
yet enough indulgent over them with a Christian moderation :
a wise and discreet mistresse towards her servants, whoe loved
and honoured her in theire obedience, truly affectionate to all
her relations in generall, and courteously affable to all neighbours and freinds. And, indeed, a great losse to all amongst
whom she lived, doeing much good and imploying her time in
helpeing the diseased, and doeing many cures, following the
example of my mother in all these things. She lived, affter
the birth of this child, about a month, dieing on the 30th of
September, 1645, and was buried that night * att Sir Thomas
Danby's owne towne, in Massam church, in the night, by
reason of the parliment sett and Scots, who would not let a
sermon be preached. Butt there was great lamentation made
for her death.

The death of my cosen, John Norton, 1646.

My cozen John Norton died of a consumption, long in a
languishing condittion, but at length it pleased God to take
him to Himselfe in the yeare 1646.† He was a sweete good
natured youth ; he died at St. Nicolas.

---

* Sept. 22, 1645, Katheran, the ladye to Sir Thomas Danbye, of Thorp
Perrye, was buried. (Masham Par. Register.)

† Richmond Par. Register is wanting, 1645—1654.

The death of Sir Edward Osborne, 1646.

My uncle, Sir Edward Osborne,* who was my mother's half-brother, was a very good, wise, and prudent man, under whoes tuition my father left the hope of his house, my brother George, as being joynt gardian with my mother. He had soe fraternall a love for, and parentall caire over, my deare mother and us all, that we weare most happie in him, and during his life this our familie was kept in much peace and tranquilitie, he seeing that each party had its right and dues, with a caire for the due observance of my father's will, of which he was an executor. But affter his death, we (that is to say) my mother and her children, was much opprest and injured through the bad managerie of all that estate, and that was all seised on by my uncle Wandesford for the debts, which he was much wronged of too by one he made a leace of it for seven yeares takeing many hundred pounds more then his due, and before he gott it againe he put him to a suite; but in this time all the children was maintained by my deare mother from her joynture. My deare uncle Osborne beeing att Keeveton with his ladie, and desireing to eate some mellons att the time of yeare, sent for severall from his gardens at Thorpe† and Keeveton. And, finding some excelent good, did eate a little freely, but that fruit was too cold for him, and strooke him into a vomiting and purging so violently that it could not be staied till his strength was past recovery, soe that in a few daies time he was deprived of his life, to the great and exceeding loss to all his owne family and ours, as allso of his majestic's and countery, he beeing a most excelent good Christian, true and orthodox to

---

* Sir Edward Osborne, of Kiveton, in the parish of Harthill, co. York, son of Sir Hewett Osborne, created a baronet 13th July, 1620; vice-president of the council in the north, and lieut.-general for the king. (See Mon. Inscription. Hunter's South Yorkshire, vol. i., p. 146.)

† Thorpe-Salvin, in the parish of Laughton, an estate theretofore of the families of Sandford, Rogers, etc. By the marriage of Ellen Sandford, second dau. and coh. of Henry Sandford with Henry Nevile, the mansion and manor came to Francis Nevile, of Chevet, who sold them to Sir Edw. Osborne in 1636. (See Hunter's South Yorkshire, vol. i., p. 311.)

the church of England, a faithfull loyall subject to the king, and of a sweete and affable disposition to all; in whoes death I suffered the losse of a father, and my mother a husband. But he was very happie in a holy good life, an high esteeme in his countrey, and of a great fame for vertue, and much lamented in his death; makeing a sweete and comfortable conclusion of his life with an abundance of pieious and religious expressions. He died about the month of July, in the yeare 1646,* att Keeveton, in the furthest part of Yorkeshire.

My cozen Edmund Norton, eldest son to my uncle Norton, was married to Mr. Dudly's daughter and heire, of Chopwell, in the bishoprick of Durham, Mrs. Jane Dudly, an excelent, fine and good gentlewoman, Feb. 10th, 1647, att Chopwell.† My cozen Edmund Norton died of a plurisic, att Yorke, the 30th of November, 1648.‡ A gentleman of a sweete, good disposittion to all, obedient and dutifull to his parents, and true freind in time of adversity, a religious young man, a faithfull subject to his majestie, for whom he suffred much ;§ he lived an honest, good, sober life, doeing good to all, died religeously, and is, I hope, now very happie in peace and rest, loveing a peaccable temper, and was beloved of all that knew him, and an unmeasurable losse to his parents. My cosen Julian Norton‖ died at Richmond Greene, at her father's, the 9th of Aprill, 1649.

* The date of his death upon his monument is 9 Sept. 1647.

† See Surtees' Hist. Durham, vol. ii., 276. In the pedigree, p. 280, Jane, dau. and sole heir of Toby Dudley, of Chopwell, Esq., is stated to have married Robert Clavering. She was at that time Mr. Norton's widow. 15th July, 1651, Robert Clavering, Esq., and Mistress Jane Norton married (Ebchester, Par. Register).

‡ Nov. 19, 1648, Major Edmond Norton, of Richmond, buried (Par. Register, St. Michael-le-Belfrey, York).

§ Major Norton, of Richmond, and Edmund his son, compounded for their estates for the sum of £756.

‖ Gillian, filia Majoris Norton generosi, bap. 6 Jan. 1632–3 (Richmond Par. Reg.) The Par. Register is missing at the time of her death.

Uppon the beheading of King Charles the Martyr, Jan. 30, 1648.
(i., 94.)

Our blessed King Charles the First, whoes memmory shall live to etternity, was cruelly murthered by the hands of blasphemous rebells, his owne subjects, att Whitehall, London, the 30th of January, 1648. Lett all true Christians mourne for the fall of this stately ceader, whoe was the chiefe suportt of the church of God. A holie, pieous prince, whoe fought God's battles against His enimes, beeing a nursing father, a good Josiah to his three kingdomes; whoe, for the defence of the true catholique religion of Jesus Christ his Lord, and for the defence of the noble lawes of this kingdom of England, the protestant faith, and the priviliges of the parliament and subject, ruling them in peace and happinesse many yeares, he laid downe his life; beeing sacrificed by the iniquitties of his subjects : their sinns pulled downe his ruine on him and our selves. Lett his admirable booke * speake his etternall glory and praise, the best of kings (as meere man) that ever this earth had; never defiling himselfe with sin or blood, of a tender, compassionate, sweete disposition. Incomparably chaste, and free from the least tincture of vice or profainenesse. Oh ! how may we take up justly those bitter lamentations of Jerimie,* the annoynted of the Lord, the joy of our hearts, the light of our eyes is taken in theire pitts, the crowne is fallen from our heads; woe unto us that we have sinned, lett every soule gird itselfe with saccloth, and lament the displeasure of God which has smitten our head, and wounded the defence of this our English church, our Solomon. Hezekiah, in him our staffe and stay is gon. O repent and humble yourselves, you daughters of Jerusalem, for him *that clothed you in scarlett** is taken from you; what will you doe in this your day of calamitty ?

* Εικων Βασιλικη.

† Lamentations of Jeremiah, iv. 20 : "The breath of our nostrils, the anointed of the Lord, was taken in their pits, of whom we said, Under his shadow we shall live among the heathen."

‡ 2 Sam. i. 24.

O that my head were waters, and mine eyes a fountaine of teares, that I might weepe for the slaine of the daughter of my people ; nay, that our eyes might gush out with teares for this holy saint and martire of the Lord.   *   *   *   *   *

O Lord God, give them a most sad and deepe repentance and humiliation for this bloody fact, all whoe has had their hand therein, either explicittly or implicittly; and affter a sharpe and salutary repentance give them pardon and remission of this horrid sin. And further, O Lord our God, still preserve thy church in this our Israell, and bring to us in peace and safety our lord and soveraine King Charles his son to rule peaceably and religeously over us with the establishment of thy true religeon in this land. *   *   *   *   *   *

Uppon the death of my brother George Wandesforde, March 31, 1651, *and of his sequestration and other troubles, affter his returne into England* (i., 97.)

The fatall blow given to my father's familie, by the death of our excelent brother, was very great, but the effects thereof fell out most heavy upon myselfe in the sad losse of soe deare and loving brother ; nay, I may say, a father to us all. He was a gentleman exceedingly qualified with sutable endowments both naturall and acquired, giveing him selfe over in the qualifications for the service of his God, his church, his king, and countery, and such as rendred him much beloved and lamented at home and abroad for the great losse and sad conclusion of soe brave a person. Yet injoyed he in his time, affter my father's death, not much comfort, for since his returne out of France, in the publicke calamities of church and state, he was driven to many straits and hardships. Beeing sequesterd through a false oath of his adversary's suggestion, and his estate, with all the other apoynted for widdow, children, and creaditors of my father, seised on for the parliament uppon that account. This don under the pretence of godlinesse and

* Jeremiah ix. 1.

religion, because he did not joyne in such practices of rebellion against the church of God and our lawfull king, whom God had commanded to be obeied ; nor could any adheare to such designes, whoes hearts was sencable of those duties of faith and alleigeance, without the danger of etternall damnation, and the curse of God upon them who seperated from the knowne lawes and commands of God Almighty, and the lawes of the land, wherein we are happiely placed our peace and safetie. According to that of the wise man, *My son, feare thou God and the king, and medle not with them that are given to change, for who knowes the ruine of them both ?** Yet, notwithstanding, this threatning evill was soc established by a law, that there was noc man of estate which did not lift up his hand against the Lord's annoynted, that could be freed either from plundering, sequestration and imprisonment, robed or murdered by secrett or open hostilitie, if any gave information against them.

As for my brother's crime, it was for dispossceing of the parsonage of Kirklington in his owne right as heire, and of my mother as a guardian to him yet under age, beeing but nineteen yeares old, unto Mr. Siddall,† a very picous, godly minister, but not of the priesbyterian faction. The liveing, beeing of too good a valew for a royalast, was looked upon by one Mr. Nesbitt‡ of the other oppinion, and so the more confiding person, which could not be invested into it till my brother, etc., was made a delinquent. Affter which it was conceaved, upon such a crime as loyallty to his God and prince, this privilege of the disposing of this, with the injoyment of his owne estate, was sufficiently forfited. Upon the poynt thus

---

* Proverbs xxiv. 21.

† Michael Siddall, youngest son of Thomas Siddall, of York, was baptized at St. Martin's in Micklegate, York, 30th September, 1614. He became vicar of Catterick, and by will dated 3rd January, 1658-9, founded an hospital. He died five days afterwards.

‡ Philip Nesbitt, son of Philip N. of Easington, co. Durham, married Susan, dau. of ... Hemmingway, of York. (Dugdale's Visitation of Yorkshire, 158.) The following children of theirs occur in the Kirklington Register :—Philip, bp. 20th Feb. 1647. Obadiah, bp. June 25, 1650. Susanna, born 20th, bp. 25 Aug. 1653. Thomas, bp. Jan. 30, 1655, bur. Nov. 19, 1657. Joseph, bp. Feb. 6, 1657. Elizabeth, born 12, bp. 20th Oct. 1660.

much was confest by Mr. Nessbitt to my uncle William Wandesford, affter my brother's death, beeing the cause why he was sequestered. In this condittion was my deare brother amongst many others most faithfull in this realme. And, therefore, they might soone make a fault where there was none, and poor Naboth must suffer, that an occassion might be found to take his possession. Albeit he saw, too evidently, that the king's forces and power declined, yet could not his loyall heart be gained to joyne with the actors in this rebellion, allthough there wanted not solicitations, but his heart could not without abhorrency looke on such practicies more abominable then that of Ireland, because masked with a faire shew of true religeon and pietie, to fight against the most Christian king that ever this nation had, under whose government we might have still continued happie if our owne sins ripe for judgement had not prevented God's mercys, and stirried up the Philistines with the discontented scismatticks instruments for our punishment in theire rebellion. It must not be denied that my dear brother's affections and conscience carried him in judgement to serve his king, the church, and state, by way of armes. Yet, as things then fell out, such was his prudence for the preservation of his family, according to his gracious majestie's command to his freinds, that he saw all was lost, and that they should sitt in quiett, and preserve themselves for the good of himselfe or sonne affterwards. So that he saw it was in vaine to strive against that impetuous streame, and involve himselfe in utter ruine willfully, when noe good could possibly be don by his service to the king, otherwaise then by our praiers and teares for him. This was the reason made him decline the ingaging into that warre. Butt his enimies vigilancy of all opportunitys to gaine his estate, and this living afforesaid, had spies upon his actions, wherein they might take an advantage against him, and had theire designes furthered uppon this accident.

I formerly shewed how my brother was disposed of for travill into France, for his improvement in education. At his returne into England, and in his passage betwixt my uncle Osborne's house, Keeveton, to his owne estate, and my mother to Kirklington, he beeing ignorant of the armies ingagement that day on Hessome Moore, was to passe that way towards Yorke home. But, most unhappiely, it fell out, contrary to his expectation, and before he could retreat any way, found a necessity to secure himselfe from the stragling company, and soe by Providence light into the company of my cosen Edmund Norton's troope that day, till he gott towards Yorke, for the securing my second brother there at schoole. Affter which escape he came to Kirklington. But this was the opportunity his enimies sought, and without any questioning in to the true state of this bussinesse, sett severall, (as Mr. Luke Wastell* by name, whose family had bin raised by my father) to examine too poore men which had bin upon the Moore that day, who weare carried to Yorke on purpose to sweare they saw him fight. But the wittnesses would not take oath they saw him fight, beeing more just not to perjure themselves then theire masters,† they would give in evidence only that they saw him on the Moore. Soe when the kites could not prevaile with them for a more full oath to theire purpose, they were dismissed without any reward, save much anger and reproaches, for theire charges in that jorney.

This dealing much incensed the poore men, who said afterwards they were trapan'd into that bussinesse, and would not for the world have gon up if they could have forseene the designe to have prejudiced my brother. Neverthelesse, this formalitty of the projectors was sufficient grownd to proceed against him as a delinquent against the parliament (though according to theire owne rules he was not liable, being under age), yet where such selfe interestts, as by Nesbitt's solicitation, it was legall, and all the right in the world that his good service should be gratified. And thus it was performed. Immeadiatly there was his estate

* A younger son of Leonard Wastell, of Scorton, by Anne, dau. of Edmund Danby, of Kirkby Knowl, and brother of Colonel John Wastell, who died in 1659.

† "The poore men perceiving they agreed to make them sweare to a falls thing, tould the comitees, that they never would take a fallse oath against any man for any gaine in the world; to take any man's life or estate from him." (iii., 37.)

all seized upon, he proclamed a traitor to the parlament, with
my mother, my two younger brothers, my selfe, all of us three
beeing young, for I was but fifteen yeares old and the eldest of
them. This was don in the church of Kirklington by Mr.
Nesbitt in a triumphing manner, and thereupon my brother's
person should have bin seized upon, but he was secured through
a disguise.* Mr. Siddall also upon this account was sequestred,
injoyed that living from my mother and brother's donation
since the death of Mr. Daggett. Such practices cannot subsist
with primitive pietie, or the purity of our true religion, what
ever pretext is with our new reformadoes. In this confusion
and streights, wherein my father's family was fairely designed
for ruine, through the desperate malice of our unjust adversary,
whoe did worry the lion for his skin, there happened a propos-
sittion of marriage, made betweene my uncle William Wandesforde, who was then endevouring to gett of my brother's
sequestration with my cosen Richard Darley,† for to be had
because he would not relinquish his title to Nessbitt, he haveing

* "And my deare brother compelled to fly into the Dales for shelter against
their prossecution, for haveing bin sequestred, as an enemy to the state, it was
noe matter to take his life, by any meanes they could obteine it." (iii., 39.)

† "My uncle William Wandesford, desiring to seeke what remedy he could
to remove or cleare the sequestration, and releive this family then under this
oppression and apparant ruine, applyed himselfe to my uncle Richard Darley;
one, and the most witty, of the then ruling comittee att Yorke; a leading man
of the rest, who, having formerly married a kinswoman of my father's, Sir
William Hilliard's daughter, he pretended a kindness for the family, and that he
would do what service he could for it; and, haveing an eye of some prospect of
advantage to his owne relation, inquiered what children my father, the Lord-
Deputy, left; was tould by my uncle of my three brothers and my selfe; and
finding I was likely to have a considerable fortune, and other desirable perqui-
sitts in a good match, immeadiatly pressed forward in the mater, and said to my
uncle, that he had a nephew, which was a good man and a good estate, about
£700 per annum, which he judged might make a good match for me; and if
my uncle would be a meanes to obteine me for his nephew in marriage, he
would assure him of the clearing my brother's sequestration. I supose my
uncle was not backward to promise his uttmost assistance, and it should not be
his fault, if he did not prevaile. Thus the bargaine was strucke betwixt them,
before my deare mother and my selfe ever heard a silable of this mater. When,
as it most concerned me, in a case on which all the comfort of my life, or missery,
depended; which for the gaining this advantag for the clearing the estate of

betwixt a nephew of my cosen's and my selfe, which motion of Mr. Darley's was att that time relished by my uncle William, and thought to be the only expedient to secure my father's estate, and accepted by him, through whoes solicitation at first (though he deserted it affterwards) that affter some time it came to such a progresse as uppon that account my cosen Richard Darley was instrumentall in putting my brother George uppon the traversing his delinquency, and in the end cleared his estate from the ruine of sequestration. As to my owne perticuler, beeing willing to be advisable by my friends in the choyce of a husband, deeming theire judgments above my owne, was perswaded that this proposall might tend to the good of the whole family, and was inclined upon these grand motives and inducements to accept of this motion for Mr. Thornton, contrary to my owne inclination to marriage, as allso to that judgement which was oppositt to my owne in his relations, which probably might bring me to severall inconveniences; neverthelesse, for so generall a benifitt to my family, and hopes of finding a sober religious person, I waved all other opportunities of greater advantages in estate, etc., which was propounded by severall persons of qualittie, and of my owne perswasion with myselfe, and presently there was a treaty of marriage entred into by Mr. Thornton and my deare mother, which was depending till a good time affter my brother's death. But it so pleased God, for our greater affliction, when wee hoped to have injoyed the

the sequestration, my uncle William followed most earnestly to propose this match, with all immaginable indeavours he could, to us ; and threatned if denyed, that we should certainly be ruined, and the sequestration would proceed, for Mr. Darley would not cleare it, or doe ought to releeive the family. Which manner of perswasion to a marriage, with a sword in one hand, and a complement in annother, I did not understand, when a free choyce was denyed me. 'Tho' I did not resolve to change my happy estate for a misserable incombred one in the married ; yett I was much afflicted to be threatened against my owne inclination (or my future happiness), which I injoyed under that sweete and deare society and comfort of my most deare parents' conduct. But my dearest mother, willing to serve the family in what she could, with reference to some comfortable settlement for me, in her judgement could have otherwise, to have disposed of me nearer hand to herselfe, and my freinds."

benefitt of the clearing his estate from that tiranny of sequestration, that we receaved a very grand blow by the sad infor-
tunate losse of my dearest brother, which was the preludium to
our many afflictions and troubles in that poore family, when we
lost such a head and piller, in whoes life consisted much the
contineuance of that noble extraction and galantry, not leaveing
in it his second behind him. The occasion of his death and
our misery was this. Uppon the dispatch of that bussinesse at
London by my cozen Darley* of the discharge of his estate
from sequestration, my brother George deemed it his part to
returne thanks due for such a favour, non more gratefull for
a kindness don then himselfe, haveinge laid at Mr. Harry
Darcy's† that night, came to Hipswell to consult my mother's
advice about writing to London to Mr. Richard Darley about
that bussinesse. Affter his obeisance, and craving her blessing,
tould her he was now goeing to Richmond to my uncle William,
where he would write to Mr. Darley, desiring to know what
she pleased to command him further in it. My mother said
that her service and thankes must be returned him for all his
kindnesse in that bussinesse, which she would have don herselfe
by writting, but that she was sudainly surprised at that instant
of his comeing up to the chamber with much feares for me,
who was soe violently tormented with a paine in the right
side of my necke amongst the sinnews, etc., which caused
me to cry out in extreamity; nor could she imagine what
was the cause, only she still anoynted it with oyle of roses.
My brother, seeing me in such paine, asked how it came, of
which I could give noe other account, haveing bin as well
before as ever, till I was combeing my head towards the
right hand, and binding my necke as he came up the staires,
and ever since it had held me grieveously. This was the cir-

---

* Richard Darley, a younger son of Sir Richard Darley of Buttercrambe,
married Elizabeth, daughter and coheiress of Sir William Hildyard, of Bishop-
Wilton, by Isabel, daughter and heiress of Ralph Hansby. The cousinship with
the writer arose through the marriage with a Hansby.

† At Colburne, not far from Hipswell. Mr. Darcy died, in York, in 1667, and
was buried at St. Olave's.

cumstances of that strainge paine which held me strongly till
about halfe an houer, which was the very time of his drowning.
But to proceed to the circumstances of himselfe; he pittied me
much, and would have staied with me, but that his uncle
William staied for him, at Richmond, for letters that post;
and affter his walking three or four turnes about the chamber
in his studieng of his bussinesse, till my thoughts* I saw a
great deale of change, he looked so scariously and soberly, as if
there was some great change neare, but what I knew not, only
feared the worst that we should be deprived of him whom I so
dearly loved. He in a very reverent manner kneeled downe
and asked blessing at his goeing out againe not long before;
which my mother .tooke notice of, praieng God Almighty to
bless him, and said, "Sonn, I gave you my blessing, but even
now how cometh it that you take so solemne a leave of me?"
He answered, "Forsooth, I cannot have your prayers and
blessing for me too often;" and so with her praiers for him in
his preservation, and his most humble obeisance in a dutifull
manner, he took his leave, bidding me "Faire well, deare sister,
I hope to find you better at my returne home." I likewise
praied him to have a caire of him selfe; and, lookeing affter him,
I thought he had the sweetest aspect and countenance as I ever
saw in him, and my heart was even full of feares that we should
losse him, there was soe great and intire an affection for him
on whom we did all much depend;† and speaking of this to him,
he said, I was allwaies full of feares for him, but hee did not
deserve it; and this was the last parting we had in this world,
with abundance of deare love and affection betwixt us as we
ever had in our lives together. Going, affter this, down staires,
hee called for his horrse, and although he had two men my
mother kept for him, yet tooke he neither with him, but bid
his footeman, James Brodricke (an Irishman, and an excelent
runner), to meete him at Richmond at two o'clock where he
was to [have] mette my uncle William. Soe my brother went

---

* i.e., *methought.* "Coming events cast their shadows before."

† The exquisite and yet simple pathos of this chapter will place Mrs. Thornton
very high in the list of English lady-writers.

towards the river, and as he rid by our chapell,* where there was a wedding that day, he asked the people whethur the Swaile might be riden. They said that there had bin a flood, but it was fallen, for some had crost the water that morning. Soe he, biding the people joy in theire marriage, went very slowly towards the river; and, as we heard affterwards by two men which saw him on the other side, he went down as cairfully and slowly as foot could fall. Nor was the second flood come so high till he was in the midest of the river; but when it comes from the Dales it falles with a mighty mountaincous force sudainly, as I can myselfe testifie, whoe (through the mercys of God) was very nigh perishing in that water, once or twice, but was delivered. For as I was coming betwixt St. Nicholas and our house at Hipswell, if I had bin but two yards of the shore I had bin lost by its force; but, by Providence, I was not above halfe the horrse length from ground, and yet the horrse was taken to the midle girths, albeit it had bin all the time I passed through before the flood came downe but a little above the fettlocke. Thus wonderously was I preserved from drowning, the Lord's holy name be praised even for ever, for my eminent deliverance from perishing in and by these floods of waters.

But to returne to the sad relation of my brother, which we was informed of by two men which walked beyond the river; they perceaving a gentleman goeing downe to the water, imagining it some [one] from Hipswell, seeing afarre of that the flood came sudainly and mightely downe, made haste to the Swale, and see only his horrse getting out of the river, where he had bin tumbled in all over head, and by swiming had gott out and shaked himselfe. They gott hold of his bridle but missed the person that rid on him, perceaved it to be his horse, made a great search for my brother but could not find the bodie; with great sorrow and lamentation they ran to Easby† and Richmond,

---

* A little, humble place of worship on the top of the bank before the slope towards the river begins. Floods of this nature are not so common in the Swale as they used to be.

† A parish about a mile E.S.E. from Richmond, where are the ruins of an Abbey, and an ancient church dedicated to St. Agatha. It comprises the townships of Aske, Brompton-upon-Swale, Easby, and Seeby.

raising all the townes, flocking in exceedingly with lamentable mornings and outcries for him whome they dowted was lost in that unhappy river. The most lamentable news came to Hipswell, where our very hearts weare allmost broken with this greevous, dismall, heavy blow and losse of our dearest brother, and for the harty greifes and sorrowes I sustained, it well nigh had brought me to have died with him ; and if God had seen it fitt that my poore unworthy life might have gon, soe hee might have lived for the good of his family, and but that the hand of our gracious God was scene mightily in my mother's preservation, we had bin deprived of her life allso. This great blow added to her former afflictions, and to have brought her with sorrow to her grave, beeing deprived in such a heavy manner of the hope of her house. A man of so great accomplishments and goodnesse, that I have heard many lament and say that few came neare to him for excelent abillities, temperment of bodie, and humours, faculties of minde, ingenious, and of great ingenuity. A most obedient and faithfull son to his parents, which increased there comfort in him. A deare and affectionate brother ; a faithfull friend, a loveing landlord ; to his very enimies ever courteous and affable, not disobleiging any by his morrocity or perversenesse. His very enimies then could not but lament his losse, said he was the greatest losse that Yorkshire had for a brave gentleman, and, if thus much came from the mouths of adversarys, noe incomium his frinds can sett upon him can speake his worth and merritt at whoes hands he had deserved soe much, and I am sure the country generally had a great losse of one soe pieous, understanding, and loyall to his king, soe that if it might have gained him the world he would not have taken a fallse oath or covenant to wrong the church or his soveraine. His death was uppon Munday morning in Easter week. March the 31, 1651, was his blacke Munday. The strange paine which seized on my necke portended this sadd losse. Great and infinitt was the search by thousands of people from that time till Wednesday following, his bodie not beeing found till on that day, and about the time when he was lost. And then one of those men which was

a wittnesse against him was the first which discovered his
bodie, it beeing fallen into a poole neare Catterick Bridge,*
above a mile from the place he was drowned. John Plummer
the man's name.

After they had drawn him up, caire was taken of his bodie,
which was as sweete and comcly in all parts as in his life, except
one bruise on the nose, which was thought to be don when he
fell uppon some great stone, theire being abundance in that
wathplace. Allbeit he was an excelent swimer, yet was it not
the Lord's pleasure that it did him any helpe to be saved
thereby. The corps was laid att Thomson's on Catterick Brigg
that night, because it was deemed the bringing him to Hipswell would too much have agravated my mother's excessive
sorrow and indangered her life allso. He was carried by
coach to Kirklington, in the company of all the gentry in
that part of Yorkshire, with a greater lamentation and sorrow
then was for any within the memory of man at his funeralls.
He was buried in Kirklington church† neare Sir Christopher
Wandesford's tombe, my great grandfather, Mr. Siddall preaching his funerall sermon, as I take it, and with as much solemnity as those times and such a sudaine accident could admitt.
And this is the true relation of his death, of the fall of this
stately ceader of our wood, our staffe to my deare father's
family ; whoes death cannot be spoken of without teares. I
have taken on me to inlarge more fully as to the sircumstances
of the latter part of his life and death, as allso of my honred
father's, with the inlargement of severall sircumstances and
passages belonging to both, because this age of the world and
sad times is so apt to raise and report fallse things of persons
of quality and worth, bespattering there dead ashes, according
to the malice of Satan, whom they durst not presume to touch

* Over the Swale, about four miles from Richmond, and one mile from Catterick. On it was formerly a chapel. Here is an inn, which in coaching and
posting days was one of the principal hostelries on the road from London to
Glasgow.

† 1651, Apr. 3. George Wandesford, Esq., bur. (Par. Reg. Kirklington). It
is observable that the dates in the Parish Registers rarely accord with those given
by Mrs. Thornton.

when liveing. And allthough I am not worthy to undertake
this taske according to each mirritts, I could not in my con-
ssience be sattisfied without the commemoration of some of
those resplendant virtues in them which I was a daly wittnesse
of; beeing obleiged in point of gratitude, according to my
capasity, to relate this truth of these sad afflictions wherein I
had a deepe shaire, and to leave them for the right information
to my posterity of theire finishing this life, according to my
knowledge. He was buried upon the first day of Aprill, 1651.
Sir Christopher Wivill,* who had a great love for my deare
brother, made an excelent paper of verses upon him in bewaling
his losse, which I will insert hereaffter.

*A Lamentation and Prayer uppon the death of my honored
brother George Wandesforde, Esquire (i., 109–115).*

Alas! O Lord, most great and mighty, wonderfull in Thy
powerfull attributes and judgements, what. shall I say or doe
unto Thy glorious majestie, Who hast looked downe uppon us
with a mighty breach, adding great sorrowes to our publicke
calamitys? Thou hast a controversey with this whole nation,
and allsoe with this poore familie, by takeing away our brother
by an unnaturall death, when he was in hopes to have lived in
peace and quiet. Yea, then hast Thou, Oh Lord, deprived us of
our head, and suffered men to breake in uppon our estate, to
disturbe our quiett injoyment of this good land Thou gavest to
us, and now at last smitten the cheife branch of our family.

Ahlas, Lord our God, we have bin rebellious before Thee,
and adding sin to iniquities by our disputes and disturbances,
and now we have lost a maine piller which preserved the peace
and quiett of us all; yea, in a suddaine and sad manner. Oh,
what have we don in displeasing this great and dreadfull God,
walked unworthy of the mercys of soe gracious a Father, whoes
dealings towards us has bin in much mercy and clemency,
having preserved him and us all from the violence of our enimies,

* Of Burton Constable. See afterwards.

and the churches, in many great and eminent deliverances. Yet hast Thou now taken him away (who was the joy of our hearts) in these sad times, to our great discomfort. But what are we, O Lord, sinful dust and ashes, in disputing Thy pleasure? Thy will be don in us, and by us, and on us, in all things.

O Lord, teach us humility and patience, and grace to repent of our iniquitics, whatever it be which is displeasing or hath provoaked Thy anger and displeasure in his death. Lett us bewaile it all our daies; beeing humbled for our miscarriadges and non proficiencys in Thy schoole of afflictious.

The murders, warres, bloodshed, that especially of the horrible murder of our gracious king, that wicked doers was lett in upon him and us for our crieing sinns.

O Lord, pardon, O Lord, forgive, and doe for Thy mercy sake make us not a by word and scorne to our neighbours in these signal punishments; returne to us againe, and lett not sin prevaile to our distruction, nor Thy corrections to desolation, but correct us in Thy judgment, not in Thy anger, lest we should be consumed and brought to nothing. Put an end, I humbly beseech Thee, O Father of mercys, to our confutions and distractions, publicke and private. Sanctifie this heavy chastisement in our losse to me which had a great shaire in what troubles that fell to us all; and pitty Thy humble, repenting, returning servant, who is smitten with Thy rod, and desires to receave instruction.

Lord, comfort my deare mother, in these her sadnesses and sorrowes by the losse of soe dutifull a son, and make us that remaines to be stayes to her in her age, and my father's friends to be comforts and succours in this world. Unite our divissions in the family, that none may wrong Thy widow and her children depending on Thy providence. Lett us all rest on Thy mercifull favour for provission, without invading each other's rights unjustly. Lett it suffice, O Lord, that this blow is given, and stay Thy sword of vengeance against this nation in generall. Lett this Thy punishments have this effect, to drive out our corruptions and purge away our sins; and then heale our soules, and receave us to Thy favour.   Forgive all our malicious persecutors, and turne their hearts that is the cause of our distruction.

As this affliction came by Thy holy pleasure and permission, soe teach me, and us all, patiently to submit to Thy dispensation, blessing Thy name that he fell not by the hands of the Philistines, whoes cruelltys was great.   But before his change (though it was sudaine) didst shew him Thy mercys, in considering his wayes, and reconsiling him selfe to his God, and giveing him the opportunity of Thy holy Sacrament, a pledge of our salvation, with great desires to serve Thee faithfully in his generation, with many many other testimonies of Thy love, as that of his estate, and great abilities and understanding in religion, severall good gifts and graces, fitting him to walke uprightly in Thy sight.   And it may be this providence was better for him then to live, to see and passe through those evills to come when there was noe king in Israell, every one did what was right in his owne eyes, but he was brought to his grave in peace.   *   *   *   I beseech Thee, O Lord, humble us for this affliction and breaking the head of our number, that the rest may lay it to heart, and become wiser thereby.   Give us not over to fall into the hands of unmercifull and cruell men, that fights against Thy church and annointed, but deliver us and Thy whole church in this kingdome from rapin of sacrilegious persons as would destroy the seamless cote of Christ, tearing it in peices by factions, divisions, and heritticall oppinnions ; from proud and covetous prettenders to reformmation, laid in the foundation of blood and murder. Lett not their prosperity allure, theire oppression inforce or draw any of us to joyne in theire designes, noe not soe much as by consent, or compliance in their wickednesse, least wee eate of such things as please them, and sin against so great and glorious a God in robing Him of that honor His only due (and to non other creatures) of those services, ordenances, sacraments, tithes and offrings, all Thy owne peculier right, or detaining our king's due obedience to his power derived from Thee and Thy church which Thou hast graciously established heere, by all which we rob Thee of Thy praise and glory Thou should have asscribed, for Thy goodnesse in these things, by us, and may thereby heape to our selves swift distruction by invading Thy right, the king's and churche's. But, on the contrary, as we have hitherto bin preserved from such iniquities by Thy mercy, soe through Thy contineued grace we may be delivered from either doeing such, and if it be Thy will from suffering by and from such practicies, as much as Thou shalt see fitt in Thy gracious providence. That soe we may still live in this good land, injoying once again Thy peace in the restoration of our right lawfull soveraine, with the restoration of Thy church and holy good bishops to feed and governe and direct this flocke aright in the waies of Thy truth, and salvation of our soules. That errours, schismes, and rebellion may be extinguished and extirpated, Thy good lawes, devine and humaine, re-established, and we of these kingdoms fixed upon those axes againe of truth and peace, righteousnesse, and obedience. * * * * * * * *

Uppon the reconsiling of my two brothers George and Christopher Wandesford, March 29, 1651, on Easter Eve, before my brother George was lost (i., 300).

It was no smale greife and trouble to.me that the wickedness of my eldest brother's servant, by idle stories to my deare brother George against my poore brother Christopher, had soe fare prevailed with him as to make a very great breech in there freindship, soe that the yonger did apprehend himselfe much injured and wronged thereby to his brother George by them : and the other, tho' a very wise and understanding person, had bin highly incensed att some lies which was tould of his brother to him, and by this meanes caused a very great anger against each other, which procceded so hy, and caused them to have such animossity, as that they neither could be sattisfied to receave the holy Sacrament. But it pleased God to make me the happy instrument to perswade and intreat each of them to such moderation and charity, to aske each other pardon (and God in the first place) for what bin amiss, and to freely forgive one annother, and put away all former disgusts or displeasure, and to be cordially reconsiled for His sake Who died for us; and with great comfort I prevailed with them to receave this holy feast of love to which we were to come, and on the Easter day I bless my God we did receave that holy Sacrament in zeale and devotion, uppon Easter day, and had a full sattisfaction of there true love and affection to each other ever affter to his death, for which I doe bless and praise the God of Heaven for ever.

An elegie upon George Wandesford, Esq., on his unfortunate death, by the Honble Sir Christopher Wyvill, Barronett (i., 115).*

ON THE DEPLORABLE LOSS OF OUR HONORED FRIEND AND NEIGHBOUR
GEORGE WANDESFORD, ESQ., MARCH 31, 1651.

Ere since the Bishops, Parliament, and King,
(A blest conspiracie) agreed to bring
The faith of Christians and baptismall seal
Free denisons into this common weal,
To the late famous streame of Swale adheres
Through the long current of a thousand years
A sacred reputation; there, whole bands
Of forward converts, by the reverend hands
Of old Paulinnus† did at once begin
To shake hands with there God, and of theire sin.
    Those waves did then a font to the banks afford
    An acceptable temple to the Lord.
Oh, what meant the rash flood, by one act, to throw
A ruine on its owne fame, and us too,

---

* This 'elegie' does not appear in that choice and rare poetical volume which contains many of the effusions of this accomplished gentleman. "Certaine Serious Thoughts which at severall times and upon sundry occasions have stollen themselves into verse and now into the publike view," etc., 12mo, London, 1647. The only 'elegie' in the volume is one "on the death of our vertuous and deare friend Mistris Dorothy Warwick at Marsk, Aug. 6th, 1644." She was a Hutton, and the wife of the well-known Sir Philip Warwick.

† Anno 627, Edwino Rege.

Soe brave a vessell, and soe richly fraught,
That guiltty channell has to ship wrack brought
As bankrupts all our contrie; noe man here
Soe unconserned but must lett fall a tear,
Whilst the sadd murmur of those waters call
On every passenger to mourn his fall;
His family, noe greifes can tell its fatall loss,
Dum in admiration at this dreadfull crosse,
All joyes in him they hoped to find
Who fraughted full with treasuers of the mind.
> What though three daies submersion did entomb
> All that was mortall of him, in the wombe
> Of a regardless eliment, wee know
> Our great Redeemer from the parts below
> Did, by Divine Power, on the third day rise
> To open a neare way to Paradise.

C. WYVILL.

An Act of gratitude for my deare mother's preservation to us
(i., 116).

When the determinate will of our God is shewed towards us,
it is then our duties quietly to sitt downe, and patiently to
acquiesce our desires to His divine pleasure Who is the great
Creator and wise Disposer of all things and times, least we show
our selves ingrate for those infinitt mercys we injoy, both
spirituall for the good of our soules, and temporall for our
bodies. All which we have long since forfited, and deserved
to have bin deprived thereof, and then we should be most miser-
abley wretched. Therefore 'tis my duty to recolect those
favours and mercys I have injoyed under the wing of my deare
and vertuous mother, when I call to mind her sufferings, and
ours, for many yeares, what cause have I of deepe consideration
of the goodnesse of God towards us all, which has not deprived
us of our sole comfort and stay, by takeing away my deare
mother, in whose life was our suport, with whome we were all
preserved from death and ruine, in Ireland, at Kirklington, at

Chester, and in all places, ever since my father's death; in all these sad times, in the opposition of freinds, the fall of the church and state. When her joynture in England, beeing but £300 per annum at best, fell under £50 a yeare, and when the Scotts devoured all her patrimony, eating up her owne and children's provissions, even then did our gracious Lord remember mercy in the midst of judgement, and caused her house at Hipswell to be a Zoar, a sanctuary for us all; out of that little estate then (not beeing the tenth part of the whole) she releived my brother George, which had a perticuler estate of his owne, as heire (though under sequestration), with the some of £500. And, since my father's death, she hath expended uppon her three younger children's maintenance, out of her owne at Hipswell, the some of £500 in our education and maintenance, as she has declared by her owne relation before wittnesses, none of us ever having receaved any thing out of that part of my father's estate of Kirklington for the same, as was appoynted by my father's last will and testament. Therefore will I give glory to our God on high Which still has preserved this deare and tender mother, thereby testificing His miraculous favours to the desolate widdow and children in all times of desersion and troubles, and beeing mindfull of His servant, my father, in the blessing powred downe upon his family. The Lord our God make us ever gratfull and thankfull to His gracious Majestie for ever. Amen.

My cosen Mary* Yorke was married to Mr. John York, at her father's house, my uncle Norton's, on the Greene in Richmond, April the 12th, 1651.

My brother Christopher Wandesforde married Sir John Lowther's daughter, Mrs. Eleanor, the eldest daughter, at Sir John's house (Lowther in Westmoreland), the 30th of September, 1651.

---

* Mary, daughter of Mauger Norton, Esq., bapt. at Richmond, 12th July, 1635. Mr. York was afterwards knighted, and died in 1663.

The mariage of Alice Wandesforde, December 15, 1651 (i., 118).

After many troubles and afflictions under which it pleased God to exercize my mother and selfe in since the death of my father, she was desirous to see me comfortably settled in the estate of marriage, in which she hoped to receave some sattisfaction, finding age and weaknesse to seize more each yeare, which added a spurre to her desires for the future well-being of her children, according to every one of their capacities. As to myselfe, I was exceedingly sattisfied in that happie and free condittion, wherein I injoyed my time with delight abundantly in the service of my God, and the obedience I owed to such an excelent parent, in whoes injoyment I accounted my daies spent with great content and comfort; the only feares which possessed me was least I should be deprived of that great blessing I had in her life. Nor could I, without much reluctance, draw my thoughts to the change of my single life, knowing to much of the caires of this world sufficiently without the addittion of such incident to the married estate. As to the fortune left by my father, it was faire, and more then competent, soe that I needed not fear (by God's blessing) to have bin troublesome to my freinds, but to be rather in a condittion to assist them if need had required. Especially more in regard that I was confident of what my deare mother could doe for me living, and at her death. Soe that to shew my deare affection towards my brother George in the time of his straights, for his better helpe in his estate, beeing sore burthened with debts, anuities, etc., I was willing to transferre £500 of my English portion to be receaved out of Ireland, which would have eased that of Kirklington. But since his death, when my second brother came heire, there was not that cause to contineue the same; by reason that both the sequestration was taken of, and the wardship mony of his brother denied to be paid to Sir Edward Osborne's executor, and that he was better by £200 a yeare in his estate, with many other considerable arguments arriseing towards my mother and my selfe. For there was such unhansome dealings to us, not to say dishonest, since my brother's marriage, as could neither induce her or my selfe to part with our estates without security. But I shall be silent in these things, which afforded us too much troubles and sorrowes, wishing rather to cover all things of the nature of disputes betwixt such neare relations. And withall my youngest brother John, beeing fallen into a grievous distemper, through greife uppon harsh dealing affter the marriage of my brother Christopher, who, by ill councell given him, detained his right of anuity of £100 per annum (to his great prejudice), and John was likely thereby to leave both that £100 in England with his whole fortune (then descended upon John by his brother George his death) of £6000 out of the Irish estate to my brother Christopher. Weighing all these reasons together, and that I had noe maintenance from Kirklington, as I ought to have had, by my father's will, but was willing to foregoe that to my uncle William Wandesforde, towards the payment of debts, I had noe reason, from all these considerations, to lose the payment of the said £500 from Kirklington. Yet I do believe from hence proceeded much displeasure that I would not consent to wrong myselfe of the whole, in soe much that affter the bussinesse of sequestration was cleared, he desisted the acting any thing in my behalfe. Neverthelesse, such was my deare mother's affection to the family for itt's preservation, that she harkened to the proposall made for Mr. Thornton's* marriage, albeit therein she disobleiged some persons of very good worth and quality which had solicitted her earnestly in my behalfe, and such as were of large and considerable estates of her neighbours about her. And, affter the first and second view betwixt us, she closed soe farre with him that she was willing he should proceed in his suite, and that cordially, if I should see cause to accept. For my owne perticuler, I was not hastie to change my free estate without much consideration, both as to my present and future, the first inclining me rather to continue soe still, wherein none could be more sattisfied. The second would contract much more trouble, twisted inseperably with those comforts God gave

* An account of Mr. Thornton's family will be given elsewhere.

in that estate. Yet might I be hopefull to serve God in those duties incombant on a wife, a mother, a mistresse, and govornesse in a family. And if it pleased God soe to dispose of me in marriage, makeing me a more publicke instrument of good to those severall relations, I thought it rather duty in me to accept my freinds' desires for a joynt benefitt, then my owne single retired content, soe that Allmighty God might receave the glory of my change, and I more capacitated to serve Him in this generation, in what He thus called me unto. Therefore it highly conserned me to enter into this greatest change of my life with abundance of feare and caution, not lightly, nor unadvisedly, nor, as I may take my God to witnesse that knowes the secretts of hearts, I did it not to fulfill the lusts of the flesh, but in chastity and singleness of heart, as marrieing in the Lord. And to that end that I might have a blessing uppon me, in all my undertakeings, I powred out my pettitions before the God of my life to direct, strengthen, leade, and counsell me what to doe in this conserne, which soe much tended to my future comfort or discomfort. And to order my waies aright, so that if He saw in His wisdome that the married estate was the best for me, that He would please to direct me in it, and incline my heart towards it; but if otherwise it were best for me to be, that I might still contineue in the same, but still referring my will to His; and allso to order my change soe that Hee would in mercy give me such a one to be my husband as might be an holy, good, and pieous Christian, understanding, wise, and affectionate, that we might live in His feare and favour, praing Him to give unto me sutable graces and qualifications which should fitt me for that calling, and this for our Saviour's sake I humbly begged in Jesus Christ our Lord. Amen. After which petitons to my God, I was the more inclined to accept of this proposition of my freinds' finding; allso that the gentleman seemed to be a very godly, sober, and discreet person, free from all manner of vice, and of a good conversation. This was the greatest incouragement to me when I considered the generall decay of true religion, in profession and practice, especially in the gentry, and with men of quality; too many being given to a sad course of life, through debauchery, made me more cautious in chusing, feareing to meete with such as neither knew God nor caired for theire soules, to preserve themselves in a holy course of life and conversation. Nor could I ever have injoyed comfort in this world to have bin matched with the greatest estates or fortunes, had I wanted that first and principall qualification in a husband, which is to be regarded above all the sattisfaction this world can afford. I cannot deny that his estate, which was then favourably given in to my mother, was the least in valew which had bin offred;* yet did my mother hope to finde a hansome

---

* " There being two parents living with five younger children, undisposed or provided for, and a hous to build from the ground, and uppon inquiry found not cleare £400 per annum. She deemed Mr. Thornton's estate, considering the circumstances mentioned, too much below my fortune, which my honored father and her selfe could give me. Besides, att that time a cleare mattch or two proposed, as Collonell Anstrooder, and my Lord Darcy's son, Collonell Darcy, of £1500 per annum and more. She doubted I should enter uppon an incombred estate, and reduced to very great trouble; wished me to consider what I would do, desireing God to direct me; but, considering the ill consequences might follow a deniall, if I could consent in my owne judgment, was willing, but not to impose to sattisfy them. Oh! what a strait was we brought to in this great affaire! Againe, I considered that Mr. Thornton's relations was oppositt to my oppinnion of the Church of England and religion; and if he himselfe had bin of the same ridged oppinnion of the Presbeterians, I could by noe meanes have granted to dispose soe of myselfe, to be misserable in the great conserne of my soule, and to bring forth children soe to be educated. In this poynt I was resolved to put to the tryall, by declaring to Mr. Thornton that I suposed he was not ignorant of my judgement and religion, wherein I was educated in the faith of God, and the profession of the true protestant Church of England; in it I have lived, and did by God's grace intend to dye; so that if he was not of the same faith with me we should be miserable, and I would not for all the world match my selfe to soe great misfortune, nor could he have any satisfaction to have one of a contrary oppinion to himselfe. Therefore desired him to forbeare any further suite in that way, not being comfortable to either, for he might match with such which was more suitable in all regards then myselfe, and I was soe happy in my condition of a single life, that I loved it above all, haveing the excelent company and example of my honored mother. After this discourse, most seriously and candidly delivered to him, I perseaved his great trouble in mind; and tould me that he was well sattisfied with my oppinnion and religion and all things ellse conserned me, beeing much above his hopes, desert, or expectation; and allso did assure me faithfully that he himselfe was of the same

compotency, without much charge, as was represented to her, only the want of a house, which he must builde; his brothers and sisters being provided for by his mother, that would cleare his estate, which was given in to be £600 per annum. This was very well, considering the addittion of my father's portion given me by his will and deeds, namely, £500 out of England, at Kirklington, and £1000 to be paid out of his Irish estate of Edough, which would be an addittion to increase Mr. Thornton's reveneus. Allso my deare mother was willing to give me what assistance she could out of her love and affection. The treaty of marriage with Mr. Thornton was very earnestly pursued by himselfe and freinds, and as discreetly mannaged by my deare mother as she could, for she was in a manner lett alone by all our relations. Especially affter my brother's death, in regard that selfe intresst too farre prevailed for those to hinder my disposall to any person, by the which they would be deprived of

oppinnion, and was for a moderated episcopacy, and kingly government; owning that the best; and that I should injoy my owne conscience as I desired (if I honored him to marry with him), and to bring up my children in the same faith, he did profess to me, both now and att all times. Haveing this assurance from himselfe, whereby the maine poynt of my religion was secured to me and my posterity (if I had any), I was the less conserned for riches or the splendor of this world, and hoped in God I might injoy that one thing necessary, as many did, which might never be taken from me, if I chose heere; he having the carracter all his life of a very honnest, sober, and consiencious man, and much beloved and esteemed in his countrey. Altho the estate was not soe cleare or great as others, yett I hoped to live with comfort in the cheifest matters of a married estate, with comfort in the obedience I owed to my deare mother's choyce; and, which was more incoragement to me, that I might be serviceable to my honored father's family in beeing instrumental to preserve or deliver it from that inevitable ruin fallen upon it. And by this meanes of my acceptance of this match, I might be a blessing to that noble family of my honored father from whence I am decended, and prevent the greedy lion which watched for his prey, to have devoured us up, roote and branch. I cannot deny my great unwillingness (contrary to my resolves to contineue my single condition) to consent to that change which involved me into a thousand misseryes, which I could not foresee or immagine, that fell uppon me, which made my life very uneasy in most of the periods. For, instead of deputing much of my fortune to pieous uses, and bestowed in Christian-charity on many urgent necessities, as I designed when single, I was plunged into great troubles and burdens uppon the estate " (iii., 40).

theire sinister expectations of my fortune. But, through God's blessing, this treaty was brought to a period to the sattisfaction of each party, and with a generall consent, and the articles of marriage drawne up by Mr. Thornton for the right settlement of all things concluded uppon betwixt my deare mother in my behalfe and himselfe weare both just and honest don by him. The articles of agreement were according to the presidents of his father towards his mother, vidz., that all his estate should be passed by fine and recovery to inable him to intaile the same upon his issue by me, male or female. That his lordship of Easte Newton, then valewed at the yearely rent of £250, should be estated on me for a joynture, and affter the decease of the longer liver of us two, to descend uppon his sons and theire issue successively; for want of such heirs male to his heires females by me, and without impeachment of any manner of waiste. That Laistrop, valewed at the yearely rent of £160, affter the decease of his mother, married to Mr. Gate, and then her joynture, was settled on Mr. Thornton for his life, affter his deccase uppon his heires males, and for default of such issue to his daughters by me. As for his land at Cottingham, Richmond, called Burne Parke, the inheritance estated as the other of Laistrop, affter a long leace made for the provission of his younger children's portions and maintenance paid out of it. The valew was accounted £100 per annum. As for the security of my portion, he was to receave the summe of £1500 out of Kirklington, which he might dispose of for himselfe and his owne use, beeing secured to me. And for the £1000 payable out of Ireland, he gave bond to my mother to purchase land of inheritance for me during my life, and for my children at my deccase. And withall my mother was willing to give us our table, with all our familie, for three yeares. These were the tearmes betwixt them. Affter which agreements, articles, and writtings done, there followed a pretty space ere his mother had passed a fine with him, in regard that his father-in-law would not joyne in the fine, and my mother's councell did not approve of it to be legall for security without it, but Mr. Thornton did faithfully ingage to doe the same legally, and passe the fine affter his death. But in the intrime I was left in an uncertainty for the security of a joynture in case of his death before me, and when my portion was disposed of by him could have noe benifitt thereby, soe that my mother could proceed noe further, least any ill consequences might follow, but wholely this bussinesse was left to my own choyce, what I would doe in this case. She beeing loth as upon her owne account to undergoe such a conserne, in which there was such a hazard, wherein she was not to be blamed; but Mr. Thornton was very much troubled uppon this unjust deniall of his father-in-law, by which he was likely to have undon his desires, fell into much sadness and discontent, which perhaps might hasten his sicknesse that he fell into on his goeing from Hipswell. His ague began in the way to his mother's, when, finding himselfe not able to goe through, came backe to Hipswell, falling exceeding ill into a feaver, but, uppon the advice of Dr. Wittie,* he was lett blood, and had all meanes used for his recovery, but was brought dangerously ill. At the last it pleased God he recovered beyond all expectation; and uppon his recovery I was willing to relie upon his promise to my mother, and his infinitt expressions to my selfe. I rested upon Providence in the fulfilling of his desire, in soe much that about the December following proceeded our marriage. This is the true relation of this grand conserne of my life, which I have bin more teadious in, because I would leave to posterity the right understanding of that conserne.

Alice Wandesforde, the daughter of Christopher Wandesforde, Esq., late Lord Deputy of Ireland, was married to William Thornton, esquire, of Easte Newton, at my mother's house in Hipswell, by Mr. Siddall, December the 15th, 1651. Mr. Siddall made a most pieous and profitable exhortation to us, shewing our duties, and teaching us the feare of the Lord in this our new estate of life, with many zealous prayers for us. My deare and honored mother gave me in marriage, in the

* The celebrated York physician and author, the only person known, perhaps, in whom arthritic pains have let loose the floodgates of song. See Dugdale's Visitation of Yorkshire, 221, etc.

presence of my owne brother John Wandesforde, my uncle Norton, my uncle Darley* (Francis), my cozen Dodsworth of Wattlosse, George Lightfoote, and Dafeny, Robert Webster, Martha Richison, Ralfe Ianson, Robert Loftus the ellder.

A relation of the remarkable passages of my life since my marriage, beginning from the 15th of December, 1651.

After my marriage it was my duty to humble my soule in praier and suplication to the God of all the earth, Who had guided me in all my youth and virgin estate to live in His feare and service, and directing me to chuse a godly and religious husband, with whom I might, through His blessing, spend the rest of my daies; and to this purpose I powred out my humble pettitions and requests, with hearty thanks and praise for all my deliverances, both spirituall and temporall, ever since I was borne, to the present houre, beseeching Him that as He in abundant mercy had heard my unworthy requests in the beginning of this treaty, soe He would now multiply His free grace and loving kindnesse to me His vilde creature, giving both to my husband and myselfe all those graces and spirituall comforts we stood in need of in this our mariage; that we might be maried to Him as verily as to each other, and that we might behave ourselves as becometh the members of Christ to each other in this band of wedlocke, being instruments of each other's salvation. And if it weare the Devine pleasure to give us the comfort of children, they might be heires of the king-dome of heaven, when He should call them, and in this life instruments of building up His church, and the raising up of my husband's family. But this temporall blessing, as all others of that nature, with subservency to His wisdome and good pleasure, that if He saw it good we might not want a comfort-able beeing in this world, nor want any thing without the which we could not serve Him comfortably. All which things

* Francis Darley of Buttercrambe, gen., about whom see elsewhere.

"Cozen Dodsworth" was, no doubt, John Dodsworth, Esq., who married Frances Hutton of Marske.

I craved with whatsoeever else He saw fitt to give us for the Lord Jesus his sake.   Amen.

A deliverance from death that day on which I was married, December 15th, 1651 (i., 126).

That very day on which I was married, haveing bin in health and strength for many yeares before, I fell sodainly soe ill and sicke affter two a' clocke in the afternoone, that I thought, and all that saw me did beleive, it would have bin my last night, beeing surprised with a violent paine in my head and stomacke, causing a great vomitting and sicknesse at my heart, which lasted eight houers before I had any intermition; but, blessed be the Lord our God, the Father of mercies, Which had compassion on me, and by the meanes that was used I was strengthned wonderfully beyond expectation, beeing pretty well about ten a' clocke att night.   My deare husband, with my mother, was exceeding tender over me, which was a great comfort to my spiritts.   What the cause of this fitt was I could not conjecture, save that I might have brought itt upon me by cold taken the night before, when I satt up late in preparing for the next day, and washing my feete at that time of the yeare, which my mother did beleive was the cause of that dangerous fitt the next day.* But, however it was, or from what cause it proceeded, I received a great mercy in my preservation from God, and shall ever acknowledge the same in humble gratitude for His infinitt loveing kindnesse for ever.   I looked uppon this first bussinesse of my new condition to be a little discouragement, allthough

* " Which condition was extreamly bewailed by my husband and mother and my freinds, and looked uppon as a sad omen to my future comfort.   And I doe confesse I was very desirous to have then delivered up my miserable life into the hand of my mercifull Redeemer, Who I feared I had offended by altering my resolves of a single life.   *   *   *   *   Thus was the first entrance of my married life, which began in sicknesse, and continued in much afflictions, and ended in great sorrowes and mournings.   Soe that which was to others accounted the happiest estate was imbittred to me at the first entrance, and was a caution of what trouble I might expect in it, as was hinted by St. Paull's Epistle, *Such shall have trouble in the flesh*,"

God was able to turne all things for the best, and to my good, that I might not build too much hopes of happinesse in things of this world, nor in the comforts of a loving husband, whom God had given me, but sett my desires more upon the love of my Lord and God.

Meditations upon my deliverance of my first childe, and of the great sickness followed for three quarters of a yeare; August 6, 1652, lasted till May 12, 1653 (i., 127).

About seaven weekes affter I married itt pleased God to give me the blessing of conseption. The first quarter I was exceeding sickly in breeding, till I was with quicke childe; affter which I was very strong and healthy, I blesse God, only much hotter than formerly, as is usuall in such cases from a naturall cause, insoemuch that my nose bled much when I was about halfe gon, by reason of the increase of heate.*   Mr.

* "Beeing helped more forward in the distemper by the extreame heat of the wether at that time, when the extreame great eclips of the sun was in its height, and a great and totall eclips fell out this yeare 1652. At which time I was big with child, and the sight of it much affrighted me, it beeing soe darke in the morning at breakfast time, and came soe sudainly on us, that in a bright sunshine morning that he could not see to eate his breakfast without a candle. Butt this did amaze me much, and I could not refraine goeing out into the garden and looke on the eclips in water, discovring the power of God soe great to a miracle, Who did with draw His light from our sun so totally that the sky was darke, and starres appeared, and a cold storme for a time did possess the earth. Which dreadfull change did putt me into most serious and deep consideration of the day of judgment which would come as sudaine and as certainly uppon all the earth as this eclips fell out, which caused me to desire and beg of His Majesty that He would prepare me for this great day in repentance, faith, and a holy life, for the judgements of God was just and certaine uppon all sinns and sinners. O prepare me, O God, for all Thy dispensations and trialls in this world, and make me ready and prepaired with oyle in my lampe, as the wise virgins, against the comming of the sweete Bridegroome of my soule.

"About a month affter, Mr. Thornton desired and his relations that I should goe to see them both at Crathorne, Buttercrambe, Yorke, and at Hull and Beverley, att Burne Parke where his mother lived then, * * * * and by God's mercy did I goe to all those places where his freinds lived, and most kindly receaved and entertained. I bless God Who gave me favor in there eyes of my husband's freinds. When I came to Hull, Dr. Witty would have had me advised

Thornton had a desire that I should vissit his freinds, in which I frely joyned, his mother living about fifty miles from Hipswell, and all at Newton and Buttercrambe.* In my passage thither I sweat exceedingly, and was much inclining to be feaverish, wanting not eight weeks of my time, so that Dr. Wittie said that I should go neare to fall into a fever, or some desperate sickness, if I did not coole my blood, by taking some away, and if I had staied but two days longer, I had followed his advice. In his returne home from Newton, his owne estate, I was carried over Hambleton towards Sir William Askough's house,† where I passed downe on foote a very high wall betwixt Hudhill and Whitsoncliffe,‡ which is above a mile steepe downe, and indeed so bad that I could not scarce tread the narrow steps, which was exceeding bad for me in that

to be lett blood. * * * * In my returne home by Newton when I saw the old house the remanes of it, as I was in the great chamber, the dore into a little roome was so low as I gott a great knocke on my forehead, which strucke me downe, and I fell with the force of the blow, att which my husband was troubled. But I recovering my astonishment (because he should not be to much conserned), smiled, said I hoped I was not much worse, but said I had taken possession, which made him smile, and said it was to my hurt, and inded soe it was many waies. For in my goeing homeward he carried me to that place of the great rockes and clifts which is called Whitson Clife. * * * * But this my husband would not have had me goe downe this way, but by Ampleford, about, and plaine way, but for Mr. Bradley, who tould him it would not doe me noe hurt, becaus his wife went downe that way and was noe worse. However, the effect to me was contrary, for I beeing to goe to my cozen Ascough's, she did admire that I came that way, and wished I might gett safe home. It was indeed the good pleasure of my God to bring me safe home to my deare mother's house, Hipswell. Butt my dangerous journey the effects of it did soone appeare on me, and Dr. Witty's words came true. For as soone as I gott home I fell into the most dreadfull sickness that ever any creature could possibly be saved out of, and by a strong and putrid feaver, which was on me eleven daies before Dr. Witty came from Hull, had soe putrified my whole blood that both my selfe and poore infant was like to goe. * * * * The more perticuler description of this great and long lasting sickness I have related in my first booke of my Life, and with the miraculous deliverance was towards me in all that time " (ii).

* Newton was Mr. Thornton's paternal house and estate ; Buttercrambe the residence of the Darleys.

† At Osgodby.

‡ Hood Hill and Whitstone cliff, two lofty hills in the Hambletonian range.

condition, and sore to indure, the way soe straite and none to leade me but my maide [Susan Gosling], which could scarce make shift to gett downe herselfe, all our company being gon downe before. Each step did very much streine me, beeing soe bigg with childe, nor could I have gott downe if I had not then bin in my full strength and nimble on foote. But, I blesse God, I gott downe safe att last, though much tired, and hott and weary, finding myselfe not well, but troubled with paines affter my walke. Mr. Thornton would not have brought me that way if he had knowne it soe dangerous, and I was a strainger in that place; but he was advised by some to goe that way before we came down the hill. This was the first occassion which brought me a great deale of misery, and killed my sweete infant in my wombe. For I continued ill in paine by fitts upon this journey, and within a fortnight fell into a desperate fever att Hipswell. Upon which my old doctor, Mr. Mahum, was called, but could doe little towards the cure, because of beeing with childe. I was willing to be ordered by him, but said I found it absolutely necessary to be lett blood if they would save my life, but I was freely willing to resigne my will to God's, if He saw fitt for me, to spaire my life, yet to live with my husband; but still with subservency to my Heavenly Father. Nor was I wanting to suplicate my God for direction what to doe, either for life or death. I had very offten and frequent impressions to desire the later before the former, finding noe true joy in this life, but I confesse also that which moved me to use all means for my recovery, in regard of the great sorrow of my deare and aged mother and my deare husband tooke for me, farre exceeding my deserts, made me more willing to save my life for them, and that I might render praises to my God in the land of the liveing. But truly, I found my heart still did cleave to my Maker that I never found myselfe more desirous of a change to be delivered from this wicked world and body of sin and death, desiring to be disolved and to be with Christ. Therefore indured I all the rigours and extreamity of my sicknesse with such a shaire of patience as my God gave me. As for my freinds, they were soe much conserned for me that, upon the importunity of my husband, allthough I was brought indeed very weake and desperately ill aboute eleventh day of my sicknesse, I did lett him send for Dr. Wittie, if it were not too late. The doctor came post the next day, when he found me very weake, and durst not lett me blood that night, but gave me cordialls, etc., till the next day, and if I gott but one hour's rest that night, he would doe it the morning following. That night the two doctors had a dispute about the letting me blood. Mr. Mahum was against it, and Dr. Wittie for it; but I soon desided that dispute, and tould them, if they would save my life, I must bleed. Soe the next day I had six or seven ounces taken which was turned very bad by my sicknesse, but I found a change immeadiatly in my sight, which was exceeding dime before, and then I see as well as ever clearly, and my strength began a little to returne; these things I relate that I may sett forth the mercy of my ever gracious God, Who had blessed the meanes in such manner. Who can sufficiently extoll His Majestie for His boundlesse mercys to me His weake creature, for from that time I was better, and hee had hopes of my life. The doctor staied with me seven daies during my sicknesse; my poore infant within me was greatly forced with violent motions perpetually, till it grew soe weake that it had left stirring, and about the 27th of August I found myself in great paines as it were the colick, affter which I began to be in travill, and about the next day att night I was delivered of a goodly daughter, who lived not soe long as that we could gett a minister to baptize it, though we presently sent for one. This my sweete babe and first childe departed this life halfe an houer affter its birth, beeing receaved, I hope, into the armes of Him that gave it. She was buried that night, beeing Friday, the 27th of August, 1652, at Easby church. The effects of this feaver remained by severall distempers successively, first, affter the miscarriage I fell into a most tirrible shakeing ague, lasting one quarter of a yeare, by fitts each day twice, in much violency, so that the sweate was great with faintings, beeing thereby weakened till I could not stand or goe. The haire on my head

came off, my nailes of my fingers and toze came of, my teeth
did shake, and ready to come out and grew blacke. After the
ague left me, upon a medecin of London treacle, I fell into the
jandice, which vexed me very hardly one full quarter and a
halfe more. I finding Dr. Wittie's judgement true, that it
would prove a cronicall distemper; but blessed be the Lord,
upon great and many meanes used and all remidies, I was at
length cured of all distempers and weaknesses, which, from its
begining, had lasted three quarters of a yeare full out. Thus
had I a sad entirtainment and begining of my change of life,
the comforts thereof beeing turned into much discomforts and
weaknesses, but still I was upheld by an Allmighty Power,
therefore will I praise the Lord my God. Amen.

*A praier and thankesgiveing. for my deliverance of my first
childe, August 6th, 1652 (i., 129—133).*

O Lord most great, and yet our gracious and loving Father in
our Saviour Jesus Christ, Thy deare Son, tender and deare as a
loving mother, Who hadst a love to me in my preservation from
death and distruction, in Thy Devine wisdom hast Thou ordered
all things and passages in this my great sicknesse of my life,
not laing more on me then Thou gavest me strength to undergoe. O Lord, this dispensation of afflictions and great sicknesses is the way and meanes to bring me unto Thee, and the
fittest for me to injoy, letting me see thereby Thy mighty
power to cast downe and raise me up againe, even in my
desperate condition; when all men had given over to expect my
life, then did the great Phisician of soule and bodie raise
the one and heale the other; raising mee up againe and giveing
mee strength, and setting me on my feete affter six months
sicknes in my bed. I called uppon my God, in mine anguish
of spiritt and heavinesse I did complaine, and made my suplications unto my God the Lord of my life and joy. For my
desires was to cleave unto Him that I had offended, and made
my suplications unto my Judge. O Lord, I have offended

many waies, but Thou art He that canst wash and cleance my defiled poluted soule, for whoe is there that liveth and sinnest not? As my desires was alone to cleave on Thee, so Thou didst send this to me this sicknesse unto Thy servant, and by degrees did remove the same in Thy due time. Thou heardest my praiers, accepted my teares of repentance, my sorrowes, when death had compassed me about. Lord, heale my soule, for I have sinned. And now, O Thou most Holy One of Israel, blessed be Thy glorious name, and magnified for ever, that Thou hast put fresh opportunities of praising Thee and serving the Lord in the land of the liveing. Stirre up my heart and soule in true and unfeigned thankfulnesse to Thy Devine Majestie, and never to be unthankefull or ingratefull, or unprofitable in Thy world, or forgettfull of these inexpressable mercys and deliverances in my childe-birth and all my other extreame weakenesses, which my soule had never seene before till now. Lord, lett me be kept by Thy grace from any displeasing thought of Thee, for Thou art good and doest good allwaies; and that this may doe me good, sanctifie this Thy dealing unto Thy handmaide; lett it incourage me to put my whole trust and confidence in Thee alone, and that I my accept of the punishment of my iniquities, and learne by this not to offend. And tho' Thou, O Lord, art pleased to give me the lesse comforts heere on earth, I shall not much caire if that I may injoy the more of Thy preasance heere and the full fruittion of Thyselfe in heaven. And that Thou wilt also make Thyselfe known to be a gracious God to me and to all such as relie upon Thee by faith. I know also that it is through Thy dispensation that I am brought into the married estate of life, and that Thou in wisdome hast ordered each change and accident about this my sicknesse, as to my danger and cure. I beseech Thee therefore, O Lord my God, leave me not, for I am Thine, and freely willing to be at Thy disposittion, desiring Thee to give me sutable gifts and graces to serve Thee in this calling which by Thy providence I am entred into. And as I did not foolishly or lightly put myselfe upon itt, without begging Thy direction, in which my desires was unfeinedly to serve Thee, and trusting

and relieing upon Thee my guide, so, deare Lord, leve me
not, but lett me still find Thy goodnesse and clemency in
comforting me in all crosses, afflictions, sicknesses, and calamities, in soule and bodie, giveing me faith, patience, humility,
chastity, charity, hope, and fortitude; with fixed resolutions to
love, serve, and follow Thee to my live's end, that soe I may receave
the end of my hope in the salvation of my poore soule.   Lord,
as Thou has united our hearts in a holy union in marriage, so
contineue me faithfull, loyall, and obedient to my deare husband,
liveing according to Christ's institution, loveing him with that
conjugall love Thou requirest.   Blesse him with a wise and
an understanding heart and loveing affections to me his wife,
that we, liveing together in Thy love and feare, as Thou hast
appointed, may receave a happie crowne of glory hereafter.   I
beseech Thee allso support me in all my sadnesse, and sorrowes,
and sicknesses;   receive my humble and hearty thanks and
praise for my deliverances and preservations.   Make this fire of
affliction instrumentall to purge the drosse of all my sinns of
negligencys, ignorances, and willfull transgressions, that I may
come out like gold out of the furnish.   Then shall I praise the
Lord most high for all His benefitts showred downe upon my
soule.   Give us grace allso to lead the rest of our daies in Thy
service, not swerving from Thy lawes or waies, but love Thee
and delight in Thee.   And sanctifie us with Thy free spiritt,
that we may make good use of all those opportunitys Thou
puttest into my hand to serve Thee uprightly even all our life
long, that we may give up our accounts with joy and not with
greife.   All which humble requests and pettitions I crave with
pardon for our neglect in duties, and the meane performances
that I present, craveing all things Thou in wisdom seese fitt for
me or my husband, in soule and bodie, I most heartily begge
in the name and for the sake of Jesus Christ Thy Sonn, to
whome with the Holy Spirritt, One God in Trinity, be all
glory, power, thanksgiveing, and dominion, now and ever more,
Amen; calling uppon Thee in our Lord and Saviour's prayer
that He taught us, saing, *Our Father,* etc.

Uppon the birth of my second childe and daughter, borne at Hipswell on the 3rd of Janeuery in the yeare 1654 (i., 134).

Alice Thornton, my second childe, was borne at Hipswell neare Richmond in Yorkshire the 3rd day of January, 1654, baptised the 5th of the same. Wittnesses, my mother the Lady Wandesforde, my uncle Mr Major Norton, and my cozen Yorke his daughter, at Hipswell, by Mr. Michell Siddall, minister then of Caterick.*

It was the pleasure of God to give me but a weak time affter my daughter Alice her birth, and she had many preservatious from death in the first yeare, beeing one night delivered from beeing overlaide by her nurse, who laid in my deare mother's chamber a good while. One night my mother was writing pretty late, and she heard my deare child make a groneing troublsomly, and steping immeadiatly to nurrse's bed side she saw the nurse fallen asleepe, with her breast in the childe's mouth, and lyeing over the childe; at which she, beeing affrighted, pulled the nurse sudainly of from her, and soe preserved my deare childe from beeing smothered. * * * Affter I was delivered, and in my weary bed and very weake, it fell out that my little daughter Alice, beeing then newly weaned, and about a yeare old, beeing asleepe in one cradle and the young infant in annother, she fell into a most desperate fitt, of the convultions as suposed to be, her breath stoped, grew blacke in her face, which sore frighted her maide Jane Flouer. She tooke her up immeadiatly, and with the helpe of the mid-wife, Jane Rimer, to open her teeth and to bring her to life againe. Butt still, affterwards, noe sooner that she was out of one fitt but fell into annother fitt, and the remidies could be by my deare mother and aunt Norton could scarce keepe her alive, she having at least twenty fitts; all freinds expecting when she should have died. But I lieing the next chamber to her and did hear her, when she came out of them, to give great

* At the end of this chapter is "a praier and thanksgiveing for my deliverance of my second daughter, January 3rd, 1654" (i., 135-7).

schriks and sudainly, that it frighted me extreamely, and all the time of this poore child's illness I my selfe was at death's dore by the extreame excesse of those, uppon the fright and terror came uppon me, soe great floods that I was spent, and my breath lost, my strength departed from me, and I could not speake for faintings, and dispiritted soe that my deare mother and aunt and friends did not expect my life, but over come with sorrow for me.   Nor durst they tell me in what a condition my deare Naly was in her fitts, least greife for her, addid to my owne extreamity, with losse of blood, might have extinguished my miserable life : but removing her in her cradle into the Blew Parlor, a great way off me, least I hearing her sad scriks should renue my sorrowes.   These extreamitys did soe lessen my milke, that tho' I began to recrute strength, yet I must be subject to the changes of my condittion.   Affter my deare Naly was in most miraculous mercy restored to me the next day, and recruted my strength; within a fortnight I recovred my milke, and was overjoyed to give my sweete Betty suck, which I did, and began to recover to a miracle, blessed be my great and gracious Lord God, Who remembred mercy towards me.

Meditations uppon the birth of my third childe (i., 187).

Elizabeth Thornton, my third childe, was borne at Hipswell the 14th of February, 1655, beeing on Wednesday, halfe an houer affter 11 aclocke in the forenoone.   She was baptised the 16th of February, by Mr. Anthony ;* wittnesses, my mother, my aunt Norton, and my brother, Christopher Wandesforde.   Mrs. Blackburne stood for my mother, beeing sicke then.†

* This is Charles Anthony, afterwards vicar of Catterick.   He died in 1685, desiring by will "to be decently buryed at the upper corner of the east end of the chancell in Catherick church, adjoyning to the south side" (Richmond Wills).
† "A thanksgiveing affter the birth of my third childe, Betty" (i., 140).

Death of my mother and father-in-law Gates (i., 142).

My mother Gates, who was my husband's mother, died att Oswoldkirke of a flux of blood by seige, as it was suposed to have a veine broaken inwardly, which by fitts troubled her many yeares, haveing broaken it by a vomit of antemony to strong for her stomacke. She departed the 10th of May, 1655, and was buried at Stangrave,* in her husband's alley, my father Thornton, whom she had outlived seventeen yeares, haveing allso bin married to him seventeen yeares; and was buried on the 11th of May, 1655.

My husband's father-in-law, Mr. Geffery Gates, died att Hull the 18th of May, 1655, and was buried at Hull the next day, May 19th, 1655.

My brother Richard Thornton died in Dublin, in Ireland, of the flux, the 3rd of July, 1656, and was buried in St. Patrick's church the 4th July, 1656. This gentleman, becing twin with my deare husband, was the likest to him in all respects, both to person and condittions, a most sweet, affable, curteous nature, allwayes ready to serve his freind, and very well disposed towards religion.

Meditation uppon the birth of my fourth childe, Katherine Thornton, June 12th, 1656, borne at Hipswell June 12th, 1656 (i., 144).
A prayer before the delivery of my daughter Alice Thornton, June the 12th, 1656, by Alice Wandesforde (i., 144-147).

Katherine Thornton, my fourth childe, was borne at Hipswell, neare Richmond in Yorkcshire, the 12th of June, 1656, beeing on Thursday, about halfe an houer affter foure a' clocke in the affternoone, and was baptized the 14th of June by Mr.

† The numerous entries in the Parish Register of Stonegrave will be made use of elsewhere.

Siddall; witnesses, my mother, my neece, Katherine Danby,* and Mr. Thornton.

My deare mother feared me much from those ill simptoms she saw in my labour, which caused her to pour out her humble petittions to heaven for me in a most excelent praier of her owne composure for that purpose, which is at large entred by me in my first Booke more at large, as also her humble thanksgiving for me affter my safe deliverance.

A thanksgiving affter the delivery of my daughter Alice Thornton, being my fourth child, June 12, 1656, baptized the 14th (i., 147-149).

Elizabeth Thornton's death, the 5th of September, 1656 (i., 149).

It pleased God to take from me my deare childe Betty, which had bin long in the riketts and consumption, gotten at first by an ague, and much gone in the ricketts, which I conceived was caused by ill milke at two nurses. And notwithstanding all the meanes I used, and had her with Naly at St. Mungno's Well† for it, she grew weaker, and att the last, in a most desperate cough that destroyed her lunges, she died.

That deare, sweete angell grew worse, and indured it with infinitt patience, and when Mr. Thornton and I came to pray for her, she held up those sweete eyes and hands to her deare Father in heaven, looked up, and cryed in her language, ' Dad, dad, dad ' with such vemency as if inspired by her holy Father in heaven to deliver her sweet soule into her heavenly Father's hands, and at which time we allso did with great zeale deliver up my deare infant's soule into the hand of my heavenly .

---

* "Katherina filia domini Thomæ Danby militis bap. 10 Junii, 1637 " (Richmond Par. Register). She married Henry Best, of Middleton Quernhow, Esq., and died in 1688.

† This was at Copgrove, a small village not far from Knaresbro. Dr. Witty, speaking of it, says that "it is a quick spring of great repute for curing the rickets in children, whom they dip into it naked, and hold them in a little while, but they must observe to dip five, seven, or nine times, more or less, according to custom, or some think it will not do " (Life of Marmaduke Rawdon, 118, 119).

Father, and then she swetly fell asleepe and went out of this miserable world like a lamb.

Elizabeth Thornton, my third childe, died the 5th of September, 1656, betwixt the houers of five and six in the morning. Her age was one yeare six months and twenty-one daies. Was buried* the same day at Catterick by Mr. Siddall.†

Uppon my great fall I had, being with childe of my fifth, Sept. 14, 1657, at Hipswell.

Meditations on the deliverance of my first sonne and fifth child at Hipswell the 10th of December.

It pleased God, in much mercy, to restore me to strength to goe to my full time, my labour begining three daies; but upon the Wednesday, the ninth of December, I fell into excceding sharpe travill in great extreamity, so that the midwife did beleive I should be delivered soone. But loe! it fell out contrary, for the childe staied in the birth, and came crosse with his feete first, and in this condition contineued till Thursday morning betweene two and three a clocke, at which time I was upon the racke in bearing my childe with such exquisitt torment, as if each lime weare divided from other, for the space of two houers; when att length, beeing speechlesse and breathlesse, I was, by the infinitt providence of God, in great mercy delivered. But I having had such sore travell in danger of my life soe long, and the childe comeing into the world with his feete first, caused the childe to be allmost strangled in the birth, only liveing about halfe an houer, so died before we could gett a minister to baptize him, although he was sent for.‡

* —— dau. Wm. Thornton, bur. 3rd Sept., 1656 (Catterick Par. Register).

† "A praier after the death of my third childe, Betty Thornton."

‡ "And where it was not neglected by us, and the meanes could not be had, I trust in the mercys of the Lord for His salvation, He requiring noe more then He gives. And His infinitt grace was to me in sparing my soule from death. Tho' my body was torne in pieces, my soule was miraculously delivered from death."

I was delivered of my first sonne and fifth childe on the 10th of December, 1657. He was buried in Catericke church the same day by Mr. Siddall. This sweete goodly son was turned wrong by the fall* I gott in September before, nor had the midwife skill to turne him right, which was the cause of the losse of his life, and the hazard of my owne. The weakenesse of my bodie was exceeding great, of long continuance, that it put me into the begining of a consumption, non expecting for many daies together that I should recover; and when I did recrute a little, then a new trouble seised on me by the losse of blood, in the bleeding of the hemords every day for halfe a yeare together. Nor did I recover the lamenesse of my left knee for one whole quarter of a yeare, in which I could not touch the ground with it. This I gott in my labour, for want of the knee to be assisted. But, alas! all these miseries was nothing to what I have deserved from the just hand of God, considering the great failings of my duties is required both as to God and man. And though I am not given over to any sinnfull inormus crimes which thousands are subject to, yet am I not pure in the sight of God, for there is non man that liveth and sinneth not. What cause therefore have I to cry out, Oh, the hight, the depth, the breadth, the length of the love of God, Which had great compassion upon the weake handmaid of the Lord which was destinated to destruction, and did shew me mercy in the land of the liveing. The Lord Most High make me truly remember His goodnesse, and that I may never forgett this above all His mighty and streached-out hand of deliverances to me His vilde creature. That I may extoll and praise the Lord with all my soule, and

---

* "I most infortunately goeing over the hall at Hipswell, my gowne skirt wraped about my feete and soe twisted that I could not loose it before it cast me a desperate fall, which I fell uppon my hands and knees to save my childe. * * * * Sept. 14, 1657. My case was soe ill that Dr. Witty was sent for, who used all his art to preserve my selfe and the child, saing that I was with child of a son he was confident, but should have dificult labour. He haveing used all his skill to preserve the stocke, by the blessing of God I was preserved from death and mervelously restored to health and strength, beeing lett blood and other remidies, which made me go to my full time."

never let goe my hope from the God of my salvation, but live the remainder of my life He gives me to His honour and glory, and that, at the last, I may praise Him eternally in the heavens. Blesse the Lord, O my soule, and forget not all His benifitts.*

My cure of bleeding at Scarbrough, August, 1659 (i., 155).

It was the good pleasure of God to contineue me most wonderfully, though in much weakenesse, affter the excessive losse of blood and spiritts, in childebed, with the contineuance of lamenesse above twenty weekes after, and the losse of blood and strength by the bleeding of the hemorides, which followed every day by seige, and was caused by my last travell and torment in childebirth, which brought me soe low and weake that I fainted allmost every day upon such occasions, when I daily lost about four or five ounces of blood. And it was the opinion of Dr. Wittie that I was deeply gon in a consumption, and if it contineued longer I should be barren; all which beeing considered by my deare husband and mother, they were resolved, from the doctor's oppinion, that I should goe to Scarbrough Spaw† for the cure of the said distemper, and accordingly I went with Mr. Thornton, staing about a month there; in which time, upon drinking of the waters, I did by the blessing of God recover my strength affter the stay of the former infirmity of bleeding, it leaving me within two daies totally, and was cleared from those faintings this carried along with it, returning to Oswoldkirke by my sister Denton‡ homewards. Affter this great cure which the Spaw wrought on me, for

---

* After this, "A praier upon my preservation affter the birth of my first sonne, and his death" (i., 153).

† In the following year Dr. Witty published a small work on the history and merits of the Scarborough Spaw, which involved him in a maze of angry controversy. He was one of the chief persons who brought the Spaw into notice.

‡ Mr. Thornton's eldest sister, Elizabeth, married John Denton, of Manningham, who was vicar of Oswaldkirk, and afterwards rector of Stonegrave and prebendary of York. He died in 1708, aged 83. He ceased to officiate for a while in 1662, in consequence of what was called the "Black Bartholomew Act."

which I most humbly returne my hearty and faithfull acknowledgement of His mercy, we returned home to Hipswell,
where we found my deare mother somewhat recovered of a
very ill fitt of the stone, in which she had bin in great
danger about two daies before, and had sent for me home, her
servant meet me at my sister Crathorne's* in my way to
Hipswell. I was very joyfull to find her any thing recruted
from her extreamity, blessed be the Lord Most High, Which
had compassion on my deare mother in raiseing her from
death, and easing her from those violent fitts of paine and
torment, giveing her to me, and spairing my life allso from
that languishing sicknesse caused by my child-birth, and might
have caused my death. About this August, after our returne
from Scarbrough, it pleased God to give me much strength
and health, soe that I conceaved with childe, which affter
Mr. Thornton perceived, he with my mother greatly rejoyced,
hopeing that I might at length be blessed with a son. For
four months together I injoyed a great deale of comfort and
health, beeing much stronger and lively when I was with my
sons then daughters, haveing great cause to admire the
goodnesse of God, which evere contrary unto hope caused me
to recover of that sad distemper wherewith I was afflicted,
and giveing me hopes to bring forth a son to be a comfort to
my deare husband and us all.†

The state of England (i., 157).

1659.—About this time wee weare all in a great confussion
in this kingdome, none knowing how the government of this
land would fall, some desireing the contineuance of Oliver
Cromwell's race to stand ; others desired the returne of the
blessed king ; and to establish theire arbetrary power againe,
others intended through the weaknesse of Richeard, son to
Oliver, and then ruled as Protector, to advance the intrest of

---

* Margaret Thornton married Ralph Crathorne, of Crathorne, Esq.
† "A thanksgiveing affter my recovery" (i., 156, 157).

·Lambert in publike authority, which was a man highly for Independency, and soe would have utterly destroyed both church and state, in lopping of all whoe had affection or dependancy on either, rooting out the very face of a clargie-man, or gentleman, or the civiler sort of the commonalty. In this distraction each man looked uppon other straingly, none knowing whom to trust, or how to be secured from the raige, rapine, and destruction from the soldiery, in whose sole power was both the civill and ecclesiasticke sword since the yeare 1648. And we had all suffered soe deepely under those oppressions, that even the contrary party to the king did heartily wish an allteration from those pressures.

Insomuch that most sober, wise people of this nation began to have a good oppinion of the antient government of this realme, under which they had lived soe many peaceable yeares, when they had smarted for theire ficklenesse in changeing it, made them experience which was the best and most desirable, for its happie productions of peace and truth. Thus did it please the Divine Wisdome soe to order it, in great and miraculous mercy, that when we had felt the evils of our sad devissions, and our growing higher towards utter destruction in theire contineuance in them, He hereby taught the nation wisdome, and did incline theire hearts to returne to theire old station, under the notion of a free parliament. As all the world stood amaised att our unheard of follies and confusions, when the best frame of government was puled downe and destroyed, soe was theire great combinations against us of all sides by our enimies, to have rooted out our name and nation. And this by all people of severall perswasions and religions would have bin glad of soe rich a prise. But He Whoe is the keeper of Isracll, That neither slumbers nor sleepeth, watched over us for good, and was a tower of defence against all our secrett and malitious enimies, and out of our owne miseries made a way for to escape, even when they little thought of such a thing. Yet, till that time was come, great and heavy was our feares and burdens, groaneing under that tirany, both church and state, haveing our deare soveraine King Charles the 2nd bannished, and not injoyeing those rights, nor indeed any thing, from his three kingdomes, which was unjustly detained by usurpation, which caused us daily to poure out our complaints to God, with uncessant cries and teares for His church, and annoynted to be restored againe, which might be the meanes of re-establishment of the gospell of peace amongst us, and the true religion in these once flourishing kingdoms.*

A Relation conserning my deare and honored mother the Lady Wandesforde, and of her death, December 10th, 1659 (i., 160).

My deare mother was sole daughter to Sir Hewet Osborne and lady Joyce his wife, which lady Joyce was eldest daughter to Sir Miles Fleetewood of London, in the reigne of Queene Elizabeth, of happie memmory. She was borne at Sir John Payton's house, January 5th, 1591, at Islellome† in Cambridge-shire, my grandfather and grandmother liveing then att my aunt's house att Islelome, beeing the eldest childe of my grand-father's, and intended by him to have inherited his estate, have-ing soe intailed it uppon her att his first goeing beyond sea in Callis' voyage.

After some yeares he returned into England, and it pleased God to give them a gallant son and heire, which aftterwards proved a most excelent, wise, and good man, Sir Edward Osborne,‡ of Keveton, barronett. A faithfull, prudent man, zealous for God, the king, and the church; of great abilitties, to serve his king and country, beeing advanced to be Lord President of Yorke; and lived and died in much honour and fame.

To returne to my mother, who was bred up in her youth

* "A praier to God for the church, and restoration of the king, November, 1659" (i., 159, 160).

† Islcham, four and a half miles from Mildenhall. An hospital for five widowers and five widows was founded here by the lady of Sir Robert Peyton, who died in 1518.

‡ See p. 54.

and infancy with much caire and sircumspect by the eye of my grandmother, a discreete and wise woman, giveing her all the advantages of breeding and good education that the Court and those times could afford, which was indeed excelent for gravity, modestie, and pictie, and other sutable qualities for her degree, as writing, singing, danceing, harpsicalls, lute, and what was requisit to make her an accomplished lady,* as she did aprove her selfe in all her time. At the age of twenty-one yeares she was married, by the consent of her mother, beeing then her selfe married to Sir Petter Frechvile, having lived seaven yeares a widdow since my grandfather's death. The portion which my father receaved was very faire in those daies, beeing two thousand pounds, paid the next day of their marriage. Nor was she awanting to make a fare greatter improvement of my father's estate through her wise and prudentiall government of his family, and by her caire was a meanes to give opportunity of increasing his patrimony, as my deare father is pleased to leave upon record in his owne booke,† for her eternall honour, soe that it might be said of her, "many daughters have don well, but yow exceedest them all."‡ It pleased God to inrich my father and mother with (the cheife end for which marriage was ordeined) the blessing of children, my mother bringing forth to him seaven, hopefull enough to live, and to be comforts to theire parents, fower sons and three daughters. The eldest beeing Katherine;§ the second, Christopher, who died att six yeares old, was a wise and beautifull childe, endowed with pictie and parts, whoes lose was very deepely resented by his parents. The third was George, whom I have had occassion to mention in this booke. The fourth was Joyce, a sweete and comlie

---

* "One only daughter have I, no kin else,
    The maid is fair, o' the youngest for a bride,
    And I have bred her at my dearest cost,
    In *qualities* of the best."

                        Timon of Athens, act i., sc. 1.

† This book has been alluded to elsewhere.

‡ "Many daughters have done virtuously, but thou excellest them all" (Prov. xxxi. 29).

§ A sketch of this part of the Wandesford pedigree will be given elsewhere.

childe, died about four yeares old. The fifth, myselfe, Alice Thornton. The sixth, my brother Christopher Wandesforde, now heire to my father affter my brother George his death. The seaventh and last childe was John, borne att London before she went for Ireland, a sweete, beautifull and pregnant childe and young man, an excelent scholer, and of pietie and parts beyond his yeares. My father beeing called over into Ireland, to serve the king in the Roles Office in that kingdom, by reason of my mother's late weakenesse affter her delivery of my brother John, went into Ireland one yeare before my mother and her family. Affter which she had a saife passage thither, liveing in much comfort and hapienesse all my father's life, doeing much good to all people in each spheare wherein she actted, laing out her selfe to the best for her husband, whome she highly honoured. Her children, freinds, and servants found theire, as in England, a perpetuall effluance of all graces and vertues flowing from soe full a spring which God had indowed her noble soule with all, lived in great peace, tranquility, and charity, full of meeckenesse, humility, chastity, modestie, sobriety, and gravity; yea, was she indowed with great wisdom in the constant course of her life, of a sweete and pleasant composure of spiritt, not sullanly sad, nor vainely light, but of an excelent temper in soule and bodie, neither of them wanting those due ornaments which might make her lovely in the eyes of God and man. And indeed exactly studious to advance the intrest of her duties, in pietie and religion, in herselfe and all her children; whoes caire was very sedulous for theire soules' happinesse as well as the imbellishments of theire persons, desiring to yeald her accounts to God in righteousnesse and truth, according to the sincerity of her soule in His service. Thus weare wee happie and blessed, that we weare childeren and offspring of such a holy and sanctified a couple, whom God Almighty had filled with such a measure of His spiritt, makeing them great ornaments of religion. After my deare father's decease, she lived his widdow till her death, which was the space of nineteen yeares and seven daies, dieing in that same month of December, and in old age. But she was not one of those that lived in pleasure, or spent her daies in vanitie, for what time could be spaired from workes of necessitie and duty to her children and family, all the rest was given to the service of her God, either as workes of pietie and devotion, in private and publick, or charitie towards her breathren, whom she saw did stand in need and necessity. Especially haveing a due regard and compassion uppon the clargy, which through the rigour of those times of oppression were banished from theire own homes, wanting all manner of releife, with theire families, very offten and frequently found the bowelss of a good Samaritaine in her's, she opening her armes to receave Christ in His poore members, accounting it a great happinesse that He vouchsafed her the honour to be instrumental for the releife and suport of such as were precious in His sight.

I have formerly made a discourse of her travills and severall accidents that befell her person and family affter my father's death, till she came to live att her joynture att Hipswell, and allso what troubles and trialls, losses and crosses, she underwent allmost all the time she lived there, as well from the unnaturall actions and unkindnesse of freinds, which had repining thoughts that she should injoy her joynture, as from the publicke enimies and disturbances from the publicke calamities of church and state.

All which she endured with a noble and invincible spiritt, beeing fortified by her religion, and the testimony of a good conscience, that she laid out her selfe for God's service and glory, and the good of my father's whole family, and the generall benifitt of Christians amongst whom she lived ; yea, even in those sad times of loseing all, many hundreds were releived and suplied at her doore. For her exceeding kindnesses don for the helpe of the heire, yonger children, and debtors of my father's, lett her owne narration, delivered from her in writting before wittnesses, declare, what and how she expended upon that account, she beeing in a manner compelld to leave such a testimony from some unworthy prejuedices which said she did not much from her estate for them. But it was requisitt, for such an act of kindnesse which she did, spending all she receaved upon it, which should not be forgotten by that family whoe receaved soe grand a blessing in her life and preservation, without the which it is too probable that we might have bin made marchandise of. Should I forgett her unparalelld wisdome, goodnesse, tendernesse, love, and parentall affection by which she governed all her gracious actions towards us, in our maintenance and education, I should be worse then an infidell, who had forsaken the faith, and bin ingratefull to that God Which made them, and the very oxe and asse which knowes his owner's cribb would rise up in judgement against me. Therefore doe I desire in point of gratitude to God my Father, and that gracious mother whom He gave me, to mention those great mercys we receaved from her in generall, and in perticuler for those exceeding goodnesse and favours wherein she extended her bounty towards me; whoe was pleased to provide an habitation for me affter her decease, and disposed me in marriage, affter which I, with my husband and children, did live with her eight yeares affter my marriage, bringing forth four of my children in her house; and had all manner of charges, expences, and houshold affaires, in sicknesses, births, christnings, and burialls, of and concerning ourselves and children, with the diett, etc., of nurses, men-servantes and maides, and our freind's entertainments, all things don of her owne cost and charges all her daies while she lived, which could not be of lesse valew to us clearely then £1600. And noe smale addittion of helpe to my husband's estate was her disposall of her reall estate in land, which she had purchased for £550, settling it uppon myselfe, and my childeren. Allso her exceeding affection extended itselfe in her settling all her personall estate by deede of guift, and her last will and testament, saving her debts and legacies and funeralls, in feofees in trust for the use of myselfe, husband, and childeren.* All which I confesse farre exceeding my merritt, but not her intire affection, for my constant beeing with her in her sorrowes and solitudes. And albeit she had in our minorrities disbursed

* See notes from will, *postea*.

uppon us out of her owne joynture, which should have bin don out of Kirklington, the some of £2000, besides above £500 to my brother George, the heire, with the payment of £300 debt of that estate, and the losse of all my father's personall estate given her by will, as allso her losse of her annuity of £300 per annum, out of Ireland, to the valew due unto her at her death, the sum £300 per annum, which nineteen yers a widdow [£5700] never receaved any part thereof: yett, notwithstanding all the afforesaid goodnesse of her's to that estate, there wanted not some whoe putt harsh thoughts into the heire's minde, that she dealt hardly, because she did not give all her widdowe's patrimony to him, when as all her former helpes did redound to his benifitt; and with all they knew our estate was more burthened att that time, which might require such helpes from her, because we weare contented, for the ease of Kirklington, to receave my portion from thence yearely, and not in an intire summe. Besides this, she fitted my youngest brother, John Wandesforde, with the opportunity of good schooles, as Beedall, Chester, Richmond, with all other provissions of maintenance, bookes, and all necessarys for Cambridge, leaveing him under the tuittion of Dr. Widdrington* in Christ's Colledge; maintaining him there all the time, which, by reason of a sore feavour that seized on him there, he cost her after the rate of above £100 per annum. All which time his anuity lay dormant in the estate of my father, which I supose was some advantage to the heire. In fine, great and many were the good and charitable acts this most deare and excelent mother of ours did to us all; she soe wisely and justly diposeing her estate amongst us, that none had the least cause to complaine, but blesse God for her wise dispensation, beeing truly thankfull for the safe protection, caire, and preservation we injoyed under her wing, in all our sad times of calamitie which our eyes beheld. She restraining and moderating her owne expences most frugaly, and good huswifery, that she

* Ralph Widdrington, D.D., fellow of Christ's College, public orator, etc. Mr. Mayor gives an account of him in the appendix to his life of M. Robinson, 196—208.

neither lived in a penurious, but a noble, hansom manner, to whom both our freinds and her owne was freely entertained and welcomed. Her poore tennants was more happie in her then many of her bordering neighboures, whoe although exceeding poore att her first comming, yet by God's blessing upon her discreet ordering her affaires in her estate, that the tennants grew rich affter little time in those distractions, and since have infinittly bewailed her losse, whose person liveing they had soe great an honour for.

It was very observable that she out lived those sad troubles upon the kingdom in part, though not till the restoration of our happie king Charles the Second, whose comeing in was daily prayed for and heartily wished. And the last soldiers which quartered att Hipswell proved to be such as turned to Generall Monke from Lambert; and within a short time the mighty power and providence of God turned the minds and hearts of the people, as a mighty river towards its owne channell, affter her disease, which she had put up soe many praiers to God for, and would have bin a joyfull day for her to have lived to see. But I hope God had prepaired a great reward in heaven for her, for all her toyle and sorrowes she indured in this Bochim and vaile of teares, and affter three weeks' sicknesse gave her the full fruittion of her long desired happinesse.

The relattion of her sicknesse heere followes.

It pleased God to vissitt my deare and honoured mother, the lady Wandesford, with her last sicknesse, uppon Friday the 17th of November, 1659, beginning then with an exceeding great cough, which tormented her bodie with stitches in her breast, and troubled her with short breathing. These stitches contineued about fourteen daies together, hindering her from almost any sleepe or rest, insomuch that it was wonderfull how she could subsist. But uppon the use of bagges with fried oates, butter and camomiell chopt, layed to her sides, the stitches removed, and the cough abated, as to the extreamity thereof. But then she was seized with a more dangerous simnttome, of a hard lumpe contracted in her stomacke, that laid on her heart, with great paine and riseing up in her throat, allmost stopeing her breath, when she either swallowed any thing or laied to sleepe. Which lumpe was conceaved to be contracted of winde and phlegme in the stomacke for lacke of voydance. She had allsoe an exceeding sore throate and mouth, soe that she was deprived of the benifitt of eateing or swallowing allmost any kind of food, save a little drope of beere, beeing the most she tooke inwardly for four or five daies, and that but with a seringe. Her tongue and mouth at first was blacke, then it turned white, soe that with the paines my deare mother tooke in washing and cleanseing, the skinn came of, and was red till the blood came; this contineuing till, in the end, her mouth grew white all over. In this most sad condittion of weakenesse was my deare mother, allmost quite without food, rest, ease, or sleepe for about a wecke. In which time, as allso in all the rest of her sickenesse, she expressed extraordinary patience, still saing it was the Lord that sent it to her, and none else could take it from her, and if He pleased to see it fitt, He could ease her, or give her patience to indure His hand. Often would she say that the way to heaven was by the gates of hell, and that the Lion of the tribe of Juda would deliver her. Likewise would she frequently breake out and say with the sweete Psalmist of Israell, in the midst of her inexpressable paines and torments, "*Why art thou soe full of heavinesse, oh my soul, and why art thou soe disquietted within me ? I will still hope in my God, and putt my trust in the God of my salvation, who is the helpe of my countenance, and my God.*"* She frequently re-peated the seventy-first Psalm, which she said was pend for old age. Surely she was a great example and patorne of pietie, faith, patience, of fortitud and resolution, to withstand all the fiery darts of Satan, which he, in her weakenesse, cast to affright and hinder her journey to heaven. But He in whom she putt her whole confidence, and served from her youth up, did not

* Psalms xlii. 14, 15 ; xliii. 5, 6.

now leave her in extreamity, but soe asissted her in soul and spiritt that it was an heavenly sight to the beholders. Even to her last period, and notwithstanding all her torments, still she putt forth her selfe for the glory of God, and the good of her family and beholders, in good instructions, severe reproofes for all sins in generall, with a contineuall prayeing to God and praising Him in psalmes sutable for her condittion, speakeing to God in His owne phraise and word, saing that we could not speake to Him from ourselves in such an acceptable a manner as by that which was dictated by His owne most Holy Spiritt. She offten desired her freinds to pray with her, and for her, and tould them that she desired that they would not pray for her contineuance in this life, for she was weary of it, and desired to obteine a better, and to be fitted for it. And that these should be the heads on which they should pettition God, for her, videlicet—that the Lord would be pleased to grant her true and unfeined repentance for her sinns, which He had mercifully pleased to begin in her allready; and to perfect the same; to give her pardon, remission and forgivenesse for them, through Jesus Christ her deare Saviour; to grant her true faith in Him to beleive all His promises in the Gospell, and layeing hold on Him for salvation, with the sanctification of His Holy Spiritt; and att last, to gloryfie her in heaven in His good time. Which pettitions, said she, whoesoever shall make for me, the Lord heare and grant the same. This sweete saint of God had alwaies a great and unfained love for all God's faithfull ministers, and offten desired theire praiers, giveing great attention to them, haveing much comfort in her soule after that ordenance. Her desires was earnest to receave the Holy Sacrament, which she did with great comfort, on Thursday was sevenight before her departure, from Mr. Petter Samewaies,* allthough it was

---

* Peter Samways, A.M., instituted rector of Bedale and Wath, 31 Dec., 1660, died 6 April, 1693. He was a prebendary of York and Ripon.

1690, Nov. 28. Will of Peter Samwaies, prebendary of York, rector of Bedale and Wath—of Trinity College, Cambridge. To Sir Robert Darcy (at whose father's house, when I was vicar of Cheshunt, I lived) £10. To the poor of Eltham, in Kent, where I was born and baptised, £5. To Samuel Collins, Esq., doctor of physick, and his virtuous lady and two daughters, guineas apiece to

with great difficultie of swallowing, she never tasting dry bread affter, for that excessive weakenesse. Her desire was to Mr. Kirton* he would preach her funerall sermon, the text to be out of the 14th of the Revelations, verce the 13th, *"Blessed are the dead that die in the Lord, for they rest from theire laboures."* This blessed soule had the guift from her God to contineue till her last breath her perfect memory, understanding, and great wisdome and piety, ever preparing her soule for God and recommending her selfe in devout ejaculations, crieing out with St. Paull, *" I desire to be desolved, and to be with Christ."†* And all that Friday night, before she departed, haveinge this sweete saing in her mouth, *"Come, Lord Jesus, come quickly;"‡* she makeing Dafeny to pray with her that praier of Dr. Smith made in his booke for a person at the point to die; and tooke great notice of each pettition, praing with zeale and ardency. It was very observable in all her sickenesse, as indeed she was not wanting of her gratitude to God for His exceeding testimony of His love and mercy to her in all her preservations and deliverances of her and her children, which she very offten repeated and severally innumerated in her best health; soe was it now in her grand weaknesse and torment, even till her death, still the subject of her discourse; calleing to minde the wonderfull and infinitt goodnesse of God to her even from her childehood, setting forth His favours to her soule, and spirituall mercys innumerable, which she perticulerly mentioned. And then she mentioned all her manifold preservations and deliverances of her person from death and destruction, makeing such an excelent cattalogue of all that it was a great consolation to the hearers, and proved by these things as a great argument of the suport of her drooping speritts now at the houer of death; beeing a strong barre of defence against her spirituall

---

buy them rings. To Thomas Dalton, Esq., 20s., to his daughter Mrs. Dorothy Dalton, 10s.—(Richmond Wills.)

His inventory is dated 2 May, 1693, in which a fine library is mentioned. Mr. Samways was a scholar and an author.

* John Kirton was rector of Richmond 1658-1664.

† Phil. i. 23.   ‡ Rev. xxii. 20.

adversaries, that God had appeared gloriously for her that was His servant, Who had delivered her from time to time whenever she called on Him; her Lord never forsaking her; but brought her to the gates of death in a happie old age, and to the sight of heaven, where she faine would be. And in Him she alone trusted, through the mirritts of Christ, He would still deliver her from hell, and sin, and Satan, and preserve her to His kingdome, theire to live with Him for ever, where she might spend the whole etternity of praise and thanksgiveing and halcluias of glory to the Blessed Trinity. Till which time she was thirsting and longing, and desirous to be desolved, and to be with Christ Jesus her Redeemer. For noe thing of this world, nor in it, could hinder her fixednesse for heaven; nor indeed did the concernes of this life come into her thoughts, saveing to leave her pieous and Christian instructions and holy admonitions amongst us her children and servants; and to learne by her how to live well, and die happiely, joyfully, and comfortably, imbraceing and offten calling for death, to lett her in to the injoyment of her Lord. She had made severall times in her sickenesse, uppon occasion of ministers vissitting her, many very excelent confessions of her faith, and proffession* of those Christian foundations uppon which our faith was built, and of her true zeale to the service of God in His holy ordenances of our most pieous and Christian church of England. Wishing us, as we would eskape the danger of damnation, not to dishonour that great God Whom we served by renounceing that faith and profession which was taught us by the holy cleargy and bushopps of England; never to listen to the insinuations of any factious, new doctrines whatever, but serve God truly and sincerely therein; and He would accept of our soules, and we should be happie, if not in this world, yet hoped in a better. And that she did beleeive, that if we humbled our selves for the abominable sins of this nation, and pray to God faithfully, and serve Him sincerely in heart, God would returne in mercy and restore His decaied church in England, and His servant's son,

---

* These professions were very frequently made on the deathbed in the sixteenth and seventeenth centuries.

blessed King Charles the First's posterity, to rule in this nation. Praing heartily we might be delivered from popery, which these devissions and schismes might tend to, if not prevented by the all wise providence of Almighty God.   As to her owne perticuler, she blessed God for making knowne to her the truth, and preserving her therein, declaring that she made it her constant endeavour to walke therein all her daies, haveing her direction and guidance from God.   And now she found the comfort of His service and the hopes of the rewards of His grace which He gave her throughout the course of her life, and fellt the sweetenesse of influences upon her soule, for which she most humbly rendered all the powers and faculties of her heart in thanks and praise to His name and mercy for ever.   She powred out her fervent, admirable praiers to her God, for all her children and relations, begging to each perticuler childe those graces and gifts they wanted; and forgivenesse to all who had any way wronged or injured her in all her life, nameing some, who had more nearely and highly wronged and greived her, with the bowells of compassion for the good of theire soules, that they may repent and be forgiven, and receaved to mercy in His kingdome, where all hearts are united in the holy bond of charity.   As to my owne private consernes, she pettitioned God that I might finde comfort in my husband's family, and be rewarded with the same blessing that God had bin graciously pleased to give me in my children (as she was pleased to say I had bin to her); and that I might be strengthned by His grace to indure those afflictions with patience which I must find in this world affter her death; and that I might have hope in God's mercy that He would lay no more on me then He would inable me to undergoe; and that they were signes of His love to me; and that I must not greive too much for her losse, since the Lord had contineued her soe long to me, for He could make up her losse in a greater comfort by giveing me a son, which I wanted, and that I was then with childe of one.   Wished me contineue as I had begun, and then we should receave each other with joy in heaven, which she was confident of, through the merritts of Jesus Christ, according to His speech to St. John, *"Be thou faithfull, and I will give thee* *a crowne of life:"** with abundance of other heavenly rich expressions that I am not able to write downe.

She tould me she had fully finished her will, and settled her estate according as she desired, and she hoped with a good conscience, settling all she had in such a manner as would breed noe trouble; and that she hoped her son Christopher would be sattisfied with it, because she had not bin a wanting in the discharge of a good conscience towards him ever since he was borne, by takeing paines with him and caire of him in his minority, and disbursing the greater part of her widdowe's estate upon him, or for his brother John, or the other part of Kirklington, whereby he had the benifitt of her maintaineing the children: and that now he would lett me injoy with my husband and children what she had don for us, considering my husband's estate needed it; and he was heire of a great large estate of his father's, and by her death the joynture came in cleare to him. All which estate would amount to yearely to him in England and Ireland three thousand pounds, which she praied God to blesse to him and his posterity, that they might injoy it in righteousnesse soe long as *the moone and sun indureth.*† "And now," she said, "I have don my worke and finished my course, which the Lord had given me to doe; *hence-forth, I hope, is laid up for me a crowne of glory, which the Lord shall give me; and not only to me, but for all those that love the Lord Jesus and His appearing.*"‡

About Thursday night she sent for her children to take her last fairewell in this life, when Mr. Thornton and myselfe came with our two children, Alice and Kattherine, she desiring my husband to pray with and for her, as he had don severall times; in which she was much pleased and sattisfied, ever joyn-ing most devoutly, reverently praing with her heart and soule in each pettition, finding great joy and refreshment upon such occasions. After which praier, she imbraced us all severally in her armes, and kissed us, powring out many prayers and blessings for us all; like good old Jacob, when he gave his last

* Rev. ii. 10.
† Psalm lxxii. 7.   ‡ 2 Tim. iv. 7, 8.

blessing to his childeren, she begged of God Almighty for us all. Affter which I tooke the sadest last leave of my deare and honored mother as ever childe did to part with so great and excelent a parent and infinitt comfort. And yet the great greife I had was increased by reason of her exceeding torment which she indured, which made me more willingly submitt to part with her, who I saw indured much paines and extreamity, not desiring she should long indure that which it was the pleasure of God, for the excercise of her patience, to lay on her. Allso, when she see me weepe much, for this affliction of her's did indeed conserne me nearely, she said, "Deare childe, why will you not be willing to part with me to God? Has He not lent me to be a comfort to you long enough? O part with me freely, as I desire to injoy my Saviour in heaven. Doe not be unwilling that I should be delivered from this miserable world; give me willing and frely to Him that lent me thus long, and be contented in every thing. You never have bin dis- obedient to me in all your life; I pray thee obey me in this, that you submitt chearefully to the wise and good determination of our Lord God. And fill your heart with spiritual comfort instead of this in me He takes to Himselfe. And soe the blessing of God Almighty be uppon the head of you and your's for ever. Amen." Certainly the words of a dieing freind prevailes much; and I doe beleive the Lord had put words of perswasion into her mouth which prevailed more then all the world with me to moderate my excessive sorow, and build me up in hopes, as she said, of our meeting againe, never to part; which soe hapened, for I was affter this even desirous that if it were the determinate pleasure of God to take her from my head, that I might patiently submitt when He should free that sweet soule from all those burthens of pressures and extreamitys. It pleased God she contineued till Satterday. About noone she spoke to my uncle Norton, and recomending myselfe and all her children to his caire, with much good praiers for him and his, she then tooke her leave of him. About four a'clocke my aunt Norton came to see her, when she saluted her gladly, biding her "Wellcome, deare sister, what comfort is it to me to see my deare and honored husband's sister" with her at that time, there ever having bin a strict league of affection and freind-ship betwixt them; she was then come to see her make her last end and sceane of her life, whome she had knowne neare forty yeares, and soe tooke her solomne fairewell of her. I forgott to declare, that, about Wednesday before, she called for her last will, it being made a yeare before that, and ratificing the same, and publickly declared the same to be her last will and testament, before my husband and myselfe, and many other wittnesses, makeing the same to be indorsed on the backe of her will, etc.*

* Will of Dame Alice Wandesford, of Hepswell, co. York, widow, dated 10th of January, 1658. To be buried at the parish church where I shall decease, Appoints John Frecheville, of Stavley in co. Derby, Esq., my dearely beloved brother, and my trusty and welbeloved freind, Francis Darley, of Buttercranbe, in s^d co. Yorke., gent., executors, desireing that they will shew their speciall love and care to my daughter, Alice Thorneton, wife of William Thorneton, of East Newton, co. York, Esq., and her children. To bee privately and decently interred as best suiteing to my present condicon and estate, and for that purpose I doe onely give £30, and £10 more to bee distributed amongst the poore at the time of my exequies, and then the poore within the lordship of Hipswell are cheifly to be regarded. To Mr. Sidall for funerall sermon, one mourninge cloake. Noe ribbons or gloves, except to my children. Quicke goods, viz., horses, sheep, etc., to be sold. Discharge £50 oweing to my brother Norton. My sonne Christopher Wandesford. To dau. Alice Thorneton use of plate, jewells, etc., for life. To her all wearing linnen and apparrell, bookes and writeings, my lute and vyoll, and my late honoured husband's picture, also harpsicall virginalls for her life, after, to my grandchild, Alice Thornton, for her life; after, to my grandchild, Katherine T. for life; after, to the eldest dau. of Alice Thorneton, my grandchild, successively for their lives.

Whereas William Wandesford, one of my husband's executors, intreated mee to become bound with him as surety for £200 to one Mr. Thomas Edmunds, which monie he told me he borrowed for the management of the estate of my honoured husband of Castle Comer in Ireland, but the said bond was putt in suite against mee, and I was forced to pay £184, which has not been repaid; also, my husband, by his will dated 2^d Oct., 1640, bequeathed unto me £100 for a legacy out of the Iresh estate, which is not yett paid; I entreat my executors to recover both the said sums, and, when recovered, lay out the same in landes in England, which shall inure to Alice Thorneton, my daughter, for her life, and after to the use of her younger sonnes and all her daughters equallie. Alsoe whereas I have taken a survey of all the landes in Hipswell and Watewth, which cost mee £20 at the least; if my sonne, Xofer W., desire to have it, it shall be delivered unto him uppon the payment of £20. To the said Christopher W. all

To returne to her last actions in this life. About six a'clocke att night this sweete saint of God began to be speachlesse, haveing still all that time imployed that toung in nothing but praiers, prayses, and pettitions to God with most heavenly, spirituall, and pathaticall recomendations of her selfe to the Lord, ever saing, " Come, Lord Jesus, make haste and receave my soule," and at the last immeadiatly before her speach failed, "Lord Jesus, into Thy hands I commend my spiritt." And when it failed, still lifting up to heaven her eyes and hands to God. And Dafeny perceaved she drew her breath short, and goeing to depart, praied her that she would give them that was with her some signe that she found the comfort of God's Spiritt in her soule, with a taste of the joyes of heaven, which she immeadiatly did, to all theire great comforts, for she lifted up both her eyes

the iron rainges in my house at Hipswell, and the lockes and keyes of the doores there; all which I bought since my comeing thither, except five old lockes and keyes I found there; also the Iresh tables in the kitchin, with all the severall blockes to cutt meate uppon, with the tables and the shelves in the milke-house, with two cheese presses, and one kneading-trough in the boulting-house, all which wooden things I made at my owne charge since my comeing hither; alsoe one brewing-lead standing in the brewhouse, which cost mee in repaires as much as would have bought a new one, etc. I declare that the great long oaken table and frame in my greatt chamber at Hipswell was left there by my cozen, Anthony Norton his wife, when she went away; to be restored to her. To Christopher W., 40s. To my sonne, John W., 20s. To my sonne, Sir Thomas Danby, 20s., to buy him a ringe. To my sonne Thorneton, 20s., to buy him a ringe, To my daughter Thorneton, 20s., to buy her a ringe. To my grandchild Christopher Wandesford, 20s., to buy him a ringe. To my grandsonne Thomas Danbie, 20s. To my granddaughter, Katherine Danby, 20s. To my servant, Robert Loftus the elder, 20s. To my servant, George Lightfoote, 20s. To Daphney Lightfoote, my servant, 20s. To my manservant——, 10s. To my three women——, ——, ——, 10s. apeece. To the two boyes, 5s. apeece. Residue to executors for the use of my daughter, Alice Thorneton, and her children. And whereas by my deed under hand and seale, d. 3ᵈ Jany., 1658, I did give to yᵉ said John Frecheville and Francis Darley all my personall estate, in trust to pay all my funerall expences, debts, and legacies, and doe all such other acts and duties to my daughter, Alice Thorneton, and her children, as shall be most proper to the execution of my will, I confirme the same. Wittnesses, William Etherington, Richard Mahum, Mathew Bellamy, William Wilson, Robert Loftus, + mke., George Lightfoote, George Wood, scr. Proved P. C. C., London, by John Frecheville, Esq., and Francis Darley, Gent., the joint executors, 19 July, 1660 (Nabbs., 105).

and hands stedfastly to heaven three times distinctly, one affter another, and closeing her eyes her selfe then laid downe her head and her hands, this holy saint and patterone of true pietie sweetely fell asleepe in the Lord, betweene the hours of eight and nine a clocke at night, upon Satterday, the 10th of December, 1659, beeing the day of her coronation, I hope, in heaven, with her Father, receiving that wellcome of *" Come, ye blessed of my Father, receave the kingdom He has prepared for you. For I was an hungery and ye fed me, naked and ye clothed me, sick and imprisoned, and ye ministred unto me. In as much as ye did it unto these, ye did it unto me."** And I hope she is now entred into the joy of her Lord.

My brother Christopher Wandesforde was then att London, where he was writt to informe him, both of her sicknesse and death. Her funerall was solomnized with as much hansomenesse as those times would afford, and considering the condittion wee weare in, the souliers haveing bin quartered amongst us, though not according to her worth and quality. She was intterred uppon Tuessday, the 13th of December following, in the cheife place in her owne quire att Cattericke church,† she haveing repaired the same all that summer, att her owne charges, to the valew of above twenty pounds. Her corpes was carried out of her house by the Lord D'arcy,‡ his son Coll. D'arcy, Sir Christopher Wivill, baronet, and divers other persons and kindred of quality. Then from Hipswell greene her tennants tooke her, and soo carrieing her to the towne of

---

* Matt. xxv. 34 *et seq.*

† There is no entry of this funeral in the Catterick Register. The Hipswell aisle in Catterick church was on the south side, that on the north belonging to the Lawsons of Brough.

Beneath a blue marble slab in this aisle is buried " The body of Dame Alice, daughter of Sir Hewit Osborne, sister of Sir Edward Osborne, of Kiveton, Bart. (aunt to the most noble lord, Thomas, Duke of Leeds), relict of the Rt. Hon. Christopher Wandesford, Esq., of Kirklington, Lord Deputy of Ireland. She died, aged 67 years, 11 months, and 6 days, 10 Dec. 1659." (Raine's Catterick Church, 17). The mention of the Duke of Leeds in the inscription shews that the monument was not prepared till very late in the seventeenth century.

‡ The heads of the noble house of Darcy. Sir Christopher Wyvill was the poet. His wife was a Darcy. The Darcies and Wandesfords were cousins,

Catterick, where the ministers whoe was appointed by her owne nomination carried her in to the church; and affter sermon laid her in her grave. The ministers' names were these: Mr. Petter Samois, Mr. Kirton, Mr. Ferrers, Mr. Edrington, Mr. Binlows, Mr. Robinson, Mr. Smith, Mr. Brockell, Mr. Parke.* Infinitt numbers of poore were served by dolle at the doore; above fifteen hundred; besides in the church of Catterick. This blessed mother of mine was thus gathered into her grave, haveing lived many peaceable yeares together with my father, brought him a compotent number of children, beeing the suport of his house and family, preserving it and the branches under her caire and prudence, liveing his chaste wife and widdow for above nineteen yeares. Her whole age wherein she lived was three score and seaven yeares, and eleven months and ode daies; soe that she died in a good old age, full of good works and vertue and honor to all of her famalie and countery. To the Lord's most infinitt Majestie be all glory and praise, for His great goodnesse and mercy extended to me and us all, through this dear parent of ours. He make us to possesse those graces and virtues which Hee bestowed upon her, that we may be the better capable to doe Him true and faithfull service to our live's end. Amen.

Severall prayers made by my mother proper for the time of the Holy Sacrament as ejaculations before receaving of the bread. Before receaving of the wine affter consecration. After both bread and wine. (i., 178).

O most gracious God, Which hath sacrificed Thine only be-gotten Sonne to appease Thy just wrath for my sinnes and to ransome my soule from hell, sealle unto mee by this blessed

---

* A party of the neighbouring clergy. Dr. Samways was rector of Bedale, and Mr. Kirton of Richmond; Mr. Edrington in 1665 became vicar of Gilling; Mr. Binlows was incumbent of Scruton; Mr. Robinson rector of Burneston; Mr. Brockell was a native of Richmond; Mr. Parke was curate of Hipswell.

Sacrament Thy promise and covenant made in Christ, that Thou wilt receave me, a penitent siner and true believer, into Thy grace and mercy; and that, for the death and passion of my deare Saviour, my sinnes past and present may be remitted and forgiven, as verily as I shall now be partaker of this blessed Sacrament. Amen.

O sweete Saviour, from Whom I have receaved the inestimable benefitt of my redemption, grant that I may receave the spirituall graces signified by these outward simbolls and pledges of Thy love. And that, as my bodie is fed and strengthned by corporal foode, soe my soule may (from the hunger-starving of sinne) bee strengthned by Thy blessed bodie and washed by Thy precious blood from all her sinnes. Amen.

Grant, O mercyfull Redeemer, as Thou hast vouchsafed me to sit att Thy table and be partaker of Thy pretious bodie and blood, soe my sinfull soule may be washed from all her sinnes in that blessed lavacre, and buried in Thy grave, never to rise up in judgement against mee. Forgive, O Lord, the want of the preparation of my heart to come to soe heavenly a banquett, in which are all the treasures of mercy displayed. Accept the poore and true endeavours of my heart to the reverent receaving of this Holy Communion, and grant that, being now made partaker thereof, it may be effectuall to confirme faith, to renue all Thy heavenly graces in me with the assurance of my salvation, being guided and established by the sanctification of Thy Holy Spiritt to walke in newness of life, by a holy, pious, and charitable conversation before Thee all the daies of my life. Amen and Amen.

Of my deare mother's last will and testament. (ii., 166).

After my deare mother's death I remained still at Hipswell a while till I could remove safely, by reason of my owne weakness and greife; and watching with her I had gott a very great cough, yett I could never doe enough for soe tender and deare a parent, nor shew my duty to so excellent vertue, whose loss

all the country extreamly lamented.   Allso, it was a great
frost and snow, soe that I could not be removed safely with my
life till March following.   Besides, there happned to have bin
suits depending amongst the family by want of my father's
will, which was not comprimised till after my mother's death,
and she haveing given me by her last will and testament and
her deeds all her estate, reall and personall, except what she
had excepted in her will, appoynted that her goods should be
removed with what convenient speed might be, in regard that
my brother Christopher Wandesforde was not willing I should
injoy her estate according to her disposall.   Nor was he willing
I should stay in her house at Hipswell till I was delivered,
haveing some ill persons that putt him uppon very unjust waies
with his freinds : but, by the good providence of God to me,
He raised me up my deare aunt Norton and uncle, who tooke
me into there house and many of my deare mother's goods and
my owne, being all presed* and the will proved and don
according to law by the order of her executors, my uncle
Fretchvill, her only brother by the mother's side, and my uncle
Francis Darley, my husband's uncle, which two friends did
take caire of me and my deare children affter my deare mother's
deceace, and order all her goods to severall places for security,
till I was in a condition to goe to Mr. Thornton's country,
which could not be don till it pleased God I was delivered.
But affter my deare mother's will was proved and put on the
file, it behoved us to be cairefull to prevent any trickes about
——, because of the maters which fell out conserning my
honored father's.   Soe that the Master of the Court had orders
from the executors not to be put on the file till some affaires
was don which conserned the said will, but to preserve it in
safe custody till further order.   My brother Christopher
Wandesforde, who had given notice to his steward, Robert
Loftus, that his mother's goods shud not be removed out of the
house till [he] heard from him, was very strict in search of the
will at London, to see how she had disposed of her estate.   Tho

* Appraised.

what she had of her widdowed estate att Hipswell was very
faire, but nothing to his which he injoyed of my father's in
Ireland and England, yett he was in expectancy to have gott
all her personall estate she left, and not satisfied with the four
thousand pounds a year left him by my father, but aimed to
have gott that of his good mother's, which she, out of her
great kindness and affection, she had bestowed uppon me; as
she is pleased to mention in her deeds and will, with a singuler
carracter of my duty and obedience to her, as well as on her
death bed; which is great matter of comfort to me, to have the
testimony of soe pieous and holy a parent, beeing the motive
to induce her to dispose of her estate towards my releife and
my children's.   Aftter he had caused the court to be searched
for probate of wills at London, I beeing then removed to St.
Nickolas, he tould me that he had made a search att London
where the wills are proved, and there was no will on the file,
and the men of the court said they never saw any, and if soe,
he beleived my mother did make no will or disposall of her
estate, it did all fall uppon him as her heire. This did much
surprise me to heare my only brother, formerly pretended soe
great an affection to me, now to seeke to defraud me of my
deare mother's blessing, and I tould him that tho he was now
the heire, as being a son, yett I was two years elder by my
birth, and though he had got the birthright, yett I ought to
have a shaire of her blessing, if she had not made a will. But,
God be praised, she had made one in perfect forme and manner
and deed, by which she disposed all as she thought fitt, and the
will was att London long since, and proved fully, and he might
repaire to it if he pleased and be sattisfied. He did not beleive me then, but since that did find the will on the file, and
soe receaved satisfaction how she had ordered all her estate.
Which since I am speaking of, it may not be amisse to
acknowledge God's great goodnesse and mercys to my selfe
and my deare husband and children in those provissions she
made for us in her will and deeds, besides her excelent kindness
she expressed to us in giveing my husband, my selfe, and all
my family, one man and three maides and nurrses, and all the

occassions of my sickneses, christnings, and deaths of my
children, all our table gratis, with all necessaryes of hous,
beding, linning, furniture, coles, hay, corne, etc. And this
contineued for above eight yeares affter I was married, as long
as she lived, with a great deale of hearty love and freedom did
this deare Saint of God entertaine us. Which constant housekeeping for our perticulers, besides her owne, she did account
it stood her in above the somme of twoo hundred pounds a
yeare, which she has tould me if she had not don she might
have given me sixteene hundred pounds more in money, which
would have purchased land, added to that her land at Midlham
which cost her five hundred and fifty or sixty pounds. As to
her personall estate in monneys, plate, linning, beding, etc., I
have heard Mr. Thornton say he had as good of what my deare
mother left me to the valew of one thousand pounds more,
which amounts to the valew in monney from my mother
receaved by Mr. Thornton and myselfe and children £2,550 or
£2,600. Besides which she made a deed of guift to feffees in
trust of all her arrears in Ireland, due to her out of my father's
estate of Edough of £300 per annum, in lieu of her joynter.
She outliveing my deare father nineteen yeares, there became
due to her, which she maide over by deed, the somme of £6,000;
which somme or any part of it was not paid, but remaines in
my brother's estate still; together with £200 as a debt my
deare mother paid for my father's estate, and ought to be paid
me by her will. But I know in all these things my poore
brother has bin imposed uppon, and maide believe not due to
be paid to my deare mother or myselfe.

I have all the reason in the world not to concealle the
great goodness of my gracious [God] in due acknowledgement
and humble gratitude to His Devine Majesty, Who raised and
preserved this deare parent to me for my releefe and suport
ever affter He tooke my deare father from me, who gave me all
my maintenance as well as to my three brothers during our
minoritys, which should have bin done out of Kirklington.
But she has given it in on account that she had expended uppon
our three persons, myselfe and two younger brothers Chris-

topher and John Wandesforde, to the somme of £1500 in maintenance and education; all which monneys, if she had gotten for our maintenance in her widdowhood, she would certainly have pleased to have given it to me and my children and husband; but since that was not paid to her, yett did she expresse her bounty in what she was able to me. For besides what is mentioned before in her will and deeds, she did send me by Dafeny her servant in monney and gold, which she charged her not to tell me of till after her decease, above one hundred and sixty pounds putt into my trunke one night when my husband and I was in bed; at our bed feete the said trunke stood, which I affterwards tooke and disposed of, much of it for to furnish Mr. Thornton's hous and to pay Lettleton's bailis* and other necessarys to his use, as I can shew on account. Besides, there was a great some of monney that was of her arreares of rents receaved at Hipswell tennants, which was disbursed by me for his use in accounts for housekeeping, as may apeare, which did amount to above £300, as may apeare. And if the rents which I have receaved out of her land att Midlam for soe many yeares since she died, be computed, affter £28 per annum, allowing the £2 a yeare for abatements and public charges out of that perticuler land and lett at £28 ycrely, it will amount in thirty yeares time, she dieing in December, 1659, till Lady Day, 1680, at £28, to £840.

Alice Thornton's preservation, 1659 (ii., 173).

I must not forget to glorifie my gracious Lord God, Who did deliver my deare Naly from faling into the fire in my chamber at Hipswell, when I was sitting in the chaire; then did the child stumble on the harth, and fell into the fire on the rainge with one of her hands, and burned her right hand three fingers of it, and by God's helpe I did pull her out of the fire by her clothes. I catched her out of it before she was exceedingly

* Bailiffs.

burned, only three of her fingers sore burned to the bone, which
I beeing but three weekes laid in of Betty could not dresse, but
was cured by my deare mother's helpe, for which eminent
deliverance I humbly blesse and praise the Holy One of Israel.
Amen.

I had allso a great deliverance at Hipswell when Besse
Poore was makeing of balsom. She would needs do it herselfe,
and when we went to diner she sett the chimny on fire, which
did indanger the whole house; but blessed be allwayes the
Lord our God Which did deliver us out of all dangers, and att
this time more especially. Praise His name for ever.

My Dream, 1660 (ii., 174).

Upon my removall to St. Nickolas, and Mr. Thornton was
gon to London, about the suits of my brother Sir Christopher Wandesforde,* I, beeing great with child, dreamed one
night that I was laid in childe-bed, had the white sheete
spread, and all over it was sprinkled with smale drops of pure
blood, as if it had bin dashed with one's hand, which so
frighted me that I tould my aunt of it in the morning; but she
putt it of as well as she could, and said dreams was not to be
regarded; but I kept it in my mind till my child died.

My delivery of my son William, my sixth childe, and of his death, April the 17th, 1660, at St. Nickolas (i., 180).

It was the good pleasure of God to contineue me in the
land of the liveing, and to bring forth my sixth child at St.
Nickolas. I was delivered of a very goodly son, having Mrs.
Hickeringgill with me, affter hard labour and hazardus, yet,
through great mercy, I had my life spaired, and was blessed
with a happie childe about 3 or 4 a'clocke in the morning upon

* He was created a baronet, 5th Aug., 1662.

Tuesday, the 17th of Aprill, 1660. That day allso was my childe baptized by Mr. Kirtton of Richmond, called William affter his father.* His sureties were my cozen John Yorke,† my cozen William Norton, and my cozen James Darcy lady of Richmond. Thus was I blessed with the life and comfort of my deare childe's baptisme, with its injoyment of that holy seale of regeneration; and my pretty babe was in good health, suckeing his poore mother, to whom my good God had given the blessing of the breast as well as the wombe, of that childe to whome it was no little satisfaction, while I injoyed his life; and the joy of it maked me recrute faster, for his sake, that I might doe my duty to him as a mother. But it so pleased God to shorten this joy, least I should be too much transported, that I was vissitted with another triall; for on the Friday senitt affter, he began to be very angery and froward, affter his dressing in the morning; soe that I perceaved him not to be well, uppon which I gave him Gascoyne powder and cordiall, least it should be the Red Gum in children, usuall at that time, to strike it out of his heart att morning affter his dressing. And haveing had three houers' sleepe, his face when he awaked was full of red round spotts like the smale pox, being of the compasse of a halfpeny, and all whealed white over, these continueing in his face till night, and being in a slumber in my arms on my knee he would sweetly lift up his eyes to heaven and smile, as if the old saying was true in this sweet infant, that he saw angells in heaven. But then, wheather through cold uppon his dressing then, or what else was the cause, the Lord knoweth, the spotts struck in, and grew very sicke all night, and about nine a'clocke on Satterday morning he sweetely departed this life, to the great discomfort of his weake mother, whoes only comfort is that the Lord, I hope, has receaved him to that place of rest in heaven where litle children beholds the

* Gulielmus, filius Gulielmi Thornton, arm., bap. April 17, 1660. (Richmond Par. Reg.)

† (Sir) John Yorke married Mary, dau. of Major Norton, of whom William Norton was a son. James Darcy, a younger son of Conyers Lord Darcy, married Isabel Wyvill.

face of theire heavenly Father, to his God and my God; Whom
I humbly crave to pardon all things in me which He ses amisse,
and cleance away my sinns by the blood of my dearest Saviour
and Reedeemer. And that my soule may be bettered by all
these chastisements He pleaseth to lay upon me, His vilde
worme and unprofitable servant, under all His dispensations that
hath laid heavy upon me for these many yeares, whereby He has
corrected me, but not given me over to death and destruction, for
which I humbly magnifie His glorious name for ever. And I
most heartily beseech Him to sanctifie these fatherly rebukes,
and make them profitable to my poore soule, to bring me in the
possession of patience nearer to Himselfe by a strict communion
to see Him with joy above all this earthy comforts or injoyments, that soe I may be better prepared for acting to His glory
heere and heereafter; even for Christ Jesus His Sonne's sake.
Amen.

My son William Thornton was buried at Easby in the same
grave with his eldest sister, which died before baptized, by Mr.
Kirton, he beeing scarce fourteen daies old, near my Lady
Wharton's* grave at Easby, Aprill 29th, 1660: his father bceing
much troubled at his losse, whom the child was exceding like
in person, and allso his eldest sister.

> " Tax not thy God, thy owne defaults did urge
>   This toofould punishment, the mille, the scourge,
>   Thy sinns the authour of thyselfe tormenting,
>   Thou grindest for sinning, scourgded for not repenting.
>   I do not begge this slender inch to while
>   The time away, or falsely to beguile
>   Myselfe with joys;
>   Heere's nothing worth a smile.
>   What's Earth, or in it,
>   That longer then a minuite
>   Can lend a free delight, that can indure?
>   Oh, who would droyle or delve in such a soile,
>   Where gaine's uncertaine, and the paine is sure."

* One of the wives of Philip Lord Wharton, who was then residing at
Aske, in the parish of Easby.

Uppon this sad affliction of the losse of soe brave a delicate son who we tooke delight in, my Lady Francis Darcy* comming to see me desired me to beare it as patiently as I could, for she was persuaded that God would at length give me a son to live (and my husband), but he was to be borne att his house where God would make him the heire of, and the Lord would looke in mercy uppon me, and that I should not dy without an heire. I was then resolved in my mind, if it should please the Lord to grant me that blessing of a son, to be an upholder of my husband's family in its name, that I would freely give him unto the Lord as Hannah did to Samwell in the service of the Lord at His holy alter. But I only desired my will should be submissive to His heavenly pleasure; not my will but His be don in me and myne, and he should be dedicated unto the Lord my God from the wombe. Amen. * *

Affter the death of my deare Willy Thornton I tooke the crosse very sadly, that he died soe soone, and had many sad thoughts of God's afflicting hand on me, and one day was weeping much about it. My deare Naly came to me, then beeing about four years old, and looked very seriously on me, said, " My deare mother, why doe you morne and weepe soe much for my brother Willy ? doe you not thinke he is gon to heaven ? " I said, " Yess, deare heart, I beleive he is gon to heaven, but your father is soe afflicted for his losse, and beeing a son he takes it more heavily, because I have not a son to live." She said againe, " Mother, would you or my father have my brother to live with you, when as God has taken him to Himselfe to heaven, wher he has noe sickness, but lives in happines ? would you have him out of heaven againe, where he is in joy and happiness ? Deare mother, be patient, and God can give you annother son to live with you and my father, for my brother is in happiness with God in heaven." Att which the child's speech I did much condemne myselfe, beeing instructed by the mouth of one of my owne children, and beged

* Wife of Colonel Conyers Darcy, the eldest son of Conyers lord Darcy and Conyers. She was a daughter of Thomas Howard, Earl of Berkshire, and was buried at Hornby, 10th April, 1670.

that the Lord would give me patience and satisfaction in His gracious goodness, which had putt such words into the mouth of soe young a child to reprove my immoderate sorrow for him, and beged her life might be spared to me in mercy.

A thankesgiving for the restoration of King Charles the Second of his Coronation, May 29th, 1660 (i., 182).

Affter the Lord had taken my childe from me, I had some weaknesse upon my bodie by reason of the returne of my milke ; but in much mercy I was restored to a pretty degree of strength, and staing att St. Nickolas till I was perfectly recovered. In this time we had that grand blessing to the whole nation given to us in the restoration of our dread soveraine lord King Charles, when we, each moment, feared ruine and destruction, beeing in that conserne soe wisely and prudently ordered through the providence of God, that notwithstanding the opposittion of the soldiery and other great factions, yet was he brought into his owne kingdome, city of London, and parliament, in great peace and exceeding much joy from all parts of the kingdome, without the power of one dogge that durst open his mouth, or the losse of one drope of blood shed in the whole kingdome. A maine instrument of our deliverance was Generall Monke, whose faithfull heart God stirred up to be instrumentall for this blessed change, desiring to joyne with the consent of the best in the nation, whoe pettitioned him for a free parliament; all the way as he came out of Scottland from following the factious army of Lambert, through each county, was hee alarumd with there cries and pettitions, hoeping thereby that this might be the best way to establish peace in church and state, and re-establish the king in his throne in honor and safety. Thus, by the infinitt goodnesse of God, this was effected accordingly, for immeadiately affter that parliament was caled and sett, they votted with great alacrity his majestie's returne in honor and safety to his kingdome, affter twelve yeares' banishment or thereabout. And now the hearts and

tounges of all faithfull loyall people in these kingdomes was
even full of joy and admiration, not knowing how to shew forth
there exceeding content and sattisfaction with gratitude to the
great and etternall God of Gods and King of Kings, Whoe had
delivered our soules and bodies from those thraldomes, restoring
His true and faithfull doctrine, and His vicejerent upon earth
to us, which requires our uttmost possibility of thankes and
praise to our great Lord Whome we serve. Oh that our hearts
might never forgett what He hath don for us in restoreing our
king, our priests, our prophetts, to this our land of our nativity,
but adore the glorious name of Jehova for ever. Amen.*

*Uppon my deare Naly deliverance from death by convollions,
May 29th, 1660, at St. Nickolas (ii., 183).*

That day on which there was a great deale of joy and mirth
uppon the King Charles the Second his birth and returne from
his banishment into England, and his coronation, beeing
matters of great and excelent gratitude to heaven to the
Church of England, they had a shew att Richmond of all kindes
of sports and country expressions of joy, and, amongst the rest,
they shott of musketts, and had soldiers, and the townsmen of
Richmond appeared in armour. The maides at St. Nickolas
did beg leave to goe and see the shew, and would not be pleased
till I lett my deare Naly goe with them; but I refused, and
thought it would fright her and doe her hurt. But they gott
Mr. Thornton perswaded, and my aunt to lett her goe, and
they would take great cair of her, but I was still very unwilling,
nor could be convinced of the fittnesse; tho they went and
carried her with them against my mind, having Mr. Thornton's
consent. Butt before two houers they returned with my childe
home in a very sad and changed condittion, for alas! she never
having had seene any such things as soldiers, or guns, or
drums, or noyses, and shouting, she was soe extreamly

* Then follow a " Praier and thanksgiveing for deliverance from destruction
of the kingdom, 1660."

scaired att these things, and when the musketts went of soe
fast did soe affright her and terrify my poore child that she
was ready to fly out of Jane Flour's armes, her maide. And,
beeing allmost out of her poore witt, did scrike and cry soe
extreamly she could not be pacified for all they could doe.
Butt in extremity fell into most dreadfull fitts of convoltions
there, while she was att Richmond, in Mr. Smithson's shop.
Haveing had three or four of them soe sadly and soe dreadfully
that they had much to do to save her alive or bring her to herselfe againe, but started extreamly much, and then falling
downe againe. Att last, they doing all [they] could do to her,
did bring my deare childe halfe dead to me, which was a sad
and dismall affliction to my weake heart, and she continued
very ill all that night. But I gave her all meadicins for it,
and oyle of amber and pieony and other things, which, by the
Lord's great and infinitt mercy to me, did at length preserve
and restore her from them. O Lord God of mercy, what glory
shall I give to Thee the God of heaven and earth, which hast
delivered my sweete infant and spared her life againe. O
blesse the Lord, O my soule, and all within me praise His holy
name for this and all Thy mercy to her. O lett her be saved,
I pray Thee, and live to Thy holy praise for ever. Amen.

*Uppon my deare Kate's deliverance from beeing choaked with a
pin at St. Nickolas, May 17, 1660 (vol. ii., 185).*

Affter dinner, we were in my chamber at my aunt Norton's
house, St. Nickolas, and my deare Katy was plaing under the
table with her sister, (beeing about three yers old, but a very
brave, strong childe, and full of mettle, beeing much stronger
then her poore sister Naly, she never haveing had either ricketts
nor convoltion fitts to keepe her downe, but allwaies contineued
very healthfull and strong, and full of trickes, and indeed apt
to fall into dangers,) as she was plaing with pinnes, and putting
them into her mouth, her sister see her, and cried out for feare
she should doe herselfe hurt. But she would not be councelled

with her, and at last she gott a pin crosse her throate, at which her sister cryed out that she had gott a pin in her throte. By God's pleasure I was just neare her, and catcht her up in my armes, and putt my finger immeadiatly into her throate, and the pin was cross, and I had much to do to gett it out, but, with all the fores I had, it pleased God to strengthen me to do it. I gott beyond the pin, and soe got it out of her throate, but in a great deal of danger; her life was well nigh gon, and she was as blacke as could be, and the blood sett in her face with it. Soe nigh to death by this accident was this my poore childe, for it had stoped her breath.*

Uppon my husband and familie's removall from St. Nickolas to Oswold Church neare Newton, June 10, 1660 (i., p. 186).

After my strength was againe recruted, through God's mercy, for travill, we removed with my husband and those children the Lord had blessed me with, Alice my second and then eldest, and Katharine my fourth childe, and came to Oswoldkirke,† liveing a fortnight at my sister Denton's house till our owne in that towne was ready. Then we gott to it, with all my deare mother's household stuffe, which was brought thither, where we lived two yeares, affter I had taken leave of my owne countrey and deare freinds and relations, parting with them, with a sad heart, amongst whom I had lived many comfortable yeares. But God was pleased to goe along with me in a strange place, makeing me to find many sweete influences of His favour, both in sicknesse and in health, and giveing me comfort of my husband's freinds instead of my owne, and to find a great deale of favour amongst strangers where I lived, soe that in all places, and at all times, and upon all occas-

* "As allso through His providence I preserved her maide Anne Robinson from the like death by a peice of a goose pinnion which was crosse soe long that her breath was stopt, and almost dead, att Oswoldkirke, 1661" (vol. i., p. 228).

† Oswaldkirk, a parish three and a half miles south from Helmsley, in the north riding co. York. Roger Dodsworth, the antiquary, was born at Newtongrange, in the township, in 1585.

sions, I have daily fresh cause and occassions to admire the infinitt goodnesse of that God Whome I serve, desiring to speake well of His name, Whoo has pitty upon His weake servant. Heere I lived for two yeares till our owne house at Easte-Newton* could be finished, which we had bin in building severall yeares before my deare mother's death, which if we could have finished before, she would gladly have lived with us heere, but it was not begun time enough for that. In this time, while we were att Oswoldkirke, my brother Denton preached there, and did that with much gravity and piety, beeing indeed a very excelent good and wise man, from whom all our family had receaved many assistances and helpes by way of advice; and cheifely my husband, whoe depended much on his councell affter our comeing thither. But he, haveing some scruples, did not conforme to the now established government of the church, soe that he did leave that church affter a while,† and retired to live with us att Newton. I confesse his non-conformity did much trouble me, and I endeavoured with my smale mite to discourse that bussinesse, but I supose he had bin otherwise ordeined then episcopall, soe that it was fruitlesse to perswade, otherwaies it might have bin better for us all, though he was ever of a quiett and peaceable temper, free from faction or disturbances of the State. And indeed, I injoyed much comfort in his ministery, and great assistance, as toward the building of our house at Newton, Mr. Thornton not giveing himselfe to take pleasure or trouble in any thing of that nature, beeing much addicted to a melancolicke humour, which

---

* East Newton, four miles from Helmsley, in the north riding co. York, an estate held by the Thorntons from the time of Edward I. By the marriage of Alice, dau. of Mrs. Thornton, the estate passed to her husband the Rev. Thomas Comber, D.D., Dean of Durham, from whose family it was purchased by Sir George Wombwell, Bart. The old hall is now occupied as a farm-house. In the gardens might be seen, in 1824, in a state of tolerable preservation, the square tower or turret in which the dean is said to have pursued his studies. A broad gravel walk formerly led from the mansion to it, and the space between was tastefully laid out in shrubberies and pleasure grounds, not a vestige of which remains (Eastmead's Historia Rievallensis, 1824, p. 198).

† On account of the Bartholomew Act in 1662.

had seized on him by fitts for severall yeares before he was twenty yeares old. Neverthelesse, affter the use of great meanes, which God directed me in by Dr. Wittie, etc., as leaches, and gentle course of phisick, Spring and fall, as there was occassion ever since we weare married, those weare much abated, and he offtener was in a more chearefull frame of spiritt then formerly, as both he and his freinds has offten times acknowledged, to my great comfort, whoes uttmost endeavours and caire was ever to study his good and sattisfaction in whose life and wellfaire my owne did much subsistt. Yett affter his house was don, and we in it, he tooke much content in itt, when he was well. In this time while I lived there, about Shrove Sunday,* '61, I was in the church, when it was a frost and snow, sitting in the minister's pewe, I feltt myselfe exceeding cold, and by fitts contineued till the Tuesday following, very ill.

My greatt sickness att Oswoldkirke, Feb. 13th, 1661 (vol. i., p.188).

I began a dangerous sicknesse which brought me very nigh to death att Oswoldkirke affter my deare mother's death, which was caused by that cold I gott and aguish temper on the Sunday in the church, causeing a very violent vomitting, comeing greately upon Shrove Tuesday, Feb. 13th, 1661, beeing that day my birthday; and soe contineueing perpetually in paine and vomitting till I was not able to receave any kinde of sustenance, beeing then fallen into an intermitting feavour, soe that at five daies' end, I was compell'd to send for Dr. Wittie.† He saw cause to let me blood, giveing me many cordialls to strengthen the stomacke; but noe thing would stay with me till I dranke a draught of cold water, which more refreshed my thirsty soule then all what art could give. That

---

* "On Shrive Sunday," "and very chill and shakeing by fitts." "I feltt the sting of that distemper and paines creeping into my backe as I satt."

† "The doctor was extreame angrey that he was not sent for sooner till I was at the last cast."

night, beeing the 17th of February, I did verily beleive should be my last in this life,* I beeing brought into an exceeding weaknesse and feeblenesse of bodie and spiritt.   *   *

But loe, I asked spirituall, and the Lord gave me great addittion of temporall mercys, filling my mouth and soule† with abundant gladnesse and praise, when I looked for nothing but death and destruction, shewing that the mercys of the etternall God are not to be measured by the weake apprehensions of men, but admired and adored, in all His wisdome, goodnesse, and free grace to poore, wanting mortalls. For He appointing meanes, blessed the same to me, soe that by degrees I was strengthned in bodie, and in a great part recovered health, though not perfectly for a quarter of a yeare, beeing brought soe exceeding weake in my sicknesse.   *   *   *   * The Lord inlarge my heart in all gratitude and thankefulnesse to walke uprightly before His presence all my daies. Amen.

Uppon my deare daughter's preservation from a wound in her belly, 1661 (ii., 209).

My two children was plaing at Oswoldkirke, in the parlor window, and Kate beeing very full of sport and play did climb into the window, and leaping downe fell uppon her sister Alice and thrust her uppon the corner of the same with a great force and strength she had, and her sister cryed out with paine and soreness which had greivously hurt the inner rind of her belly soe sore till I was affraid she had broaken it. But it contineued a long time, tho I putt a searcloth on it, yet doth it now very offten hurt and paine her, soe that I have cause to blesse and praise the name of my God for ever that she was not wounded soe as to breake her bowells, it beeing in soe dangerous [a] place and hazard in her bearing of children. O

* "Expressing this my lamentable condition in patheck grones, which is more fully inlarged in my first book, in page 189, 190, 191, 192, 193."

† "I have written a whole paper booke uppon this great deliverance of my soule, and in expresing of my humble gratitude; as allso in the first booke, meditations heere uppon it, page 192, 193 " (vol. ii., p. 196).

praise the Lord for this His great mercy to my poore child and make her Thy servant.

A deliverance from fire at Oswoldkirke, 1661 (ii., 221.)

We had a great preservation from the house beeing burned by fire in the night time, my maide Nan Wellburne haveing carlesly stuck the candle at her bed head, and fell asleepe, soe it fell downe on the pillow and her head, and burned her clothes, and beeing stifled by the smoke it pleased God she awaked and put it out. O praise the Lord my God for this and all His deliverances of us. Amen.

Uppon our comeing to live at Newton affter the house was built,
in the yeare 1662, *June the* 10*th* (i., 193).

At the last, affter six yeares' worke at the dwelling house of Mr. Thornton, Easte Newton, haveing builded it from the ground,* it pleased God to give us all leave with our family and two daughters to come to live at it, beeing soe finished, as to dwell therein, about the midest of June, 1662. I beeing then great with childe walked from Oswoldkirke with our company, haveing a great deale of strength and health given me from God, blessed be His holy name. Also He gave us a comfortable settlement at our owne house, which I gott ready furnished with what my deare mother gave me, in five daies' time ; and all the ground stocked with her cattell. After which, within a little of our commeing to house, Mr. Thornton was called to London by Nettleton's bussinesse, goeing purposely to prevent the breakeing up an execution against him from that Nettleton against his estate for a debt of my father's, which Mr. Thornton had bin advised by some to secure out of his owne estate, and to ingage for it soe till he could receave the monneys

* " The old house could not stand longer, for age and the antiquity thereof."
(vol. ii.)

" The building of this house att Newton, I have heard Mr. Thornton declaire, cost us above £1500; which went out of my portion " (vol. iii.).

from Ireland, out of my father's estate there, which was by his leace for forty-one yeares apoynted to pay all debts, legacys, and portions, in feoffee-in-trusts hands, and he had bin advised formerly to take upon him the maunegment of it from my uncle Mr. Norton, by way of assignment, and to pay those things chargeable thereupon. But albeit there was a good estate, which was £1000 per annum there from where these debts should arrise, yet it was altogether against my deare mother's or my owne judgment or advice that he should take uppon him soe great a trouble as that must be, in regard that neither his purse nor person was suting such an enterprise; beeing in annother nation, soe a hazard to his person, and like-wise not suited in other respects to withstand the disputes which she foresee would arrise from some that were conserned for themselves. Nor was there the least necessity for him to ingage in it for gaining my £1000 theire; by reason both that and all other rights and dues which could be challenged by my mother and myselfe were sufficiently secured to us by my deare father's last will and deeds, and non could prejudice us therein, whatever sinistor pretensions were made by others, whos advice he unhapily followed, as it affterwards appeared. And besides, my English portion was suficiently and undoubtedly safe and secured to him of £1500 by will and leace from my uncle William Wandesforde, out of Kirklington, and by articles tripartite, before my marriage, betwixt my uncle Wandesford, my brother Christopher and myselfe, securing both the £1500, and the £1000 out of Ireland in its due order to be paid. But it soe hapned that he was advised without our knowledge or consent, as aforesaid, to ingage to Nettleton (as well as to the businesse of the assignement) for a debt of £1000 payable out of his owne estate by statute, because Nettleton would not accept of security out of Ireland, nor stay till Mr. Thornton receaved it thence, but he prosecuted Mr. Thornton with soe much violency and fearcinesse that he compelld him to borrow monnys to sattisfie his clamor ;* and he had payd him £900

* "As more at large may apeare in my first booke in pages 194, 195, 196, with all circumstances about the affaire."

and above ; nor would he be sattisfied, because the bond was for a thousand pounds, and, not being taken in by Mr. Thornton, he sued for the whole and for charges. And most unjustly and deceitfully watcht an oportunity when Mr. Thornton was at London to have dispatched it, he gott an execution broake up, and by his owne man with four other balifs came early in a morning to seaze upon all our goods, monneys, plate, etc., till he were all sattisficd; att first very stiffely demauded £800 then to be payd; but at last, by my brother Denton's endeavours, knowing the debtt was paid, prevailled to give them £200, which they would have, or plate, etc., to that valewe, both in regard it was a debt of my father's, and ought to have been paid out of his estate.

And besides it was a great disparagement that when we were new come into the house where we were to live in reputation, as formerly, and I brought a good fortune to my husband, and deare as any was by father and mother, yett such a misfortune to happen to entertaine my first comming into the world was very unhapy and uncomfortable to me. * * But still, in all accidents, whatever befalles me, this or other consernes of my life, the Lord my God, Who is my only life and suport, preserver and deliverer, doth still shew His most gracious and mighty hand of Providence over me. Tho' it was but a dreame, He gave me soe much warning of the evill to happen upon me, which did prepare me with more patience for this accident which was to come on me that day. By which meanes I was not soe extremely sudainly surprised as otherwise I should have bin, which might have without it have bin fatall to us, both mother and the childe.

My Dreame.—Nettleton.

For that very morning, before the balyes came, I dreamed for a certaine that Nettleton had sent his bailys to drive all our goods, and to seize on all we had, for the debt which Mr. Thornton ingaged. And I was in deepe conserne as soone as I

wakned out of sleepe affter it. Butt case that he should send to
distreine uppon me in Mr. Thornton's absence, what could I
doe in it, and how could I be preserved? It might not be impossible, I thought, such a thing should, though he went up to
London to hinder it; but, however, I was glad that he was not
at home, who they would be ruide withall. When I was in these
thoughts in my mind, at that very tourne of time came my
maide, Jane Flower, to my chamber, and unlocked it very
softly, and came soe to the bedside, and with a sofft voyce, for
fear of frighting me out of my sleepe if she spoke sudainly,
spoke softly to me, "Forsoth, are you awake or asleepe?" I
immeadiately answered her, "Jane, I am awake; but pray
answer me truly to what I aske you:—Is Nettleton's bailies
heere?" At which she was so surprized, and said: "Has
anybody bin here with you to-day to tell you soe?" I said:
"Noe, nobody; did you not locke me in? But tell me truly,
are they not below?" To which she said: "Yes, indeed, they
were below; but how, in God's name, did you know?" I
said: "None; but my God gave me warning in a dreame
which I had dreamt this morning." She praied me, for God's
sake, not to be affraid, for they should not come to me, and
they would take what caire they could to make them quitt, for
there was Mr. Denton and Mr. Darley with them. Soe I
blessed God for giveing me this notice beforehand, which did
me much good, and prevented the extreamity of the fright to
fall on my poor spirritts. My uncle, Francis Darley, promised
to make it up, £200.

The further discreptions of this is in my booke, page 196.

This accidant was very afflicting to me, in regard that
I hoped Mr. Thornton's beeing there would have prevented
it; and being bigg with childe, the greife I had with the fright
and the rudenesse of those men had nigh gon to make me mis-
carrie, what for the injustice and unhansomenesse of that conserne which came soe sudainly on me in that bussinesse. Yet
the providence of God had soe ordered that there was £100 of
Mr. Thornton's newly the week before come in, and with £57
of my owne, part of what my mother gave me, that sattisfied

them at present, or else it might have proved farre worse with me then, in that condittion; which if I had wanted, peradventure they might have taken my bed from under myselfe and children, and those quick goods my mother gave for our reliefe. I pray God forgive all those by whoes evill councell my deare husband was brought into those snaires, when he intended most good to all parties in the acceptation of the assignment; and the very troubles, vexations, and afflictions it carried along in the whole course of transactions offten times brought us into streits, and great danger of my life; proveing one sad ingredient to my other sorrowes. And indeed I did feare some hard measure to fall unawares to Mr. Thornton, and partly tould him my conjecture, offering to pay Nettleton off with those monyes my mother gave me before he went to London; but he, good man, did not beleive, nor could imagine, that he might find such treachery in those lawyers he imployed.   *   *   *

On the first coming to Newton; of the Country's kind respects to me. June, July, 1662 (ii., 235).

Upon my first comming to live at the new house at Newton, in the months of June and July, before Mr. Thornton's returne from London, or that Nettleton's baylies made this disturbance, it was matter of somme comfort to me that all the best of the gentry and neighbourhood shewed soe great a respect and kindness to me in there regard for the family and my husband, who, in his absence, made there severall vissits to me, although but a stranger amongst them; yett did they all comme to drinke with me in my new house, as they said beeing glad that Mr. Thornton did comme and settle amongst them, and had a good wife to uphold the house. I gave them, in there severall quality and degrees, the best welcome I could; bid them all very wellcome as I could in my husband's absence, who I am sorry that he was not heere to do it, but tould them I tooke it extreame kindly from them to give me this incoragment to comme amongst such good neighbors, and did assure them I would

indevour to returne there respects with the best service I could,
to be a good neighbour to them, and do what good I could to
them all. They all answred very kinde and affectionatly, and
I believe that day my brother Denton and my sister came, I
had at least fifty or sixty people with them, which did much
comfort me in there respects for me. And I bless God for these
mercys towards me.

Of a dangerous Fall (ii., 245).

While this affaire* was in acting, one day was goeing downe
the staires to the parlore with bottles of ale, etc., to entertaine
the company there, my hands beeing full, there was Celia
Danby heere, with her mother Mrs. Danby, my nephew Christopher's† daughter, a childe of four yers old, when she was
goeing downe before me, tumbled downe a great part of the
staires, and fell desperatly on her head, att which I was much
frighted, and, in making hast to save her, I gott a very desperate
fall downe four staires with my knees, which did shake and
bruise me much, and had like to bring me to my labor before
my time. But, by the mighty power of my Gôd, I was preserved from great extreamity, and did not bruise the poore
childe within me.

*Uppon my deliverance of my sonne Robert Thornton, my seventh
childe, borne at East Newton, the first childe that was borne
in the new house, September 19, 1662 (i., 204).*

Almighty God, the wise disposer of all good things, both
in heaven and earth, Who seest what and how much of the
comforts of this mortall life is conveniently fitt for us to injoy

---

* Viz., Mr. Thornton's settlement of his estate by Mr. Colvill, August, 1662
(vol. iii., p. 50). See afterwards.

† Christopher, second son of Sir Thomas Danby, became lord of Mashamshire in 1683, and died in 1689. He married Anne, daughter of Edward Colepepper, Esq.

in this earth, hath at length had pittie on my afflictions, and gave me such a mercy and deare injoyment to myselfe and husband, affter all his and mine severall troubles and losses of sonnes, as I could not hope for or expect; making me a joyful mother of a sweete son, borne at full time, affter five great trialls and hazards of miscarige when I was with him, the one of sicknesse, a second* through griefe att a strange accident,—this hapned me of a fright, which caused a marke of blood upon his heart of most pure couler and severall shapes, contineuing till hee was about a yeare old, and seene by many persons at severall times; the third, the trouble of Nettleton bailifs; and the fourth, that before the settlement was made of his estate on my children; the fifth was a great danger I escaped of him by a fall I gott downe the staires to preserve Celia Danby from hurt, when she tumbled downe the whole staires before me. The least of which mercys and deliverances were subject of a hearty praise and thanksgiveing to the Lord of Lords. But it still pleased the Most High God to adde this blessing when I was delivered, after great danger and pirill of my life in travill of my son Robert Thornton, upon Friday, the 19th of September,

---

* "The second, through greife att a strainge accident that hapned me when I was pretty big of him of a fright which came on me by a surprize of the sight of a penknife which was nigh to have hurt me. The fear and dread apprehension thereof did cause a marke of a deepe bloody couler uppon the child's heart, most pure and distinct, and of severall shapes, contineuing soe as noe thing could washe them of. The first appearance like a stab or cutt with a penknife, with many pure, distinct drops of blood all about it, as if one should have sprinkled little drops with there hand on it. The second forme it came into the direct forme of a Tee, with the like dropes about it of pure blood. The third forme it came into was exactly like the shape of a heart, with dropes of blood about it, which contineued soe long till Mr. Thornton and myselfe was much troubled at it, and humbly begged of the Lord that He would be gracious to us and the childe, and to pardon what was amiss, and to remove this great marke uppon the childe. Affter which it pleased God that the couler did faide by degrees, and grew paler and bleuish, and about a yeare or neare it they was quite gon. This was seene by many persons at severall times—my brother and sister Denton, my husband and my sister Frances Thornton, the nurse and all the maides, with many more. All which is the token of the goodnesse of God to preserve him from death in my wombe" (vol. ii).

1662.* He was borne at Easte Newton, betwixt the houres of eight and nine o'clocke att night, haveing bin since the night before in strong labour of him till that time.† But as though this grand mercy should not passe alone, without its severer monitor to my unbridlled passion of joy, and that I might be cautioned not to sett my affection too much on things below, be they never so neccessary or desirable, it pleased the great God to lay on me, His weake handmaid, an exceeding great weaknesse, beginning a little affter my childe was borne, by a most violent and terrible flux of blood, with such excessive floods all that night, that it was terrible to behold to those about me, bringing me into a most desperat condittion, without hopes of life; spiritts, soule, and strength seemed all gon from me. My deare husband, and children, and friends had taken theire last fairewell. In this deplorable condittion layd I in for severall houers together, not being able to utter one word. All the meanes could be was don in that fright, but did not prevaile. After five houers' torment it pleased my gracious Lord to have compassion ou His languishing creature, and brought to my remembrance a pouder which I used formerly to others, and with His blessing had good successe in the like kinde, and hardly could I gett the name of it to my lady Yorke‡ for my feeblenesse; but affter she had given me some of it, through

---

* "On Thursday my lady Cholmely and my dere aunt Norton, my lady Yorke and Mrs. Wattsou, with my sisters Denton and Frances Thornton, was with me and staied till evening, then went home to Oswaldwirke. The next day came againe."

† "And I laid in bed while all the company was gott together to veiew that goodly childe and admire him, soe large and big, newly borne, and all soe fond of him beeing a son, with great joy."

‡ "My lady York out of her fright came to my bedside and wept over me, and said : 'My deare cozen, you that helpes every one to save them, cannot you tell me what would do you good in this extreamity to save your owne?' On which it pleased my good God to inable me, she laing her eare to my mouth, to say only : 'Goe into closet, right hand shelfe, box, pouder, syrup of cloves, give me.' And by Devine Providence she gott the box and powder which I tould her of, and had laid ready for myselfe before my sicknes, and tould my midwife and maide of it, to give me in such a case, but they had forgotten it in their trouble for me" (vol. ii).

the mercy of my Saviour, Who healeth and helped all that came unto Him, by it helped me, soe that the flux stayed by degres till Dr. Wittie was come, when, affter the use of other meanes, I was delivered and spaired at that time from that death soe nigh, but brought soe exceeding weake that the effects lasted till Candlemas upon my body by fitts; yet did I recover my milke againe.   But oh! O Lord, most high and loving Father, wherefore are Thy miraculous favours and mercys extended thus to such a vild worme as myselfe, whoe am not able to recount the unmesurable goodnesse, nor tell what Thou didst for my soule.   Doubtlesse to sett forth Thine Almighty power, glory, and infinitt perfection, that canst raise from death and bring to the grave in a moment.

A Thanksgiveing affter my deliverance of my son Robert
(vol i., p. 205).

*   * The Lord God had great pittie upon my distress, and gave me after this a compotency of health and strength to be able to give my childe sucke, which, by His blessing, I did till Robin was above two yeares old, he contineuing very healthfull and strong.*

My son Robert was baptized on Saturday, the 20th of September, 1662, by Mr. Luckock, att our house in East Newton, in my owne chamber, where the Lord gave me opportunity to see his admittance into the church millitan by holy sacrament of baptisme, when I hope the Lord did enter into covenant with him to be his God, and he to be His faithful servant to his live's end.   The Lord give him allso the grace of His meanes as well as the meanes by which He gives His grace unto us.   Amen.   His godfathers and godmothers were Mr. Thornton for my nephew Best,† Dr. Wittie, my lady

---

* "The fuller description is related in my booke of meditations on this subject, and allso of the first booke of my life, page 203."

† Henry Best, of Middleton-Quernhow, Esq., the husband of Catherine Danby, Mrs. Thornton's neice.

Cholmely.* The God of all consolations and comfort preserve
his life and health, with happie opportunities of religeous and
holy education, that he may be an instrument of great glory
to God, comfort to his parents and relations; and for the
building up in righteousness and hollinesse his father's family
to posterity for many generations; and at the end of his life he
may receave the comfort of a sanctified old age, with a crowne
of glory to praise his Redeemer and mine for ever for our beings.
Finding what the goodnesse of God had beene to me in giveing
me the requests of my heart, and beeing these mercys receaved
by and from a gracious Father, Who hath at length bestowed
on me His servant this hopes of contineuing our memories by
a sweete son of my vowes, beeing obtained from God, as Samuell
was, by the fervent prayers and teares of a poore wretched
mother. To Thee, O Lord, I humbly dedicate my son of my
wombe. O lett him be established before Thee for ever in Thine
everlasting covenant. Amen. (Looke Meditations on 1 Sam.
i., 10, 11, 12, 13, in my booke on purpose made on that
occasion.)

He was born that very fatall day to me of his father's
buriall (the sixth yeare of his life), being observed to be a very
remarkable sircumstance that his deare father, who had rejoyced
soe much att his son's birth, should make his excit that day six
yeares, and leave his great joy in expectation so soone, and not
live to see his only son, whom he had begged of God, to continue his family, to be brought up, but left him so young to my
poore indevors and caire.†

As to the education, maintenance, and learning of my
deare son Thornton, will amount to soe prodigious a somme as
perhaps may not be creditted. But it was the great conserne
of my daies how to find suplyes for him when he was to goe out
abroade to the University, in order to make him a scoler, to
which he was designed by God's grace and his owne choyce and
inclination, and my sacred vowes to Almightie God, if He would

* Catherine, daughter of Henry Stapleton, Esq., the wife of Sir Henry
Cholmeley, of West Newton Grange, a near neighbour of Mrs. Thornton.
† Vol. iii., p. 24.

please to grant my humble pettition of a son. As His servant Hannah dedicated Samuell to the Lord, even soe did I dedicate my son to the caire of the Lord, *   * to serve Him at His alter and ministery of His holy Word and Gospel. To which pettitions the Lord my God did please to say Amen, and in His due time gave him that happy opportunity to preach His Gospell; and I trust in His mercy he became an instrument of saving soules. Glory be to the Lord God of Heaven for His infinitt Providence, and calling him to the faith and way of salvation.*

Mr. Thornton's preservation from drowning, October, 1664 (vol. i., p. 208).

After Robin was two yeares old, Mr. Thornton went to London about wittness for Sir Christopher Wandesford's suite with Mr. Robinson conserning the bounders. In this jorney, when he was returning home, he escaped drowning at the waters neare Newarke,† when the floods was soe high that they had nigh have carried him downe with the streame. But the Lord was pleased to deliver him from that death. His holy name be glorified and praised for ever, Who brought us safely to meete againe with joy, to enjoy each other still in peace and temporall comforts, joyned with spirituall mercys. Oh that we might make a right use of these temporalls, that we finally lose not the hopes of eternall mercys, through Jesus Christ our Lord. Amen.

Upon the birth of my eighth childe, Joyce Thornton, September 23rd, 1665, *att Newton* (i., p. 208).

It pleased God to give me a new hopes of comfort of beareing Mr. Thornton annother childe, although these are accompanied with thorny caires and troubles, and more to me then others. But yet I was contineued in much health and strength, affter I had given suck to Robin, all along while I was with childe, and

---

* Vol. iii., p. 132.

† Thoresby, in his Diary, alludes to the great dangers he encountered in his passage of the waters about Newark.

till about a fortnight before my delivery, when my travell began upon me, and then the panges of childe-beareing, often remembring me of that sad estate I was to passe, and dangerous pirills my soule was to find, even by the gates of death. Soe that I being terrified with my last extremity, could have little hopes to be preserved in this, as to my own strength, if my strength were not in the Almighty. However, I tribled my diligence and caire in preparation, haveing with comfort reccaved the blessed Sacrament as a pledge of my redemption; which we had the opportunity of doeing in our family, with Mr. Thornton and his servants, receaving it from Mr. Comber, minister of the parish at Stonegrave. After this great mercy in the renewing of our vowes and covenants with God, I was fully sattisfied in that condittion, whether for life or death, haveing committed my soule in keepeing to a faithfull Meadiator and Redeemer, hopeing for me to live is Christ and to die was gaine;* when I should exchange sorrow for joy, and death for life and immortality. I was the most conserned for my poore children, who might peradventure want some helps from theire weake mother, and haveing noe relation or friend of my owne that might take caire of them, if theire father should see cause to marry againe, according as I had bin tould that it would be necesary for him for his health. I was indeed the more solicitous for my three young children, casting in my mind what friend of my owne to desire to intrust with theire education, if he did soe. For my son, the hope of my house, I humblie committed him into the protection of Almighty God, as allso his two sisters; and for his education, into the caire of my deare and honoured uncle, my lord Frechvile;† my daughter Alice to my deare aunt Norton; and my daughter Katherine to my deare neece Best; with strict charge to bring them up in the nurture and feare of the Lord, and the true proffession of the Prottestant religion, as it was my faithfull endevours soe to doe while I was with them,

---

* Philippians i. 21.

† John, son of Sir Peter Freschville, knight, created Lord Freschville of Staveley by Charles II., the half-brother of Mrs. Thornton's mother, Mrs. Wandesford.

that I might give a good account of theire soules unto my
Saviour. They had allso a very good begining of knowledge
through the due examination and catechising of Mr. Comber,
each sabbath day, as well in the church as at home. Next in
order was it my duty to take caire for the right settlement and
devission of the goods and personall estate of my deare mother,
according to her will and testament, which she left me power to
doe by deed, amongst my children; having left theire maintenance and portions settled as by the deede made formerly, in
as good a condittion as could be for the many incumbrances
and debts upon Mr. Thornton's estate, soe that it only remained
for me to depositt the safe custody of all the deeds, intails, and
writings about our whole estate for our children into a safe
hand; which, in case of my mortality, should be delivered to my
lord Frechvile affter my death. This was seriously considered
and agreed upon by and with the approbation and command of
my deare husband, that they should be delivered in keeping to
Mr. Comber, whoe, as a friend to all, should preserve them and
give them to my lord Frechvile.* Haveing intrusted all the

---

* " Before I fell sicke of my son Robert, I delivered the little red truncke of
my deare mother's, which she kept her writings in, to my cozen Roger Colvill,
for safe custody, till it pleased God I was recovered of my childe, and then he
restored me them. Butt my cozen Colvill beeing dead now, and I farre of all
my relations, was in a great strait who to intrust soe great a concerne withall for
safety, beeing not willing to leave the said trunke in the hand of any stranger ;
and accounting my deare husband my nearest and only interessed for my children
in case of my decease, I begged of my deare husband that he would please to take
this trunke of my mother's, with all the writings, into his caire and keeping, and
to keepe them for me and my poore children till it should please God to restore
me againe; but if the Lord should take me away from himselfe and my children,
I begged hee would please to deliver this trunke, with the writings, unto my
Lord Frechevill, who was my mother's brother, and allso her trustee and executor of her will and testament. I allso desired my husband to deliver to my
Lord Frechvill these monneys which he had the use of, which was my mother's,
and he had given to me againe to keepe, but I gave them, being about £60 or
£70, praing him to give it to my Lord Frechvill for the use of my deare mother's
will expressed for my children, as it may appeare in her deeds and last will and
testament. It did belong to my lord, as her executor, for the use of my children,
as by her will expressed. To which request of mine my deare husband gave me
this answer : ' My deare heart, I thank you for beeing soe kind as to repose soe

cheife consernes and evidences for my deare children within a little
red lether trunck, locked, I delivered the same to him according
to our agreement, laing a great charge and injunction, with my
earnest desire that he would keepe that truncke safe, and if it
pleased God to take me, then to deliver the same with his owne
hand to my lord; as I had charged the same to George
Lightfoot and his wife Dafeny with it, in my sicknesse of my
son I bore at St. Nickolas, affter my mother's death. For in it
was contained all children's provission and subsistence; and if
any thing should happen to that truncke they might be ruined.
It pleased my gracious Lord God to give me space and time to
doe all these things as well as I could, affter which I fell into
travell, beeing one day and night in travill of my eight childe,

much trust in me as to leave the trunk of writtings in my hand, and your
mother's monney, to keepe for yourselfe and children; but I desire thee to
excuse me for haveing them in my custody, the trunke of writings and your
mother's monney; for though I would do ten times more for thee and thine
then that comes to, yett if in case God should take thee from me, I would not have
them found with me, because they conserne thy children, and some of thy friends
might thinke I had alltered them, or not don right to them, and I would avoyd
all suspittion.' * * He would advise me to leave them all, both the trunke of
writings and the monney, with Mr. Comber. * * And from hence did arise
that abominable scandall that I had robed my husband of his monney, and had
given it away to this man, with many other horrid lyes and invented sircumstances. * * That very money which Mr. Comber had in keeping for me, for
which I was soe abused, did Mr. Thornton know that I laid it out for his use
and occasions. Though it was my dear mother's, he had it all freely. Soe farre
was I from purloyning or robing of him, and taking his estate or money from him
to any bodie's use, that I can make it appeare, uppon account with him, that I had
disbursed for his house building and keeping, and many other occasions, of my
dear mother's monney and estate, above the summe of £500 for his debts and
children's maintenance. Nor did I maintain, and subsist, and uphold, the family
of the Danbys, my dear sister's children, for twenty yeares together out of my
husband's estate, as he did very well know; but what I had of my deare mother's
estate, which she bought and gave me to live on, that was purchased by her
widdowe's estate at Midlham. Paying above £600, the yearly rent maintained
myselfe and assisted me to do what I did for the Danbys and other freinds
in charity, besides my constant laings out for my deare husband's occasions."
(vol. iii. 89.)

Roger Colvill, who is mentioned above, lived at Fremington, in Swaledale,
and married Anne Norton. He died in 1665, his widow administering to his
estate on June 10th in that year. (Richmond Wills.)

and then it pleased the Lord to make me happie in a goodly strong childe, a daughter, affter an exceeding sharpe and perillous time, beeing in the same condittion of weakenesse affter I come into bed and of my son Robert, which I escaped very narrowly the blow of death. But, by the providence of God, I was prepared with a remedy which prevented that extreamity, and within fourteen daies I began to be in a hopefull condittion of recovery, blessed be the great and gracious Father of mercys, He allso giveing me strength, and the blessing of the breasts to give sucke, with much comfort in my infant, with my deare husband and children, Who then had increased my number to four sweete children. O Lord, I beseech Thee accept the humble addresses of my soule, bodie, and spiritt, for these infinitt mercys,—give me a thankfull heart to rejoyce in Thy salvation, and in that Thou alone didst raise me up from this death, and my deare childe, not suffering our sins to prevaile, but had pitty on Thy servant my husband, and myselfe, giveing us this addition to our number on earth. The Lord make her a vessell of glory to all eternity. And I humbly addore Thy gracious clemency and mercy, magnific Thy name. Amen. Joyce Thornton, my eighth childe, was borne at Newton upon Satterday, about four a'clocke in the afternoone, on the 23d of September, 1665; baptized on the 28th day at Newton, I haveing the satisfaction of seeing her entred into the role of Christians, and a member of the millitant church of Christ. The godfathers, my lord Frechvile by proxie, my cosen Legard,* Maddam Grahme, and my cosen Cholmley. It pleased the Almighty, in much mercy, to give me great comfort in the nursing of this sweete childe, inabling me with pretty strength to goe through this duty. Therefore doe I praise the God of heaven for ever, Who had preserved my life, and given me this great temporall blessing. For all good comes from Him alone. Lord, sanctify this mercy to us all.

---

* "Cosen" Legard was one of the Legards of Ganton; "Maddam" Graham was of Nunnington; "cosen" Cholmley was Ursula Thornton, Mr. Thornton's half-sister, wife of Marmaduke Cholmley, of Brandsby, Esq.

A relation of Mr. Thornton's dangerous fitt of the palsie at Steersby, November 16th, 1665 (i., 211).

But peradventure I might be too much lifted up by this mercy, and therefore it seemed good to the Divine Providence to lay a very sad affliction uppon Mr. Thornton and myselfe, in a most dangerous sicknesse seized upon him, as he was returning from Yorke, in his way home, commeing soe neare as the moore nigh Steeresby,* November 16th, 1665, at which time he, through cold and the distemper of the palsie violently prevaileing more upon him in his jorney as he rid, soe that he scarse could be gott to my sister Cholmeley's house. For three daies that greivous distemper of the palsey, convoltions, and feavours was soe high upon him that, notwithstanding all possible remedies could be used by Dr. Wittie, he was not able to assist himselfe, nor capable to receive others' helpe at some times, and shewed to all his freinds there present that he was more like to die then hopes of his recovery. Which sudaine and most dismall newes of my deare husband's lamentable condittion beeing made knowne to me, when I expected him each houer to have receaved him home with health and comfort, did soe surprize my spiritts, that I was brought into a violent passion of griefe and sorrow, with fitts of sounding, which I never knew before; and prevailed soe exceedingly that I immeadiately went sick to bed, beeing soe weake upon that occassion that all gave me for dead, soe that it was an impossibility to carry me alive to see my deare husband, although I could not be pacified without it, till I fell soe weake myselfe I could not speake. Thus was I deprived of seeing or doeing my faithfull duty to my beloved husband, through the Lord's hand upon myselfe in such extreamity. Nor had they hopes of the spairing either of our lives, in all appearance. Only our hopes was in the miraculous fountaine of inexhaustible mercys of the Almighty Lord God, "Whoe turneth man to destruction,

* Stearsby, a hamlet in the parish of Brandsby, seven-and-a-half miles from Easingwold, N.R., co. York.

and saith, Turne againe from the grave, yee children of men."
Nor had I any comfort or freind that could assist me in my
sorrowes at that time, nor who to leave my fower young children
too, in that excigent of both our sad calamities, but only to the
gracious Father of mercies, and begging my husband's relations to have pittie on my deare children then like to be left
young orphans to the world of troubles. Yett, blessed be the
Lord, Who did not give us over to death; but when we were
nigh it, behold the goodnesse of God was intreated for us to
restore both our lives. And lett me ever returne Him the glory
of His power and mercy in the returne of our praiers be ascribed
to his Majestie, Who immeadiately gave us hopes of recovery,
upon calling upon His name. For that very night, about that
houer when we weare at praiers for him, my deare husband
wakened us out of sleepe when Dr. [Wittie] expected his
departure; and at three a'clocke at night called for a toste
and butter, not haveing eaten ought of fouer daies, and
changed soe fast in a way of recovery that it was admirable
to all.*

Uppon my dear Joyce her death, Jan. 24, 1665 (i. 214).

It was the pleasure of our God to vissitt my deare childe
childe Joyce Thornton with a great sicknesse, falling exceeding
ill on Sunday, the 20th of January, 1665, begining, as we
thought, with a cold which strucke in many red spotts all over
her bodie and face, affter which she mourned and cried exceedingly, beeing tormented with her sickeness. We used all
meanes that could be don to so young a childe by the advice of
Dr. Wittie, yett noe thing did prevaile, it beeing the pleasure
of God to take her out of this miserable world. She contineued,
with some intermittions of slumbers, and in much strength did
resist the sickenesse, till the Thursday after, when it was past
hopes of recovery; and about one and two a'clocke in the after-

* After this follows "a prayer after Mr. Thornton's recovery, November 28th,
1665" (i. 213).

noone on Friday, the 26th of January, 1665, the Lord was
pleased to free her from all paines by takeing her to His mercy,
when she sweetely fell asleep, without any paine or extreamity
to the appearance of all. She was buried at Stonegrave,* by
Mr. Comber, the next day, who preached a funirall sermon. I
dare not, I will not repine at this chastisement of the Lord,
though it may seeme never soe troublesome to part with my
suckeing childe of my wombe, but say, Good is the will of the
Lord, inasmuch as He hath spaired my dearc husband's life,
which I soe earnestly begged of Him, spairing my owne allso,
who is the vildest of His creatures, and has given me still the
lives of my husband and my three children, for which I will
praise the Lord our God, and begge of Him patience to sustaine
the losse of my sweete infant. * * * *

*Upon my daughter Alice preservation in a sirfitt,
June 13th, 1665 (i., 215.)*

It pleased God to deliver my daughter Alice from a sirfitt,
which brought her into a violent and dangerous illnesse, which
came upon her in her sleepe, as she laid in bed with me, when
1 wakend sudainly in a fright with the noyse she made, being
almost choaked, and her breath stopt with undigested turbutt
eaten the night before; but with the helpe I made her, and
taking several cordialls, she vomitted what did offend her
stomack. Blessed be the most gracious God of mercys for ever,
that raised this childe of mine up from death very offten, even
from a yong infant. Therefore I humbly dedicate her to the
Lord to walke before Him in righteousnesse for ever. In her
sound, she afterwards tould me, she was even overjoyed and
ravished with the glorious sights she then saw, as if heaven
opened to receave her, and she was angry to be disturbed from
that hapinesse.

---

* Extracts from the Stonegrave Register, and a pedigree of the Thorntons,
will be given elsewhere.

Of my dangerous sickenesse, August 16*th,* 1666 (i., 216).

After the drinking of Scarbrough waters,* Mr. Thornton sent
for me to Yorke, about businesse with my Lord Frechvile, in
which jorney I thought I receaved some harme,† beeing lately
conceived before, as Dr. Wittie apprehended. So this, together
with a griefe that befell me at my returne home, about a settlement last made by Colvill for my children's maintenance and
portions, which had bin undon, without my consent and knowledge, when Mr. Thornton was sicke at Steersby, for the
chargeing of Mrs. Raines‡ and Mrs. Portington's debt of £1,400
by mortgage upon Laistrop.§ In soe doeing, there was not one
penny could be secured for my two poore daughters, either
maintenance or portion, till after the payment of the debt, and
there was but £100 per annum for all. And also that my
brother Christopher rent-charge out of Ireland was secured
to them allso for seven yeares, £200 a yeare. Which condition I could not but lament, nor had I got a sight of this new
disposittion of that estate, which I doe beleive Mr. Thornton
was partly necessitated to doe, in regard that they would not
be sattisfied with that security alone out of Ireland. After this
hapened, I fell into a very sad and desperate condittion, upon

---

* There is much about the Scarborough Spaw, and the cures wrought by it,
in the controversial works of Doctors Wittie, Simpson, and Tunstall, which were
printed about this time.

† "My uncle Francis Darley was in company with us, and my nephew Kitt
Danby. I was very faint in the morning, and eate nothing before I went, and
the water wrought with riding. I tould Kitt Danby I was sicke and faint, and
would have lighted to refresh myselfe a little at Strenchall. But uncle Darley
would not grant it; said we should be soone at Yorke, and soe I did not take
any refreshment for displeasing of him, which indeed my deare husband was
sorrey for, and would have had me don. This did somewhat disorder me then,
but I got home pretty well." (vol. ii.)

"Mr. Francis Darley, of Aldby," bur. at Bossall, Dec. 31, 1679 (Bossall
Register). Strensall is a village between Newton and York.

‡ Mrs. Raines, of Appleton-le-Street, not far from East Newton; Mrs. Portington was Mr. Thornton's sister, and lived at Malton.

§ Laisthorpe, a small hamlet in the township of East Newton and parish of
Stonegrave, co. York.

Satterday, the 16th of August, 1666, beeing then about eight weeks gon; the violency thereof contineued a long time affter Dr. Wittie was with me. And for three daies he did not expect my life, soe that he was compelled to use all his art for my preservation. But it pleased God, upon the use of his meadicens, that extreamity a little abated, he leaveing me in a hopefull way of recovery, only said I must not expect to be restored till about the latter end of October. All which time I was in continuall faintings upon the reneuall of the extreamity, soe that my losse of spiritts and strength, etc., was soe great that it was expected I should have fallen into a deepe consumption. And I contineued exceeding feeble and weake till the Candlemas following. The cheife remidie which I found for restoreing strength was a meadicine made of muskedine, which I was directed to by my noble and worthy freind, Madam Grahme, upon which I grew to gather strength by degrees, to passe through that tirrible vissitation and languishing condition all that winter. * * * In my booke of medittations, there is discourse upon this deliverance, upon those words in St. Matthew ix. 21, 22; Luke xvii. 15, 16.

After these weaknesses seized soe extreamely upon my person with such violency and danger to my life, I could not be insensable of my daily decay and dieing condittion, which these frequent incussions of my health might too sudainely bring to its period. Death in itselfe beeing desirable to those whoes affections had came to be weaned from the comforts and vanities of this life, wishing to be freed from this world's troubles and to be receaved into the armes of everlasting rest; yett, as a Christian wife and mother, was there a duty incumbant upon me to discharge with faithfullnesse and godlinesse towards my deare husband and children, according to each capacity, soe that I was obleiged to be a comfort to the one, and a suport to the other, while I was contineued in this world; which duties I made it my studie to observe, and though I could not be in such a state of perfection, doeing all I was commanded from God, yett, through His mercy strengthening me, I may affirme that I made it my endeavour to performe to my uttmost

capacity with a good conscience towards all.   And for as much
as the future well-being of my children did then represent
itselfe to my thoughts, and it had pleased God in mercy to
spaire me till that time, liveing to see myselfe blessed with
three hopefull children, for whose soules I was the most conserned in theire education in the true faith of Jesus Christ.   I
was the more induced, uppon this account, to accept of a proposittion formerly made, and begun in the yeare 1665, by
Mr. Comber* to my 'deare husband, that he would except of
himselfe for my daughter Alice Thornton in marriage,† whoe,

* The Rev. Thomas Comber, son of James Comber, by Mary, widow of
Bryan Burton, of Westerham, co. Kent, born at that place 19 March, 1644;
admitted of Sidney-Sussex Coll., Cambridge, 1659, B.A. 1662, M.A. 1666.
Ordained deacon at the early age of nincteen.   Came into Yorkshire as curate to
the Rev. Gilbert Bennet, of Stonegrave.   In 1699 instituted to the rectory of
Stonegrave ; created D.D. between 1676 and 1679.   Prebendary of Holme in
Cath. Church of York 1677, which, in 1681, he quitted for that of Fenton in the
same church.   Collated to precentorship of York 1683-4, which he resigned,
being nominated to the deanery of Durham in 1691.   He was also chaplain to the
Princess Anne of Denmark, and to King William and Queen Mary.   Manifested
considerable zeal in defending and illustrating the principles and formularies of
the established 'church.   Died 25 Nov., 1699, aged 55, when his credit as an
eminent divine was fully established, and he was making rapid advances to the
highest ecclesiastical honours.   But though the duration of his life was short, yet
it became in effect long, by having had each hour of it actively and usefully
employed.   Buried at Stonegrave.   (Eastmead's Historia Rievallensis, 1824,
p. 466.)

† "My owne great illness, and many weakness on myselfe, uppon every such
fitt, did pres much uppon my spiritt, least we both should be snatched from our
deare children, and they left in a forlorne condittion of both theire parents gon,
and soley left orphants.   This consideration did move us to accept of the motion
to dispose of our eldest daughter in marriage, when she attained some yeares fitt
for that change, unto Mr. Thomas Comber, then minister of Stongrave, who my
deare husband deemed to be a man of great abillityes, learning, and parts ; and
in his owne phraise did say, 'If he lived, would be a very great man in the
church, and he beleived would be a bishop before he died' (vol. iii. 26). * * *
"And makeing all the faire testimonyes to proove a good man, pieous, learned,
and understanding ; with a great prospect of his deserved mirrits to be capable of
preferment in the church ; and of a true and loyall education, and zeale for it.
These was great inducements to choose heere for her to a wise, discreet person,
rather then to a great estate, without those good qualilications ; and these was
the motives and ground of our choyce of this match ; becing more inlarged on
this subject in my first booke of my widdowed condition.   I humbly made my

though her yeares were but young, beeing fourteen then, yet
such was his great affection towards her, that he was desirous
to attend for her seven yeares, if he might by his leave obtaine
her att last, haveing discerted all other opportunitys for her sake,
and the favours he had from him. And allso, that whatever her
fortune was, it should be wholey for her use and her's, and with
all he did not dispaire but that God, Whoe had preserved him
hitherto, would provide a hansome compotency, and to make a
better provission for my daughter by adding to her owne. This
proposittion was answered by a faire respect of Mr. Thornton's
side, and he was incouraged to proceed. Nor could I be
sattisfied in a businesse of this nature, on which might depend
the well-being of our familie, without serious and deepe consideration of all our affaires, and the condittion that our estate was
in; which, beeing well knowne to my good brother Denton,
more then to any in the world, I consulted and advised with
him all along in this transaction, whose prudence and discression was a great suport to Mr. Thornton and myselfe in all our
bussinesse and actions; he also haveing had knowledge and
acquaintance of this gentleman for severall years, might the
better judge of his life and conversation, together with his
qualifications for the great and high calling of the ministery;
which, in itselfe considered, carries allong with it the most noble

pettitions to Heaven that He would please to direct and guide me in this great
and weighty conserne of my deare child's marriage; that we might dispose of
her for a blessinge to herselfe and to us her parents, and to me who had, with
great and exceeding sorrowes and paines, brought her out into this world (as it
may be more at large seene in my first booke of my life expressed, in her birth
and deliverances more at large); how deare she was to me. Soe the Lord would
contineue His most signall caire over her, and mercy towards me, her poore
mother, as to provide such an one to be her husband and her guide, that she
might be a happy wife, and live comfortably in this life, and bring forth children
to the glory of God and salvation of their soules, and be a comfort to each other
in this great change of her life, for Jesus Christ His sake, Amen. To all these
humble pettitions, I bless the Lord God of mercy, I hope He did vouchsafe to
grant; and gave her a great share of happiness and prosperity as a blessing to
her from heaven, for her reward of beeing a good and gracious childe even from her
infancy, beeing both deare and tender to me, and obedient to us both; full of virtue,
piety, and modesty, and many graces, eminent in her youth and more riper
years" (vol. iii., 60).

title that man is capable of in this world, and wherein the highest acts of piety and religion is vested, beeing honoured by God himselfe in the Old and New Testament above all other dignitys, and haveing the greatest opportunity of drawing neare to the throne of grace, from whence proceeds every good and perfect gift, shewing to us mortals the way to everlasting life. After the consideration of all these motives, as principally to be regarded, I was in the next place confirmed in my resolves to proceed in this buisnesse for my daughter, whom I hoped to be placed neare us and her freinds at Stongrave, beeing our owne church, where I might have better advantage for my sonne Robert and his sister's instruction. Allso, I perceaved by this last un-settling of the estate from my daughters and yonger children, they were brought into an incertainty for their provission, which might fall too heavily out for them, and be the worse for them after my decease. Soe that, uppon consideration of the whole bussinesse I have mentioned, it was conseaved convenient to entertaine this motion, and to close with such a happie opportunity which, by the providence of God, was directed; and by reason of her youth we resolved to keepe it secrett till a fitter time, when this intended bussinesse should be consumated, there beeing still an affectionate correspondancy of these persons by chaste and religious conversations in our family. Neither was I out of hopes that Sir Christopher Wandesforde might duely pay his £2000 out of Ireland, which was to redeeme the estate and pay Mr. Thornton's ingagements. But, in the meane time, I might more probably die in some of these sick-nesses, and my deare husband, who was often falling into his pallsie, when, affter our decease, my children would be left in an uncertaine condittion for assistance. Behold the good-ness of God, which taketh caire for mine, even out of strangers, makeing me see His mercy in His providence manyfold to me and mine. "Praise the Lord, O my soule, and forgett not all His benifitts." Amen.

About the 2nd of September, 1666, began the great fire in London, which, in four daies' time, consumed 13,200 houses, 89 churches, and, without the miraculous providence of God, it had devoured that whole citty.

*My daughter Katherine Thornton's preservation in the smale
pox, the 29th of September, 1666 (i., 220).*

Uppon the 29th of September, when I was yett very weake,
began my daughter Katte with a violent and extreame pain in
the backe and head, with such scrikes and torments that shee
was deprived of reason, wanting sleepe, nor could she eate anything. For three daies she contineued, to my great affliction,
not knoweing what this distemper would be. At last the smale
pox appeared, breaking out abundantly all over; but in her
unguidablenesse stroke in againe, soe that my brother Portington*
used many cordialls to save her life, affter which they appeared,
and then we had more hopes, but was in great danger of losseing
her sight. She was all over her face in one scurfe, they running
into each other. But loe, by the goodnesse of God, for which
I humbly blesse and praise His holy name, she passed the danger
of death, begining to heale. Her extreamity beeing soe great,
criciug night and day, that I was forced to be removed, though
very weake, as before, into the scarlett chamber, for want of
rest. Blessed be our gracious God, through His infinitt mercy
directing to good helpes, and prospering the meanes, she was
preserved and healed againe. Hanna Ableson and Mary Cotes
was her keepers. About November she went abroad in the
house, only losst by this sickenesse her faire haire on her head,
and that beautifull complection God had given. The Lord
suply her soule with the comelinesse of His grace and spirit in
her heart, makeing her lovely in His sight. And praised be
the Lord my God Which was intreated for my childe's life. The
Lord give me a thankfull heart, and that she may live to His
glory, for Christ's sake. Amen.

*My son Robert's haveing the smale pox, Jan. 5, 1667, and of his
recovery perfectly againe (i., 227).*

The 5th of January, my deare Robin Thornton began his

* Timothy Portington, of Malton, married Frances Thornton.

sicknes of the smale pox, beeing very ill and weake for two daies; the 7th, 8th, and 9th he was in great danger of death, they not comeing well out till the 10th, on which day he lost his sight by them, beeing very great ones and full. About the 14th, his feavor and disscase was at hieght, and on the 15th he altered for the better, soe that a change was discerned; the 17th, he began to see againe; the 18th, had his sight clearly recovered; affter which he recovered very fast, for which I most humbly bless God with all my soule, and magnifie His mercy to me in the deliverance of this my deare and sweet childe, in not quenching our cole in this family. "O praise the Lord, O my soule, and forgett not all His benifitts;" this His favour to thee for ever. Amen. The 24th, Robin first gott up, and was perfectly well, groweing strong, and was not soe much disfigured as his sister Kate. But he never recovered his sweete, beautifull favour, and pure couler in his cheeks; but his face grew longish; his haire did not fall off; he wanted nine months of beeing five yeares old and some daies. Hanna Ableson and Margery Millbanke kept him in his sicknesse.

It pleased God, affter my sonne Robert was well, to vissitt my daughter Alice Thornton, which began with annother dangerous fitt in her sleepe, which much frighted me, she beeing almost choaked by the phlegme, makeing her exceeding sicke, before she vomitt up some ill-digested meate, and with extreamity she was blacke in her face. But, by the mercys of our gracious God, affter she vomitted, she did recover, though it kept her weake. I will praise the Lord our God of our salvation for this great deliverance of my childe. Amen.

My daughter Alice Thornton her smale pox (i., 228).

About the 25th of January, Naly tooke phisicke to prevent the smale pox, when she fell to be very ill, pained in her head and backe; on the 26th, she beeing very ill and sicke and in an aguish temper the 27th and 28th, till the smale pox appeared, beeing for two daies in a cold sweate without heate and In very great danger of death; the 29th, she was in great hazard, yet lay very patiently, and did not talk idle, as usuall in such diseases, though there was little hopes of her recovery, they beeing stroke in through her cold sweats. Yet was all remidies used to her for warmth by Hanna, etc., and cordialls by brother Portington. But on the 30th it pleased the great and gracious God. He did begin to give us better hopes, the smale pox then comeing out and apeare. She was in a warmer temper, not soe sicke as formerly, and we, by the mercys of God, hoped for a recovery. At the 31st day she fell blind, intermitting till the 5th of February, beeing exceediugly choaked in her throat, and could not swallow allmost anything without a pipe, for the smale pox and streit throat. Nor did she gett any sleepe till the 3rd February, after which she gott a little, and the 4th, her eyes began to unclose, the 5th, saw perfectly, and they blackned, and her throat mended, and the feaver abated; the 8th day of February she began to be pretty well, though extreamely full and sore. About the 18th Naly rose out of bed, and recruted in strength by degrees. The haire came of, and that favour cleane taken from her. But oh that our hearts weare inlarged in thankfullnesse to the great Lord our God for the preservation of this my eldest childe, whoes speciall deliverance must not be forgotten, to give glory to the great God of Israell, which had pitty uppon myselfe, husband, and three children, by restoring theire lives when they weare all soe nigh many deaths. O Lord, accept, I beseech [Thee], my gratefull and humble heart, Which had compassion upon Thy servants and our children. Let us all live to be instruments to Thy glory and honor, heere and heereaffter. Amen.

The death of my brother John Wandesford, Dec. 2nd, 1666 (i., 221).

It pleased God to vissitt my deare brother, John Wandesford, at London, with his last sickenesse, beeing an ague, joined with violent fitts of the stone, haveing had severall of them the last halfe yeare. His sicknesse contineued soe strongly that he was very weake in bodie, though I blesse God perfect in mind and spiritt. I am the better able to shew the same from the relation of his owne servant, and the people where he lived, testifieing this truth to Mr. Comber, who was then at London, and intreated by me to vissitt my deare brother in his affliction. At the newes of hearing of me, he did much recover, and faine would have seene his deare and beloved sister; but when he understood I was in Yorkeshire, he praied them to remember his deare love to me, and thanke me for sending to see him, with abundance of testimonys of his affection and love to me and mine, praing for us. Then did he more zealously prepaire for his change and departure out of this miserable world, God haveing given him a taste of heaven and happinesse, haveing bin long since weary of it, and banished from the comforts of its injoyments. For severall years since my brother George's death, he had laid under the most sad and afflicting hand of God, by reason of the want of the use of his understanding, which came to him by a deepe melancolie scising upon his spiritt, partly for the losse of my said brother, and the greife he tooke upon ill usage in the detaineing of his annuity; he beeing of a sweete, noble nature, it wrought the more to his prejudice. But I do beleive that what things of this nature to any of the prejudice of our family did not proceed from the heire's owne inclination, beeing naturally of a good and sweete dispossittion, but from the councell of such by whome he had bin acted [upon] since his marriage, who had advised my brother George to destroy the intaile and settlements of his father, by which he might be free to settle his estate wholely upon his daughter, to the ruine of all his family. But my brother George abhorred such treachery, nor ever harkned to such designes; nor could my brother Christopher understand the depth of such insinuations, not beeing experienced in the transactions of bussinesse of this nature. However it was, this poore brother was the greatest sufferer, both in bodie and minde, haveing bin offten recruted and fully restored, was againe brought downe through trouble and want he sustained. Nor was it in my power to helpe or releive him, otherwise then by my praiers and teares for him, our owne sufferings beeing soe great. Yet did the God of mercy give him many intervalls, in which times he was religeously disposed and constant in duties, with a conscience to spend his daies holely and uprightly, and in great penitence for anything that might offend his God. About halfe a yeare before his death he was more strict in his severe dutyes of pietie, saing that he should not live long; soe that he prepared for his desolution each day.

The morning before he departed (though he was very weake in bodie) he would kneele in bed, and most devoutly and seriously praied to his God, and heartily recomended his soule to his Creator, and soe laied himselfe quietly downe. He drew his breath shorter each minuitt, and at last sweetely fell asleepe in the Lord. Thus was the conclussion of that deare and sweete brother, soe much afflicted, and under soe long a weakcnesse. His condition was much to be lamented, and it was indeed a continueall greife and daily corrosive to myselfe, whose neareness in affection and consanguinity had a sufficient simpathy in his sufferings. He was a very great losse to our family, by his trouble and visittation, whose parts, pietie, learning, and quick witt was not infeariur to any that was remaining of it. Beeing of a most sweete, affable, and injenious nature, nimble and ready in his acqute answers in disputes, as well at skoole as Cambridge. At both places he carried himselfe soe obleigingly that all persons of his acquaintance loved and admired in his sigacitie, comeing nearest to his brother George for witt and parts. My deare mother had given him the best education she could, sending him to Cambridge, about fifteen yeares old, under the tuittion of Dr. Widdrington,* where he made a great improvement of his time in the sciences and learning, and was soe studious, even at nights, and when his houers should have bin for recreation, that his tutor was forced to forbid that severity. His sabaths were spent allwaies (as much as he could) very strict, in acts of religion and pietie, truly from his childhoode and youth, studieing to serve and feare God. In fine, he was

---

* Dr. Ralph Widdrington, brother of Sir Thomas Widdrington, Speaker of the House of Commons and antiquary. He was fellow of Christ's College and public orator, etc., and died in 1689. (Life of Matthew Robinson, 196-208.)

so hopefully good and pregnant, that my mother had much comfort, and all his relations joy in him, beeing full of expectations that this early plant might flourish to the honour and happinesse of the whole family. But it soe hapned, to our great greife, that this malancoly seising on him, first at Cambridge in a great sickness; then by an infinitt caire and cost of my mother he was perfectly well againe; but, upon the former accidents mentioned, he fell very ill. And yett all her caire was contineud over him, even at London, where he had bin inticed to goe from her, contrary to her mind, and suffered great hardships and injuries, for the want of some caire over him, and negligence to performe that duty, till my deare mother committed him under the tuittion of Dr. Bathurst, which he did faithfully performe all his life towards him, when he wanted nothing for his comfort and helpe that either hee or my mother could doe for him, she every yeare giveing the doctor a gratituity of £10 for his paines and caire over my brother, soe long as the doctor lived; allthough even then he wanted to discharge the man's house, where he laid, out of his owne dues and annuity. But I am sorrey there was cause to speake thus much on this subject; I shall therefore returne to speake conserning his buriall. He departed this life upon the second day of December, 1666, and buried in the parish church of Hodgeden,* with as hansom a solemnity as could be in that time. Mr. Comber preached a funerall sermon, text Eccles. . . . . . . there being abundance of people on that occassion. He was buried the 3d December, Mr. Tirrill and his wife and servant all expressing very great sorow and lamentation for him, whoe had lived soe innocently, and carried himselfe soe hansomely and well, that had gained there affections and pitty towards his person very much in that place, God makeing him to finde favour in his distresse amongs straingers. And now the Lord God of mercys has, I hope, freed him from all misery, want, and oppression. His most sad afflictions for severall yeares had prepared his soule for his Saviour, Who had kept him in all his

* (?) Hoddesdon, Hertford.

health and sickenesse from any grosse sinns, nor was he inclined
thereto in the least, but given himselfe to God in his youth and
childehood. He was never heard to sweare an oath. Before
he went to Cambridge I heard him make the most fine exposit-
tion extempory upon those words of David's advice to Solomon,*
"And thou, Solomon my son, know thou the God of thy father,"
etc., and the other three verses, that I never heard the like from
soe young a person, laying downe our duty to God and service
of Him. I hope he now injoys those hapinesse this world is not
capable of, whoe sett himselfe to seeke God soe early, and so
with an upright heart. * * * *

About this Christmas, 1666, my cozen William Norton† was
inhumainly murdered at London, neare Gray's Inn. It was the
permition of God, for the affliction of us all, in the losse of soe
brave a gentleman, to lett a dismall stroake fall heavy upon the
person of my nephew Thomas Danby, beeing the hope of his
familie; and just at that time when he had ingaged to cleare of
all debts, portions, etc., in the due performance of his father's
will, when all things would have bin don to all persons' sattis-
factions. But allasse! this poore gentleman was sudainely
surprised and murdered, without any provocation or malice
begun on his side, comitted with the most barbarous sircumstances imaginable, by one Berridge, a stranger to him, but a
camrade to Ogle and Jenny, which was then with Tom Danby,
but did not assist. The pretence was about Ogle's sword, that
Tom had redeemed from pawne, and unluckily had on that day,
and which Berrige upbraiding him for, picked a quarrell. But
it is too probable that they had a spleene again his life, because
non assisted, but wittnesses of this bloody tragedie. The murderer fled; they were catchd; but by the too remisenesse of
the jury, escaped punishment, notwithstanding the displeasure
of the judge. But Jenny that summer went home, and was
convicted in conscience, never apeared affter, but died very

---

* 1 Chron. xxviii. 9.

† Eldest surviving son of Major Norton, Esq. He was a barrister of
Gray's Inn, and is said to have been killed in an affray in a London tavern.
(Fisher's Mashamshire, 277-8).

penitent.   He died in London, neare Grayse Inn, August the first, in the yeare 1667.

My brother Denton's son John fell into great extreamity, upon the takeing of phisicke, on the 25th of January, which did not worke kindly, and soe contineued three daies deprived of sleepe or foode, falling into a feaver, with violent paine, all which deprived him of his understanding, beeing in a dangerous condittion; but it pleased God at last, getting some sleepe about four a'clocke in the morning, he knew every one.   When the pox apeared the feaver abated, and he recovered very fast, haveing but a few.   Blessed be God for his deliverance.

The 8th of Aprill, 1667, Nally had a pearle on her eye affter the smale pox, which indangered the losse of her sight; but by waters and a meadicen to the wrests of her arms, which sweate Mrs. Bucke did advise, she recovered that danger, beeing well againe about the 30th Aprill, 1667.

About the yeare when Kate was ten yeares old, plaing with her cozens in Newton barne and swing crosse by a rope, she gott soe high a fall by his swinging her from him (T. D.) that she was taken up dead, beeing blacke and without breath for a long time, at which sudaine blow I was much affrighted for my childe, rubing and usueing all meanes for her recovery; and it was halfe an houer before any signes of life apeared.   But it pleased God in mercy at last she did breath againe, and by degrees came to herselfe at an houer's space, after warming, etc., in bed; but knew nothing of the fall a long time; it had don her much harme in her head, with great paines.

The birth of my sonne Christopher Thornton, my ninth childe, Nov. 11, 1667, and of his death Dec. 1, 1667 (vol. i., 230).

Of my ninth childe it was the pleasure of God to give me a weake and sickely time in breeding, from the February till the 10th of May following, I not having fully recruted my last September weaknesse; and if it had bin good in the eyes of my God I should much rather (because of that) not to have bin in this condittion. But it is not a Christian's part to chuse anything of this nature, but what shall be the will of our heavenely Father, be it never soe contrary to our owne desires. Therefore did I desire to submitt in this dispensation, and depend uppon His providence for the preservation of my life, Who had delivered me in all my extreamities and afflictions. I had not my health till about the 10th of May, when I perceaved myselfe with quicke childe. Aftterwards, during the time of beeing with childe, till within a month of my delivery, very well as of any other, walkeing a mile to the church each Sabath day. I humbly blesse the God of my life and strength that restored soe much health and strength againe to His handmaide, giveing me great comfort in my deare and beloved husband, who all this summer and spring was soe well and strong as he never had bin since his first ill fitt at Steersby, the Lord giveing a blessing to those meanes appointed by Dr. Wittie for his preservation, which order we observed till towards September following. But when I grew soe bigge and ill, neare my delivery, about Mick [aelmas], he intermitted those rules of directions, wanting my assistance about his person. In my illnes he relapsed severall times, and had the doctor sent for to him very offten, by which helpes, through God's blessing, was restored to me againe. Praised be our good and gracious Lord God for ever. Amen. The birth of my ninth childe was very perillous to me, and I hardly escaped with my life, falling into pangs of labour about the 4th of November, beeing ill, contineuing that weeke; and on Munday, the 11th of November, 1667, I fell in travell, beeing delivered betwixt the houers of ten and eleven a'clocke at night. * * * It pleased the Lord to give annother mercy that night, for my daughter Alice, with feare and greife for me, fell so sicke in my labour that she was in much danger of death; but blessed be the Lord which preserved her then, and recovered her from that illnesse the next day, November 12, '67. Christopher Thornton, my ninth childe, was borne at Newton, on Munday, the 11th November, '67; baptized the 12th at Newton. His godfathers and godmother were my brother Denton, my brother Portington, and Mrs. Anne Danby.

Affter this comfort of my childe I recovered something of my weakness, better recovering my breasts and
milke, and giveing sucke, when he thrived very well and grew
strong, beeing a lovely babe. But, least I should too much
sett my heart in the sattisfaction of any blessing under heaven,
it seemed good to the most infinitt wise God to take him from
me, giveing me some apprehensions thereof, before any did see
it as a change in him. And therefore, with a full resignation to
His providence, I endeavoured to submit patiently and willingly
to part with my sweete childe to our deare and loveing Father,
Who see what was better for me then I could, begging that His
will might be mine, either in life or death. When he was about
fourteen daies old, my pretty babe broake into red spots, like
the smale pox, and through cold, gotten by thinner clothing then
either my owne experience or practice did accustom to all my
children, they following the precept of M. D.; it presently,
though then unknown to me, upon this accident, with the extreame cold wether, fell into great loosenesse, and, notwithstanding all the meanes I could use, it contineued four daies,
haveing indured it patiently; then fell into some little strugling,
and at length it pleased his Saviour and mine, after the fifth
sicke night and day, to deliver him out of this miserable world.
He sweetely fell asleepe on Sunday at night, beeing then the
1st of December, 1667, who was at that time three weeks old
on the next day the 2nd, when he was buried at Stonegrave by
Mr. Comber, who preached a funerall sermon December
2nd, 1667.

After my deare childe's death, I fell into a great and long-
contineued weaknesse by the swelling of my milke, he haveing
sucket last, in his paine, of the left breast, had hurt the niple,
causeing it to gangareene, and extreame pained with torment
of it, made me fall into a feavour, which, together with excessive
paines in my head and teeth, uppon much greife from the unhansome proud carriage of those I tooke to be a comfort in my
distresse, proved the greatest corisive in my sicke and weake
condittion, I beeing then the lesse able to suport my spiritts
under such afflictions; soe that such strainge, uncharitable

dealing kept me from gathering strength, I not beeing able to stand nor goe for four months till February following, wittnessed by those servants that attended me then, and was compelld to be carried to and from my bed in a chair. Even at that time did those which had a secrett hatred against me (though I neither knew it nor its cause then; for I never in my whole life, by word or act, had the least prejudice or don her any injury to make it, as I must speake to the Lord for truth), yet then she undermined my peace and quiet, and scornfully presenting my reall weaknesse and sad condittion to some in secrett, saing that I ailed nothing, and I was as well as she, and made myselfe a talke to my neighbours; all which she carried with much subtilty for the dishonour of my poore despised person, sufficiently afflicted without this addittion. Yet were these but the begining of sorrowes to me upon that account, endeavouring to bear all with abundance of patience, which my God did please to give me in part, hopeing with all that, when I mett with Tom Danby's wife, I should prevaile for her restoration to her children, which she did object daily to me that she had bin kept from, because her sister was angery she came, as before, to be with me while I layd inne. But I still tould her if I had suspected her sister's displeasure for that, I would never have putt that to hazard for the world. Nor did she in the least give me notice thereof. But my nephew Kitt's wife did make this an objection, and I bellive owed me noe good will for it, though she reserved more for an affter game (secrett) to my ruine. Butt Thou, O Lord, seest and knoweth my integretty for this woman's good, and the love I bore her ever since I knew her; and therefore I desire Thee to pardon what occasion of evill has befallen me from her, and receave my humble and faithfull thanks for Thy inexpressable mercy and goodnesse to me Thy poore creature.   *   *   *

Of the illness of my deare husband (vol. i., 234).

After the recovery of my health and strength againe, I had returned another affliction, which was not at the time soe heavy, when I was sicke myselfe, I blesse God; but like two bukettes in a well, it pleased God to deale with us; when the one was downe the other was up; soe I beeing recruted, had my worke in the assistance of my deare husband, whoes offten and frequent relapses into his pallsie fell on him, to my abundant greife; soe that from November, '67, till August, '68, Dr. Wittie was allmost each month fetched to him when he relapsed, or the degrees begining on him, which most sad condittion made me I never injoyed myselfe, with feare of losseing him, my cheifest comfort and suport; and for his sufferings, although the Lord did please to give him intermitions, and allso we could not perceave that he was in any extreamity, but slumbring all the time of his illnesse, till after glisters he was brought to himselfe againe; they beeing the speediest reamidies at present, then afterwards all other reamidies was applied by Dr. Witty direction. And he was well againe, even to people's admiration, which was soe ill of a sudaine and better againe, and according to the earlinesse of begining with reamidies, they wrought, and the fitts longer or shorter in contineuance; soe that we saw too aparantly that my deare husdand's distemper might be a meanes to shorten his daies at last; and we weare much conserned to gett all the settlements don and perfected, least we should be deprived of him. And to that end, my brother Denton, with Mr. Comber and myselfe, was exceedingly imployed att all times almost when he was in a condittion for bussinesse; hastening the draughts of writtings and settlements with councell, how to give all persons sattisfaction in there just debts. And not till the 28th day of May, 1668, was our settlement perfected, from the time of my cosen Covill's beeing destroyed, for either portions or maintenance, which went most sadly with me. But now, by the great paines and industery of my brother Denton and Mr. Comber, who we did, for my children's good, imploy as a freind to them in generall, as well as in his perticuler respect for my daughter Alice, had much caire for them. Allso, it was most true that I lived remote from my owne relations. That day wherein my deare husband signed his deed for my children's provision out of Laistrop, he did signe my brother Denton's three *(sic)* rent-charge for his part of portion by my sister of £250 out of the other part of Laistrop, which ought in conscience to be payd. I humbly blesse our gracious Father, Which gave me leave to get this don for provission of my yonger children, and that the estate was in a better frame then it had bin of late, by the payment of £1000 in debts of his rent-charge of Mr. Sayer, which he had but newly sould, and payd of with it this yeare many great ingadgements secured out of the land at Laistrop, by which it was made clearer.

About the 20th day of May, on that night, my deare husband had a dreame which he tould to my brother Denton, Mr. Comber, and myselfe in the morning severally, which did very much trouble me to heare, that he should live but forty-seven daies longer. Nor was he ever apt to take notice of such things, but rather condemne me for relating severall ominous dreames that I had before the death of my father, my uncle Osborne, my sister Danby, my brother George, before whoes death halfe a yeare I dreamt soe fully conserning it, the manner and all sircumstances about it, that he refrained that river affter I tould him my dreame till the time which was the last, beeing compelled by his bussinesse to doe itt; allso before my mother's death and severall of my children's; soe that now he himselfe was more apt to make use of this as a warning to him, beeing offten heard to say he should not live very long, and with much diligence endeavoured to prepare his soule for God; in which time I, whoe had my comforts soe intirely bound up in him, could not with patience allmost to think of this change. Possibly it might be the good pleasure of the Lord to spaire him to us. We repaired (upon the next illnesse) to Dr. Wittie, he not beeing willing for any other's advice, to consider what course could be taken for his preservation; soe that, upon a serious consideration of his distemper, then inclining to malanlolicke, he advised him for the Spaw,* where he had bin other yeares with good successe; upon which Mr. Thornton was very desirous to goe, beleiveing it would helpe him; and the doctor

* *i.e.* Scarborough Spaw.

firmly ingaged to be as cairfull of him as his owne life. Soe upon the 5th of June, 1667, we sett forward in a coach with him to Malton,* with my three children, I thinking to have gon to Scarbrough with him, but it soe pleased God that I fell exceeding ill, that I could not goe, but was forced to returne home to Newton, and left him under the caire of my brother Portington and sister; and in the company of Dr. Wittie, the 8th of June following, he went by a hired coach to Scarbrough; and about a month affter he returned home, on horsebacke, it beeing his own desire: all which time we had a deare and comfortable corrospondancy betweene us, by our mutuall and frequent letters, I heareing of him, or from him, three times in a weeke and offener, each one bringing me the good newes of his haveing cast off his malancoly. It cannot be imagined what my joy was in his returne to finde him soe prettily recruted by a chearefull temper and spiritt. But I quickly saw that his weakencsse had left much dreggs of his distemper. Yett had I great cause of thankefullnesse to the Lord, Which gave me hopes of him, and that if he could have bin prevented of cold, he would remaine well.

My son Robert Thornton preserved July 25, 1668 (vol. i., 264).

It pleased God to give my sweete Robin Thornton a very great deliverance uppon the 25th of July. In his play with his sister Kate and cosen Willy Denton, standing in the window in the hay laith at Newton, which is above four yeards from the earth, he fell downe into the laine, neare a great stone, which, if he had light on, might have killed him, falling soe high; soe that the danger was very great, and his deliverance also, and ought to be had in remembrance with gratitude, and hearty thanks to the God of Heaven, Which sent His angell to preserve my poore childe from death or any harme, save a tumble on his face. The glorious name of Jehovah be praised and magnified for his life, and the preservations thereof from all casulties, dangers, sicknesses, dislocations, and evills, and giveing

____
* On the river Derwent, about twenty-two miles from Scarborough.

him a compotent shaire of understanding, witt, memory,
a loving and affable nature, with severall other good guifts
tending to the accomplishment of his person with naturall endowments. But I doe adore the Lord's name and mercy, which
hath begun upon dawning hopes of His grace in his heart;
appearing in his beeing affected with good instructions in the
knowledge and feare of God, and his desire to be informed of
all things conserning God; with notions of feare in hearing
His judgments, with severall pathaticall expressions of God and
His wayes. One day, beeing about four yeares old, he tould me
of his owne accord that God was a pure, holie, wise, and mercifull
spiritt; but the devill was a wicked, lieing, malicious spiritt.
Was it not better to beleive the holy good God and serve Him
then that wicked evill spiritt, which woulde destroy us? I must
therefore, with humble gratitude, take notice with comfort in
His mercy, which did not dispise the prayers of His handmaide,
but given me a gracious answer to my humble suplications,
when I wanted a son; for this blessing I begged of the Lord as
Hanna did Samuell, and has dedicated him to His service, even
all his daies, further craveing the contineuance of His favour
and grace of His spiritt upon my sonn; endowing his heart from
his childehoode with all Christian virtues, faith, knowledge,
wisdome, and true understanding, to guide and direct him in his
youth to his riper age, to follow Him and walk in His wayes
with a perfect heart even to his live's end; preserve him from the
sinnes and vanities, follies, evill inclinations, either of custome,
examples, or naturall habitts, which might staine or polute his
soule in Thy sight; and from all temporall evils, soe farre as
shall seeme fitt in Thy wisdome to give him; and finaly, I
beseech Thee, preserve him from etternall sorrow and misery in
the world to come; thus consigning this my childe as a blessing
to his family, comfort to his weake mother and relations, and
an instrument of the glory of Thee, His Creator, in this life,
serving Thee faithfully in this generation in righteousnesse; and
at the last may joyfully praise Thee in heaven; all which I
humblie and heartily begge, for the lone sake of our dearest Lord
and Saviour Jesus Christ, His holie Son. Amen and Amen.

A relation of the last sicknesse and death of my deare and honoured husband William Thornton, esquire, whoe departed this life at Malton, September 17th, 1668 (vol. i., 265).

While I am in this vaile of teares and shaddow of death, I must not desire nor expect more comforts of this life and temporall mercys then will preserve me from sinking in sorrow or despaire under the crosse. Even that shaire was denied my Saviour, the Captaine of our salvation, when He fainted under it, and allmost dispaired by the sadder loade of our sinns. Well may I, miserable creature, take up His cup and pledge His love with love againe. His life heere had little or noe mixture but gall and bitternesse. I have the beames of IIis sweete influences, injoying sometim the sunshine of His favours behind the clouds of dispaire and afflictions. Fare be it from me to repine at the great and wise Disposer, the Lord of heaven and earth's most infinitly wise disposittion, or to grudge at His dealing with me; for heere I am, Lord, make me Thine, and doe what Thou wilt with me, either for life or death. The Lord best knowes how to propose and intermixe crosses with comforts, smiles with frownes, to His servants heere, as shall be best for them in proportion to theire etternall happinesse; and not as they shall thinke fitt, which are but of yesterday, but Himselfe, Whoe sees not as man sees, haveing all things in [His] Omnipotent and Omnicient power, and shall tend most to His owne glory and devine gracious pleasure. Noe sooner was my strength in part recruted, begining to returne againe, affter my deare aunt Norton's departure home, and my deare husband's goeing that day to Malton, when I was soe weake that I kept my bed a week before and since her goeing away; soe about the 14th day of September, they goeing away upon the 11th, I gott up, begining to rejoyce att my deliverance from the late weaknesse and illnesse, both of the plague of slanderous tounges; and the faintings abated something affter Dafeny Lightfoote came to see me. But on that day when first I arose out of bed, I had the sad newes of my deare and tenterly-loving husband falling sicke at Malton, brought to me in a letter to my brother Denton,

which soe sudainly surprized my spiritt, yett exceeding weake,
that I fell to a great trembling, with excessive greife and feares
upon me for his life and safety; soe that I went sicke thereupon to my sorrowfull bed, immeadiatly sending for Dr. Wittie
to come to him, each day and night posting thither to let me
know how he did.*   Nor could I possibly, without the losse of

* "It pleased the Devine Wisdome to deprive me of the comfort of my deare
husband's life, bringing me into annother sad dispensation, which I had much
rather, to have had my choyce, have bin deprived of my owne, who was weary
of the world and myselfe.   Even then did the Lord take from me the joy of my
heart and the delight of my eyes, adding one affliction uppon the other, by which
meanes my poore dejected hart was drenched into a deep abyse of sorrow and
misserys, and by which I was reduced into a more dangerous condition.   I had
reason to call the aydes of heaven and earth to my assistance, least I should be
overwhelmed with dispaire.   Often had I pettioned Heaven to spaire him, and
to call me to Himselfe, when I have seen him in his pallsie fitts.   But my deare
would reprove me, and say that I offended God in too much loveing him, and not
to be willing to part with him; wishing that we might all be freed out of this
miserable world and enjoy God for ever" (vol. ii., p. 18).

"My deare husband went to Malton to my sister Portington's on Friday,
the 11th September, 1668, beeing in health much as of late, pretty well of his
infirmity.   He rid into that faire upon Satterday; to church on Sunday; upon
Munday he was not well, and had pills given him as he used to have by my
brother Portington; but they did not worke kindly, and we had a glister given
him, beeing the method ordered by Dr. Wittie.   On Munday he sent for
Mr. Sinkler, and tould him that he knew formerly that he had bin in much
trouble and sadnesse for his sinns, and walked uncomfortably for the want of the
sence of God's favour, in great feares and doubtings.   But now the Lord was
pleased to make Himselfe knowne to him to be a reconciled Father in Christ
Jesus; and that he was at peace with Him, he perceaving a great deale of joy
and comfort inwardly in his soule and minde, blessing the Lord for this His infinitt mercys; and hoped that he should blesse His name for evermore that he
had bin soe troubled, for now he was reconciled to Him againe.   These, with
many such like expressions, to the great sattisfaction of Mr. Sinkler, who staied
a good while with him.   Then, towards night, this sweete saint of God grew worse,
and more heavy and drousie, according to that distemper, and they sent to me
for the doctor, which came to him on Wednesday after dinner.   My deare was
then very weake in bodie, but, I blesse God, perfect in mind and understanding.
Mr. Comber goeing to see him, he tooke his leave of him, and bid him to remember him to his deare wife, bid me be patient and contented with God's hand,
and to submitt to His will, which he uttred as well as he could for his speach
beeing taken.   After which he had his haire taken of, by order, beeing the
last remidie, and this with his owne consent.   But alass! noe remidies or

my life, be carried to see him; albeit they could not keepe me from him, till I was brought soe feeble by reason of another accident that befell me in my greife. Then was the grandest affliction upon my heart that could be, under which I had surely fainted, as it was my desire rather then to have lost my joy and comfort, had not the Almighty power and mercy of God miraculously upheld my spiritt from sinking. On Wednesday I sent my brother Denton and Mr. Comber to my deare joy att Malton, longing all that day to heare from him, still earnestly desiring to have gon myselfe, but my freinds would not lett me, for feare of my poore and miserable life, which yett I despised in comparison of him. Soe with much impatience, great feares, and some hopes, I waited till night, when word was brought me from Dr. Wittie that I should be of good cheere and not cast away my life, for I should have my deare husband home as well as ever I had him in my life; soe that I endeavoured to comfort up my hopes in God the Almightie, Whose power was infinitt as His mercy and sweetest cleamency to us His poore servants had bin offten shewed; and poured out my praiers and teares abundantly that night, for the preservation of the life and health of my deare husband with me, if it weare the good will and pleasure of our God that that deare and sweete union and affection intire in our lives together might not be broke, nor we seperated by death from the injoyment of each other in Him. If this might stand with the gracious pleasure of our gracious God, I made these the requests of my soule to Him. That night was spent in somme little slumbers, but very unquiett and

meadicine nor art could prevaile, it beeing the determination of our God to take him to Himselfe. And yet to mixe this bitter cup of death with the alay of a quiett framed temper, free from any torment or signes of paines, lieing as if he were in a sweet sleepe; and by degrees growing colder at his feete, and soe dieing upwards, and drawing his breath shorter all the Thursday morning. And towards eleven a'clocke in the fore noone he fetched one litle sigh, and soe sweetely resigned up his spiritt into the handes of his deare Saviour and Redemer Jesus Christ." "The full relation of all these things, and of his interment in his own quire at Stonegrave with his father, and all concerning this tradegy, is related by me in the first book of my life, and in the beginning of my widdowed booke." (vol. iii.)

full of feares, trimblings, and sad apprehensions. In the morning my brother Denton came home and very discreetely prepared me with good advice and councell to entertaine the Lord's determinate will in all things with patience and submittion, if the worst should fall upon me according to my feares. But withall said that God could raise my dearest joy up againe, were he never soe weake, as I had experience of, if He see it fitt for us, although, indeed, my deare heart was then very weake; at which words my faintings renewed with my exceeding sorrows, for the feares of beeing deprived of this my sole delight in this world next under God. The Lord pardon my impatience in this conserne, which had for the three last past yeares bin weaning him and myselfe from this world, through great and manifold tribulations. Thus, betwixt hopes and feares, I remained till the next messenger came, at four a'clocke on Thursday in the afternoone, at which time I receaved the sad newes (for me) of my most tirrable losse that any poore woman could have, in beeing deprived of my sweet and exceeding deare husband's life.*

He departed on Thursday, the 17th of September, 1668, betwixt the howrs of eleven and twelve att noone; he beeing on the 2nd day of June ('68) fortey fouer yeares of age; we haveing lived a deare and loving couple, in holy marriage, almost seaventeen yeares. My deare husband's bodie was brought home to Easte Newton on Friday, the 16th of September, in company of many of our neighbours, gentrey, and other freinds. Those that weare about us and I did desire that his interment might be deferrd till we could acquaint our remote freinds and relations. But the doctor tould them that he had laid not long sicke, and taking of phisicke would hinder that. Those that were helpers to beare his corpes were of his kindred and relations : My brother Thomas Thornton, my brother Denton, my brother Portington, my cosen William Ascough, my cosen Ralphe Crathorne, my cosen John Craithorne, my cosen Bullocke, my cosen Ed[ward] Lassells. There was a very great congregation at that time, he beeing most generally beloved of his countrey;

* Here follow " Prayers and pettions upon this sad dispensation of the death of my deare and honoured husband" (vol. i., 271—273).

a man of great pietie, peace, honesty. There was a great lamentation for him, God haveing given him much love and affection.
But my sorrowes and laments cannot be weighed for him which
parted with the great and sole delight and comfort I esteemed
of my life. The Lord grant me some measure of patience to
sustaine, that I may not displease the great Governer of heaven
and earth, but desire to submit, for the Lord's sake, with resignation to His will; and in hopes of a joyfull resurrection at
the last day, then to be united in haleluiahs to the God most
High for ever. My dearest heart was interred in his owne
alley at Stongrave church, neare his mother and two sweete
babes, Christopher and Joyce. Buried on Friday, the 18th of
September, betweene four and five a'clocke, by Mr. Thomas
Comber, who preached his funerall sermon. The text was in
Ecclesiast. 12th, verse 1st,—" *Remember now thy Creator in the
daies of thy youth,*" etc., applieing it fittly to that occasion.
Lord, hee loves Thee the lesse that loves any thing with Thee,
which he loves not for Thee. (*St. Austin.*)

THE WIDDOWE'S PRAIER FOR HERSELFE AND CHILDEREN.

" The Just shall live by faith."   Mr. Thornton's motto and my owne.

Nisi Christus nemo. } None but Christ. } God.
Tout pour l'Eglise. } All for the Church. }

ANNAGRAME.

Christ and His Church in love soe well agreed,
That He for her, and she for Him, has bleed.
Thus imitate thy Saviour in His frequent love
And then thy joyes, my soule, will lasting prove.
Oh groundles deeps, O love beyond degree,
The offended dies, to sett the offender free.
But now
The Churche's head to heaven is gon,
Leveing her heere on earth alon,
Much like a widdow in disstresse,
Washed in teares, teares that expresse

Her dailie greifes, with sighes, to be deprived
Of her deare Soveraine, the world denied.
But what although thy Lord is gon
To sitt in glory, placed on His throne,
Has He not left His pledge of love
To thee His loyal spouse, His holy dove?
Bequeathed thee His sanctifieing Spiritt
For to conduct thy weary steps to inheritt
Those everlasting joyes He has prepaired
For thee?   A glorious tabernacle's shaired
Wherein noe sun needs shine, for He alone
Is all the light in that vaste horrison.
What then, if through a sea of brinie teares
Thou swimmest?   Hee'l free thee from all feares
Of sinking; canst thou but hold Him fast
In armes of faith, thou shalt come safe at last.
Nay, weart thou dead, yet shalt thou live
A life much more superlative
Then heart can thinke or tongue can tell,
Those glories all they doth excell.
I'le strive till death, but shall my feeble strife
Be crown'd, I'le crown thee with a crowne of life.

AGAINST THE FEARES OF DEATH.

Since Nature's workes be good, and death doth serve
As Nature's worke, why should we feare to die?
Since feare is vaine, but when it may preserve,
Why should we feare that which we cannot flie?
Feare is more paine than is the paines it feares,
Disarming humaine mindes of native might,
While each conceipt an ugly figure beares,
Which weare not evill, well vieued in reason's light,
Our only eyes, which dimm'd with passions be,
And scarse discerne the dawne of commeing day.
Lett them be clear'd, and now begin to see
Our life is but a stepe in dusty way.
Then lett us hold the blisse of gracious minde,
Since this we feele, great losse we cannot finde.

AN INDUCEMENT TO LOVE HEAVEN.

Leave me, O love, which reachest but to dust;
And thou, my minde, aspire to higher things;
Grow rich in grace, which never taketh rust,
Whatever fades, but faiding pleasure brings.
Draw in thy beames and humble all thy might
To that sweete yoake where lasting freedomes be,
Which breakes the clouds and opens forth the light
That doth both shine, and gives us light to see.
O, take fast hold, lett that light be thy guide
In this smale course which birth drawes out to death,
And thinke how evill becometh him to slide
Who seeketh heaven and comes of heavenly breath.
Then fairewell! world, thy uttermost I see;
Eternall love! maintaine thy life in mee.

A FAIREWELL TO THE WORLD.

Fairewell! ye gilded follies, pleasing troubles,
Fairewell! ye honored ragges, ye cristall bubbles!
Fame's but a hollow eccho; gold poore clay;
Honnour the darling but of one short day;
Beautie's cheife idoll but a damaske skin;
State but a golden prison to live in.
To vex free minds, imbroidered traines
And goodly pageants proudly swelling veines,
And blood alied to greatnesse is but lone,
Inherited, not purchast, not our owne.
Fame, riches, honour, beauty, state, traines, birth,
Are but the faiding pleasures of the earth.
I would be rich, but see man too unkind
Diggs in the bowels of the richest mine.
I would be great, but yett the sun doth still
Levill his beames against the riseing hill.
I would be faire, but see the champion proud,
The world's fair eye, oft setting in a cloud.
I would be wise, but that the fox I see
Suspected guilty when the fox is free.

I would be poore, but see the humble grasse
Trampled uppon by each unworthy asse.
Rich, hated; wise, suspected, scorn'd if poore,
Great, feared; faire, tempted; high, still envied more.
Would the world then adopt me for her heire,
Would beautie's queene intitle me the faire:
Fame speake me honor's minion, and could 1
With Indian angells and a speaking eye
Command baire heads, bowed knees, strike justice dumb
As well as blind and lame, and give a tongue
To stones by epitaphs, be called great master
In the last lines of every poetaster.
Could I be more than any man that lives,
Great, wise, rich, faire, all in superlatives,
Yett I these favours would more free resigne
Then ever fortune would have had them mine.
I count one minute of my holy leasure
Beyond the mirth of all this earthly pleasure.
Wellcome pure thoughts, wellcome my sadest grove,
These are my guests, this is the joyes I love.
The winged people of the skies shall sing
The anthems by my sellers gentle spring.
A praier booke shall be my lookeing glasse
Wherein I will adorre sweete virtue's face.
Heere dwells noe heartlesse loves, noe palefac'd feare,
Noe short joyes purchast with etternall teares.
Heere will I sit and sigh my weake youth's folly,
And learne to affect an holy mellancholly.
And if contentment be a strainger, then
I'le neare looke for itt butt in heaven againe.
Ah, foolish, faithlesse, fickle world, wherein
Each mottion is a vice, and every act a sin!

MY FAITHFULL SOULE'S WISH.

Oh, had I of his love but part
That chosen was by God's own heart,
That princely prophett David, hee
Whom in the word of truth I see

The King of Heaven soe dearely loved,
As mercy beyond measure proved;
Then should I neither gyant feare,
Nor lyon that my soule would teare;
Nor the Philistines, nor such freinds
As never were there Christian's freinds.
Noe passions should my spiritt vexe
Nor sorrow soe my mind perplex,
But I should still all glory give
Unto my God by Whom I live.
And to the glory of His name
Throughout the world divulge the same.
My walke should be but in His waies,
My talke but onely in His praise:
My life a death but in His love,
My death a life for Him to prove:
My caire to keepe a conscience cleane,
My will from vaine thoughts to weane:
My paine and pleasure, travell, ease,
My God thus in all things to please.
Nor earth, nor heaven should me move,
But still my Lord should be my love.
If I am sicke, He is my health,
If I am poore, He is my wealth.
If I am weake, He is my strength,
If dead, He is my life att length.
If scorned, He only is my grace,
If banished, He my resting place.
If wronged, He only is my right,
If sad, He is my joy and soul's delight.
In summe and all, all only Hee
Should be all above all to mee.
His hand should wipe away my teares,
His favour free me from all feares.
His mercy pardon all my sinne,
His grace my life anew begin.
His love my light to heaven should be,
His glory thus to comfort mee;
And, as 'tis writt, such honour shall
Even unto all His saints befall.

UPPON RASH CENSORERS.

Judge not thatt feild, because 'tis stubble ;
Nor her that's poore, and full of trouble ;
Though th'one looke baire, the other thin,
Judge not, theire treasure lies within.

GEORGE WANDESFORD—ANAGRAM.

Feareing God's Word.

(Seventy-six lines of verse, including great part of Sir Christopher
Wyvill's Sonnet.)

Of Mr. Thornton's affairs (ii., 29).

There was provission by a deed of settlement for maintenance,
education, and portions for the younger children out of Burn
Parke before marriage. By his unfortunate ingagement in that
affaire of the assignment of Major Norton, dated August 2,
1658, of the resignation of the Irish estate* of my father to pay
debts and 'portions and leguacies * * * * he was forced
to give Mr. Nettleton bond and judgment for his debt, and
entred into a statute. Whereupon Nettleton sued him to an
outlawry, and prosecuted my deare husband with soe great
mallice till he compelled him to take that coarce, which he was

* "And that estate, gotten out of the rebells' hand in Ireland, as allso possession
from Captaine Preston, son-in-law to Mr. William Wandesford executor. * * *
I have seen a great bill under his hand of charges uppon that account, which
account amounts to a great somme of monney, £3548 16s. 11d., since Aug. 1686
and October 1689, insomuch that he was forced to borrow great somes to
discharge those suits; * * * * he beeing bound to Mr. Nettleton and Mr.
Skinner, (a) of Hull, in £1000 to Nettleton, and £600 to Skinner, both in
statutes staple, and of a dangerous consequence if not paid punctually. As for
Mr. Skinner, I find his statute discharged by Mr. Thornton (entred into May 6,
1658) and paid and acknowledged before Mr. Charles (b) Foxley, maire of Hull,
April 27, 1668."

(a) William Skinner. merchant, and alderman of Hull; mayor in 1664;
died 19 Sept., 1680, æt 53 ; married, firstly, Jane, daughter of Mr. Foxley, alderman of Hull; she died in 1652.

(b) His name was William. William Foxley, alderman and twice mayor of
Hull ; died 24 Sept., 1680, æt. 71.

very sorrey to do ; that was, to sell the estate att Burne Parke, which was settled for his younger children's provission, and to pay with £1000 of that monney Mr. [Robert] Nettleton, which otherwise would have cast him into prison; that estate beeing sould for £2000.   As for the other part of the monney, beeing £1000, I desired Mr. Thornton he would be pleased to pay with it his two brothers, Thomas and John, and his two sisters, Elizabeth and Frances, theire portions with it; for I could not indure to see theire portions unpaid which was due to be don by his owne ingagement when they cut of the intaile to inable him to make settlement of marriage for himselfe, without which he could not expect a fortune with a wife.   But Mr. Thornton said he would not doe it, for he could purchase a rentcharge with it of £80 per annum of his nephew Ralph Crathorne, which was a great advantage to him, and pay his brother's and sisters' intrest out of that.   I was neither convinced nor sattisfied with that way, but rather desired the other, because that debt had bin sooner sattisfied, and his estate more cleare, and there portions paid.   But Mr. Thornton took his way with it, and it proved to be worse, and that rentcharge was affterwards sould to Mr. Danby to pay debts.   *   *   *   *   Mr. Norton had noe mind to act in that trust reposed in him by my honored father's last will and testament, beeing an excequetor; but, to be quit of that trouble, very politickly did persuade my unkles Richard and Francis Darley, who came over to Hipswell at that time, to advise my husband to undertake that trust and to free my uncle Norton of that trouble, and give Mr. Thornton (as they thought) a better advantage to gett his dues, being in my behalfe, and for my deare mother's, the greatest creaditor.   But alass! it proved otherwise to him (and that we feared), for he beeing a meke, peacable man, and did not love the trouble of mannaging of his owne, could not be able to graple with such spirritts as he had to contend withall in the trust.   *   *   *   *

What for the charge of solicitor, and journeys into Ireland, and high returnes, tooke up much of that monney was receaved there, and soe his own went to make it up; together with great trouble this created him, by my brother Sir Christopher

Wandesford's suing him for that estate, which was putt on him by his father-in-law Sir John Lowther, who would have had him to injoyed that estate of Edough,* without sattisfaction of debts or portions. And to that end, perswaded my poore brother to deny my father's will, and to come into that estate uppon the intaile. But this was soe hainous a thing, that the great God of heaven would not suffer it to proceed on to destroy soe just and honnest settlements in a family as my deare and honored father had maide. But when we were all ingaged in suits with Sir Christopher to preserve our just rights, and that he was in hopes we could not find the originall will in Ireland; beeing not then on the file, but taken off, behold! the goodness of our gracious God, in the very nicke of time, caused the said will of my father to be found out, which had bin of the file many years,† and thought to be burned by the rebells, or the Protector's soldiers, who had don soe to all the wills which was found then on the file; and it being of soe great consequence to many people and familyes, it will become me to keepe in memory the providences which prevented both our ruine, and that of many more, which might never have had there debts paid by Sir John Lowther's good will. But the accident was as followes :—

A discourse uppon the preservation and discovery of my deare and honored father's last will and testament, in the rebellion of Ireland, from the yeare 1640 *till the yeare* 1658 (ii., 36).

That my dearely honored father, the Lord-Deputy of Ireland, did make and ordeine his last will and testament in full power and strength of body and mind, with wisdome and piety, is sufficiently proved and attested, both by his servants and wittnesses at that time when it was made; as allso by many

* Now called Castlecomer.

† There is not a single will on the file between January, 1639-40 and 1650, except this will of Wandesford's. It was found again 1653.

wittnesses which was then liveing in Ireland* when Sir
Christopher did call it in question, beeing many yeares affter
the publication and proving the said will by the executor, my
cousin William Wandesford, in Ireland; all which time the said
will was put uppon the file,† and laid in the court for probat of
wills, as was order of law in such cases; but more perticulerly
my deare mother and myselfe was sommoned in to give uppon
oath (by Mr. Nettleton, one of the creaditors) to the court in
England, what we knew conserning the said will, whether there
was one made or not, and to declare our knowledge conserning
the same, which we did, before a master of chancery, at Hipswell, November 3d, 1658, our testimony being affixed by him to
the copie of the said will, which was writt out by my brother
George Wandesford in part, out of the authentique copy he had
taken out of the court in Ireland, and attested under the hand
of Sir William Reives, the then Master of the said court for
probat of wills; and had bin soe ever since the said will had bin
proved, Aprill 1st, 1641. The orriginall will, dated October 2,
1640, in Ireland, and was ratified and confirmed by my father
two daies before he died, in presence of many noble persons,
when he called to my cozen Wandesford to fetch it to him and
read it before him, then and there before them all declared it to
them to be his last will and testament, and did ratifie and confirme the same, and revoked all other wills but this, which
should stand and be in full power and vertue, and praied them
to beare wittness of the same, and sett to his hand before my
Lord Dillon, Sir George Ratcliff, my Lord of Ormond, my Lord

* Two of them, John Burniston and Ralph Wallis, were still living.

† " Remained on the file for severall years, till the yeare 1647, when my brother
George Wandesford went into Ireland to get a true copy of it, and not having
mony to discharge it, the said will was laid by in a chest by the clark who had
writt it out, and ther was secured for severall years of the warre affter my brother
George died, and non knew what became of it; upon which great suits and
troubles arose for the want of it, by Sir John Lowther's bad councell to my
brother Christopher Wandesford, who married his daughter, and would have
come into the estate by the intaile. But att last, by the providence of the great
God of heaven, this said will was discovered, and produced in the yeare 1653,
which did put an end to all the troubles. This is fully related in my 2nd
booke."

Bishop of Derry, cozen Wandesford, my deare mother, and many more of her servants and others, with strict charge to my Lord Bishop of Derry and my cozen Wandesford that they would see it faithfully performed, and to pay all his debts whatever, justly proved, be it by bill or bond in any other way due, and to be cairefull of his deare wife and four children ;* and this same charge allso he gave to his son George, as he and they would answer it to him in annother world.† Affter this so solemne and sacred a charge, they all answered that, by the grace of God, they would performe his command to the best of there power ; uppon which he gave it into my cozen Wandes-

* See pp. 22, 23.

† Prerogative Court of Dublin. Register Book 1626-1686, page 369.

1640. October 2. Christopher Wandesford, Esquier, Lord Deputie of Ireland and Master of the Rolls—had left his wife Alice £300 a year, by a deed executed a short time before ; refers to a deed executed on his marriage, by which Sir Peter Frechvile, Kt., Sir Edward Osborne, Kt., Mauger Norton, Esq., and others were named trustees ; affirms the same, and appoints John Lord Bishop of Derry, Sir Edward Osborne, his brother Norton, his brother William Wandesford, trustees for his children George, Christopher, John, and Alice, desiring the Lord Deputy Strafford to assist and aid them. To Lord Strafford, who was godfather to his son George Wandesford, £20 as a remembrance ; to the Lady Ann Wentworth £5 ; to the Lady Arabella Wentworth £5 ; to the Lady Margaret Wentworth £5 ; to his godson Lord Raley £— ; names his late grandfather Ralph Hansby, his cousin Michael Warton, his cousin Sir George Ratcliffe, one of the Privy Council in Ireland. To his daughter Alice Wandesford £1000, besides what he had given her before this will. His sons not to marry under age without their mother's consent. To his brother William Wandesford £30 a year. Hopes that his lease in Ireland will be continued to his wife and children ; names his house in Dammask-lane, Dublin ; his estate of Castlecomer, in Ireland ; and his manors and lands at Kirklington, Hipswell, Hudswell, Easby, Pickhall, etc. Gives to the churchwardens of Catterick, Yorkshire, the sum of £100 to form a stock for apprenticing poor boys of his tenantry at Hipswell. Desires the sum of £6000 to be raised and laid out in land of inheritance, entailing the same on his second son and his heirs male ; failing such, to the issue male of his third son John ; failing such, to the issue male of his late father ; failing such, to his own right heirs.

Codicil dated the same day, 2 October, 1640, as to a certain share of money due to him, which is to go into the bulk of his personalty.

Witnesses, John Burniston, Ralph Wallis. Proved in Prerogative Court, Dublin, 23 September, 1641, by the oath of William Wandesford, Sir Edward Osborne, knight, renouncing ; and is the only will on the file between 1639-40 and 1650.

ford's hand to lay by where it was.   These things I have often
heard rehersed ; and after my deare father's decease my cozen
Wandesford gave it into my dere mother's hand to keepe till
he called for to prove the same ; in which time, which was
about a quarter of a yeare, I had much occasion to reade it, and
be acquainted with the contents thereof, being advised to do so
by my deare mother, saing it conserned me to know it, for in it
was all the provission for me that I was like to injoy, which
I had by my deare father's noble disposition to me, who he
loved soe dearly.   Affter which time, my cozen Wandesford
came and called for my father's will, and said he would goe and
prove the same, but my mother must needs lay downe money,
for he had non till he gott out of the estate, and faithfully
promised to pay her againe ; but he never did that, nor £100
more he got her to borow for him, to mannage the Irish
estate with ; but had her bound with him to Mr. Edmonds,*
which, tho' he did get many hundreds from the estate of Castle
Comber, yett never sattisfied those moneys, but lett my deare
mother be sued by Edmonds many yeers affter, and gott himselfe fred, and left her in the lurch to the mercy of that Jew,
who sued her to an outlawyery, and put her to great greife ; who
was forced to pay £200 and all charges, beside the trouble my
deare mother had about that bussiness.   Alltho', when he had
proved the will, and had taken administration, he came to my
mother and (I beeing in the chamber) did solemnly protest,
with his hand on his breast, that, by the grace of God, he would
performe that sacred and just will of that holy, good man my
Lord Deputy Wandesford, to his uttmost ability.   But, affter
this, he went with his family to Castle Comber, and there lived
like a lord on the land, and receaved rents, and did what he
would amongst the tennants, but paid noe body, nor debts, but
cast them uppon my deare mother, which had all the hard
trouble of children, servants, debts, etc., while she lived in

* Probably Thomas Edmunds, secretary to the Earl of Strafford, the first of
that family who settled at Worsborough, co. York. See pedigree in Hunter's
South Yorkshire, ii., 290. Wilkinson's *Hist. of Worsborough*, pp. 32-54. He
died 9th Jan., 1662, aged 66.

Ireland, to her great damage and losse; and was ready to do all acts of kindness to the family, and for the honor of my father's memory. She staied in Dublin till affter the rebellion broke out in October 23d following; paid of servants, and bills and creaditors due befor his death, haveing sent my brother George, her eldest son, into England, with the countess of Strafford, in order to be with my uncle Osborne, for his better opportunity of education.

Of the loss of my father's Book of Advice, 1643 (ii., 41).

At Chester, my deare mother was desired by my uncle William Wandesforde to give him my father's "Booke of Advice to his Son George,"* writt with his owne hand, which he would keep for my brother George. She made many excuses, and would not willingly have given it him, but don it herselfe, as most proper for her. But, at last, she found him discontented, and was willing to oblige his kindness to herselfe and children, she commited it into his caire and custody, with charge to preserve it as the richest jewell she had, to be contineued in the family, and given to her son George on the first opportunity, which he did protest faithfully he would, but alas! it was afterwards in the warrs lost, as he said, with all his writings. But the sudainess and sirprize my uncle William tooke her in, did prevent her intentions of takeing a copie of my deare father's booke befor he gott it from her, and she was but newly come into England, and but a stranger, wanted time to take a copy, therefore desired to lett her have a copy of it from him, which he did promise her. Tho' the warres growing hot betwixt the king and parliament caused my uncle to fly for safety, and leave the said booke into the custody of somme

---

* "A Book of Instructions, written by the Right Honourable Sir Christopher Wandesforde, Knt., Lord Deputy of Ireland, First Master of the Rolls, then one of the Lords Justices, and Baron Mowbray and Musters, to his son and heir, George Wandesforde, Esq., in order to the regulating of his whole life." Cambridge, MDCCLXXVII. There are several MS. copies of it, one of which is in the posssession of Mr. Comber, of Oswaldkirk.

freindes with his owne evidences of all his estate, which the
parliament party seized on ; yet, blessed be God, I have great
cause to acknowledge His great goodness in the preserving one
copy of the said booke, which now I am soe happy to injoy, one
writt out by it.   And, altho' the manuscript itselfe has soe unhappily gon from the whole family, and that non of his chilldren
was soe happy to see our deare and blessed father his advice,
under his owne handwriting, to his deare son George, but myselfe, who read it severall times over, when in my mother's
keeping, the benefitt whereof I would not have wanted for great
riches; when I had his advice to us by his owne pen, and
esteemed it a great mercy to me in perticuler, whose councell
was most percing to my heart ; and when I could bear witness
myselfe, that his advice to his children was zealously practised
by himselfe in his life and holy conversation.   And it has bin
my great greife that noe good freind's pen could have leasure,
in those sad times, to write us an account to the world of his
eminent, holy, wise, prudent, and picous life and conversation;
whose virtues was soe eminent that he lives fresh in the
memoryes of all that knew him ; if it had been writ out 'twould
continue his memory for ever.   We must therefore rest ourselves contented in the injoyment of what he left behind him,
and since we are deprived of the orriginall of that excelent
manuscript itselfe, be thankfull for what we have of him, in the
copy which I obtained, by a providence, to my great joy;
praising the Lord my God, Who brought to my memory fresh
againe soe much of that good booke, which, alltho' I had not
seene, nor heard of, for many years, vidz., from the yeare 1641
till the year 1657 (or 1664), yett did those carracters remaine
soe deeply ingraven on my poore hart, that I could have testi-
fied the truth to have bin my honred father's meathod, stile, and
councell; and have gott it copied over, since I had it, for my
brother, Sir Christopher Wandesforde, his son, and for the
Earle of Straford, who desired them very ernestly of me.

*Of the providence to me in finding the copy of my honored
   father's Booke of Advice to his Son George Wandesforde
   (ii., 44).*

Uppon the agrement and compromise of all the suits in the
family (when the will was a-wanting, and affter it was found
againe, to our joy and comfort, and all belonging, who had an
interest in it), made by Baron Thorpe, and all things settled
betwixt Mr. Thornton and Sir Christopher Wandesforde, and
he ordered to deliver up the Irish estate on trust to performe
the will; they were to meete with Mr. John Dodsworth, of
Watlous,* who was, as a common friend, intrusted to keepe
somme writings for all partyes.   Mr. Thornton and my brother
Denton was to goe thither, in order to signe and seale writings
with Sir Christopher Wandesforde, who had yelded to pay my
thousand pounds out of Ireland, and to sattisfy Mr. Thornton
for Mr. Nettleton's debt (for which he suffred soe much, and
was soe much perplexed by him).   I say, when my husband was
then at Watlous, my cozen Dodsworth careing him into his
study to looke uppon his bookes, haveing a very fine library
there, my cozen Dodsworth tould him, "Cozen, I have one
little booke in my study, which is but a little manuscript—a
paper booke—a copie—but I valew it above all the bookes in
my library, and that is my Lord Deputy Wandesford's Booke
of Advice to his son George."   Uppon which my deare husband said that he had heard much of it, and a very high
carecter of it, but nere had seene it, and that his wife had many
times with tears lamented the losse of it extreamly, and would
be overjoyed to have but a copy of it.   Asking my cozen how
he had it, and came by it, because the orriginall was lost many

* Thornton Watlass, near Bedale, co. York, where the Dodsworths have been
for many generations the principal proprietors.   From a younger son of this
family descended Roger Dodsworth, the eminent antiquary.   See Whitaker's
Hist. Richmondshire, vol. ii., pp. 76-298.   This John Dodsworth was connected
with the Wandesfords through his marriage with a Hutton of Marske.   His
eldest son and namesake increased the connection by marrying a daughter of
Sir John Lowther.

yeares agon, as I tould him ; my cozen tould him the truth of
it, that it was indeed writt out in Ireland by his sonn* Timmothy Dodsworth, who was my Lord Deputy's servant, and one
whom my lord had a peculiar kindness for, intending to make
him his secretary. And when my lord had come home from
the councell table, did every night, for an houer or two, write
in that booke, before he went to bed. And affter that he was in
bed, made him read in some good booke, and instructed him in
it, and soe contineued till my lord was overcome with sleep, he
not goeing to bed till twelve or one o'clocke att night, and rise
again by five or six in the mornings. My lord leaving the
booke on the table at his goeing to bed, his son Timmothy
knew something of the subject, that it was of an excelent
nature, as this that came from him ; thought it would be of
great advantage to himselfe in poynt of instruction, bceing a
young man, and but comming into the world. And soe, without my lord's knowledge, did copy it over himselfe, as well as
he could, by nights, when my lord was asleepe ; and soe he satt
many nights up the most of it, to doe it, for he durst not have
don it, if my lord had discovered him. " I confess," said my
cozen, " it was a very bold part in him to doe it, and what he
ought not. But since it soe fell out that the orriginall of my
lord's booke was lost, I thinke it was very well, that we had
something of him, though it be not so perfectly writt as by
day, and might correct the mistakes that uer a scoller [would
make] where it is not true spelled."

Mr. Thornton begged the booke of him for me, and said he
would correct anything of that kind, and did assure him I
would take it for the hiest favour he could do me, and it would
be the greatest kindness in the world. Soe he lent it to him,
for me to have a month to read, and take a copy of. Which,
by great kindness, I gott my good brother Denton to do for
me, he writing it in carracters could not, for his other imploy,
gett don till severall years affter. I beging the kindness of
him, he gott it writt out for me, and I got annother copy writt

* Baptized at Thornton Watlass 27th December, 1618 (Watlass Register).
Although a younger son, the family estate came to his children.

by Mr. Smith for myselfe, and soe gave my son Robert Thornton that copie, which my brother Denton writt for me first out, to Cambridge.

Thus have I made a long discource of this booke, but not in vaine; for I humbly blesse and praise the name of my God for it, and that I have receaved a copy, which was don for a good end, tho' not in such a manner. But I am sure we ought to express our signall gratitude, in liveing up as neare as we can, both I and mine, to the pieous rules and dictates of our holy good father. And if the Rechabites retained so great a reverence and obedience for there father's commands, as they did, and soe obteined a blessing of there God in there obedience, oh! would to God He would please to indow the hearts of myselfe, my children, and children's children, and my father's allso, of his family, that He would give us all (that are of his seed) His grace to walke in His commandments, and in the wholsome precepts which he has commanded us by our blessed Father, which he was teached by the Spirritt of his God, and has confirmed it by his practice, and instructed us by his holy booke, that soe we may all injoy the said blessing on us and our posterity, which befell upon the Rekabites for there obedience, and that for Jesus Christ His sake. Amen.

Haveing, in the best manner I could, writ downe, for the use of my children, the mercys of God to preserve the copy of this excelent father of our family in memory amoungst us the blessing we injoyed in his life, and wherein he immitated the great father of the faithful, Abraham, to instruct and teach his house and children in the waies of God, and to command us by his holy writeings, a pledge of his lasting love and caire of our precious soules to all posterities, not only of us, but even of many more good people; O lett us, my deare children, walke worthy of all these favours of God, and learne to love God, feare Him, and serve Him with all our hearts, and to keepe His holy commandments, which not only teached us by His owne Word and Spiritt, but confirmed it to us, by the examples and precepts of this my deare and naturall father. I charge you, therefore, all my deare children and grandchildren, to keepe fast those good instructions, advice, and councells, which are writt in my said honored father's booke, and to make it your indeavours to walke answrable to those precepts in the frameing your lives and conversations uprightly and just, in your thoughts, words, and actions; and observe his wise and prewdent councells, which will be a meanes to draw downe God's blessings uppon your heads, and to make your families to prosper in this life, and by your pieous examples to intaile an etternall blessing uppon your seed's seed after you; that sinfull habitts may not poyson your younger yeares with those follies your age is too proue to, and too much incoraged by the vanities of this wicked age; and least those mercys you injoy by this holy Saint of God be turned into judgement; you haveing the true faith and light made known more unto you then the world: yet walking contrary to it may prove a greater condemnation in the day of judgement, who having receaved more knowledg of the truth, in so plaine, and easey, kinde, and oblciging tenderness of a deare father to his children, that it will be the greatest act of ingratitude to Heaven and your honored father's memory not to make this your rule to walke by, who left this carracter for the wisest, [most] vertuous, and justest man in his time. Oh then, lett not, I beseech you, his honor be stained in you that are his branches. Soe shall you, I hope, all receave the same reward of your vertue in heaven. Which I hope you and he may possess together, which is the incessaut prayer of her who is your most affectionate and afflicted mother, Alice Thornton.

Of my brothers George and Christopher, their different dealing as regards my honored father's last will and testament (ii., 50).

It is now more then time to returne to mention the preservation of the last will and testament of my deare father; who first tooke caire of our spirritualls in his booke, and then for our temporall estate by his will; disposing his estate in a just manner to all his children, and which had certainly bin soe performed, if not prevented by the succeeding rebellions in Ireland and England, that destroyed the estate, we should have had our education out of, and we was all of us obleiged to my deare and honred mother, who out of her joynture gave us all the bread we ate, and cloths, and all things we injoyed. For which great act of charity and affectionate kindnes her children can never enough acknowledge her goodness, nor speake too much in honor of her holy memory. Nor ought we to forgett our most humble thankes to Almighty God our Heavenly Father, Who contineued this our deare parent soe long, and to give her the hart to imbowell herselfe and estate for us; when the estate was seized on by the parliment, and so we all at a losse; when Kirklington was sequestered for my brother George, who they prosecuted, beeing for the blessed King Charles the martyr and sufferer.

But since I must take notice, where I left of, of the will beeing left on the file in Ireland by my cozen Wandesford, I must goe backe to speake of my brother George, eldest son of my father, and who went into France with Mr. Anderson for education, and staied soe long till there could not be any monney got out of the estate to suport him there, and therefore called home to my uncle Sir Edward Osborne, my deare mother's brother, beeing his guardian, joynd with my mother. After his returne to Hipswell, which was her joynture, he tould her " that he perseaved my uncle William Wandesford was much incombred with my father's debts and trouble, and the creaditors was very pressing, soe that he had a desire to goe over into Ireland on purpos to gett a true copy of my father's will, that he might see to do every one right, and to pay them there dues." To which my deare mother answred, " Son, it will be very well don of you to do soe, and God would bless you the better to do justice to all, and pay debts, as your deare father ordered by his will." Thereupon my brother George did goe into Ireland, about the year 1647, and at his returne home shewed my mother the copie of the said will out of the court in Ireland, and attested by Sir William Reives his hand, to be a true and authentique copy of the orriginall will of my father, S[r] William beeing the master of the court for probat of wills. But my brother George tould us he owed some mony to the court for the copying the said will out. My brother then saing to my mother, " Madam, I went into Ireland on purpose to gett a copy of my father's will and heere is one, and by God's grace I will perform it, to a tittle, as much as in me lyes, and do right to you, my sister and brothers, my uncle William, and to all the creaditors, according to my father's charge att his death." My mother said, " Son, it is a very good act of you, and you will be the happier in the good performance of it, and receave a blessing from God. But, in regard you must keepe that copie for your owne use, and your sister wants one to repaire to, I would have a copy of it, to keepe by me." My brother said she should have one, and that he would write it out for her, and, if he could not gett time, his brother Kitt, and John, and his sister, might gett it don amongst them. After which he began the copieing the will out, and with his owne hand writt on the outside of the leafe in great letters, THE WILL, APRIL 1ST, 1647, and then proceeded to write the first leaves, all with his owne hand, which copy I have yet. But the treaty of marriage being then began betwixt Sir John Lowther's eldest daughter and himself, he was soe full of bussiness that he never gott time to write out any more of it; but the rest of the copy was writt out by my two brothers, Christopher and John, and by myselfe, part of it; all our hands beeing at it; but the last was my brother Christopher's hand, as may apeare by his name at it, and writt " Copia vera," to testify the same.

The wittnesses to my father's will weare as follows :—John Burniston, Ralph Wallis, George Straherne, James Foxcrafft, Ezra Wollstone. And this very copie has bin ever since in my deare mother's hand and my owne, beeing forced to give our testimony uppon oath conserning the said will, when Sir Christopher Wandesford came heire, uppon the sad losse of my deare brother George, and that the authentique copy was delivered to my brother Christopher by my uncle William Wandesford; who, uppon the delivery of it to him, promised me and my

mother to lett us have it to take a copy by at any time, and
never denied to give us one a long time. But affter his marriage with that lady which his brother George should have had,
Sir John Lowther's daughter, Mrs. Eleanor, beeing many times
asked by myselfe and my deare mother when he came to Hipswell, that he would please to give us that copy of the will which
was my brother George's (and that he had gon into Ireland on
purpose to gett one out of the court, to do right to every one of
us by it), and allso he himselfe promised faithfully to us he
would do soe too, when my uncle gave it him in our sight, and
would lett us have it to copy one by it, after my brother George
his death; he would somme times have said, " We should have
it, and he wold bring it with him," and other times say, " He
had forgotten it; but indeed we should have it next time."

And afterwards, about halfe a yeare, I begged it, and
praied him for God's sake to lett me have it, for I could not
gett my dues of the tennants which was to pay me by my
uncle's assignment out of Kirklington, which he knew to be
true, and had gon with me to helpe me to get it of them before
he was mared. Then he tould me that " he had laid it wher
he knew not how to find it, nor knew not where it was, except
Sir John Lowther had it." At which answer I was much surprized, and much conserned, fearing some ill consequence to
follow to us, because he had got it into his hand. Tho' I was
hopefull that my poore brother wold not be prevailed with to
doe any thing contrary to his knowledge of the will of my
father, if he did but understand the thing rightly; soe I still
intreated him to look for it, and gett it from Sir John, but
durst not speake my feares to shew any distrust of Sir John.
But after this time my brother Christopher would never be
knowne that he had found the copy, nor had we any other, but
that which was writt out by us all, in parts, which we repaird
to on all occassions. It was about this time that the will was
begun to be questioned; tho' I believe Sir John had a designe
to have destroyed both the will and deeds of my deare father in
my brother George his life-time (as I have heard, and attested by
my deare brother George and my uncle), att the last time of

there meeting with Sir John Lowther about the termes of the match, which was the very last time of the treaty; for my brother George would not grant to that Sir John proposed, and soe they parted in displeasure. It beeing very late, they had there discourse that time, I thinke at Sober's in Richmond, and my uncle William fell asleepe on the couch, when Sir John Lowther and my brother George discorsed on there bussiness. At last Sir John tould my brother George that "he would never have his estate his owne, nor free to settle as he would, till his will and deeds of his father were all distroyed, and then he might settle or dispose as he would his estate."

At which motion of Sir John Lowther my deare brother, beeing extreamely offended, said, "Sir John, I will never do soe unworthy and unjust an action, nor have my hand in the destruction of my honored father's will and deeds while I live, and you shall never perswade me to it; and if I cannot have your daughter without it, I will never consent." "Then," said Sir John, "the bussiness is don," and parted, for that time and ever; for, God knowes, he was drowned in goeing over the river Swale, on March 31, 1651 ;* beeing most sad and misrable for all our family to lose soe good and honnest a man, who would not do an unworthy or unjust act, tho' it were in secrett, and for his advantage. That night, after Sir John had made this motion to my deare brother, as before, and my uncle was sleeping (as I tould you), my brother George awaked my uncle William, and chid him, saing, "You are sleeping heere, and never mind your bussiness, when all lies at stake. You little knew what Sir John and I have don; I might have destroyed you all, and you nere heed." "Why," said my uncle, "what's the matter?" My deare brother George tould him what Sir John said, thus: "Did not Sir John make a motion to me, and would have had me consent to it, for to destroy all my father's deeds and his will; and said I should never be master of my owne estate till I had destroyed my father's will and deeds?" Then said my uncle, "God forbid! did you yeald

* See page 65.

to do it?" "No," said my deare brother; "do you think that I will ever be such a rogue? God forbid! and I will see the old dog hanged before he shall ever make me to do soe wicked a thing, and soe, on some other words, we parted; and the bussinesse is at an ende, if he require such termes of me."

At which my uncle rejoyced to heare such resolute honest principalls from soe young a man, and that he would not gaine a wife, to do an unjust action, against his father's just will and testament. This one act doth speake much for the honor of my deceased brother's memory, and I hope he now injoyeth that blessed happiness of keeping his father's commands, when he was tempted to have broken them, and that uppon the advantage of a match, and to have advanced his temporall estate, if he had don it, by many thousands. But then he might not have had that blessednes, he, I hope, now injoys with the God of justice for ever. I wish this good action in him may be a president for my son and family to walk by, which makes me be more punctuall to sett downe the sircumstances of this story. And secondly, it too much confirmes the bussiness to proceed from Sir John Lowther advice and councell to my second brother Sir Christopher Wandesford, of conscallment of the copy aforesaid; and then they proceeded to search the Roles'-office, where the will was proved, and putt on the file, as I have related before. But since that time, in the yeare 1647 and the yeare 1652, or 1653, there had bin a great revolution and change or changes in the Government, since my brother George Wandesford had taken the copy of the will, as before related. And when search was made for it there, there was found noe will on the file, nor any footsteps of such a will; all things beeing changed by the Protector Cromwell and his instruments, and all those wills and testaments then on the file they found was all destroyed by the mallice of the soldiers and others. Soe that all the kingdome was att a most sad loss and damage, and many familyes was destroyed, for want of those settlements that was then a wanting. I supose this newes did not a little please them at Lowther, whose end it served, and forthwith putt these designes in agitation, declaring publickly that a dilligent search was made by Sir John meanes in the Roles' office in Ireland for the will of the Lord Deputy Wandesford, but there was non, nor the officers that was then in the office said there never had bin any since they came to it. This sad newes was very surprising and afflicteing to all the family (except to the heire), who came in very unfortunatly so to be, by the sudaine and lamentable death of the bravest person then in the North; and had often bin heard to say before his death, that "If he thought he should dy without issue he would cut the intall of, and give the estat to his brother John and myselfe, leaving him only what portion and anuity my father left him." But the will of our Heavenly Father be don in all things, for I never wished nor desired anything save what I had nobly given and bequeathed by my honored father's last will and testament. And that even now, by the want, or, as we feared, to be in danger to be lost, and so deprived of all the maintenances and portion which I was to injoy in the world. All the creaditors and relations was like to suffer in this generall calamity, who had not gott a copy out of the orriginall will, but was forsed to repare to that copy I mentioned, taken by my three brothers and myselfe, out of that authenticke [copy] my brother Christopher had given him by my uncle William Wandesford, which he pretended to be lost long before. Soe that Mr. Nettleton compelled my mother and myselfe to give in our testimony on oath before a Master of Chancery, whieh we did accordingly, to the best of our knowledge and memory, at Hipswell, November the 3d, 1658, which was fixed to the said copy, writ by my brothers, April 1st, 1647   *   *   *   which did make it fully apcare to the world, and to the conscience of my said brother (Christopher), that it was noe forgery, nor false pretentions, of a will made by his father, but such by which he himselfe did acknowledge in his owne behalfe, before he was come heire, and very strictly demanded his owne education money, as well as my portion, out of Kirklington. Soe that this consideration as touching his honor, and of that of the family in him, did much move my deare mother and myselfe, not to lett it apeare in publick as a wittness against him; but did putt Nettleton of as much as we could, and only kept it private, that but in case of absolute necessity never to apeare; out of our tenderness of affection to my poore brother, whose case, as well as our owne, we did lament, he beeing of too good a nature, and soe much imposed uppon by cunning pollocy; and not diserning the sin at the bottom of entring upon the estate, on the intalle's account, soe well as his brother George, did goe too farre in this affaire,   *   *   *   suing Mr. Thornton, my uncle William, and the trustees for the meane profits of the whole estate in Ireland; and laid it to there charge above twenty thousand pounds, which by my deare husband's bond to Mr. Norton, on the taking the assignment, did all fall uppon him, because he entred uppon the trust and the estate together.   *   *   *   While we were all in the sadest trouble and confusion immaginable about the want of the will, and just like to be devoured up by Sir Christopher Wandesford's suits (beeing egged on to that which he would have died before he had don it, before), Mr. Thornton haveing sent over into Ireland a solicitor to mannage those affaires, and to seeke after the inquiry to find the will, if possibly to be had. The name of this man was William Mettcalfe, a servant to my uncle William Wandesforde. The account he gave of the will was, that all those wills which were on the file when the Lord Protector's son, Richard Fleetwood, came over, not one of them was left, but all was gon, or cutt in peeces for tailors' measures, or any idle use, and had no regard to them; and, for anything he could learne, he feared that my Lord Deputy's will had the same fortune as those on the file had.   *   *   *

Of the maner how my honored father's last will and testament was found, affter the losse of it many yers (ii., 68).

   *   *   *   I tooke notice before, when my dere brother George had bin in Ireland to get a copy of the will, he said that he had not monney to discharge the court for the

copieing of soe large a great will, and that he would send the somme over to pay for it, which, as I remember, was £5 or £6, with fees, and all the charges belonging to it. But he could not gett monneys to pay with. We gott very little out of my mother's estate for her selfe to live on; and soe the warrs came still on, and my poore brother George was forced to fly for safety from one place to annother, till his sequestration was gott of by the meanes of my uncle Richard Darley, who traversed it for him. And noe sooner that was of, but he goeing to write the acknowledgement of his gratitude to him, but in goeing over to Richmond by the wath at the end of the grownd of my mother's pasture, a flood did arrise while he was in the river and overcame him, and he was lost. The perticulers is more at large related by me in my First Booke of my own Life.* And that money was never paid into the court, but remained a debt all that time. The clarke, to whom the fees was due, for the securing of his monneys, did keep the will of my father, with the probatt of the same, by my cozen Wandesforde, of the file, and laid them very cairefully up in a large iron-bound chest, together with many more writings of the said nature, deeds of evidences, which belonged to persons of quality, suposing those that wanted them would inquire for them. This same clerke lodged at one Mr. Kerny's house in Dublin, and fell sicke there, and, before he died, owing this Mr. Kerny somme monney for his table, called to him, and tould him he owed him moneys, but could not pay him, for he had a greate deale owing to him for those writings and deeds. And that he gave him into his charge an iron-bound chest with the key, which he charged him to have a great caire of, and to deliver them into the hands of such as should inquire for them, and assured [him] they were of soe great valew that the parties would pay well for them, and that he could not lose by them. The poore clerke died, and Mr. Kerny still kept the chest under safe custody, and non came to inquire for there writings, and there was such a disturbance in Ireland, and that city of Dublin, that, till there

* See page 65.

was somme peace and respit from troubles, he did not see fitt
to looke into the chest.   But now, as it was soe ordered by our
good God in His Providence for our releife, was the time that
Mr. Kerny did first open this chest, finding many deeds and
wills and evidences, put up very safely; he takeing them all out
of the chest, till he came at the very botom of it, and findes a
large stately writing in five sheets of parchment, and, looking
at the bottome, the name of my Lord Deputy Wandesford, with
his hand and seale, and which was [attested to be] his last will
and testament; finding allso Mr. Ralph Wallis his hand as a
wittness to the will, with four other men's hands to it; allso
the probat of the said [will], as it had bin out of the court, and
put there for custody.   Mr. Kerney, knowing Mr. Wallis his
hand, went forthwith to him, and asked him if he knew my
Lord Deputy Wandesford [his hand].   Mr. Wallis answred
" Yes, he had reason to know," and spake greatly in his incomium.   " But why doe you ask that question ?"   Mr. Kerney
said, " Doe you know your hand when you see it ?"   " I think
I doe," said Mr. Wallis.   At which Mr. Kerney produced my
dere father's will and shewed it to him.   Uppon this Mr. Wallis
cryed out, " Oh, my deare lord, how joyfull am I to see this
blessed hand againe," and with affectionate teares he kissed
his deare lord's hand and name, saing, " I will be deposed of
the truth of it, that this is my lord's last will and testament,"
and that he himselfe ingrossed every word of it, beeing written
by his owne hand, and that it was the last act his lord did, to
confirme and ratify the said last will and testament.   Saing,
with a sad heart, for the want of this will, to sett all right
amongst the family, we were all most destroyed.   Asked him
how he came by it, who tould him all the said sircumstances as
before related.   To which he answered, " It was the greatest
providence of God that it was of the file in those sad times, for
they would have bin destroyed; and was allso the mercy of
God to have it now found and restored againe, which he hoped
would be a meanes to preserve that noble family from ruine for
want of it."   He did allso assure him " He should be gratefully
paied for those moneys due for the copy Mr. George Wandes-

ford had, tho' God knowes what a loss there was of that brave gentleman in that family." After this, Mr. Wallis did with speed and great joy acquaint Mr. Burniston with it, which did much rejoyce of its beeing found, and attested his hand as wittness to it also. * * * Soe Mr. Burniston did write to my uncle William, and William Metcalfe writ with speed to Mr. Thornton, and the sircumstances of the strange preservation of this excelent will of my dead deare father. Which most happy newes was soe great a joy to my deare mother and myselfe as was not immaginable. * * * According to Mr. Wallis's promise to Mr. Kerny, all his monneys due to the dead clarke and himself was by my husband's order to William Metcalfe fully paid, and by advice of Mr. Wallis and Burniston the said orriginall will was againe putt on the file, with all the essentiall scrimoncys belonging to it; and there, I hope, it will remaine preserved for the use of the family for ever.* Butt it was a long time before Sir John Lowther and my brother's agents was sattisfied of the truth of the said will beeing found. And they putt us to a great deale of trouble and cost to produce wittnesses, and such evidences on oath that compelled them to be sattisfied of the truth of the thing, which we were forced to prove upon oaths of Mr. Kerney, Mr. Wallis, and Mr. Burniston. The adversarys to it, beeing unwilling to alow soe great a blow to there designe as to enter uppon my father's estate without sattisfaction of all dues out of it, therefore was raised in court objections against us of forgerye and fallshood, with designe to cheat the heire of his estate and right; which suites and charges and objections lasted for severall yeares against my uncle William Wandesford and my deare husband, to the great loss and damage of us all. * * * The mercys of my gracious Father in heaven did still contineue to me and us, in beeing pleased to blesse the indevours of freinds, and moveing the

* It is on the file, the only will between the years 1640 and 1650.

"A copy of my letter to Mr. Graham to desire him to write to my uncle William Wandesford to deliver up Mr. Thornton's bond about the affaires of Ireland, which Sir Christopher Wandesford had given him sattisfaction, Jan. 26th, 1668-9" (iii., 214).

heart of my brother Sir Christopher Wandesford to be inclinable
to an end, and to have the state of the case to be made knowne
to Baron Thorpe, who tooke cognizance of the matter, and an
agreement was stated amongst us.   *   *   *   There beeing
three deeds then made, viz., on by Sir Christopher Wandsford
to Mr. Thornton, bearing date April 15th, 1664; the second
deed by William Mittchell and John Hall, dated April 16th,
1664; the other deed by William Mitchell and John Hall,
April 16th, 1664.   *   *   *   I having due to me in all by
my father's will and testament the somme of £2,500 as portion.
Besides, I ought to have by his will a sufficient allowance for
maintenance and education, till I came to the age of twenty-one
yeares or marriage, which first happned, with consent of my
deare mother; to be maintained according to my degree and
quality.   Which maintenance I never yett gott one penny of it,
tho' due for many years, soe that I was not furthersome for
that, yet it doth still remaine due to me.   *   *   *   If
Mr. Thornton had onely stucke to my mother's intrest of £300
per annum out of the estate anuity for her life, which was due
for nineteen years affter my father's death, and was first charged
on the trust, beeing in lieue of the estate due by law for thirds,
and soe settled by my dere father by deed of anuity, and confirmed by his will.   The somms which was due to her beeing to
the valew of six thousand pounds, I heard Sir John Lowther
promise my mother for it fifteen hundred pounds for to quit her
intrest there.   I do beleive she would have accepted of it if left
to herselfe, but the same parties which advised Mr. Thornton to
the taking on him the trust, did advise my mother to the contrary, and so she did not accept of Sir John's motion, when he
was to pay her that monney all downe at a payment.*   However,
she would have made over her dues there to Mr. Thornton, by
which he might have entred on the estate in her right, and soe
have had an intire intrest before debts, however might have bin
sharers with them.   Allso, there was a right due to my poore

---

* " My mother gott not one penny of all that great right to her, nor Mr. Thornton neither, but was quite lost from us by this assignment." (Book iii.)

brother John Wandesford of £6,000 out of Ireland, which fell
on him by my father's will, when Christopher became heire, by
my brother George Wandesford's death without heires, as now itt
was, and he made me, his only sister, his excequtor, and gave it to
me.   Besides, there was my owne portion of £1,000, which was
to have bin paid from that estate without dispute.   Now, if all
these intrests should have failed, it would have bin strange, and
an unaccountable thing, when there was such an estate worth
two thousand pounds a yeare to pay it out on, besides a great
colliery.   *   *   *   We have great reason to blesse and
praise the Lord our God that it was noe worse, which it would
have been without doubt, had not Devine Providence so ordered
that the will of my deare father was first out of harm's way,
and of the file, when those lawless times indured ; and yett to
be found in due time, when we were like to be overthrowne by
our adversarys, and even in the nicke of time to be produced,
to preserve us, and all who had an intrest in it, from destruction.   Therefore we may say, in regard of this Providence of
the will, as a good man said of himselfe, " Had it not bin lost,
we had bin lost ; and had it not bin found againe, we had bin
lost."   Thus mercys express themselves by meanes, with meanes,
without meanes, and above meanes, all to the glory of God our
great Creator.

Of the grand mercy I had in the first Sacrament at Easte Newton
affter we built the house, August, 1662 (i., 196).

Since the sad and dismall times of distraction in church and
state, the people in most of the northerne country was much
deprived of the benifitt of those holy ordinances of the Word
and Sacraments ; but especially of the latter, which, with the
use of the Lord's Praier, was wholey laid aside, as under the
notion of reliques of idolatrie and popish supperstition.*   Soe

---

* De la Pryme, writing under date of Sept. 16, 1697, says :—" I have heard it
from many ministers and old people that the sacraments of baptism and the
Lord's Supper was so regarded in Cromwell's time that they were in many towns

that least wee should offend God by serveing Him in His own
way and command (supperstitiously), and pray to Him in His
owne words, there was found out another manner of worship,
by presenting to His Majestie praiers contineually out of our
owne braine composed, and that with not premeditation too
often. And the Lord's Praier was by too many despised as
drie and insiped; by others neglected out of a compliance
with the times. Alsoe, the Holy Sacrament, which was the
testimoniall of the highest act of our Saviour's love to us lost
men, was had in contempt, as uselesse to the Church of Christ,
through some men's high flowne puritie and gifts, imagining
themselves above those ordinances, who was comd allready into
the state of perfection. In what a condittion then may it be
thought the true Church of God was in heere in England, and
the members thereof, when we weare cutt off from the comfort
and joy we receaved in and by the holy and reverent use of
these transendant ordinances, given and apoynted as His last
will and testament to us, and all His who should be pertakers
of the benifitt of salvation through His bloodshed; and the
breach of His loveing command, *Doe this in remembrance of
Me*, when in and by the use thereof, it was the comfort and
confirmation of all those holy martyers and saints of God which
suffered persecution for the testimony of the gospell of Christ.
Noe wonder then if we were brought into such plagues and confusion in this land, whoes pride was soe great, and devotion so
dead; but we who thirsted affter these waters of life, did still
all these times affter my deare mother came to Hipswell, as
well as at Weschester, injoy this blessing, through the mercy of
God; even all the time of my mother's life, to my exceeding
great sattisfaction and comfort; but affter her death and my
comeing from St. Nicholas into my owne house at Easte
Newton, which was above two whole yeares, I had not had any

and places quite left of. In many towns the Lord's Supper was not administered
for ten or fifteen years together, and the people, I mean especially the presby-
terians and independents, did not take any care to get their children baptized,
so that quakerism and anabaptism spread mightily," etc.—Diary of Ab^m de la
Pryme, Surtees Soc. Pub., vol. liv., p. 151.

oppertunity of receaveing. For there was not then any minister
at Stongrave which did administer the Sacrament, nor had don
there for many yeares, soe that I was holy destitute of an
opportunity to performe that comfortable, refreshing duty which
my soul longed for, and greived much for the want thereof;
and withall, beeing in such a languishing condittion, as I
formerly mentioned, without any spirituall helpe from men.
* * * But I could not obteine this happinesse in regard
that the ministers had not given it on this side during the
warres; nor was it againe established heere since the comming
in of the king. Neither, indeed, had wee any minister settled
at Stongrave, our parish church, which was a great greife to me,
that had never bin soe long deprived of all these publicke ordinances; nor was I in a condittion to travell any whither. Soe
that I called to mind that good man Dr. Samwaies, who had
given the Sacrament last to my blessed mother, desireing his
company at Newton for that necessity; who accordingly came
with Mr. Browne, and divers others, with whome, and my deare
husband, we did receave the pledge, I hope, of our salvation, in
the Supper of the Lord. Through which meanes I was much
comforted, helped, inlivened, and quickned, from that blacke
vaile of unbelcife, which clouded my hopes of etternall salvation. * * *

*The godly man Mr. Daggett att Kirklington, minister there.
His life and doctrine, sickness and death (iii., 31).*

It was my honoured father's great caire and indeavour to
provide a most wise, godly, and learned minister to supply that
great parish in the caire of soules att Kirklington, for the right
instruction and bringing them up in the feare of God, and the
true church and faith professed in England; arming them
against the scismaticks, and Scotts, and presbiterians, then
predominant; which, under hand, in there principalls joyned
with the papists. At this time, while my deare mother lived
there, we had the great happiness to live under his ministry
beeing of no smale conserne to our poore soules to have such

excelent doctrine joyned with his holy and pieous example, which was like another Saint Athanatious, to be a true light to our church and family, in the midst of the mists of those accursed practises of all contrary dissenters.

Which, next to the holy instruction and godly precepts and sweete exemplary examples of my ever-honored parents, I must attribute much of my true bottoming and confeirming my greene and younger yeares, to be strengthened and established in the true faith of Christ, to that most holy and zealous preacher of God's Word, who directed my steps aright, and teached me in the practices of the primitive times, and comforted us to indure afflictions, and not to be wavering in that true faith which was once delivered to the Saints. But alass! his doctrine was contrary to what those proud people taught, who, when the Scotch and parliament soldiers laid like caterpillars gnawing at our heart and religion till they had swallowed us up, while we were under there tyrany. The affliction which laid uppon this good patron of the church did ly soe heavy uppon him, that the greife bore his spirit downe, and by degrees brought a decay uppon that excelent person, by a decay of his vitalls, and fallen into a consumtion, but bare it upp with soe great a patience, that it was not perceaved by any, tho' he, finding his strength to abate, had bent the subject of his discourse for severall sermons to comfort our hearts against the feares of death, and to prepare us with patience on the loss of our freindes. Text, 1 Thessalonians, chapter iv., v. 13 : *" But I would not have you ignorant, brethren, conserning them which are asleep, that yee sorrow not even as others which have no hope."* He had gon through all the severall parts of his text severall days, and was intended to conclude it the next Lord's day, but God had another part to play ; and to shew us, by his example of holy dieing, as he had of holy liveing and preaching, when we non of us feared his death, had made ready to goe to church and heare him preach, was speedely called to his house to vissitt him on his sick bed ; which was soe sirprissing to us, not immaginable ; but it was the will of God to bring him to this bed, and we in great affliction for him, who to lose at that time was almost death to us. But he, sweete saint, seeing us thus sirprised, lifted up himselfe as well as he could, and said with great chearfullness of sperritt, with his hands and eyes errected up to heaven, " He was ready for his Master's call; he had don his indevor to serve Him in his station, and ministry of His holy Word. And tho' this was to others a sodaine change, it was not soe to him; he had indeavoured with St. Paule to walke uprightly, and to walke before Him soe as to give no offence, to keep a conscience voyd of offence, both towards God and man; and that he thanked God, he had lived soe that he was not ashamed to live, nor afraid to dye." With many other excelent saings, and prayers to God, for himselfe, my mother, and us all, and his parish, and this kingdom; that God would please to restore truth and peace againe in this our land. About the time of day, when the bell was ringing to church, att that time (9 a clocke) it was sent to ring this sweete soule's passing peale. And thus departed that sweete servant of God out of this miserable life to receave a crown of glory at the hand of Him who shall say to his sheepe, " *Come, yee blessed of My Father, receave the kingdome prepared for you.*" And blessed be the Lord our God, for the life, doctrine, and piety of this servant of God, by whose meanes many was taught the way of salvation. And amongst the rest I have great cause to praise and blesse and magnify His glorious name for ever. " *Blessed are the dead that dye in the Lord; for they rest from theire labors, and there workes follow them.*" Oh Lord, let me be one of them.

But now, affter the death of this pieous minister of God's Word, there fell uppon my deare mother and her family very many troubles and afflictions, for all the caire and conserne to provide for a godly and religious orthodox devine to be receved into that province, to discharge that weighty place which had bin soe much under the eye of Providence, never to want such; and was her great indeavours where to be furnished. At that time it pleased God to poynt out such an one, whoes name was Mr. Mickell Sydall, who had married my father's stuard's widdow, Ellen Hunton, liveing att Kirklington. He offred his service to performe that part, to interre that good man Mr. Daggett,* and preached his funerall sermon. Who did doe it with much sattisfaction, and could preach excelently well, soe that my deare mother and brother George heard him with great pleasure and approbation, as all others. That liveing ever belonged to my forefathers of the Wandesfords; soe, belonging to that family to present to it, of right decended on my deare brother George, who was the eldest son of my father. But he being under age then, had appointed by my honored father's will to be his guardians Sir Edward Osborne and my deare mother. In pursuance of theire power and right to present to the liveing, they did, with my brother's consent, judge him, this Mr. Siddall, fit to that liveing, and gave him a legall presentation to it, in form according to law in those cases. By vertue of which he indeverd to gett induction and institution, but he was tould that there could noe minister injoy a living without the consent of the parliament, who then did assume all power and authority, as well in ecclesiasticall as temporall consernes in this poore kingdom; hereby, not only robing the king of his throne and kingdom, but added sacreledge to God, as they had don rebellion, making all manner of crimes triumphant, while they sate in the seate of that they called parlement, without a head, a king, or governor, or house of lords, but ruled and overawed all lawes, equity, or justice. In this circumstances was the whole kingdom, and we, as the rest, truckled under this slavery. And this time did Sir Thomas Fairefax usurp the power of the sword against his gracious king, and made lord generall of the northern army. In former times, my deare mother had bin acquainted with himselfe and lady, soe she made application to him as a freind, conserning the bussiness of the living, by way of pettition; that since that liveing was voyd by the death of Mr. Daggett, and the right of presentation was in the guardians and the heire, she begged the favour of his excelency to grant that request to her, that the minister they had chosen might be permitted to injoy

---

* Mr. Daggett and Mr. Siddall have been mentioned before. See pp. 58-61.

P

the same accordingly. But, instead of granting her pettition, gave her a flatt deniall, saing that the parliment did not thinke fitt to trust the power of disposall of livings in any but themselves, and so he tooke the freedome to send one to it himselfe, which was a most inhumaine part. But when that man he sent (Clarkson) came to the church to prate, for preach he could not, beeing nothing of a scoller, the poore people in the church was soe greived, they came all out of it, and left him; nor did they ever goe againe to him, who, they said, spoke and railed against the Lord's Prayer in Yorke Minster, saing that they were all damned that used it, for it was popish invention. When he had uttered those railings against the Lord's Prayer, and blasphemous speeches against this most holy prayer, which was spoken and taught by our deare Saviour Himselfe, when He was on the earth, there was a poore old woman in the church att the time, when she heard him, rose of her seate in the ally and shooke it in her hand, ready to throw it att him, cryed out, " They weare noe more damned then himselfe, old hackle backe," and made him come down with shame. But affter this man was in a manner hissed out of the church att Kirklington for his blasphemous speeches, he was forced to turne out, and would have had Mr. Siddall to have undertooke the preaching and the cure, when he should have halfe the benifitt to himselfe, and Mr. Siddall the other halfe. But Mr. Siddall did abhorre all such sacrilegious practices. When he saw noe good to be gott, as to the confirmation of his presentation, called to mind of a freind he had bin very intimate and kind, from beeing scoole-fellowes; whose uncle was a great stickler in the committee and parliament house, whoes name was Alderman Hoyle, and of so daring and confident an humour for this rebellion, that he had too great a shaire in the king's blood, as appeared to his ruine affterward. Butt at this time, which was but at the begining of theire reigne, this Hoyle satt with them, and had a great vote, beeing a man through paced in there practices, and a deepe presbiterean. Had one Nesbitt, which was of that stampe too, which man was the man that Mr. Siddall made use of, uppon the account of confidence in his freindship, who made him believe he would be faithfull to him, and uppon his application and desire that request, he would solicitt his uncle Hoyle to gaine the parliament's consent, that he might injoy this living according to his presentation. He did fully promise to doe this act of kindnes, and was well assured that he could prevaile with his uncle, who, he said, could have any thing granted that he desired of them; was confident that he could gett this don for Mr. Siddall. Uppon which hopes he rested a long time; and att last putt Nesbitt more fully for a positive answer; was tould "that he had don his endevor to his uncle for Mr. Siddall to gett him that request granted as to obteine it for him, to injoy it as it was given by my brother and my mother. But truly, his uncle tould him it would not be granted that Mr. Siddall might have it, because they would not let any have the power to bestow livings which was suspected to be delinquents, but would present to them themselves, soe that it was in vaine for Mr. Siddall to trouble himselfe any more about it, and if he would take his councell not to doe it." Which unexpected returne of Mr. Nesbitt was very much trouble to Mr. Siddall, and he tould him that his patron was at under age, and had never don any thing contrary to the parliament, nor my lady neither, and wondered why they should be suspected. He answered he knew not; but the parliament was resolved not to doe it, and had thoughts to bestowe it otherwise. Thus went of all the sincere freindship (of a pretended one, but non in heart), for beeing halfe Scott by birth, and a strict presbyterian by profession, Mr. Siddall was not aware of this duble deceipt in him, both as to nation and oppinnion. Soe that it is a true beleife they both have a false quarter in them; and this Nesbitt made it fully appeare, both before God and man, who, while he made Mr. Siddall, good man, beleive he was speaking for him, all that while was acting for himselfe, and to gett this living for himselfe. He haveing, under the notion of freindship, gott some foot steps in his discorse, how to bend his way, tooke advice of his freindes, perceaving that Mr. Siddall and we all were of the church of England (which he mortally hated), knew by the clew how to wind up his information, and uppon that bottom proceeded against us all.   Which was a peice of the greatest treachery being acted against a poore family, that cannot be paralled but by his owne nation, who first betrayed his sacred majesty king Charles the First, and then sold him, and imbrued theire hand in his innocent blood.   But his uncle Hoyle and himselfe had time enough to repent of this guilt of the king's blood, tho' God did not give him the grace; for, affter that horid murder, he bceing one of the deepest in his actings and consent, yett when his conscience flew in his face for his wickednes, was never quiet night or day, but still cryed out, " He saw the king follow him without a head," and said he had no hand in his blood; but sometimes looked backe, said, " I am damnd for the blood of the king," and, as we were truly informed, died in this manner as if distracted, but never could find ease, nor repentance, or comfort, tho' all the godly clargy was about him.   God deliver us from blood guiltiness, and this above all !   And, as we were creadibly informed, did affterwards hang himself,* out of con-siousnesse of his cryme he was guilty of against that innocent martyer, whose blood yett cryes against this guilty nation. Nesbitt, affter some yeares injoying the liveing of Kirklington (but not peacably), died† of a sad distemper, in vomitting up his very excrements.   As to the making way for Nesbitt to gett the possession of the parsouage of Kirklington, it was found the most plausible to be don by proveing my dcare brother George Wandesford to be a delinquent to the parliament; by which meanes he not only forfited his right to present to that liveing, but allso thereby forfited all his whole estate, which struck att the family, roote and branch: which profitable prospect to injoy this poore gentleman estate, was an undeniable argument to prevaile for the guift of this liveing to Nesbitt by the parlia-ment, who gained soe well by his information, and such was his

* Alderman Hoyle hanged himself in his garden at Westminster, Jan. 30, 1649-50. (Drake's Eboracum, 172).

† Rev. (Philip) Nesbit, minister, buried in the chancel on the south side of the Communion Table, under the broad stone; his widow, Susan Hemingway, buried 19th April, 1683,—in St. Martin's, Micklegate, York.

art he used, that he prevailed for a sequestration to issue forth uppon my brother George, my brother Christopher, and my mother, and my brother John (then a child), and myself, which shewed the height of malice and covetousnesse, to grind the face of the poore (which att this time was fallen uppon us), beeing but lately fled from the horrid Irish rebellion, wherein we were designed to have bin murthered, and escaped that missery, we fell under this second persecution by the factions in England, which may be accounted from the roote of the said popery, which designed a catastrophy uppon England, allso to the true Christian faith. * * * Nesbitt gained his desire, and by a fallse wittness obteined his sequestration, soe makeing him incapable to present to the liveing, and thereby it fell into my Lord Fairfax and the parliament's hands, who immeadiately presented him to that noble living of Kirklington, of £300 per annum, and cast Mr Siddall quite out, by a speedy sequestration of him also. * * *

Of my husband's sisters, and Mr. Comber's coming to Stonegrave,
A.D. 1663 (iii., 70).

Forasmuch as I was by Divine Providence disposed in marriage, soe remote from all my owne relations and freinds, whereby I might be in a suffering condittion for the want of theire advice and assistance, either in my temperall affaires, and I was hereby exposed as a stranger to the severall humors of those factious spirritts, which was altogether fixed amongst whome I lived and was placed, there beeing not any of the profession of the church of England. As for the first match of Mr. Thornton's father beeing all strict papists, so oppisitt to our faith both to intrest consernes, whos daughters carried of a great part of the estate from Newton by the large portions, haveing £1500 a peece, beeing three of them, matched to the best gentlemen of the county, papists, vidz., the Cholmleys of Bransbey, £800 per annum, the eldest daughter was married to ; the second daughter, my sister Margrett, was married to Mr.

Crathorne of Crathorne, of £800 a yeare; the third daughter, my sister Anne, married to Mr. Langdale, in Holderness, of the best family of that name, and had as much estate as theire sisters, of a good house and quality. All soe well disposed of, with good portions out of the estate, and yet had more expectancys of injoying the whole as heires, if theire father had not married againe affter theire mother's decease, who, on her death-bed, gott her husband to settle such vast fortunes uppon her daughters, even to the ruine almost of his estate. Butt great and beautifull woods were destroyed at Newton and cutt downe to pay them portions, which disfaced that land.

Butt, affter his first wive's death, Mr. Thornton was advised by his freinds to marry a second wife,—Sir Richard Darley, of Buttercrambe, his elldest daughter,* a very good and vertuous woman, by whom he had four sons and two daughters, all of which had portions out of my husband's estate of about £1500, besides maintenance and education.† And my mother had a faire joynture of all Laistrop; and but a portion of about £400, as I have heard, if ever was paid. All these were brought up in the way of strict presbiterians, Sir Richard Darley beeing, with his family and sons, actually in the way of the Long Parliament, and I feare had too deepe a hand in the Scottch faction, and bringing them into England to reforme this church, in the way of rebellion and Scotch presbitry, enimyes to our church, episcopacy, and the kingly government. In this juncture of time was my fortune to be amongst them; and how I came to bring myselfe into it I have made a full relation before, when my marriage was laid in the skaile, to redeeme my deare

---

* Elizabeth, dau. of Sir Richard Darley, by Elizabeth, dau. of Edward Gates, born 3 Oct., 1597 at Buttercrambe, married at Stonegrave, 2nd, Geffery Gates, of the parish of Cottingham, Esq., 26 June, 1638, and was buried there 11 May, 1655.

† "As to the provission Mr. Thornton gave for the maintenance of portions of his younger brothers and sisters, it may be seene in his owne account booke, having disbursed many and constant sommes for their maintenance and intrest, and portions amounting to large sommes, more then ever my children ever had out of there father's estate, or any of my owne portion or fortune, beeing so deprived of to our ruine." (Book ii.)

brother's estate from the tiriny of our oppressor, by the sequestration of all that was a freind to loyalty or the Church of God then established in England. But since I was thus disposed, it became my duty to stand my ground in a strange place, and amongst strange people, and that I was resolved to doe, by God's grace and divine assistance, never to yeald to temptations of either faction. And tho' I had soe great trouble uppon me to defend the intrest of my poore children in the right establishment of the estate uppon them, as I have declared in part in this book, but more att large in the severall relations mentioned in some papers of collections from the first allterations from the articles of my marriage, yett these things did not sinke soe deepe with me as the danger I should leave them, in poynt of theire beeing right principalld in matters of faith and doctrine of the true orthodox religion heere established, and of which I ever owned myselfe to be a true professor, and a faithfull member; and therefore could not be any way acceptable to any of the other dissentours when I first came hither to Oswoldkirke. The house [beeing] not ready att Newton, we weare under my brother Denton's ministry there; who was a very good man and a good preacher, but was only ordained by the preisbitery ordination, and so I durst not adventure to receave the holy Sacrament of him att that time, not beeing episcopally ordeined; wanting that benefitt of my salvation, which I thirsted affter, till two yeares affter the death of my deare mother, till, by God's blessing, I had the happiness to receave it first att my owne house at Newton, by Dr Samwayes, as I have related it in this booke, with my humble gratitude to God for that inestimable bennifit of my redemption. Nor had I the opportunity to receave the Holy Sacrament affter this time, till, by Providence, Mr Bennett* came to Stonegrave, and gave me it the first time in that church, about Easter, 1663; soe that I wanted the cheife foode of my soule to comfort and strength my faith, and nourish me up to life everlasting; haveing all that time bin exersized with many crosses and accidents, happ-

---

* Gilbert Bennett instituted 19th March, 1662-3.

ning from those which was oppositt to my faith and religion, which I was like to undergo with great difficulty, beeing exersized with variety of humours, intrests, and suspitious eyes, as well on the account of my differing in judgement, and for my assiduous caire to prevent the ruine of my children by the alteration of setlements. Soe this contineued to my great trouble, till, by God's great goodness and providence, Who provides a salve for every sore, did looke on my affliction with pitty, and caused Mr Bennett, which was then our minister by the king's guift of Stongrave living, did see it fitt to send us his curate to officiate in his stead in this parish, and who constantly preached and baptized, and delivered the Holy Sacrament. Mr. Bennett gave my husband a most excelent carracter of his learning, abillitys for God's service, and his guifts in preaching, with a very high incomium of his wortheness to performe that holy function, which, tho' he was young, yett he was able to performe duty as ably as those which was much elder. When my deare husband had receaved this letter of recommendation, it made him more acceptable, from soe grave a person as Mr. Bennett, and much more sattisfied, and all the parish, with Mr. Comber, affter he preached his first sermon : Text, 19 Psalme, verse 7, which he made an excelent peece of work of it, which Mr. Thornton and the whole parish highly commended, and had ever affter a great oppinion of him. The time which Mr. Bennett sent him to Stongrave was in the yeare 1663, about the month of October. Affter, he was receaved into the parish, and preached constantly both ends of the day, besides constant prayer on Frydays, and on Wednesday. He expounded methodically uppon every holyday throughout the yeare, and catechized all the children and youth in the whole parish, which we had not bin used to that good way, tho' much desired it, and the youth much improved by his catechizing. Att the first he was tabled att Stongrave, att George Masterman ; from thence he removed to Ness, to Mr Tullye's, who was muche in love with his person and preaching; soe contineued for some time there, which was a great deale of paines he tooke in comming from thence to Stongrave so offten in a weeke, beeing two miles from

the church, which my deare husband considered to be to much
to hinder and breake his studies.   With all, I have heard him
say, "It was a great pitty that he was obleiged to be with such a
kinde of a rude house, and too much company, and such as was
not fitt for him, beeing a scoller and a civill man, did much conserne his sircumstances should not be better accomodated
then he could be in that house."   Besides, he haveing a valew
for his learning, and parts, and injenuity, would make him a
very good companion to divert him in his retiredness, and too
seariouss a temper, which he was naturally troubled with sometimes, when he was vexed about the suites and incumbrances on
him by the deed of Mr. Norton's assignment. Soe, consulting
with my brother Denton of this affaire, it was concluded to make
the motion from Mr. Thornton that he should be invited to come
to have his table att Newton, which my husband would give him,
with a horsse to be kept, winter and sommer, if he would please to
come and live with him, and to performe family dutyes of prayers,
and catechising the children.   Which motion was accepted
of on both sides, and was concluded on betwixt them before I
ever heard anything of the matter, till he was to come by my
husband's order; but I hope in God this was soe ordered by
Providence, that those good offices was performed by his endeavours, which was an occasion of a blessing uppon this family,
and instruction of them, and teaching them in the way of piety
and religion. My deare husband beeing well pleased in his
chearfull company, reading, studdy, and other pleasant accomplishments, which diverted him, and very acceptable to his
jenius, besides the daily performancy of prayers and reading the
Scriptures, and repetitions of sermons, all which things was very
acceptable, both to God and good Christians, with great comfort
to ourselves and children. Mr. Thomas Comber came to live att
Newton with Mr. Thornton about the time of March the 19th,
1665, and soe contineued, and was heere att Mr. Thornton's
death, in a painfull way of studdying and reading, improving
himselfe in his studdyes in this retyred course of life. And in
this place he began and finished his learned bookes of meditations uppon the Litturgy of the church of England, 'The Com-

panion to the Temple and Allter,' which pieous peece of worke I hope God had given a blessing to, and has bin a meanes to bring in a great number of the dissentors from our church, which had soe great prejudice against us for it that they would forsake our communion, nor by noe meanes would either heere devine service, but rediculed, scorned, and abused it; calling the whole service " a dry morcell," " cold meate," nay, " popish superstition," and soe blaspheming that sacred order of our holy faith and church, and the Holy Scriptures themselves, which is soe fully proved to be the ground and substance of our devotions, compiled into this sett forme for an excelent rule and guide to our public devotions.   I hope, as the benifitt was great to Mr. Comber to begin his first yeares and youth in this our private family, in which he injoyed the benifit of soe early a studdy and ministry, soe the blessing of God will, I hope, goe allong with his endeavours for the generall good of soules in many thousands, and convertion of many enymyes.   Soe I hope allso, he shall receave the due reward of his labours, by converting of soules and bringing many to salvation by the grace of God, given by his meanes and indeavours.   This was allso one happy effect of this worke, began at our house at Newton; that whereas my deare husband had bin brought up in a way of the presbiterian prejudice against these holy formes of prayers in our litturgy, and indeed of all formes (but what use in extempory by him and others), uppon discourse with Mr. Comber, and hearing his questions answered soe well by him, he putt him uppon the first desire to heare what he could say by way of inlargement uppon each of the prayers, which did give him so great sattisfaction that he ever affter had a more honorable esteeme of our prayers, and was willing that it should be used in our family, and from thenceforth did never neglect the receaving the Holy Sacrament with me att the church in public with the people, and allso in private with me in the house, uppon occasion of my sicknesses, or when we could not have opportunity to receave it at the church att our public communions, which we never omitted, since Mr. Comber came, to · receave it four times in the yeare, which never had bin don before, but only att Christmas and Easter. Butt he brought them to four times in the yeare, vidz., att Easter, att Whittsontide, att Michlmas, affter the gathring in of the fruits of the earth, to returne God our thanksgivings for His blessings of the fruits of the earth, and then att Christmas. * * . * My husband tooke great delight in his facetious company and exercize of his religion, and injenuity, and severall times would say to me and others that Mr. Comber, beeing a man that tooke such delight in his studyes and learning soe young, he was confident, being a man of such learning and parts, would come to great preferment in the church, if not to be a bushopp. About the yeare 1666 his time was completed, he was to commence Master of Art, goeing up to Cambridge to take his degree, beeing of Sidney Colledge, where he was much admired, and did come of with great applause, haveing bin assisted to that worke by some of Mr. Thornton's freinds, who was kinde, and loved him for his preaching.

There was much discourse then, when he was att London, that Mr. Benett would only leave a curate att Stonegrave to read prayers and give about £10 a yeare to officiate that place, and soe to save the £30 a yeare, which he now gave to Mr. Comber, he giveing in all to him £40 per annum. Uppon which Mr. Thornton was soe much conserned that I herd him affirme, if we might not injoy Mr. Comber still, and a preaching ministry, he would not live at Newton, but goe where he might injoy it ellsewhere. About Whittsontide, 1666, Mr. Bennett came to Stongrave* in order to receave his tyths then due, and brought one Mr. Roose with him to assist him in that bussinesse of the parish. My deare husband, finding Mr. Bennett's inclination to doe as before expressed, and that nothing but faire tearmes could doe with him, and haveing a perticuler respect for Mr. Comber, consulted with my brother Denton, a wise and prudent person, what to doe in this case; who,

* "Who before was resolved to marry one of his daughters to Mr. Calliss, (probably, Thomas Callis, Rector of South Dalton, 21 March, 1654-5, conformed), and for her portion to give her Stongrave living, haveing one in his owne countrey." (Book ii.)

uppon mature deliberation, judged it the best way to obteine his desire in providing for his owne sattisfaction in that poynt, which was to see if Mr. Bennett might be prevailed with to lett my dere husband a leace of the liveing for twenty-one yeares or his life; to pay him the rent of £100 per annum, and to find a suply of a minister to preach and to performe all dutyes belonging it. They came att length to this conclusion, and a leace to be drawne up in order to a resignation of the liveing affterwards. * * * But beeing that year's tythes due to Mr. Bennett then, he would not signe a leace till he had that rent of one hundred pound paid to him,* which Mr. Thornton did not know of, neither any one but myselfe, and Mr. Bennett, and brother Denton, who paid it from me. Which I did to a good end, to obteine the settlement of soe good provission for the gospell, and this family. Which £100 was paid this yeare, as apeares by Mr. Bennctt's acquitt of that date, June 25th, 1666. Affter this matter was stated about the liveing, and Mr. Thornton had obteined a leace, and resignation of this liveing of Mr. Bennett, the charges whereof was most of itt discharged by me, both myselfe and husband was very diligent and indus-treous to gett the presentation granted of the king, who, by the great affection his majesty king Charles the 2nd bore to my uncle, my Lord Fretchevill, he obteined the grant of it for Mr. Comber to succeed Mr. Bennett affter his deceace, which, by God's blessing, we did obteine.+   Indeed, there was many

* "Mr Bennet stuck uppon the whole yer's profitt due at Whitesontide then, and unless Mr. Thornton would pay a hundred pound then att entrance, he would not grant to tearmes, which my brother Denton knew my husband would not grant, nor, indeed, had it to pay." "I procured this monney out of my dere mother's land, which I lett Butterfeild have a leace of till it was run out." (Book ii.)

+ "We did both desire my Lord Frechvill, my good uncle, to procure the perpetuall advousan of the living of the king, that we might have it anexed to his estate att Easte Newton, a benifitt soe great and desirable in the consideration of this family, that Mr. Thornton indevored to get the same confirmed by the king, Charles the 2nd., which my deare lord did joyne with us in, and solicited the bussinesse soe farre, till he writt me word he had soe good and kinde a master of the king that he would deny him nothing in his power to grant; but my lord had taken advice in the thing, and councell told him it was in the king's power

obstacles and hinderances mett withall in the way to hinder it, but att length, by great strugle, the Lord granted to have it obteined, to the great satisfaction of my deare husband and the parish.   But before this bussiness of the liveing happned, Mr. Comber beeing then att London and knew nothing of it till att his returne home, he called at Southwell and was intreated by Mr. Bennett to bring downe the leace from him to my husband.

(Book ii.) Nevertheless I did ingage Mr. Comber that when ever he should remove hence to some other preferment,* that he should part with the liveing of Stongrave to my son Robert Thornton, which would be an excelent advantage for his spiritual as temporal preferment.   For as I had begged him of God, so did I make it my uttmost endeavours to have him fixed in so good a station as neare his own place of birth and his forefathers.

He had receaved a letter from Mrs. Anne Danby, who was then his great freinde (pretended soe, however,), whos advice he was ever inclined to observe, as from a wise and prudent freind. Tould him he might, in her judgement, be a very happy man in a wife,† if he could prevaile to obteine in marriage for her cozen Alice, which was very promising and vertuous, and tho' she was a little too young, yett a few yeares might worke that; and her parents having soe much respect for him, it might be very advantageous for him to settle himselfe in this place, where they would be industerious to promote him to as great prefer-

to sell the advouson for his time, but noe more, it beeing anexed to the Crown, and could not be aleinated, but if Mr Thornton would have it don, he could gett it for £300. When we heard it was noe otherwise to be gott, but subject to a change uppon the king, we did not prosecute the designe any more."—(Book ii.)

* "But we were very ready to shew our indeavours to bring him into the way and eye of preferment, and to that end I made it my request to my deare lord Fretchvill to accept Mr. Comber for his chaplain, which he pleused to doe for my sake, and gave him a confirmation by his pattent." (Book iii.)

† "Offered himselfe to bring a match about with Mrs Katherine Farrer, which she tould him would be of great advantage to him; * * and insinuated soe much that she gott his sermon notes or heads, and then writt them over, and called them her owne; soe did she with him about his Coates of Heraldrie of the Nobilitie of England." (i., 242.)

ment then ellsewhere.   And much more to this purpose, which she had conjectured by discorses from us.

She then, having made this motion from herselfe to Mr. Comber then, as well as long before, that had incoraged him to begin this sute, which he had don soe long since as when my children was att Yorke for to learne qualitye, when Hannah, my maide, wated uppon them, and can witness the ·same by his frequent letters and tokens, and his offten treats of them, as the dates of all those letters may testify to each other, and that by my consent—how then, (with what impudence and treatchery to me and my husband, and these two who she had incoraged and begun this designe of a marriage betwixt us all), could she afftterwards sit as a judge against us, in hearing and repeating such horrid lyes* was forged against us? and not

* "By these lyes I was ruined and brought to a public scorne, as poore Susana was before the judges who was wronged by the fallse witnes of two wicked Elders. Even so was I and my poore child accused and condemned before her in her chamber by her servant in a most notorious manner, and all my chaste life and convcrsation most wickedly traduced, soe that she railed on me and scoulded at me and my poore innocent child, before our faces, with the most vile expressions could be immagined, while we had noe time or liberty to justify ourselves against them, but with our teares and sorrowes to committ our cause to God, Who knew all hearts, and would justify our innocency to be wronged, and would, I hope, judge our enymyes for the false lyes and calumniations against us. Such was the fury of Barbary's mallice against us that with a brasen face she impudently cryed out against me, and said 'I was naught, and my parents was naught, and all that I came on was naught,' which, when I heard these blasphemous speeches against the unspotted honnor and holy life of my parents, it more wounded me then my owne, for they was long sence died honnorable deaths, and lived holy examplary lives, whose honor is to all etternity. To have them blemished for my cause was like a sword to my soule, soe that I fell downe before the mistres and her maide, in a swound for my great calamity. * * I was soe extremely tormented with these slanders that I mourned and wept soe extreamly, with her loud clamors against us, that my deare husband, beeing then walking in the hall, heard the sad tradegy and abuse was putt on me, and in a great anger he came to the dore of the scarlett chamber and broke it open, and hearing my complaint, and seeing my condition, did kike that wench downe staires, and turne her out in great rage for soe wickedly doeing against us; [and called Mrs Danby a most impudent, and unworthy, ungrateful woman; p. 210] and had certainly kiked out Mrs. Danby too, but that I begged he would not, because she had noe house nor harbor to goe to, and I trusted God would revenge my cause. Which few would have done; but that my God bid me render noe man evill for evill; but, 'if thy enymy

to vindicate our honors against all such, with detestation to resist and stop their mouths, by declairing the truth, of her knowledge, or to have tould me and my husband, or Mr. Comber of them? * * * Even for the discharge of my duty to my husband and children was I thus persecuted by hell, and by those I had fed at my table, and clothed with my woole, and succoured in all distresse, as wittness this woman's many letters of thanks, for many yeares together, till she turnd my unjust enemy, for her sister turning her out for her ill tongue.

hunger, feede him,' etc.; for God is suficient to revenge my cause, and in Him I did beleive that He would doe it, and to His glory be it spoken, has don it, even uppon this wretched woman, her maide; whose remarkable judgement was knowne to all, that her conscience flew in her face when she was a dieing at Malton. For she (p. 65) married to one John Pape, had one child, which fell sick of the smalepox, like to have died of them, but only had them come forth all of one side of all the body from head to foote, extreame full, but not one on the other side at all. After it was cured of them on the one side, and the child was well againe, perfectly, it broake out of the other side with the smalepox as full as before, and my brother Portington had much to doe to save her from death. This was counted a strainge accident, but, within a while this mother, who had in so vile a manner abused myselfe and childe and Mr. Comber, fell very sicke of a strong feaver, and had the advice of the doctor and my brother Portington, and all the meanes could be to save her life, but it would not doe; and when she saw she must dye, she cryed out to many that was present, her husband being one, ' that she was damned for what she had don to wrong myselfe and Mr. Comber, in those lyes she had heard and had reported them, tho' she knew we did not deserve them, and she was now damned for them if we did not forgive her, and begged of God and us to forgive her, and if we would not forgive her she was damned for them, and it was long of her mistress which sett her on against us.' * * When I was tould of this extraordenary way of punishment which the Lord chose to punish her sinn and confess His justice therein, it could not but worke a great terror in my soule to see the great reward of sin heere, and, without true repentance, heereafter." (iii., p. 191.)

" This is most certainly true, that if she had beleived him to be guilty of any of those horrid slanders which she cast on him and me, which she had long before that heard and examined, she would never have admired him soe much, and indeavored to match him to the best freind she had, as she ever called Mrs. Batt; but from that time forward she studied how to doe us a mischeife." (iii., p. 197.)

" Madam Danby comeing to see me on May-day, said * * ' Her owne insufferable pride, which would not be humbled, and her railing blacke-mouthed wench that came to Farnly and abused her there, these all did cause her to cast her out. * * She would gett Kit a place in a troope, and give them theire furniture, and fitt him with accoutrements of all things for it.' " (i., 241.)

Had not this deceaptfull person a designe to have taken this opportunity to breake this match, and that in the most bace and scandalous way immaginable, takeing this advantage by the consealment of this intended match to bringe her owne end about, to make us to be forced to keepe her, who had disobleiged her sister-in-law, and abused her with her tongue, and turned herselfe of there, for her owne and maid Barbara's odious railing.   Since which time of her beeing discarded from Beedall, where Madame Danby had kept her and her family severall years at £60 a yeare, and affter Tom Danby died, she would have given her the same, or more, uppon my solicitation for her to her sister; but she would not accept under £80 a yeare;* uppon which refusall of Madame Danby's kindness she did utterly forsake her; which was by her own willfull act. * * * Thus did this woman† requite my kindness and charity, who I had for twenty yeares space bin her continuall daily and faithfull freind, as I have made some remarkes in my first booke of my widowed condittion sett downe, but a longer account I was forced to give of my disbursements and maintaining of herselfe, husband, and children, on all accounts whatever, for the space of twenty yeares; they beeing cast out of favour by Sir Thomas Danby on her inveigling his son to marry her in Virginia,‡ and her pride affterwards, declared by Mrs. Batt to me. But I could make it appeare I had laid out for her occassions and necessitys and her family above £400, which was out of my owne patrimony given me by my deare

---

* "but stood upon her high horse." (i., 245.)

† "After my deare husband had turned her out of my house for her wicked ingratitude, * * this woman made her complaint to her brother Francis Danby att Yorke, and sent him to Newton to move my brother Denton to be a meanes to bring her into my house and favour, and if I would receave her againe into my house as formerly, she both could and would vindicate my honor and innocency to all the world." (Book iii.)

‡ The maiden name of this lady was Anne Colepepper, niece of John, Lord Colepepper, Master of the Rolls, who died in July, 1660. Her husband was Christopher, second son of Sir Thomas Danby, and their children eventually inherited the Danby estates. Mrs. Danby, against whom Mrs. Thornton has so much to say, died in York, and was buried 15 Nov. 1695, at Holy Trinity, Micklegate.

mother, with household goods, and all necessarys for house, meate, and clothing, and in theire tabling and expences of journeys to gett theire estate againe from Madam Danby, which, by my meanes and great assistance, her son Abstrupus* Danby did doe, and allso by my meanes did he make a deed of assurance to his father for his releife, and his mother and his younger brothers' portions for them, when he should have gotten the estate, by the vertue of those settlements made before he gott his father's estate, he haveing bin cheated of it by Madam Danby her freinds to make it over to her affter her husband's death, which, by my great indeavours, cost, and pains I gott her son and them to obteine. He and his father both vowing that if ever he should gett his estate againe, he faithfully promised, and did ingage to pay me all that ever I had soe kindly laid out for his father and mother and selfe any way; and if I could have suspected his fidelity conserning his dues to me, I would have made him to have given bond, as he was then willing. Butt, not doeing that, I affterwards beeing in a great straits for some debts for my son Thornton, affter he had gotten and injoyed his estate by my meanes as aforesaid, I made some application to Sir Strupus Danby in my distress for my son Thornton, for monney to releive him with, and shewing my account laid out for himselfe and family to the somme of £400. Yett I would have bin contented to have accepted £150 for it, paid in three years' time, if he would have don that. But he would not yeald one penny more, to releive myselfe or my dere son, but £50, which was gained with much indeavours by my son Comber; and that neither, but uppon my releasing all my other monneys which I had disbursed as before for himselfe and family. Which is very hard measure, not to pay me what I was forced to borrow, and pay interest for to releive him and them from starving, which just debt I now want to releive myselfe in my needs. * * *

In Dafeny Lightfoot's honest and kinde letter, since she went from me home, dated Nov. 8, 1668, she tells me that tho'

---

* Afterwards Sir Abstrupus Danby.

she came away from me, and left me soe weake and sicke in bed, yet there was a providence in her returne home ; for my deare Aunt Norton had discoursed with her conserning my affaires, and had heard how all my troubles increased by the envious mallice of Mrs. Danby, being turned out of my house by Mr. Thornton before his death for her wrongs and abuces of me (iii., p. 139).

Butt tho' she had vowed to Mr. Thornton and herselfe, that as she had never seene or knowne any thing evill in or of me in her life, soe she never would repeate or report of any thing of that nature she had heard from others, but would vindicate my honor as long as she lived ; yett now, contrary to her oathes, she was soe full of malice against me and Mr. Comber, that she made abundance of storyes up to Dr. Samwayes against him, because she could not prevaile to breake the match with my daughter, and to have had him married with that Mrs. Batt* she brought to Newton to breake this match, and have that woman to have him ; she having gotten Dr. Samwayes to dine with her att York, had soe farre prevailed with him against Mr. Comber, that he, good man, was imposed uppon by her cunning tongue, to gett my lady Yorke, my neare and deare kinswoman, and my daughter Alice, her god-mother, to be incensed against him for some misdemeanour of his to some person (but cleared me) : that it was not fitt my daughter should be married to him, and that the doctor would come with my aunt to breake this mattch, desireing my aunt that she would goe with him to doe it ; but my deare aunt answred that she would not goe to Newton till Dafeny came home, which would tell her the truth of what she knew of all things if she saw any motive in him, that he did not carry as a wise, sober person, but if he did so, as she saw no other cause to beleive, she would not designe to prevent it, which might, if itt please God, prove a happy match for her, he beeing soe great a scoller and ingenious person. Butt Dafeny did heare that there was a consperacy betwixt Dr. Samwayes, Mrs. Danby, and my lady

* "Mrs. Mary Batt."

Yorke, that my lady Yorke was resolved to come over to
Newton, in order to prevent that the match should be broken,
and that she would come to pretend to have my daughter Alice
with her to Yorke, under the pretence of haveing her to be
confirmed, and so to have prevented the match to goe forward.*
This my deare aunt tould Dafeny; upon which Dafeny did in-
form me of it, and said all those which was my freinds, and
sincerely wished me well, did advise me to putt an end to this
long designed match, which would make them dispaire of
breaking it. And she designed to come over to Newton the
next weeke, and doe me what service she could, but in the
meane time to be very carefull of my daughter, for it was intended to steale her away, and all contrivances was laid out for
it. * * * Poore honnest Dafeny writt me a second letter
to lett me know * * * the caball was soe great that
Mr. Darcy was for turning Mr. Comber out of the house.
* * * But Mr. Comber valewing his honor, and vindicating
the same, having this beleife the designe was from Mrs. Danby,
who solicited him for Mrs. Batt, did make soe full proof of his
wronged innocency, and beeing very earnest to have the bussinesse concluded, desired me to take those true freinds' advice
that knew the state of all things amongst us, and, by the grace
of God, to lett the marriage proceed with what conveniency of
speed and secrecy we could; and he did not doubt if, please
God, he lived, would make it appeare by his life and conversation to confute all those odious scandals against him; and that
if I pleased to give consent, he might injoy his long desired

* "My lady Yorke * * about the 23rd of January, 1668-9, writt a very
kind and compassionate letter of her intentions to have come to have seene me
(which was in order to have broake the match) but was prevented by a great
could, and was very ill, which prevented her; yet she desires, now she is att
Yorke, to have her god-daughter to be confirmed by the bishop, it beeing her
duty to present her to him, and she had bin confirmed herselfe. And she had
heard news of her god-daughter Alice that she could not beleive, that she was
allready married. * * I returned her thankes for her caire of her god-daughter
Alice, in her desire to have her confirmed, and that I hoped Almighty God would
please to give me leave to receave that holy ordenance myselfe, and then she shall
have the benefit with me." (iii., 156.)

happynesse in my daughter in marriage, that she should live as comfortably and as happy in a deare and affectionate husband as if she had married to a great estate; for ritches could not make one happy without the grace of God, which he humbly begged to guide and goe along with him in all his wayes. * * * And another arguement he used, that whereas he had sett his desires and affections soe on her vertues and deserts, that he had denyed himselfe of the proposall of Dr. Stones* his daughter, which had £1,500 portion, and severall others for [her] sake, soe he did beleive, if I should be taken away by death, which God forbid, that her seeming freinds would strip him of her, and he never should obteine his soe long desired happiness.   And he saw under what afflictions I lay in, which made him doubt very much my illness should prove dangerous, and soe begged of me to grant his request.   I tould him, uppon his former assurances, and that I should advise with my freinds in this conserne, which was soe great to me as the disposall of my eldest childe, and begged the assistance of God to direct me for the best; and withall did expect the full performances and agreement of those articles, long since drawne by him, to be drawne in forme of law, with his bond for performance, to establish all her fortune uppon my daughter and her issue male or female, with other clauses for the benifitt of my deare son Robert, her brother.   To which he answred, "That he was not only willing to make the best assurances I would or he could, of her owne fortune, but was resolved, if ever God inabled him with an estate, to settle all he had uppon her and hers."   And this very promise he made to Sir Christopher Wandesforde, my brother, soone affter his marriage, which Sir Christopher Wandesford tould him he did expect of him, "Because, Sir," said he, "my niece marryes you to a great disadvantage to her, she haveing a present fortune, and borne to a partition of her father, as next heire to her brother, we shall expect this from you."   To which discourse Mr. Comber did possitively answer, "he would doe all that her freinds thought fitt in this

* Christopher Stone, D.D., Chancellor of York, Rector of Boeford, Aug. 27, 1669 to 1685.

perticuler, and did binde himselfe in honor and conscience to performe by the grace of God." * * * Soe advising with my brother Denton in the case, and making him fully acquainted with the indevors to take my child from me, knowing all the wrongs and injuryes don to me by Danby and the rest, as allso of the conserne of marriage from the first motion, uppon all these reasons did joyne with us in our affaire, and was willing to draw up and ingrosse all those tearmes, articles, and agreements before marriage, to which Mr. Comber had freely and fully consented to, and drew up the first draught of those articles with his owne hand, when he had first hopes of this marriage. Therefore how fallse and abominable was those scandalls, imputed by hell and his instruments, which said I was forced to marry my childe to hide my owne blame or dishonour. * * * Having uppon mature deliberation, with the advice of my true freinds, considered of the aforesaid reasons, [I] accepted of the motion of this marriage, with the full consent of my deare childe. * * * Affter we had poured out our pettitions to God att the throne of grace, He was graciously pleased to returne an answer to us, and soe ordered all things soe as we hoped would tend to His owne glory and our comfort. * * * Thus, what our enimyes used as a meanes to breake our good designes, God our gracious Father made it the more speedy to bring it to passe ; and we were willing that affter Dafeny came to Newton, Mr. Comber should goe to Yorke to procure the license to marry my daughter Alice, which day was on the fiveth day of November, in the year of our Lord 1668.* I hope, it beeing don of a most eminent day to our Church of England, being that day in which Almighty God did shew His miraculous deliverances of all our soules and bodies, with the whole Church of God in the Christian world from that Gunpowder Plott of the bloody papists, for our utter ruine and subvertion, when we had cause

---

* " A good omen, that Mr. Comber, takeing out a licence, uppon a most remarkable day to our church for her deliverance from the popish Gunpowder Treason."

to rejoyce. I hope in God it may prove as prosperous, blessed, and happy to the good and establishment of the truth and light of God's gospell, to be established and preserved in this my poore family and blood, and shall be confirmed in me and mine as long as the world indureth, and for the salvation of all the soules that spring from my deare husband and myselfe, which will be the great blessing I humbly crave of God, for the Lord Jesus Christ His sake. Amen. And, instead of aboloshing, to establish the truth from all sects, schismes, herisics, or popery, or prophanes whatever. Because this man had sett himselfe to write soe many learned and orthodox bookes, to vindicate our religion and the truth against all fallshoods, he had contracted many enymyes against him, as well as, I hope, he had bin a meanes to convert many (yea, very many) from theire errors in there life and doctrine. Which workes of his in the church is of more valew and riches to it then if he had build great and rich ediffices, and given much indowments to its temporall advantages. For alltho' those are of great honor and esteeme, that are great patrons to the church in any kinde, yett it is of more glory to God and advantage to the soules of men to be a meanes of salvation to poore sinful soules, and to bring many to righteousnesse. Soe that we could not say we marryed for the riches of this life and glorious estate heere. Indeed, this was not my thoughts to doe soe, which, if I would have soe chosen, I might have bestowed my childe soe, for her haveing opportunitys to doe it in our nigh neighborhood. But I may apeale to God, that my choyce, and my deare husband's, was soe to chuse for the better part as Mary did, which shall, I hope, never be taken from me or my children for ever. This is my ground and bottom on which I ever desired to fix, both in my owne choyce of a husband for myselfe and my deare children; and I hope I have found a greater joy in my own soule in my choyce, then all the worldly riches could afford. And soe I humbly trust shall doe for all my deare children whom God has given me. And tho' all the world shall condemne me, yett shall not my heart condemne me, since God is on my side.

And tho' selfe interest shall blast my honest designes with falls gloses, and horrid imputations, yett in God is my trust, and in Him will I hope for deliverance. * * *

Soe affter some preparation for this marriage, the writings and deeds which Mr. Denton had ingrossed and made ready, with a bond of Mr. Comber for performance of articles and deeds being entered into for security of her fortune, dated November 17, 1668, Mr. Charles Man, the minister of Gilling, was intreated to doe this kinde and freindly office for us to joyn these two, Mr. Thomas and my deare daughter Alice Thornton, in the holy bonds of matrimony, which was performed in a very decent and a religious manner, I myselfe beeing all the freind she had to stand for her father, whom God had taken from us, and gave her in marriage, which I could not refraine to shed many tears, considering how I was left, and she in a manner forlorne of all our relations, who should have bin our comfort in this great trouble of our change. My deare child did carry her selfe most virteusly and modestly, with chastity in this holy action into which she did come, and with teares entred into it, begging a blessing of God to His holy ordinance, [which] we both did, and to which I humbly blesse His holy [name]. I hope He gave a gracious returne of our prayers. Ther was wittness of this sacred marriage, being don in the (s)charlett chamber, Dafeny Lightfoote, Hannah Ableson, and Mary Lightfoote. Which, because it was don in soe much secrecy, by reason of our adversaryes' malice, it was not thought fitt to have any more witnesses, for making itt public sooner then it was convenient to be known for severall reasons. Butt indeed, I was, with my daughter, very desirous and earnest with my brother Denton to have stood for her father to give her in marriage, or to have bin a wittness of it att least. Butt, I do not know very well on what account, butt for reasons best known to himselfe, did desire to be excused to be there, but said he wished them much happiness and joy in their marriage; soe we had not his company at that time. I supose that the rest of the brothers and sisters was never well pleased att the disposall of my children in the way of marriage, for severall reasons; and one maine one may be, that the more of my husband's children had children, the further off the estate would be of descending; as it has appeared since my deare son Thornton's decease without issue, and the daughters succeed. There was £800 to fall to them. This bussiness was transacted with great gravity and piety, affter which my daughter and myselfe went to prayer, to beg a blessing and mercy uppon our great undertaking; and tho' it was began with great sorrow and affliction on my part, I hope and putt my trust in the living God He will be mercifull to me and my deare child, and lett us receave the comfort of His presence to preserve us from all evill, and blesse us with all good, that we may be His faithfull servants in all conditions. The bridegroome, as in those cases, laid downe a weding ring and severall pieces of gold, as a token of his faithfull and conjugall love to his deare bride, over whom he expressed abundance of joy and inward sattisfaction to have obteined soe vertuous and chaste a wife of God; and we could not but hope God will give them a great shaire of His favour and mercy, to live to His glory and praise; and I begged some comfort in them to suport my sad and sorrowfull widdowed condittion. Glory be to the good God of my salvation, Who has performed this mercy to us, makeing me to live to see this soe happily ended. But in regard that it was not sutable to publish the marriage, beeing too neere the time of my sorrow and great mourning for my deare husband, it was by consent thought fitt that the solemnity of the getting the bride to bed should be defferred till it was convenient to invite all Mr. Thornton's relations to the publication of theire marriage, which was don on May following, the 19th, 1669, when we had all his relations from Malton and ellsewhere of kindred, and had what preparations of entertainment on that occasion. * * * May 17, 1669, beeing a just halfe yeare affter the marriage of my deare childe and eldest daughter Alice Thornton, did I invite all our nearest relations, and Mr. Thornton's freinds which we could gett, to as hansome an entertainment as I could be able to procure, considering my owne still weakness and ill habitt of health. Brother Denton and my sister, my brother Portington and my sister, Mr. Charles Man, the fortunate person who married them, and many other good freinds and neighbours; all who expressed there great sattisfaction at the solemnity and making the publication of this marriage, and wished the young cuple many hearty joyes in there marriage, saeing they hoped it would, by God's blessing, be a great happyness and comfort to us all. Att night they had allso a good supper, and those usuall solemnityes of marriage of getting the bride to bed, with a great deale of decency and modesty of all partyes was this solemnity performed. I blesse God, He letting me live to see this great conserne of my life performed, with such freinds' sattisfaction which wished myselfe and poore children well, and that by God's blessing [they] may be prospered in His feare; we haveing solemne prayers twice that day to beg a perticuler blessing uppon my children and family.

Be it remembred that, notwithstanding all the great and subtil indeavours of our spirituall and temporall enymyes to blast the designe, to frustrate my family of the greate blessing, and the placing a standing ministry in this place and countrey, this marriage was solemnized in my house by Mr. Man uppon the 17th day of November, in yeare 1668. And another sircumstance I desire to take notice of was, it was don in that very chamber in which Mrs. Danby had bin hatching and contriving all her malice against us three, vidz., my son Comber, which now I may call so by vertue of affinity, and my poore daughter Alice, and myselfe, beeing the unfortunate creature against whom all those arrowes was shott. But by the immence and profound goodness, mercy, and compassion of our gracious Father to the widdow and fatherless, me, His poore servant, did pitty my wrongs, heard my greifes and teares, and did bring good out of this evill, I hope, to my whole family, for whose good I may testify I am a sufferer. Tho', as David saith, *Many are the troubles of the righteous, but the Lord will deliver him out of all.* And thus I hope in mercy He will to me His handmaide make me righteous, and then He will according to His promise deliver me.

A Relation of memorable actions and afflictions befalln to me in the first yeare of my widdowed condittion since September 17th, 1668 (iii., p. 21).

I haveing now passed through the two stages of my life of my virgin estate, and that of the honrable estate of marriage, as St. Paull tearmes it (tho' with much troubles in the flesh),* the same has had its comforts alaied to me.   Yet have I great cause to render most humble thanks to the great God of Heaven for His infinitt and inexpressable favours towards me ; Who has mixed His frownes with smiles, His afflictions with comforts, and soe ordered His vissitations as to make a way for me to escape, and bestowed on me that great blessing, above many others, of a deare and pieous, virtuous and chast husband, with whom I lived and injoyed his indeared and faithfull affection in the bonds of a holy marriage, without the least taint of our conjugall vow, but our faith and holy tye most sacredly and inviolably kept to each other, as I may justly avouch, who am now left the most desolate and forlorne widow in the world by this seperation of soe dear a husband.   *But, who may say to the Lord, What doest Thou ? since the Lord giveth and the Lord taketh, blessed be the name of the Lord.*   He pleased to lend me his life, tho' mixed comforts with many tribulations of this temporall evils falling uppon our own persons, posterity, and estate, which made injoyments to bitter to us.   Yett while we injoyed each other's love (and, indeed, candid love) so intirely to each other, with the benifitt of Christian pietie and religion, it did sweeten our temporall troubles to us, and made us valew this world but as a troublesome passag into a better.   And God there by these His dispensations, so wisely framed and molded us in the furnace of afflictions, drew our hearts to Him, and there fixed our anchor of hope, that affter this miserable life ended, we shall injoy each other in a glorious etternity.   And offten would my blessed husband say, " My deare, oh that thee and I and all our deare children were now all with God ! " nor

* Hebrews xiii. 4 ; 1 Corinthians vii. 28.

could I be blamed to wish the same, and pray for it, if it might be good in the sight of our gracious Father in heaven, Who made and preserved us to this time of our daies. And I hoped, in His due time, after a few daies heere spent in His service, and doeing His worke which He has appoynted us to doe, we shall injoy the same. But as to the sett time of our departure, we dare not appoynt it to Him, but submissively wait His devine pleasure, both when, and the sircumstance of our abode, and of our worke, and allso endeavour to be ready for him att His call. Offten would my deare husband give a cheque to my great and unreasonable desire and passion of greife for him, when I have bin ready to die with greife for feare of lossing my cheifest joy by his death, gently reproving my too much doteing on him. * * * I being at, and before the death of my deare husband, fallen into a very great and dangerous condittion of sickness, weakeness of body, and afflicted mind, on the account of my evill enimies' slanders, with excesse of greife thereon, as related by me in my first booke more at large, was reduced to a very weake and fainting extreamity when I had that sad newes of his departure brought from Malton, which did extreamly highten and agravate my sorrowes, both in respect of his sudaine loss (when I expected him), and of my owne great faintings, and was most desirous to have gon with him to the grave, soe that non did expect my life to be continued affter him; and all my freinds used uttmost indeavours to administer some comfort in this sad condittion with perswading arguments. First, that as to the slanders soe cruelly and inhumainly raised on me, I had the testimony of a cleare conscience, both before God and man, of my innocency, and confirmed by an unspotted virtuous life I had given the world testimony of in all my life and conversation ; and that I might be assured in all passages, and on all occasions, I was soe clearly vindicated by my deare husband's faithfull and tender deare expressions, and constant zealous beleife and affection towards me, and assurance of my faithfull and intire conjugall fidelity of me, insomuch that he declared to my aunt Norton, and to my brother Denton, uppon my bitter cryes to stay him from goeing to Maulton, for feare he should fall in a fitt of the pallsy. He declared to them that he was much troubled to leave me in that weake condition I then was in by those slanders; but that, as he knew best my fidelity towards him, and vertue, all my daies, soe he could not be sattisfied in his own conscience till he had vindicated my cause, and righted me against that abominable beast, Mr Tankred,* who envied any one's chastity, but was alwaies an enemy to his family before I came into it, and so, out of malice, had injured me for his sake. He then did protest he went on no other bussiness but that, and was resolved to be revenged of him for it, but charged them not [to] tell me of it, for the greife would kill his most chaste and deare wife. * * *

It was my great joy and comfort in the midest of all my trials and sufferings, unjustly charged uppon me by malicious tongues, and the devill in them, that not one of the heavy slanders was proved, nor did ever my deare husband beleive any of them, or had, I blesse God, the least shadow of suspition of my vertue and chastity. He ever would say that he had had soe many yeares' experience of my modesty and chastity to have any cause of suspition of me from anything whatever my enimies could say or doe against me, and the more of there lies that they invented, the more he pittied me and loved me, and would offten abuse and reproch Mrs. Danby for her bace and in-humaine and unchristian dealing with me, and would never be sattisfied till he had turned her out of his house. And when I had bin overcome with sorrow and extreame weeping att my missrable misfortune to be thus traduced by my freinds and servants, he, deare heart, would offten say to me, " My deare

---

* " By that slanderous tongue of Mr. Tankerd, of Arden, who had laid a wager with my deare Lady Yorke of £100, that if my husband were dead I would be married within a month to Mr. Comber, which lye did soe conserne my deare husband, that he tould my aunt Norton he would be revenged of that trator for traducing soe much his chaste and innocent wife with such a fallse lye; for he knew that we designed it a match with his daughter Alice, if itt pleased God she lived." (Book iii.)

" Old Mr Tankerd's malice was against me, because I did gett that morgage cleared of Laistrope for the £100 for Hamblton, which he had gott that land secured to him for it." (Book ii.)

Joy, why doest thou thus lament and breake my heart with sorrow for thee, to see thou wilt not be comforted? Would I not spend my derest blood to right thy cause, and justify thy unspotted innocency? And I have examined these people which had heard them, and they all uppon there oathes cleare thee from the least guilt or showe of evill, by example, or words, or anything, and all are sore greived for those lyes was tould. And besides, I will make it my bussiness diligently to find out those what wronged thee, and will certainly have them severly punished. Nay, God will revenge thy cause uppon all those miscreants who has abused and injured thy precious good name. And sence I both know that bussiness which we would not have made publick, of the match of my child with Mr. Comber, which you have had many occasions to imploy him about our estate and affaires, which non but my brother Denton and myselfe and Mrs. Danby knows of, this might be some occasion that our enimies might pretend that you imployed him. But Mrs. Danby is most ungratefull and disloyall to thee, to know these things and would not discover them. And since you know my faithfull heart, and my confidence in thee, I pray thee take comfort [in] your owne conscience and my indered love to thee." Much more comfortable words would this blessed man, my deare husband, comfort me and suport my hart in the midest of sorrowes. * * * I have great cause to bless my gracious Father of heaven for His immence goodness to me, His poore creature, that vouchsafed me that mercy and providence in order to cleare my innocency from all those lieing aspersions cast on my good name, and was spread as farre as Richmond to the eares of my deare aunt Norton, who lamented much my misfortune, to have lived to the 42nd yeare of my life in an unspotted reputation, and now to be seemed by these lyeing tongues to have bin guilty of something unworthy of that noble race, and vertuous, that I came from. My deare aunt was soe conserned to heare I had bin soe belied that she immeadiatly came to Newton and found me in a manner halfe dead with greife uppon this larum that Mrs. Danby and her maide raised up against me. I was extreamly overjoyed to see her, and blessed God for that providence which brought her thither, tho' att first they had possessed her with some feares, tho' never of my giving cause of skandall, that I had bin unfortunate in lighting uppon some treatchery from those of a contrary judgement. Indeed, her apprehension had some grownd for it, beeing placed amongst soe many contrary oppinions who was glad of any pretence to make me not soe desirable; for those two factions of popish and preisbiterian had bin some occasion to chuse a match for my daughter to secure my children from that education. This, joyned with other selfe-intrests, which was contrary to myne, all made up a caball with those of my enimies, to take fire and spread my misfortune that was raised against me. But then an inward secrett malice of her that should have bin my com-purgator, and have done me right, by the discovring to me how I was wronged, and in what manner, did not doe soe, but suffred me still to goe on soe slandred in my owne house for two yeares together, which had bin raised uppon my securing my writings and money of my deare mother's, by Mr. Thornton's order, with Mr. Comber, till it should please God I was delivered of that child, which was my last. When my deare aunt understood all those bitter pills I had prepared for me, she very much commiserated my condition, and did use her uttmost indeavour to find out the injurious practices against me, nor would she be sattisfied till my deare husband did quit the house of Madam Danby. I have related the sircumstances before.* Her zeale for my honor was truly good, and allso to have as many to understand the wrong I had bin under by such abominable slanders, and I blesse God for her great paines and industery which she tooke in that affaire, who made it her bussinesse to testify the truth in my behalfe against all opposers. Thus she plaied a most Christian part to me in clearing my wronged innocency, both to my Lady Wivill, Mrs. Darcy, Dr. Samwayes, and my Lady Yorke, who had bin too much byassed by Mrs. Danby's storys. The excelent comfort, ease, and refrishment I receaved from, and by

---

* See MS. iii., 191-193.

my deare aunt's councills and praiers, and good advice in my trouble, I have great cause to remember, with hiest gratitude to my Heavenly Father Who sent me such releife, I may say, from heaven, haveing a freind nearer then a brother, which did succor me in this deepe distresse; and when she brought Dr. Sammoies with her to pray for me, haveing staid with me till she saw Mrs. Danby sent away to York, which I did, and borrid Mrs. Gramse's coach to carry her, with a maide to waite on her. I allso tooke my last leave of her, and gave her other £3 to releeive her withall, added to the £5 I sent before to her, which made up the somme of £8, which she had then. Beside all the attendance of my house and servants, she wanted for nothing I could doe for her, tho' she deserved it not, to turne soe much my deadly [foe] as much as in her laied, to despoyle me of my precious honor. * * * Att my deare aunt's goeing away she sent my good freind Dafeny to be with me and comfort me, which she did much, in her pittieing my distresse, and assist me in my weakness which this occasioned, falling into a flood on my greife and sorrow. But when she went home, which was a long time affter, she did her best to doe me right with Mr. Darcy, Mr. Ederington, and my cozen Nicholson, whose charity, tho' of annother oppinnion, was much greived att the unjust lyes which was tould of me att my Lady Frankland's, who was insenced against me, that I would not lett my servant leave me when I was in child-bed, and goe to her. They, God forgive them, had hatched lyes of me, which, when my cozen Nicholson, out of her charity, came to see me, tould me of, and examined the truth, and then declared the same att Newbrough, and Ouston, and Thirkelby, which I blesse God to putt it into the hearts of my freinds to pitty my condittion.

Of the taking Addministration of my deare Husband
(iii., p. 115).

After the solemnity of my deare husband's funeralls was over, the first and great consern to be don was to have the choyce of an administrator, to have a good and honnest person gott to doe justly in that weighty consern. They tould me that it by law did fall on myselfe, as his widdow, to take administration of my husband's goods, and to pay debts, etc., by reason there was no will made. As to the making of his will, I had very offten putt him in minde of it when I saw he did soe frequently fall into those pallsy fitts, desiring he would please to doe it for the sattisfaction of all the world, and that he would please to order his debts to be paid as he would have them don. All the answer my deare husband was pleased to give me was, " He had settled his estate at Laistrop, as he would have it to pay debts, and for his children; and he desired me to see his debts paid, as he knew I had a good conscience to doe." I tould him againe, " My deare heart, you know there is nothing to maintaine my deare son Robert but out of my joynture and estate, and if you leave anything to pay the debts withall, I was not unwilling to do it; but if they were soe many and soe great, I doubted I could not doe it, and to educate my poore child withall."* Soe Mr. Thornton did not make any will, but what he had said of Laistrop for debts. Butt, affter his decease it was necessary that one should take administration to the personall estate, and to order and pay all things according to law, and to have an apprisement of the goods as the law appoynts in that case. Soe my brother Denton tould me that it was belonging to me for to doe it, and that if I did not take administration myselfe, I might chuse one to take that office uppon him. * * * Uppon this I tould my brother Denton that there was non more fitt or proper to undertake soe great a trust, and act in that conserne, as himselfe, who was soe wise and prudent and knowing a person in all such affaires and the law, to act accordingly; nor noe man knew the consernes of Mr. Thornton's estate, and himselfe and family being soe kind and good a freind to my deare husband, and doe all things according to equity and justice. If he would please to undertake that trouble, the family would be much obleiged to him for it, and I in perticuler

---

* " To which he said * * * for his son Robert, he knew I would take caire of him, and that he doubted not of that but he would want for nothing what I could do." (Book ii.)

account myselfe much ingaged for his favour. But my brother Denton made his excuse, and said he would serve that family in anything he could, but he could not doe that ; he was a trustee for the children, and could not be both, tho' he was a trustee for the debts, too, as well in that deed of Laistrop as well as for the children. Then I said, if my brother Portington would doe as much as take that trust of addminustrator on him, I should desire he would please to doe it for Mr. Thornton. Butt Mr. Denton made the same returne for him as he had don for himselfe, soe he left me in a great conserne how or where to pittch of a right and good man to doe it. Att last he said, that if one could be thought uppon which had not much estate, but an honest man, and one of an indiferent judgement, that would be advised how to manage the conscrnes of the estate, it were better to have such an one then have any of a good estate, or were too wise, and would not be advised. So when severall was named did not please in one poynt or other, at last I desired him to nominate one, who, affter a little pawse, named Mr. Thornton's servant, who he had caused the Warrant* house to be builded for him to live in, having married Nan Robinson, what soe abused me about a great lye she tould my brother Thomas of myselfe and maide, Jane Flouer, and had made my brother ever since my bitter enemy against me. And, to please Mr. Thornton, I had granted that the Warrant house should be builded for them to live in, but this people was my great adversaryes ever affter, and a great losse and destruction to the estate of Mr. Thornton and myselfe. This man could neither write nor read, and was but of indifferent parts or honesty, not att all, in my thoughts, capable or fitt for such a matter of importance of the family, soe that I was forced to decline this motion as modestly as I could, and speake my thoughts that, in regard he could neither read nor write, he could not understand the bussinesse, nor dispattch anything of that nature. Butt my brother Denton did incline to non like him, and did pray me to thinke of it, because, if the debts should come too fast on,

* *i.e.*, warren. "As melancholy as a lodge in a warren." *Much Ado about Nothing*, Act ii.

he might plead a plea, "*neæ [ne] administravit.*" The unfitt-
ness of this man was, indeed, a great trouble to me (being too
nimble of his fingers, which I knew, and had proofe of in the
house, tho' would not be beleived by those [who] proposed him),
put me to a great trouble what to doe, least theire importunity
and fearinge to displease might have him cast uppon me, soe I
would not consent, but said I would consider of it. But behold
the gracious goodness and mercy of my God, when, in the midest
of my distress, made a way for me to escape the necessity of
having such an one to be made a slave to. He caused an unexpected providence to fall out, and as poore Dafeny said, " God
had sent me a freind affter my owne hart." And just as I was
in trouble, and powring out my prayers to Heaven to assist and
direct me to one fit for us in this great affaire, which conserned,
indeed, the right payment of debts, and all things ellse about
the administrator, Dafeny, looking out at the window, heard a
horsse at the dore, cryed out, " Oh, mistresse, God has heard
your prayers, and has sent you a good and honest man, as you
desired, to helpe you, and that is Mr. Anthony Norton, which is
come to see you only as a vissit since Mr. Thornton's death."
Affter this good man came to see me, I asked him if he would
doe me the favour to stand for Mr. Thornton's administrator, to
beare the name, and I would take caire that the charges should
be noe way troublesome to him, but should be paid for his
journeys and for his expences, but that he should be saved harmless of anything conserning that bussiness, for I was now
extreamly weake and sick, and could not be able to travell
about it, nor would any of Mr. Thornton's freinds doe it, nor I
could not have any stranger to confide in like him, and hoped
that God had in providence sent him hither. When this good
man, my cozen Norton, heard me make my request and mone
to him, it pleased God to putt it into his mind to pitty my desolate condittion, said, " Deare Madam, I am truly sorry for your
losse of good Mr. Thornton, and wish that I could doe anything
to serve you and your children, but doe not understand these
things very well, but shall be willing to doe you any kindness
for your owne sake, haveing a great honor for yourselfe and

family. Indeed, I have don it once for my cozen, Major Norton, but he directed me in all things and proceedings, and by his order I acted and finished that conserne for his son Edmund, I hope to his owne sattisfaction and all creaditors; and if you will give me your orders how to act I shall observe it the best I can, or anything ellse for you lies in my power." When I heard what this good old man said in a full answer to my desire in this bussinesse, I blessed and praised my good God for His mercy to me in granting my humble pettitions, hoping this was ordered by His providence for good to me and mine. I acquainted my brother Denton with this opportunity of my cozen, Anthony Norton, beeing come, and of my gaining his assistance in accepting to be my husband's administrator, which by reason he knew him to be an honnest, good man, and his wives relation and uncle, did approve well of; and soe, uppon full agreement about this bussiness, proceedings went on. And Mr. Flathers,* beeing rurall dean, came to Newton, with orders to take my renounsiation of the administration, and my cozen Anthony Norton's name putt in, to whom I gave up my power in it. And my cozen Norton tooke out letters of administration according to law out of the court, and entred bond to the court for right administrating, as in order of law.† Affter this great matter of the administration was settled, it was requisitt I should take the tuittion of my poore children, beeing now by this great change become both father and mother and gaurdian to them, a duty which I willingly undertooke for theire owne and father's sake, having a threefold tye uppon me, as beeing my owne, dearly bought in bringing them forth by exquisitt torments and paines in child-bearing, added to many caires and difficultyes in there bringing upp to theire severall ages. As to my son Robert, he was solely left to my charge for subsistance, since there was not out of the estate at Laistrop more than what

* Thomas Flathers, vicar of Lastingham, 20 Sep. 1662; rural dean of Rydall; living 1695.

† 1668. Oct. 15. Admon. William Thornton, Esq., of East Newton, intestate, to Anthony Norton, his kinsman, with consent of his widow. Inventory exhibited. (York Registry.)

would provide for his two sisters' maintenance and portions.
* * * For severall yeares together I receaved not towards
my daughter Kate's maintenance, or for her education, the
somme of twenty shillings, or of ten, tho' she should have had
equall with her sister, affter £40 a yeare to each of them. But
I did borow for her keeping severall yeares that I wanted out of
Laistrop, and never had it made good to me, as I ought, out of
the land. That is still owing to me the somme of —. Where
then could there be anything to bring up my only son Robert
but what, by God's providence, I could have out of my joynture
and my deare mother's estate at Midlham? all which was soe
burdened with public charges and debts, which I was forced to
contract uppon severall accounts, fell on me, that I had great
straits, which I entred on uppon my husband's death, borrowing
even from the first to pay funerall charges, and to keepe house
with, and to maintaine my children. I entred bond to the court
for the tuittion of my three children.* My poore son Robert
was butt six yeares old when his dere father was buried,
September 19th, 1668; his first tyeing cloths was mourning for
his father. My daughter Alice, her age was, January 3rd, sixteen; my daughter Katherine, her age was, June 2nd, twelve.
As for my two daughters, there was to have bin £40 a yeare for
each out of the land of Laistrop for maintainance, but such was
the great taxes, sessments, and all public charges affter Mr.
Thornton's death, with the payment of intrest for debts, that it
fell much short every halfe-yeare, and some yeres was very little
to be had, soe that I had great difficulty to live, as well to maintaine my owne family, pay intrest for those debts soe contracted,
as to keepe my son, which I had solly to provide for, without
borrowing; which cannot be immagined but reduced me to
great straits, entring into this widdowed condittion att first with
debts; and my estate att Newton, which was most of it in
Elizabeth Hicke hand, she paid noe more for all the parke and
upper ground butt £28 a yeare; which, affter she was gon of, I

---

* 1668. Nov. 11. Tuition of Robert, Alice, and Catherine, children of
William Thornton, Esq., of East Newton, to Alice Thornton, their mother. Mr.
Thomas Comber, clerk, special commissioner. (York Registry.)

made of that very grounde in my owne hand, by stocke and gaites, neare £150 per annum. Yett, haveing undertooke this charge uppon me, I did my best indeavours to discharge a good conscience towards my deare children, with a tender regard for them, both in sickness and in health ; and I hope non of them can say they wanted anything was fitt for them in all condittions ; and I hope I may with a good conscience appeale to my gracious God that I made it my duty to serve Him in the performance of my paternall caire over them whom He had putt into my hand, with all due affection and prudence, and to correct there sins, and instructing them in all dutyes of piety and religion.

Affter I had prevailed with my cozen Norton to accept of the administration, itt was the first in order to have the goods praised. And to that end there was fouer chozen to be apprizers, and that to be indifferently chosen, but was wholey in the darke where to pitch for two that might not be byased, being a stranger to them, and all for the other conserne. But I did not desire more than justice and equity in this action, since I too well knew who was to beare the burden, and the weaker horse, and non to putt to there helping hand to ease itt, or beare part. Att length I chose and desired my brother Denton to be pleased to be one to stand for me, and if he pleased, to chuse whom he would. He named Mr. Denton of Nawton, and Robert Garbutt ; then wanted one more. They putt me to name one, and I named Thomas Thompson. A day was appoynted to meete att my house att Easte Newton, when the goods was brought out in reddiness, what was Mr. Thornton's, to be prized. As for what was my deare mother's goods, I desired Dafeny (who, by the good providence of God, was yett with me heere, to assist me in my house and troubles, that she, beeing with my deare mother in her last sicknes and death, and att her will-makeing and inventory, and priseing her goods), I desired her she would goe along with them, and what she knew was my deare mother's in the house, that she would tell my brother Denton and the apprisors which they were, because she only knew them ; and I had allso acquainted my brother with it when he asked me who should goe along to showe them the goods in the house. But before they went uppon the apprisement, my brother Denton, out of his regard to me [said], That it was the law, and usually don, the widdow was to have her widdow-bed first out of all her husband's goods, choose where she would, and commonly they chose the best where she would, and if I pleased I should have one. I thanked him for his advice, and telling me of it; I knew it was my right and due, as I was his sorrowfull widdow; butt in regard there was soe many and great debts of my deare husband's, which could not be scarcely paid, I would deny myselfe of that right and priveledge, and remited it from myselfe, wishing that his goods would pay all the debts; and by my deare mother's kindeness to me she had given me beds enough for myselfe and family, or else I should be but in a sad condittion, but thanked him for his respect to me in that kinde offer. Besides, I had taken advice of Mr. Driffeld not to administer unto the goods, nor undertake or medle with them to administer in mine owne wrong, if I had medled with them and made myselfe liable to pay all the debts; for the debts farre exceeded all the worth of the goods Mr. Thornton had. * * * Affter this passage, before the apprisement begun, my good brother Denton came to me in a freindly way, that perhaps I did not know as much, but he thought fitt to tell me of it, that he knew my mother had given me her personall estate and goods by her will and testament; butt whatever was soe given to the wife will fall due to Mr. Thornton my husband, and by the law nothing which was soe given to the wife but did fall due to the husband; for the property was in him, and not in the wife, beeing under covert barr; and therefore all my ladie's goods and personall estate would fall due to be praised amongst the rest of his goods, as his was. Uppon which discource I was much surprized to heare this sad newes; which it had bin all along harped affter, as by Harry Best betraying me to that which they would have had by his fallse deed; but I bless God I was awaire of itt, and did not signe it; but now the bottom was laid oppen, it beeing all along a decine to have had the property of her estate to have paid his debts, which was my blessed mother's intention to secure for myselfe and children, which she foresaw would be left

poore enough.   Butt, affter some pause, I gave him thanks for
his kindness in acquainting me with the matter of law in this
thing and perticuler, and withall tho' my mother has given her
estate and goods to myselfe and children, as I see cause, yett,
rather then just debts should not be paid, I would quitt my right
in them.   If I must not have them according to her deeds and
last will and testament, I must borow a bed for myselfe till I
could buy one ; this beeing a surprizall to me att that time to
have the will soe broaken.   "Butt, Sir, I must now lett you
know the reason why my deare mother did settle her estate
personall in the manner she has don; to prevent what she
otherwise see might come to passe ; as 'tis, God knowes, come
to passe too true."   That my deare mother having advised Mr.
Thornton against taking uppon him the assignment of Major*
Norton, as very pernicious for him and his estate, such troubles
in the mannagry of such a conserne was contrary to his humor
or practice, and well knowing that the deeds and last will and
testament did suficiently secure both his intrest and her owne.
But that Mr. Thornton would not take her advice, not to medle
with Major Norton's assignment; but by acting in that bussiness contrary to reason, and her judgement and interest in the
Irish estate and his owne; and forseeing what ill consequence
it would be of; she did then resolve, by the best conncell she
gott, what way she had best to take by law for the securing all
her personall as well as reall estate, that she might preserve and
secure it for myselfe and children, for she said Mr. Thornton, by
acting in that affaire which did not belong unto him, would
certainly involve himself and estate into debts and suites
with Sir Christopher Wandesford. * * * Uppon these
considerations, she had, by advice of an able lawyer, made a
deed of guift to feefees in trust of all her estate personall whatever, with scudells annexed of her goods, to such purposes and
intentions, use, and dispositions as therein mentioned; for to
secure it to myselfe during life, and at my death to such child
or children as I should see best deserving.   Still the property

* Otherwise written Maulger, a Christian name common in tho family of
Vavasour.

to be kept in those fefees in trust, and not to be made liable to any other use as debts and other inconveniencys as consequence to the assignment.   *   *   *   So, affter this discource, I desired to shew my brother Denton all my deare mother's writtings and deeds which settled that poynt with the deed of guift and her last will and testament.   He having read them, was much surprized, and said that he had never seene them before; but I thought I had shewed them to him when Harry Best drew the deed for me to signe; but I tould him of them, how my deare mother had settled them.   And then he said, that my ladye's goods could not be touched, and that he had never seene any thing better don in his life, and that the property was not in Mr. Thornton, nor could they be made liable to Mr. Thornton's debts or disposall, the property not beeing in him, but the trustees. Which when I heard him say soe, I had the more cause to blesse God for, Which had in mercy soe provided for me by my deare mother's blessing, and prudence to preserve something for my necessitys, for myselfe and poore children, now in my sad and desolate condittion.   *   *   *   When the goods was to be praised, which was in the scarlett chamber, came to be looked uppon by the apprizers, I tould them that I bought them with my mother's monney, and ought not to be praised, and pleaded they were all her's, bought by me and paid for of her monney. It was quickly answered me that her monney, beeing converted into goods, and they not expressed in her will and deed of guift, did fall to Mr. Thornton's part, and soe must be prized as his. Which goods I soe bought and paid for came to the somme of ———.   But if I had had any relation or freind with me that would have stood upp for the widowe's right, either law or equity, things must not have gon soe.   But I, allas! had noe uninterested person to assist me in all these occassions, and I was left desolate, only from what Heaven was pleased to give me His helping hand; for which I returne His holy name praises for ever.   Therefore I esteeme the mercy of God was very great to me that poore Dafeny was heere with me att this present when the appraisement was made, because I had non in the world which did know which was my mother's, and which was

my husband's goods, but she. Soe she went into the house
allong with them, and shewed which was my mother's beds, and
other goods in every roome belonged to her; for she knew
all the markes, and had marked most of them. And for the
pewter, brasse, and all ellse could be don, was her name set on
them before her death, who like a wise and prudent parent did
thus to prevent any disturbance might fall out afterwards.
When Robert saw that Dafeny did owne that most of the houshold goods to be my deare mother's, by the markes and
Dafeny's testimony to them, "What," said he, "we shall
have at this raite [all] to be my lady Wandesford's that is in
the house; heere is little or non for Mr. Thornton then." To
which Dafeny presently returned answer againe, "Sir, if I
were called to my oath, I must take it, that what I say is true
conserning these goods; they are all my ladie's, and all of them
was sett downe in an inventory before her death, by her order,
she seeing them don before her owne selfe, and was prized all
after her death, which is to be yett seene, I beleive, in my
mistresse her keeping. And Mr. Thornton had not a bed, or
any household goods, in this house, or any where ellse, before
he married. But what he had [was] from my lady, and she
gave them to my mistresse to use, but not pay debts, but out of
kindness to assist them in theire house." Affter this, the
prizers went on with there worke, and when they come to the
scarlett chamber, they valewed the bed and the hangings of itt,
with the stooles and chaires, six of them, with the counterpaine,
rug, and blanketts, and a little ordinary bed which was bought
by us, the raite was sett on them to be by Mr. Denton of
Nawton to be worth £40, and soe sett it downe in the aprize-
ment. Att which, Thomas Tompson, judging it to be very high,
and above farre the worth of itt, came to Dafeny and my selfe
and tould me that he was against it, and did speake his mind; .
but that Mr. Denton of Nawton said 'he was a praiser att
Mr. Gibson's, when Sir John died,* and they had a bed which
was not soe fine a coler, nor mad so fine a show, which was

* At Welburn, June 1665. See *Visit. Ebor.*, p. 73.

prized higher.' Soe affter my brother Denton came in to my chamber, and said " he doubted they had don amiss in over valewing the scarlett bed," I asked what the raite was sett on it; he answred £40, but doubted it was too much. Uppon which I tould him, I should be glad it would give as much, and sence I desired to buy the goods and pay for them again, rather then expose them to a more disgracefull view, which was a dishonnor to Mr. Thornton, but if they could make that money of that bed, they were wellcome to itt, for I could not give it. And I could make itt apeare by my cozen Beal's notes, who bought the goods att London, that all she bought for that sute did but cost £25, soe that if they was soe prized, and I had paid soe much before of my mother's monney, I had better never owne them, it would ruine me to pay soe, and I would not have itt. On which my brother went out againe, after I tould him to answer the objection of Mr. Denton's about Sir John Gibson's bed. I knew it, and had taken good notice of it, beeing a very rich flowred silke damaske bed, with all answerable to it of the same, and a large one. The bed beeing a noble downe bed, with bolsters, pillows, blanketts and all sutable, which I am sure was never bought for £60, soe that £40 for it was an indifferent price for that. But mine was but a searge bed, and what belonged to it, but was a light couler, made a show, but that would yeld noe such price. Affter this discource, I supose they fell of that price was sett, when they heard I could not medle with it at that raite. Yett [what] ever raite was sett on that and the great parlour too was very unreasonable, haveing bought and paid for them before, which yett, out of my love I had for my husband's family, I was content to doe, tho' I borrowed every penny of it, and paid his debts with it. And I know we had not one cow for milk, butt what was my deare mother's, and the sheepe was bought with her monney, and severall of the best horrses we had was all her's, and he sould them and made use of the monney.

Of my saving the wood at Newton.   (iii. 129).

Before I passe to annother subject, I thinke it butt fitt to give an account of a very materiall accident, which fell out for me to strugle withall in the first month of my widdow-hood. Tho' I had bin given some notice of by my good lady Fairfax,* some time affter Mr. Thornton was returned from Scarbrough, vidz., she commeing to see me one day, it happned that my deare husband had bin in a fitt of the palsey, and was ordred by Dr. Wittye to have a bath, which I made according to his directions. My lady just came when he was in it, and had bin prettily recruted while he was in the bath, and would have had me gon to my lady while he was in it. But I durst not leave him soe long, only stept to her ladyship, and tould her would she stay till I had laid him safe in bed affter it. Which I did, and went downe to my lady againe ; which good lady did much pitty my condition ; asked me, did I not heare anything of Mr. Thornton making a bargain when he was att Spaw, to sell all the wood at Newton and Laistrop? Att which newes I was much conserned, and said, "Noe, madam." She prayed me then not to be troubled att it, but assured me it was soe ; "and some bace fellow, taking advantage of his illness in his head some times, had gott him in an humor, and had made him sell all his wood he had, and att a pittifull raite, as she heard, and was very sorrey for it ; therefore she came on purpose to lett me know, that I might take some cource to save it." I returned her ladyship humble thankes, and "had saved the wood severall times, and should be very sorry to live to see it destroyed." Soe my lady went away, and left me in much conserne least he might cutt it downe some time or other, but durst not owne it to him. Butt now, affter Mr. Thornton's death, there comes a man called Kendall, a wright, and cutts downe one of the best fine oak trees in the parke, without acquainting any one with it. Affterwards, he comes to my brother Denton, telling him that Mr. Thornton, when he was att Scarbourgh, had sould to

---

* Daughter of Sir Philip Howard, Kt., of Naworth, died 3rd Sept., 1677.

him all his wood at Newton and att Laistrop for a considerable somme of monney, and taken of him twenty shillings in earnest of the bargaine; and he now came to have his bargaine performed, and had wittness of it, and could make it good, and he had cutt downe one of the trees in the parke as part of the bargaine, and expected it should be performed by me for all the rest. My brother tould him he never heard anything from Mr. Thornton of itt in his life, and did beleive if it were so he should have; tould him besides, the estate is now in annother hand, and he was sure I, to whom it did belong now, would not grant that the wood should be destroyed, and he was mistaken to thinke he should have liberty to cutt a sticke downe, and was questionable for what he had don; but he would lett me know what he said. When my brother tould me this matter, I then calld to mind what my lady Fairfax had tould me, and feared it was too true, butt how to preserve the wood I was desirous to consult with him; telling him that, by the grace of God, he should never have his designe to destroy that beauty of the estate as long as I lived. I loved it, and had preserved it thus long, and this man was a knave to take the advantage of my deare husband to draw him into a snaire in his weakness. In conclusion, we had much to doe to breake this bargaine, and I utterly refused, and threatned to punish him for the trespasse he had don to come into my grownd to doe it. Soe att last, for feare I should question him for it, my brother advised either to give him the twenty shillings my husband had receaved, or to give him the tree he had cutt downe. But Kendall would have both: soe to be quitt of a knave, and to quitte the bargaine, I paid him the twenty shillings, and he was to make me a discharge under hand and seale, to renounce all his tytle, claime, or demand to the same bargaine of the wood for ever, and this tree which he had was valewed to be worth £5 or £6. Thus, by the good hand of Providence to me His poore servant, was I delivered from this great evill of destroying this benifitt of the estate, and I hope to preserve it for my husband's posterity, I ever making it my endeavor to increase the wood, by planting and setting young trees, which if I could have secured as well as I would, or as I have don to all the plaine trees or scycomors, which I brought from Hipswell, and nursed them in the orchard till fitt to sett in the rowes and walkes in the front of my house, there would have bin in the parke and ellsewhere many hundreds [more] then ever was cutt in my time. For I ever tooke a delight both in the ornament of it as well as the pleasure and profitt of it, on any land.

A collection of my freinds' letters uppon the death of my deare and honered husband, in comforting me for his losse and my great afflictions (iii., 194).

But while I am relating my sorrowes and sufferings from such ingratitude of men, and those I ever counted my freinds, I must not forgett, or passe over in silence, without expressions of most humble and hearty thankes and praises to the glory of our most gracious and mercifull Lord God, Who did not snatch me out of this misserable life before He gave me, in the midest of these sorrowes, many signall and gracious testimonyes of His mercy, which I am ever obleiged to owne to His glory and my comfort. * * * Yett will I not forgett the goodnes of God to me, abundantly shewed to my drooping spirritts, by the many kind and affectionate testimonyes of my freinds' letters, and consolatory advices, and affectionate letters written to comfort me in my sorrowes, and losse of my deare husband, as well as under that other calamity.

1. In the first number was my husband's sister, my kinde and good freind, tho' of the Roman religion, was ever my true freind. My good sister Craythorne writt a comfortable letter to me conserning his death and my other afflictions, by her son. September 19, 1668.

2. My nexte was my cozen, Allen Ascoughe, writt a kinde letter to me uppon Mr. Thornton decease, his trouble for his losse. Sept. 21, 1668.

3. The third which condoled my loss, and gave me a comfortable letter and advice in my most heavy condittion, was good Dr. Wittie, who, by the good Providence of God, on his

advice, was the meanes to raise him up at Steersby in his first dreadfull fitt of the pallsey, and had very offten bin instrumentall to his recovery of many relapses, and who was now called to him att Malton, but in vaine, for God had dettermined to take my deare joy from me. This good doctor writt a most comfortable letter, to beare his losse with patience, from the consideration that he was taken away from future evills; his dated Sept. 24, 1668.

4. Dr. Sammwayes, from Middleton,* his comforting me for my losse of my deare husband; received by Mrs. Francis Grame. Oct. 12, 1668.

5. My deare neece, Best, her most kinde letter, condoling my losse, and my great affliction on the account of Mrs. Danby's wicked tongue. This letter dated Sept. 30, 1668.

6. My deare Lord Frechevill, his very comfortable letter on the death of my deare husband, and that he will ever be my freind and assistant in all my consernes. Dated Oct 18, 1668.

7. My deare neece, Fairefax,† her compassionate letter affter Mr. Thornton death; tho' not so soone as others expressed, yet as faithfull to my affection. Her letter dated Nov. 20, 1668.

8. My deare Aunt Norton uppon the sudaine newes of Mr. Thornton decease, she beeing returned from Newton a day affter his goeing to Maulton, as I spoke of, and this she heard by a woole man, her most kinde and compassionate letter in my sadest disconsolat condition, sent by her servant to see my selfe and children; her most deare and tender conserne for me in the losse of my deare husband, and the lamentable condittion I was in by the hand of God on my body, soule, spirit, and estate; and tells me she will come over to comfort me, if she can doe me any service. Her letter dated Sept. 19, 1668.

9. I received annother kinde letter from my good aunt in

---

* Middleton Quernhow. Peter Samwaies, A.M., was instituted rector of Wath 31st Dec. 1660.

† Mary, daughter of Marmaduke Cholmley, wife of William Fairfax, whose son became the ninth viscount.

making some remarks of my great sorrow to be beyond the bounds of what I ought; for non can beleeve me to be soe fallen of or degenerate from those pieous principles since my infancy. * * * Affter which she assure me that she had come to see me and give me some comfort in my great distress, now in my conserne uppon me, as to the disposall of Mr. Comber some other way, to sattisfy all the world in my proceedings, to be wise and discreet, and that she heard Mr. Scott had some who would be proper, as she heard, which would compose the bussiness in hand. Thus farre, goode woman, she went, as to the breaking of our match.

10. Dr. Sammwayes, which had bin a great stickler in the acting about the breaking the match by Mrs. Danby's fallse instigation, God did make him very sencable what wrong he had don to me, and what a contineued greife and trouble to beare the scourge of the tongue, was soe truly sencable of his error that he writt me a very Christian and comfortable letter, to alleviate my sorrowes and compassionate my sufferings of all kindes, with hearty wishes for me, and prayers.

11. My niece, Best, Feb. 5, 1668, writt a deare and comfortable letter, and begged of me not to be soe afflicted for her sister Kitt's slanderous lyes, for she was sorry I had the ill lucke to doe soe much good to her and her husband, and she to requite me as she had don all her husband's freinds, and her tongue was noe slander.

12. Notwithstanding all good people was satisfied with our proceedings in it, yett it seemes Mrs. Danby was still the same, by her inveterate malice against Mr. Comber, and against the match. She could not lett us alone, but still imploying new emissaryes to stirre up new coles of mischeife against us, in soe much as her abuies did comme to my cozen Elizabeth Nickolson's care, one who, tho' of the Romish faith, yett had the principalls of charity soe much, that it wound her soe much to heare such horrid lyes and slanders raised by her, against such which she knew had the grace of God in them. Therefore she writt a letter to me to acquaint me with it, and allso one to my brother Denton, to desire him, as he had known all the

intregues of this family, soe he would doe as much to testify
the same, which would give a great satisfaction to all strangers,
for those of our knowledge was well sattisfied, only who she had
deceaved by her cuning tongue, which my brother Denton was
pleased to doe. * * I must observe, with great gratitude to
my gracious Father of mercy, that where ever the serpent began
to hisse and stirre up his venome, in order to make a full end
of his mallice against me, then did the gracious Jesus come in
to my rescue by His Devine Providence. So ordering such
sircumstances of my freinds, unknowne to me, as noe sooner
my enemyes began to broach there vennome by there tongues,
butt my freindes are as ready to stop there first assalt, which
was given against me by Mrs. Danby att Rippon, where
there was severall of my kind freinds lived, as my cozen Frances
Maude, and her two sisters, my cozen Maudes, Jane Wandesford, married to Mr. Aude, and my cozen Lister the youngest.
Att which time my cozen Elizabeth Nicholdson, which was nece
to them all, beeing att Rippon, and made acquainted by them
what most vild aspersions Mrs. Danby had invented and others
against my son Comber, (soe that I was made a reproach by
some, but not my freinds, for marreing my daughter to him,
beeing a clargyman, and which had come to my lady Frankland's* ears, and my lady Wivell, and others,) desired that I
would lett them see my papers and letters which did conserne
that bussinesse, and the reasons and occasion which caused Mr.
Thornton and myselfe to match our daughter there. * * *
These letters, papers, and transaction of this affaire are in
bundles, and preserved, to make out these proceedings, and in
vindication of our just and lawdable actions.†

----

* Arabella Bellasis, dau. of Henry B., Esq., M.P. for co. York, by Grace,
dau. and heir of Sir Thomas Barton, of Smithells, co. Lanc., wife of Sir Wm.
Frankland, Bt., of Thirkleby.

† 1. Mr. Comber's request made to his honored lady when she went to York
to learne quallitys, May, 1666.

2. A paper of his verses made to his honoured freind when she was att Yorke,
1666.

3. An annagram on the name of his honoured lady Alice Thornton, 1666.

4. A paper of verses to his lady affter she had the smale-pox, July 20, 1666.

* * * I am obleiged in duty to God first, and the cleare satisfaction of my owne conscience, the world, and my owne family, whose good I have ever established before my owne, to leave behind me the full evidences of truth conserning this bussiness. * * These evidences will, I hope, be kept by my children for a justification of my innocency, and a condemnation of all there wickedness, who had any hand by the murder committed on my good name and innocency, and will rise up in judgement against all those lyers and forgerys which has not repented, and asked pardon of God, and us who they wronged. * * I did send those letters and papers to my

5. A letter of Mrs. Anne Danby's advice to Mr. Comber when he was att London, and that Mr. Holland, which had bin his scoolmaster, profered his daughter and a living of a £100 a yeare to him in the south.

6. Mr. Comber's letter.

7. My letter to my lord Fretchville.

8. The payment of the £100 by my brother Denton from me.

9. Mr. Bennet's letter.

10. Mr. Bennet's lease.

11. A copy of my letter to my lord Fretchvile.

12. Mr. Comber's letter from London, June 22, 1666.

13. A copy of my letter to him in answer.

14. My lord Fretchvile's letter.

15. A copy of my letter to Mr. Comber his mother.

16. A letter of Mr. Comber's to my daughter Alice.

17. A copy of her letter in answer to his.

18. My letter to Mr. Thornton.

19. Mr. Thornton's answer.

20. Mr. Comber's letter to Mr. Thornton.

21. Mr. Thornton's answer.

22. A copy of my letter to the Marquess of Carmarthen, my deare mother's owne nephew, Sir Edward Osborn's son, which I writt to him in the behalfe of my son Comber for his advancement and preferment in the church, Sept. 13, 1689.

23. Mr. Comber's first letter to Yorke to my daughter Alice, May 25, 1667.

24. Mr. Comber's second letter, June 19, 1667.

25. Mr. Comber's third letter, July 19, 1667.

26. Mr. Comber's fourth letter, Sept. 17, 1667.

27. A copy of articles of marriage.

28. A letter of Mr. Comber's mother to me, August 15, 1668.

29. A letter of Mrs. Comber affter her son's marriage, July 26, 1669.

30. A letter of my lord Fretchvile, Aug. 30, 1668.

cozen Elizabeth Nickoldson to Rippon, and from thence she sent them by my order and Dafeny's desire to her, to shew my freinds att Richmond, and to my lady Wivill, who was much conserned for all my wrongs, and pittied me extreamly much. The letter of account which I receaved from my cozen Nickolson in answer to myne was as follows: dated Dec. 3, 1669. "Most worthy cozen, I receaved your last, and have performed your desire, and sent your letters to Dafeny by my cozen Thomas Gill,* who I mett with att Rippon, where I have don you all the right I possibly could, in makeing you appeare by your prudence from time to time truly vertuous, and not soe imprudent an act as itt appeared to som in the matching of your daughter; and in relating the truth makes Mrs. Danby apeare that she is not a saint, but an unworthy woman. Soe lett me, deare cozen, beg that you will sattisfy your selfe, and not impaire your health by your immoderat sorrow and greiving, nor offend Him Who is able to make the very stones beare wittness for your innocency, which, I pray beleive me, is beleived by all worthy and noble persons. As for my worthy lady Frankland, she doth both love and honour you as a woman of excelent parts, and pittyes you as one that hath bin soe much wronged by all your servants. I desire you not to write till I consider to see you. And I must needs tell you that my lady tould my husband that of all the sermons that ever she heard in all her life, that sermon that your son Comber preached before my lord Faulkenbridge † was the very best, and for her part she can never have an evill thought of him while she breaths, but doth beleive he hath bin much wronged."

Of Dafeny's shewing my freinds the First Book of my Life. Anno Domini 1668 (ii., 195).

Affter the aprisement of Mr. Thornton's personall estate, and all those great consernes about the administration and the

---

* Thomas Gyll, of Barton, who married Elizabeth Wandesford.

† Thomas, second Viscount Fauconbridge, Lady Frankland's brother, and son-in-law of Oliver Cromwell; lord-lieutenant of the North Riding of Yorkshire. Died 31st December, 1700.

valew of the goods, and my cozen Anthony Norton's taking on
him that kind office, and my owne taking the tuittion of my
children, Dafeny beeing a materiall witness to all these actions,
and doeing me great and considerable services; she, fearing
her husband's displeasure for leaving him soe long, returned
home, and by her I sent my owne Booke of my Life, the collections of God's dealings and mercys to me and all mine till my
widowed condittion. That she might be able to sattisfy all my
freinds of my life and conversation,—that it was not such as my
deadly enymyes sugested, and the reasons I had to take caire for
all my poore children, and what condittion I was reduced into
affter the intaile was cutt of, and many other great remarks of
my life, which I knew would take away all those scruples and
fallse calumnyes against my proceedings in the match,—this
poore woman did shew the said bookes to my aunt Norton and
severall other freinds, as my lady Wivell, which sent to her to
lett her know how much I was wronged, and to speake to her
about me, with great greife and many teares did expresse her
concerne, and pittied my case, saing that I had ever bin a most
vertuous woman all my life,* and now to be soe abused, did wound
her very hart; and soe gett my booke of her to read, which she
did with a great delight, as she said, and yett with much greife
to see me soe greatly wronged by those I had don soe much for;
and did heartily beg of God that He would judge my cause, and
revenge my wronged innocency uppon all that had a hand in it,
and prayed heartily for me and myne; and when she returned
my booke to Dafeny, did write a most excelent, pieous, and
comfortable letter to me. * * * I did allso receave att this
time my said booke home when my deare aunt Norton returned

---

* "Did viudicate me from a childe of my innocency from those abuces, for
she did resent my case as it were her owne as long as she lived. * * * She
might doe me that right, and shew my cause to all my freinds at Hornby,* and
to my lady Dalton,† and all others where I was abused for it." (iii., p. 211.)

---

* Hornby, the seat of the Darcy family.

† Elizabeth, dau. of Sir Marmaduke Wyvill, Bart., wife of Sir William
Dalton, Kt., of Hawkswell. Her will is dated 25 Oct., 1707, and was proved
8th May, 1711.

it, that Dafeny carried, which did abundantly please and sattisfy her, and said that "it was not writt as if a weake woman might have don it, but might have become a devine," tho' she knew the contents to be of my whole life to that time.   Butt she gave me her advice, that the sence of the world was in generall of the match of my daughter Alice, and that she was putt on it to come to Newton about it, butt the season bad, and her husband sicke, did prevent, and that Mr. Scott* had some daughters for a match for Mr. Comber.   She beleived the want of preferment was the only stop, and for her part she had noe prejudice against him, haveing his pieous workes with her, but wishes some other way be found to compose this matter; dated October 20, 1668. (iii., p. 154.)   I did give Dafeny for herselfe, as a token of gratitude, a young cowe and calfe to sustaine her house, with other good things, which she had deserved for her faith and fidelity to mee and my poore children, and sent her husband a bible and a pound of tobaco.

Of Mr. Thornton's debts and my deepe distress thereat, and my deare son Robert's comfortable words.   Anno Domini 1668-9 (iii., 133).

Altho' I was uppon these and many more accounts formerly mentioned forced to make use of my freinds' kindness, and to borrow many sommes of monney to discharge what I was creaditably obleiged, yett it pleased God soe to order things to be somme comfort in the midest of my sorrowes and sufferings. I found many good freinds which was willing to lend me monney,—some uppon my owne single bond, vidz., as my lady Cholmley lent me £50, my lady Yorke lent me £100, Dafeny did procure for me £50, all which I tooke as a high favour from God, to assist me till I gott them in somme time paid with due intrest.   Butt I could not compass the greater sommes I had need of without somme freind to be bound with me, soe was

* Probably George Scott, instituted to the rectory of Oswaldkirk, 18th April, 1663, who died 1699.

forced to have a freind to be joyned with me ; tho' I remember
Mr. John Hicks,* my husband's old freind, did lend me £150 of
my owne security, which is all paid with due intrest long since,
I blesse God.   Butt it was a very pinching consideration to me
that I was forced to enter the first conserne of my widdowed
condition with bonds, debts, and ingagements for others, whereas
I brought soe considerable a fortune, and never knew what debt
was, to others, but what I had bin servicable to many in necessity to lend for charity ; but it was the good pleasure of my God
to bring me into this dispensation, therefore I do humbly beg
His mercy and grace to indure it with patience.

There was many occurrences hapned to me of a fresh
supply of tryalls before I could be inabled to gett by my
sorrowfull bed, which was of many occasions.   But since it
pleased God to give me this opportunity to receave the blessed
Sacrament with my daughter Comber, and my son, and Hanah,
and some others, I was much comforted in God's mercy, this
beeing the first time I could be able to doe it since my dear
husband's death, which was in my chamber, when I sat in bed,
December 25, 1668.   *   *   *   It pleased God about January
to inable me to gett out of my bed, tho' very weake.   *   *   *
(iii., 162).

In this deepe distress of sorrowes I did much continew
for severall months together, but the greatest comfort I
tooke was in the consideration of God's Almighty power to
bring me out of all, and was my suport under it in the testimony of a cleare conscience ; and, while I was able to do my
duty, with my poore ability was in teaching my deare and only
son to read, and heare him his catechisme, prayers, and psalmes,
gitting proverbs by heart, and many such like dutys.   Butt one
day, above all the rest, beeing, as I remember, on my owne birthday, in the afternoone, haveing kept the other part seperate in
fasting and prayer, February 13, 1668-9,—as I was siting on
the long settle in my chamber, and hearing read in the gospell
of St. Matthew, my heart was full of sorrow and bitterness of

* Qu. John Hickes, V.D.M., who died 1685.

spirrit, beeing overwhelmed with all sorts of afflictions that lay uppon me, considering my poore condittion, either to pay debts, to maintaine this poore young childe, or to give him the education which I would and designed, by God's blessing, to bring him up a clergyman, and a true minister of the gospell. * * * Such was my sad affliction at this time, that passion and a flood of teares overcame my reason and religion, and made me to leave my deare childe when I was teaching him to read, and could not conteine my great and infinitt sorrowes, but scarce gott to my bedside for falling down, when I then cast myselfe crosse the bed, fell in bitter weeping and extreame passion for offending God, or provoking His wrath against me, to leave and forsake me thus forlorne. Butt while I was in this desperate condittion, and full of dispaire in myselfe, behold the myraculous goodnesse of God, even the God Who I apprehended had forsaken me and cast me off for ever, in that very instant of time did bring me an unexpected both releife and comfort, tho' a mixture of His gentle reproofe for my too great passion and impatience under His hand and correction. My deare son Robert, seeing me fallen downe on the bed in such a sad condittion and bitter weeping, comes to me to the bedside, and beeing deeply conserned to see me in such extreamity, crept on the bed with his poore hands and knees, and cast himselfe on my breast, and imbracing me in his armes, and laid his cheek to myne with abundance of teares, cryed out to me in these words: "Oh! my deare, sweete mother; what is the reason that you doe weepe and lament and mourne soe much, and ready to breake your heart? Is it for my father you doe mourne for soe much?" To which I answred, "Oh! my deare childe, it is for the losse of thy deare father. Have I not cause? for I am this day a desolate widdow left, and thou art a poore young orphant without helpe or any releife." To which my deare infant answered, "Doe you not, my deare mother, beleive that my father is gon to heaven?" To which I replyed againe, "Yes, I doe beleive and hope through Christ's merrits and suffrings for us that thy deare father is gon to heaven." Uppon which he said to me againe, "And would you have my father to come out of heaven, where he injoyes God, and all joy and happiness, to come downe out of heaven and indure all those sickness and sorrowes he did, to comfort you heere? Who is the father of the fatherless, and husband to the widdow? Is not God? Will not He provide for you? Oh! my deare mother, doe not weepe and lament thus very sore, for if I live I will take caire for you and comfort you; but if you weepe thus, and mourne, you will breake my heart, and then all is gon; therefore, my deare mother, be comforted in God, and He will preserve you." All which wordes, uttred with so great a compassion, affection, and filiall dearness and tenderness, can never be forgott by me. But this excelent councell came from God, and not from man; for non but the Speritt of God could put such words into the mouth of a childe but six yeares old and four months. Therefore I acknowledg the glory to my gracious God in it, which both did admonish my passion, and put this comfortable word into his mouth, which I bless the Lord my God for, and never affter was overcome with the like passion. * * * I was at annother time comforted from the mouth of this childe when he was very young, and I have great cause to recount the goodness of God to me and him, to put His Spirritt soe early into him. When his sister Kate had the smale-pox he was with me in the scarlett chamber, and looking very earnestly to the window, with his eyes up to heaven in a deepe meditation, with a great sigh said to me (when he broke of his catechisme which I was then hearing him), " Mother, God is a most holy, righteous, and pure spiritt. The devill is a lying, wicked, and evill spiritt. It is better to serve this holy pure God and righteous spiritt, then to serve this lying, wicked spirrit, the devill. And by God's grace I will love and serve this good God, and not this evill spirritt, which is the devil." Which he spoke with a great deale of zeale and earnestness of speech, and from his poore heart, which was a great deale of comfort to me; and blessed God for His grace putt into him, my child, and bid him follow these good things which God had graciously put into his heart soe young, that he might know Him, and love Him, and feare Him all the daies of his life. And one more I am bound by the mercys of

the great God of Heaven to record to His eternall glory and
future hopes of comfort for His salvation in the midest of many
feares.   The first time he went to church att Stongrave he was
but four yers old and a halfe, or thereabouts.   Mr. Comber
preached, but I was not well and could not goe to church, but
he went with his father.   And affter he came home I asked
him what he did remember of the sermon, and where was the
text ; for if he did not remember to tell me the text and sermon
he should go noe more ; not to be idle and looke about him, but
to heare and remember what God said to him by His ministers.
After this he looked me in my face and cryed out, " Oh !
mother, God did tell me in the text that He loved me with an
everlasting love, and His loveing kindness He did embrace me,
and He would never leave me nor forsake me; and, indeed, I
love God with all my heart."   At which unexpected answer of
this infant my heart was exceeding joyfull.   *   *   *   Long
before this time, Mr. Thornton beeing in my chamber, and my
deare child on his knee, beeing very young, his father began to
tell him that God made man of the dust of the earth, and gave
him a body and soule, and made him Eve to be his wife, and
gave her to Adam, and had made all the creatures in the world
for Adam and Eve's service, and made a garden, and gave them
all the trees of the garden for fruit ; only one tree which God
had forbidden them to eate of it, which was an aple tree, and
said that if they did eate of the aple tree they should dye, and
charged them not to eate of it.   Butt the devill, in the shape of
a serpent, beguiled Eve, and tempted her to eate of an aple, and
soe God was angry at her and Adam.   They both did eate of it,
and soe He cursed them, and said they should [dye] because of
disobeying His command ; and soe death came into the world,
and all we must dye for this sinn.   The childe beholding his
father very earnestly, looked him up in his face, cryed out to his
father, " Oh ! father, and must he dye to ? "   He, with a great
passion of teares, said, Must he dy for eating God's apple ? He
was sure he did not eat God's aple, and must he dy ? with
abundance of sorrow and bitterness, as if he had realy seene this
with his eyes. Which his father tooke hold of him and said, that

he did not eate it himselfe, but in his first parents, Adam and Eve, we beeing their children. Yett God was soe mercyfull to mankinde that He did give His only Son Jesus Christ to dy for us, as it was in his belefe, "He was crucified for us." That if we beleve in Him we shall be saved, and feare and serve God all our dayes." To which the poore infant said, "I beleive in God and in Jesus Christ Who dyed for me, and will love and feare Him all my life," with many great expressions of piety. *Oh! who gives man knowledge? Is it not I, saith the Lord ?** (iii., 170.)

My brother Sir Chr. Wandesford compelled me to strip myself of all the arrears due to me (iii., 162).

About this time I had a new affliction† befell me conserning my brother, Sir Christopher Wandesford, who, as I said before, had made over a rent-charge of £200 pound per annum to Mr. Thornton, out of Ireland, to discharge my £1000 due for part of my portion, which Mr. Thornton had before marriage given bond to secure for myselfe and children, and that I should injoy it for my life if I was a widdow, and affter my decease to be for my children. The other £100 a yeare was to repay Mr. Thornton for that debt he paid to Mr. Nettleton, which should have had it out of my father's estate in Ireland ; and these conditions made when Mr. Thornton did part with the estate to Sir Christopher Wandesford. When this rent-charge was demanded by Mr. Thornton's freinds,.viz., Mr. Portington and Mr. Raynes,‡ to whom Mr. Thornton had made a morgage of 99 yeares over Laistrop—as I mentioned uppon the cutting of the intaile of Mr. Colvill's intaile on my two children, Alice and Catherine—to secure their portions and maintenance out of Laistrop; the

* Allusion to Proverbs ii. 6.

† "Still haveing new fuell put to the first flame of my sorrowes, which was not extinct, but laid sleeping a little, till fresh occassions from without kindled a new flame." (iii., 161.)

‡ Attorney-at-law, of Appleton-le-Street ; died 8th March, 1713, æt. 73, buried at Easingwold. *Visit. Ebor.,* 1665, p. 368.

cutting of the same, when I came to the hearing thereof, in the year 1666, did bring me to that miscarage by greife, and brought me neare to death. * * * My brother, Sir Christopher Wandesford, knowing this £1000 in Ireland was my portion, and that it was made over to me by Mr. Thornton before marriage, would not pay any part of that rent-charge to the administrator of Mr. Thornton, but only to my selfe, being my due and right to have injoyed now in my widowed estate, according to articles and bond before marriage. I was forced to informe him that, for that end Mr. Thornton should settle Laistrop by Colville's deed uppon my daughters for provission for portions and maintenance (his debts beeing soe great) ; that, to pay them, and fre his land, I was willing to yeld up that £1000, to cleare his estate and make provission for his two children ; and soe I was to have noe part in it, but desired it might be paid by him as the £1000 he paid to Nettleton was, to goe to the sattisfaction of Mr. Thornton's debts; when, in the meane time, still this heavy mortgage laid uppon the estate of Laistropp, and nothing in reality formerly settled uppon any of my children, nor anything in the world to maintaine my deare and only son, then but six years old, and all swalowed up with debts from us. Nor had I ever one penny of all my father's portion to doe me good in all my life, nor my children. These was pinching sircumstances for me to begin my life with ; yet, altho' I was thus willing to rob myselfe of my right and comfortable subsistence for myselfe and poore son, who I had undertaken to maintaine and educate without any assistance, but to enter into debt the first houer of my widdowhood ! and had then a certaine and great debt due to my owne selfe, by vertue of my honred father's last will and testament, and my deare mother's ! * * * Yett nothing of this would be taken into consideration either by one or the other, either to demand the said dues for my selfe and children, or the other to give me in leeiew of it. Albeit I stood uppon it to have it demanded as my right and due, yett they was soe cold in the matter that there was noe thing don in it in my behalfe, least of offending Sir Christopher, who was then to pay that anuity (I should have had) for debts. Alltho' that was designed soe, yett it would have bin no disadvantage to debts, or my children's well-faire, to have been better inabled to have performed all, if my rights had bin gained, to the sattisfaction of my dear uncle Sir Edward Osborne's debt, which my deare mother gave first out of those arrears, which, by remissness and neglect, was quite lost. Nay, the gaining of the one would have bin the way and meanes to have gott the other arrears due to me; and the neglect of the first was the losse of the whole arrears, to the destruction of my selfe and estate. Butt, instead of my receaving any advantage from that, when Sir Christopher saw that my £1000 was thus condemned to the debts of Mr. Thornton, and that his estate could not subsist without that anuity out of *his* estate, due to me as above, he was very earnest to have me to make him a generall release of all my rights and dues to me out of my father's estate, either by my selfe or mother, or my brother John Wandesford, which he very well knew was a very great somme of money. And before he would yeald to pay one penny of the anuity to Mr. Thornton's administrator, he stood uppon this poynt, and would doe nothing or pay any dues; soe, haveing made his demand of this thing, which, I supose, was by the advice of his father-in-law, who knew I had never released my rights, or my mother's, out of that estate, but kept this as a rod over us, to make me yeald to these unjust demands, knowing how low my husband's estate was, judged we could not obteine it by course of law, or have any right from him. This sad oppression was very greivous over my weake spirritts, who had non in the world to take my part, or to assist me to gett my dues. Nor was it judged fitt to advise with my deare uncle Sir Edward Osborne's relations about this conserne, which soe much conserned them, least the acting in that might be to hinder the payment of the annuity for Mr. Thornton's debts. * * * When my son Comber saw me in such distresse and conserne, that I should destroy myselfe and children of all my dues from the estate from Sir Christopher, he tould me I might have somme advise what to doe in that case from somme lawyer, which could assist me in that poynt, which I was glad to doe;

for tho' att present noe likelihood Sir Christopher Wandesford would agree, or pay any of the rent-charge, without suite, or to make me signe such a bace release as was drawne up by Mr. Binlowes* (a turnecote, bitter presbiterian, Sir Christopher made use of), which cutt me totally of, or any of myne, from even having any benifitt of my father's will, by which I had very great dues ; yett I would not doe it, or signe any at all, till I had some advice about it. * * * To this end I advised with Mr. Hassell,† an able lawyer, about this bussiness, who did draw up a deed of guift for me to seale and signe in a leagall manner to feoffes in trust of all my rights, dues, and tytles, to what my honred father and mother had given me, by and in there last wills and testaments, references being thereunto had, as may att large apeare in all there deeds and guifts and bequeths belonging to myselfe, or mother, or brother ; and to settle them all uppon the feoffees in trust for the use and behoofe of my only son and heire, to him and his issue ; and for default of such issue then to the use and behoofe of my two daughters, Alice and Katherine Thornton, to them and theire heires for ever, to be laid out in land of inheritance purchased for them as neare as could be obteined to be neare unto my husband's estate of Easte Newton and Laistrop ; and yett, neverthelesse, reserving power in myselfe a power of revocation. The trustees nominated Renald Grahme,‡ esquire; Dr. Wattkinson ;§ Mr. Chancellor of Yorke ; and Dr. Burton. This deed of trust or guift of myne was dated * * * in the * * * before the releace was signed by me to Sir Christopher Wandesford, which was drawne up by

---

* Thomas Bendlowes, of Howgrave, near Kirklington, who gave up the living of Meldon, in Northumberland, in 1662, and afterwards practised as a lawyer.

† Thomas Hassell, of Hutton Derwent, barrister of Gray's-Inn, bur. 27 Oct., 1694, at St. Michael's, Malton. *Visit. Ebor.*, 1665, p. 75. This name occurs at Ripon in the middle of the 18th century, a George Hassell, attorney-at-law, being chosen recorder of that place, 30th October, 1767. He died 17 July, 1773.

‡ R. Graham, of Nunnington, Esq.

§ Henry Watkinson, LL.D., Chancellor of the diocese of York, 1673 ; buried 25th April, 1712, at St. Cuthbert's, York. *Visit. Ebor.*, 1665, p. 206.

my councell's advice, Mr. Driffeild.*   Nor would I doe it to rob
my selfe of every bequeth which my deare father and mother
had, out of there tender affection, given to me, but would have
that only reserved to myselfe of one hundred pounds given by
my deare father in his will† to my deare mother to buy her a
jewell, which Sir Christopher, or some for him, thought much
at, that I should not be a cast-out, or exposed from the family
in all; but with much to doe I did affterwards receave the same
£100, £50 of which I receaved and paid my lady Yorke that
£50 I borrowd of her, and the other £50 was paid by me for
the discharge of somme debts of my son Thornton at Cambridg.
Butt I humbly blesse Almighty God for the great mercy that
I receaved in this £100, which releived myselfe and poore son.
(iii., 162.)

An act of submission in my poverty.

Thus was I striped of all the great riches and honorable
injoyments I had right unto, which I yealded to do for the good
and quiett of this family, beeing unable in body or purce to
resist this great pressur was laid for me, which proved the overthrow of this poore estate, which, if it might have bin rightly
mannaged in my husband's lifetime, or since his death by some
freind or assistance to have succored me in my distresse, it would
have bin of soe great an advantage to have purchased a duble
estate to what I found, and made a most florishing family as was
in this country.   But since I am now reduced to the degree of
losse in those riches which God had given me, I humbly beg
His grace, and patience to be suported under the hand of God,
which He did see fitt to bring me to, under great burdens, and
debts, and losses, which I no waies was contributary to, either
by my pride, extravagancy, voluptuousness, excesse, or waist-
fullnesse of what the Lord had given me, nor by any way of
imprudence to the managery of what was under my caire or

---

* Christopher Driffield, Esq., was chosen recorder of Ripon 3rd Oct., 1673.
Died 1733. Mon. Ins.

† Dated 2nd October, 1640.

part to performe in my power.   I hope that God and my owne conscience will not condemn me for any of these things, since what I did doe in poynt of houskeeping, diett, apparrell, or entertainments, was ever designed and practised to keepe within bounds of moderation, decency, and necessity, nor ever I affected to conforme myselfe to the modes or quirkes of new fashions and affected noveltics, either in meate, drinke, apparrell, of the gaictyes of the world—not even in the prime of my youth, when, as Job saieth, *The candle of the Lord shined uppon me.** Butt I blesse God for His grace to me, in giving me to strive and indeavor affter the addorning of my spirritt and heart with all those Christian vertues of faith, humility, patience, meekeness, chastity, and charity, that I might put on the Lord Jesus Christ, and Him crucificd, that by following of Him in His stepts I might become acceptable in His eyes, and abounding in true and faithfull conjugal love to my husband and his family.   I cannot deny but when my deare and only sister's family some of them fell into decay, and the estate taken away by the late rebellion against King Charles the First, and so exposed to much poverty, especially the second son, who married against his father's comand, and came to be a family missrable enough; to releive himselfe and family I did expend, out of my deare mother's estate she gave me, somme considerable sommes to releive that family; but not without my husband's knowledge or consent, who never was backward in those poynts of charity.   And if in this poynt I have erred, I humbly beg pardon ; since affection, necessity, and charity, obleiged my assistance in these cases.   And if now I am reduced to want those necessarys I bestowed on them, and theire estates be now florishing, and mine brought downe to want and indigency by great and many debts, contracted by others, and for the saving the estate I am now soe low, I will not yett dispaire in the mighty helpe and releife of a mighty and mercifull Father of Heaven, Who both sees my distresse, and I hope will pitty my condicion.   And tho' He has raised three familyes by my

---

* Job xxix. 3, 4. ·

meanes, and my freinds, to great riches and glory in the world, and given me to taste of His bitter cupp of sufferings for others, yett will I humbly cast myselfe low before His footstoole and throne of grace, Who has brought me downe to the grave and raised me up, times without number. He alone both can, and I hope will, raise me up out of this poore estate, and give me sufficient sustaintation, support, releife, and deliverance out of this land of bondage, even as His mercy did to that poore widdow of Sarepthæ, and give me out of the little I have to pay all debts, pay all just dues, to live in moderate, comfortable station; not beeing burdonsom to any; but doeing good to all, harme to non; beeing helpfull, usefull, charitable to those in need or necessity, and to follow affter St. Paull's rule, *In this I exercise myselfe, to keep a conscience voyd of offence, both towards God and towards man;* * that soe I may ever live in the feare of God, dye in His favour, and for ever rest in His glory; and this I humbly beg in the name and for the sake of our Lord Jesus Christ.

Of my deliverance from the loss of sight (iii., 182).

About Aprill it pleased God my strength and sight began to recover, tho' still in a mournfull condittion, and was a great object of my dearest freinds' pitty, and of my enymyes' scorne.

It pleased God in His great mercy and goodness to myselfe and my son and daughter, to be made pertakers of that holy feast of our Lord and Saviour Jesus Christ, of the blessed Sacrament att Easter, 1669; beeing the second time I received affter Mr. Thornton's death, and affter the marriage of my daughter (iii., 216).

About March 25, 1669, I was writing of my First Booke of my Life, to enter the sad sicknesses and death of my deare husband, together with all those afflictions befell me that yeare, with the remarkes of God's dealing with my selfe, husband, and children till my widdowed condittion; as I had don ever since

* Acts xxiv. 16.

I could remember from my first youth and childehood. There hapned me then a very strange and dangerous accident to me casualy, which might have bin of a dangerous consequence to the sight of my left eye, if not to have influenced uppon both and have putt them out. Which shewes we are ever in danger, and never free from the worst of casualtyes, without the watchfull eye of Divine Providence to guard both our soules and bodies from the hostility of the devill. Even when we may thinke ourselves most safe and free from harme, in an innocent or religious imployment, then doth our enymy watch to doe us evill.

The occasion was thus which had like to have bin soe fattall to me. There was a poore little creature, harmless in itselfe, and without any gall or mallice to doe hurt, a little young chicken not above fourteen daies old, which had bin exposed, and picked out of the hen's nest that hatched it, and by her was turned out from amongst the flocke she had newly hatched, being about nine in number. All which she broked,* and made much of, but this poore chick she had turned out of the nest in a morning when the maide came to see if she was hatched; and finding this poore chicken cast out of the nest on the ground and for dead and cold; but the maide tooke it up and putt it under the hen, to have recruted it by warmth. Butt the hen was soe wilde and mad att it, that she would not lett it be with her or come neare her, but picked it, and bitt it, and scratched it out with her feete twice or thrice when the maide put it in, soe that she saw noe hopes of the hen to nurse it up as the rest, soe she tooke it up and putt it in her brest to recover it. And soe she brought this poore creature to me, and tould me all this story with great indignation against the unnaturalnesse of its mother. But I, pittiing this forlorne creature in that case, could not withold my caire, to see if I could any way save the life of it, and carried it to the fire, rapped it in woole, and gott some cordiall waters and opned its bill and putt a drop by little and little, and then it gasped and

* *i.e.,* brooked.

came to life within an houer, giving it warme milke, till it was recovered and become a fine peart* chicken.

Thus I saved it and recovered it againe, making much of it, and was very fond of it, haveing recovered it to life, and kept it in a baskett with woole in the nights, and in my pockett in the dayes, till it came to be a very pretty coulered and a strong bird, about fourteen or sixteen daies old, and sometimes put it into my bosome to nurish and bring it up, hoping it had bin a hen chicke, and then I fancied it might have brought me eggs in time, and soe gott a breed of it. This was my innocent divertion in my mallancholy houers; till one day, about Candlemas, 1669, haveing begun a booke wherein I had entered very many and great remarkes of my course of life, * * * I tooke out this poore chicken out of my pockett to feed it with bread, and sett it on the table besides me. It picking about the bread, innocently did peepe up att my left eye. Whether it thought the white of my eye had bin some bread, while I was attent on my booke, in writing held my head and eye downe, not suspecting any hurt, or fearing any evill accident, this poore little bird picked one picke att the white of my left eye, as I looked downeward, which did so extreamly smart and ake that I could not looke up, or see of either of my eyes. And the paine and blood-shot of it grew up into a little knot or lumpe, with the hurt and bruse in that tender part, that I was sore swelld and blood-shott, that it tooke away the sight of it for a long time, and had a skine and pearle of it, and with paine and sicknesse brought me to my bed, and I could not see almost anything of it, and indangred the sight of both. * * Thus had I cause to call uppon my gratious God and Father of heaven, Who had permitted soe great an evill to come uppon me, to wound that part which I had soe great a cause to make use of, by teares and sorrow in this my trouble and sad condittion. * * He did in great mercy preserve my right eye, and at length restored my sight, about six weekes or more that I had suffered by it. Nor could I suffer this poore creature to

* Peart, *i.e.*, lively, strong, active, and is still in use in Yorkshire.

be killd, as I was putt uppon for this, for it did it in its innocency.   There was some who jested with me, and said, they
had heard of an old saing* of " bringing up a chicken to pick
out there eye."   But now they saw I had made good that old
saing, both in this bird, and what harme I had suffered from
Mrs. Danby, of whom I had bin so cairfull, and preserved her
and her's from starving.   But I tould you that her cryme was
more impardonable, for what was don by her was out of mallice,
and unmerited from me; and what I did for her's and her was
out of my Christian charity, and God's cause; and only of pitty
I saved that dieing chicken.   *   *   Thus have I new occasion
uppon every action of my life to blesse and praise the Lord my
God, Who hath soe watchfull an eye over me.   For if this
chicken had light with its bill on the sight, or blake of my eye,
it had infaleably put it out, and much indangred the other eye
too, there being soe great a sympathy betwixt them in the
opticks.   Therefore will I prayse and glorify the God of mercy
for both, and humbly beseech Him that with these very eyes,
as Job saith, " *I may see God, not annother for me;* "† but with
these eyes doe I hope and long for to see God my Creator and
Father of Heaven, and Jesus Christ the Redcemer, and my
Saviour and Deliverer, and the Holy Spirritt, the Sanctifier of
all the elect people of God.

On Mrs. Ann Danby's going to Hooly,‡ April 20, 1667
(i., 237).

Uppon the complaint of Mrs. Danby to Mrs. Batte, (then a
servant to the young Countesse of Sussex, and accounted by
her to be the dearest freind she had in the world), of her hard
usuage by Maddam Danby, and severall discontents, framed by
her servant in my house, adding to her former disgust towards
me in her beeing cast out, as she said, for my sake, these, with

---

* Compare the sayings of Dr. Barnes, Bishop of Durham, to Bernard
Gilpin, the Apostle of the North.

† Job xxix. 27.

‡ Howley Hall, in the parish of Batley.

other secrett unjust reasons of her owne, by these two persons
was a mutuall compliance in there designes. And Mrs.
Danby's undermiuing me in secrett brought Mrs. Batte, late at
night, to my house at Newton, under pretence of providing
better for Mrs. Danby at the service att Hooly, to waite on that
mad Countesse of Sussex.* Mrs. Batt tould me she came to
fech her cosen Danby away, and that she would have her from
me. I, upon this first salutation, beeing surprised with her
discourse, as well as her sudaine vissitt, which yet Mrs. Danby
knew of, tould her againe that I had bin desirous to see her,
and of her acquaintance upon my neece her account, but that
she should now come to fettch her from me, whoes wellfaire I
much wished and loved her company, without giveing me any
notice, I could not tell what to say of it, and that what my
poore house could afford towards my neece's her content, and
what I could doe for her, should not be a-wanting, noe more
then what I had formerly don, to my weake capacity. And I
could not willingly part with her, hopeing that her sister, upon
my soliciting, would settle her againe. My discourse more to
this purpose, but the other said she would have her away from
me. Then I returned that I would leave it to my neece herselfe, to dettermine as she pleased. Upon the Sunday morning, they haveing lien together that night, prepaired for a
march to Hooly. But they were prevailed to stay that day,
beeing every way unfitt to breake the sabbath uppon soe
slight an occassion. Upon discourse with Mrs. Batte, she said
that she admired why all Mrs. Danby's freinds that non of them
could indure her of her husband's side, but I, that looked at
her or shewed any respect. I said that I could not soe well
know the reason, save that she brought noe fortune and was a
charge to the family, as I had heard them say, and that Sir

* James Savile, second Earl of Sussex, was son of Thomas Savile, first Earl,
who died 1644, by Lady Anne Villiers, daughter of Christopher, Earl of Anglesea,
niece of George, Duke of Buckingham, who remarried — Barde, Esq., of Weston.
The Earl, who died s. p. 1671, Oct. 11th, married Anne, daughter of Robert
Wake, a merchant at Antwerp, who married 2nd — Overton, and was buried
14 Feb., 1678-9. This must be the lady.

Thomas Danby could not be reconsiled because of Kitt's marriage to her against his knowledge or consent. Then Mrs. Batt said it was true that she had scene a letter in Virginia that came to Mrs. Danby from Sir Thomas out of England, in answer to one from Mrs. Danby to him, that was extreamly sharpe; where he tould her that she had inveagled his son to marry her without his consent, and theire marriage was not lawfull. And for her, that had not a groate portion, affter such an act to be soe proud and high as to require him to furnish her with silke stockings, sattin, and cloth, a silver mantle, and other things answrable to that state, was more presumption then any could imagine, his son beeing a younger brother, and soe had nothing but from his goodnesse. Sir Thomas Danby expressing much more to her in that letter to this purpose, and was soe incensed that he would seldom see her in all his life, but shunned her at all times, sending for his son into England without her.

I said I had not heard of such letters, but that Sir Thomas was much displeased at me and my mother for speaking for her to him, and said that we knew her not soe well as he did, and that they might curs the time of her entrance into his family, for the mischeife she had wrought in it, and that match could not prosper which was begun in such an unlawfull manner, it had bin the grand discontent of his life, and more to the like purpose, severall times. Soe my mother nor my selfe, affter many indeavors, could never prevaile for her, yet did I allwaies commiserate her condittion, whoes person was soe qualified, and seemed to be religious, and carried soe faire in her demener, having abundance of charity for her condition, having helped her with advice and assistance in all things to my poure, beleiving that she had bin wronged, according to her owne complaint. When our discource was ended, they came from church and went to dinner. Affter, it was consulted on, and thought fitt to send to Mr. Farrer* at Malton, for his advice,

---

* Probably some confidential adviser of Madam Danby, who was daughter and co-heir of Colonel William Eure, sixth son of William, Lord Eure, of Malton, who died s. p. 23rd June, 1688. Possibly his chaplain.

whether Mrs. Danby might goe to Hooly as a vissitt, who returned by word, that he conseaved she might goe thither, allthough he knew that place was in opposition to Madam Danby, and would displease her if she staied any time, but for a while she might goe, as he thought, without prejudice. This she conseaved was allowance, but he spoke very prudently for both partys. * * Att her goeing that morning she was highly displeased, I was informed [by those] that she spoke it to, that Mr. Comber, or my brother Denton, who she had much deluded with faire shew, did not waite upon her to Hooly, and was only conducted by my cheife servant and three of the earle's men, with Mrs. Batt and her maid. This was only a pretence, though pride enough; for, when I sent men and horses to bringe her home above sixty miles hence on purpose, she was not pleased because Mr. Comber came not, but sent them backe empty, save with a letter to my brother Denton to invite him under pretence, but really the other, who she then prosecuted with eager designe for to drawe him in for a husband for Mrs. Batte.

She went away with that woman to Hooly, to the Countesse of Sussex, where she was an eye wittness of all the villanyes don by the earle and his lady, most odious, and did see when six of the maides of the house servants was by the said [Earl] made to dance naked. And there was one modest chast maide which tould the countess that she would not doe it, when she presed[ed ?] her to it, and said she would not stay in such a place where it was don, and imeadiatly quitted the service. I had not writt these lines, but to sett forth the vild hipocricy of this woman Mrs. Danby.

After her returne from Hoouly, and Madam Danby to Malton, I endeavoured with Mr. Thornton, to gett her company thither, that I might have reconsiled her and her sister. But she could not be prevailed with upon noe tearmes, nor soe much as to write to her in a civill way, but said severall times, she had as leve see the dcivill as her. Soe that I went only with my brother Denton thither, and had a most teadious and ill jorney, beeing sicke as well when I came there as backe againe,

as I had like to have died.   Upon my adresse to Madam
Danby, I found her very civill to me, but soe highly insenced
against Kitt's wife as I did admire, and at first would not
scarse heare me speake for her att all.

Of the Settlements drawne by Mr. Best, Mr. Colville, Mr. Legard (iii., 50).

After our comming to our house att Newton to live, (and I
was by the wonderfull mercys of God soe well recruted that I
was able to come on foote thither), it was thought uppon to
make some paper bookes,* which was drawne att London by my
cozen Ledgard, in order to an intaile on my issue generall,
male or female.   *   *   I, not hoping to live long in this life,
so full of sorrowes and trouble, sicknesses and crosses, beeing to
pass through that dreadfull danger of child-birth, comming out
of them with dangers and difficultys, desired Mr. Henry Best,
who had married my sister's daughter, Katherine Danby, that
he would please to draw up a deed of guifft with a sedulle
annexed, which part each of my children should have, according
to my deare mother's will and deed, and to the power she had
given me, that they should not be made lyable to the debts or
ingagements which my deare husband had bin soe unfortunatly
drawn into by the assignment.   For she pleased to say the
reason why she disposed them thus, that why should my bed
be taken from under me by those debts which he ought not to
pay?   But this nephew Best forfeted his trust, and drew those
deeds affter such a manner as did flattly ruine my deare
mother's caire of me and mine, and made the deed absolutly to
give my mother's goods and monney all into the power of the
creaditors, which was a very grand wrong to me and mine,† but

---

* Drafts of deeds.

† "Which thing Mr. Thornton did declare to me he did not know, nor had
a hand in it, and was not pleased with it, soe that I never would seale the same,
tho' they cost me a great deal of charges to draw and ingrose, for fees to him and
his clark, which was don at Newton." (ii., 258).

uppon the reading the deed, affter the ingrossing, I found the pollicy to be contrary to the first bace * draught, and I would not signe it.† * * After I had powred out my complaint to God, and made my pettition to Him, it came into my thoughts that my cousin Roger Colvill was a very able lawyer and a good honnest man, a freind to our family, and had don many offices of kindness for us, and that I hoped my husband would accept of him to give his advice and assistance in the case. To him I aplyed myselfe in this case, and confided in him, as beeing an able and good councellor, and I hoped would draw up a good and substantiall deed of intaile of the whole estat to be settled; Newton for my joynture during life, and affter our decease uppon my issue, male or female, according to the articles of marriage. Laistrop was allso so settled and intailed on my issue in like manner, with such provissions first out of it made firme for my two daughters, for provission for maintenance and portion for them, before Mr. Thornton, in case of my death, or his heire male affter him, could injoy that estate and the somme of £1600 to be paid to them.‡ This deed of my cousin Colvill's dated June 3, 1662. * * But how this deed was evaded, or when, I know not, or on what occasion, only I remember Harry Best asked me if I would not grant that his uncle should have one or two of the closes in Laistrop to be made liable to secure a little debt he owed to Sir Henry Cholmley.§ I tould him

---

* Base, *i.e.*, rough.

† Some will think this the greatest proof of Mrs. T.'s talent, as it certainly is of her business-like habits.

‡ "One thing I had forgotten to mention; I was willing, out of my great love to Mr. Thornton and his family to doe, and deprive myselfe of that priviledge : I had by my first deed of joynture to have it without impeachment of any manner of waiste, by which I might have had the priviledge of cutting downe the wood, etc.; but I did desire only to leave myselfe liberty for all manner of uses of ploweboote, stileboote, houseboot, fireboote, and what I needed, beeing soe desirous to preserve the same to posterity." (ii., 245.)

"I was willing to pay all charges belonging to fees and clarkes and councell, and did, out of my owne purse that my dere mother had given me, pay Mr. Colvill's charges and fees, and gratuity, which might cost me about £20." (ii., 245.)

§ "Severall years affter, about that time when Mr. Thornton borrowed the £100 of horrse race mony (tho' I knew not of it then.") (ii.)

againe, I knew not of any debt he owed to Sir Henry Cholmley, and if he did owe him anything I hope I had don enough to cleare that and all his debts, by giveing up all Burne Parke to be sould, and my £1000, which was above £3200, beside my £1500 portion out of Kirklington; I was much conserned he owed more.*

But he pressing me to this, and he beeing a trustee nominated in the deed of cozen Covill, I thought to have his advice about it whether it were not drawne soe firme that it could not be cutt of without my consent, and soe very innocently showed him that deed, which, when he had read it,† he did tell me that Mr. Thornton could cutt of the intaile without my consent, and charged me by noe meanes to let him see it, nor know of it. * * * I beged of him, haveing non of my owne relations to stand for me but him, and he beeing a trustee in that deed, soe he would not discover that which he said he found out to Mr. Thornton, whereby that intail might be cutt of and settled for other uses; uppon which wordes he did promise and faithfully ingage to me uppon his faith that he would not betray my cause to Mr. Thornton, nor discover the failing in that settlement; on which promise I relied, nor did I think that he would have don so treacherously to me, as it did prove affterwards; for I was tould by a good freind, affter all was don, that Mr. Best immeadiatly affter he had discovered this thing, he went to Mr. Thornton and tould him that it was in his power to cutt of the intayle of Mr. Colvill without my consent.

At length it did, by God's mercy, come into my mind to acquaint my cozen Ledgard, then at Sir Hennry Cholmlie's, the

* "An accompt of morgages charged uppon Laistrop, or some part of that land, before Mr. Colvil's settlement, which I did not know of till long affter, about the yeare 1668 : 1. A bond to Sir Henry Cholmley from Mr. Thornton for the somme of £1000, dated Oct. 23, 1661. 2. A bond to performe covenants, £1000 dated Aug. 7, 1662. 3. A deed of morgage of the milne holme in Laistrop to Sir Henry Cholmley for £103, May 20, 1662. 4, 5, 6. A deed of morgage of the milne holme for £53, May 20, 1662 (ii., 260). Sir Henry Cholmley died at Tangiers in August, 1666, having gone thither to help his nephew, Sir Hugh C., Bart., Surveyor-General of the Mole." (Visit Ebor. Surt. Soc., p. 74.)

† It is thought the trustee would hardly sign a deed he had not read, especially as Henry Best was a barrister-at-law, of Gray's Inn.

Grainge,* being a lawyer.   He I desired to read my writings and
settlements of the whole estate, both as to articles and them
deeds which ought to have bin maide punctually by them, and
to give me his oppinnion of them, whether or not Mr. Thornton
had power to cutt of the intaile from my children or not.   In
regard that when I was at St. Nickolas my aunt Norton desired
if I had a son (beeing then with childe) it might be called
Charles, it bringing his name with him, and cumming at soe
happy a time as at the restoration of the king and the church.
But Mr. Thornton would not consent to that to have him called
Charles, for reasons best known to himselfe, but tould me if I
would have him called Charles, if it were a son, he should not
have any of his land, not a foote of his land, which did a little
trouble me, but said that I praied God to send me well over
that condition, and give him a son, and he might call him what
he would; and soe, God blessing me with a son, he had him
called affter his owne name, tho' I tould him, if he pleased,
not to crosse the names of his pedigree, which had for so many
hundred yeares gon in William and Robert.   *   *   *   Uppon
reading of the writings, Mr. Ledgard found that Mr. Thornton
had power by those deeds which was drawne at Chester to cutt
of the intaile of his land from my isue, contrary to the articles
of my marriage.†   *   *   *   I begged my cozen Ledgard to
prevaile with Mr. Thornton in my children's behalfe, who was
then his lawfull heires, that he would make some assurance of
provission for them for a portion, and then afterwards, if it
pleased God I should live and have a son, to settle the land
according to articles of marriage; to which my deare husband
consented, and did then enter into a bond of £6000 to secure
unto the two daughters the somme of each of them £1500 a
peece.   *   *   *   There was a paper draught drawne by Mr.
Ledgard of settlement of Laistrop affterward, when we were att
Newton, and sent by Mr. Thornton from London, which he did
give me to reade, but it was not drawne according to the articles

* Newton Grange.   Afterwards Sir Robert Legard, knight, one of the
Masters in Chancery ; died 1721, aged 88.

† Made " by Sir Robert Barwicke, uncle Darley's lawyer." (ii., 237.)

of·marriage, * * * and I did not consent unto it, beeing destructive to the heires of my owne body, and desired my husband to be more kinde to my lawfull issue, who had brought him a plentifull fortune; nor could any blame the bowells of a mother to grant her own issue to be cutt of out of what they were born to. I know my poore husband was advised to this way to preserve his name; but if God had denied sons by me, it was not convenient to make heires where God would have non. As my godfather, parson Lassells, tould my father when he was goeing to intaile his land of some affare* of in kin, and disinheritt his daughters; for where God will have a family to contineue in the name He can give them sons, and not for us to appoynt who we will.† * * * I was advised to passe a fine of Newton, which utterly destroyed it, and of Laistrop too, on pretence by Mr. Ledgard to have settled it firmer on my issue then Newton and Laistrop was don by the first joynture deed. Indeed, this was a great fallacy shewed to me by him whom I relied uppon for true and faithfull dealing, ‡and it seemes that [what] great straits I was putt uppon in my distresse, in my sicknes, to have somewhat settled for my children at present if I had died, a bond of £6000 to give them was made use of as a snaire to cutt them and all my issue from theire inheritance, which deed I would not have don for the world.

* *i.e.*, afar.

† The strongest argument in favour of an entail-general, and against an entail-male, is to be found in Numbers xxvii. 7-9.

‡ It will be observed that Mrs. Thornton finds equal fault with Mr. Best, Mr. Colvill, and Mr. Legard.

Job x. 20; Psalm xxxix. 13.

1.   My glasse is halfe unspent, forbear to arrest
     My thriftless day too soon, my poor request
     Is that my glass may run but out the rest.

2.   My time-devouring minnuts will be dun
     Without Thy helpe; see, see how fast they run:
     Cut not my thread before my thread be spun.

3.   The gaine's not great I purchas by this stay;
     What loss sustainest Thou by soe smalc delay,
     To Whom ten thousand yeares are but a day?

4.   My following eye can hardly make a shift
     To count my winged houers; they fly so swift
     They scarce deserve the bounteous name of guift.

5.   And what's a life? A weary pilgrimage,
     Whose glory in one day doth fill the stage
     With childhood, manhood, and decripit age.

6.   And what's a life? The flourishiug array
     Of the proud summer meadow, which to-day
     Wears her green plush, and is to-morrow hay.

7.   And what's a life? A blast sustained with clothing,
     Maintained with food, reteined with vile selfe-loathing,
     Then weary of itselfe again 'd to nothing.

8.   Read on this diall how the shades devour
     My short-lived winter's day, hour eats up hour;
     Alas, the totall's but from ten to four.

9.   Behold these lillies which Thy hands have made,
     Faire coppies of my life, and open laid
     To veiew; how soone they droop, how soone they fade.

10. Shade not that diall, night will blind to soon,
     My non-age day already poynts to noon;
     How simple is my suite, how smale my boon.

11.   Nor do I beg this slender inch to while
       The time away, or falsly to beguile
       My thoughts with joy, here's nothing worth a smile.

12.   No, no; 'tis not to please no wanton eares
       With feined mirth; I begg but hours, not years,
       And what Thou givest me I will give to tears.

13.   Draw not that soule which would rather be led,
       That seed has not yet broke my serpent's head;
       O shall I die before my sins are dead?

14.   Behold these raggs; am I a fitting guest
       To taste the dainties of Thy royall feast,
       With hands and face unwash'd, ungirt, unblest?

15.   First let the Jordan streames that find supplyes
       From the deepe fountaine of my heart, arise
       And clence my spots and cleare my watery eyes.

16.   I have a world of sins to be lamented,
       I have a sea of tears that must be vented;
       O spaire till then, and then I die contented.

Francis Quarles.

MEDITATIONS IN MY WIDDOWED CONDITTION.

Psalme xxxviii. 9, 15.

All you whose better thoughts are newly borne,
And (re-baptiz'd with holy fire) can scorn
The world's base trash; whose necks disdain to beare
Th' imperious yoke of Satan; whose chast ear
No wanton songs of Syrens can surprise
With false delights; whose more then eagle eyes
Can view the glorious flames of gold, and gaze
On glitt'ring beames of honour, and not daze;
Whose souls can spurn at pleasure, and deny
The loose suggestions of the flesh, draw nigh!
And you! whose holy, whose select desires
Would feel the warmth of those transcendent fires,

Which (like the riseing sun) put out the light
Of Venus' starr, and turne her day to night;
You that would love, and have your passions crown'd
With greater happiness then can be found
In your owne wishes! you, that would affect
Where neither scorn, nor guile, nor disrespect
Shall wound your tortured soules; that would enjoy
Where neither want can pinch, nor fullness cloy,
Nor double doubt afflict, nor baser feare
Unflames your courage in pursuit, draw near!
Shake hands with earth! and let your soule respect
Her joyes noe further than her joyes reflect
Uppon her Maker's glory. If thou swim
In wealth, see Him in all, see all in Him;
Sink'st thou in want, and is thy widdow's cruse spent?
See Him in want, injoy Him in content.
Conceiv'st Him lodg'd in cross, or lost in paine?
In prayer and patience find Him out againe.
Make heaven thy husband, let noe change remove
Thy loyall heart; be fonde, be sicke of love.
What if He stop His care, or knitt His brow?
At length He'l be as fond, as sicke as thou.
Dart up thy soule in groanes; thy secret groan
Shall pierce His eare, shall pierce His eare alone.
Dart up thy soule in vowes; thy sacred vow
Shall find Him out, where heaven alone shall know.
Dart up thy soule in sighs; thy whisp'ring sigh
Shall rouse His care, and feare no listner nigh.
Send up thy groanes; that sigh, that closett vow,
Ther's non shall know but heaven and thou.
Groanes freshed with vowes, and vowes made salt with teares,
Unscale His eyes, and scale His conquer'd ears.
Shoot up the bosome shafts of thy desire
Feathered with faith, and double-forked with fire.
Feare not but they will hitt where heaven bids come,
Heaven's never deafe but when man's heart is dum.

APPENDIX.

PART I.

LETTERS ILLUSTRATING MRS. THORNTON'S AUTOBIOGRAPHY.

Mr. Thornton to Lady Wandesford.

Madam,

I forbeare to relate unto you the particulars of our proceedings here, in regard that Mr. Norton can doe it more fully then I can write, and when you speake with him hee will tell you that wee have gone as farre as wee can at present, and what remaineth to be done on my part (God willing) shall be faithfully performed. I purpose, ere long, to waite on you at Hipswell, and then I hope such further progresse will be made in order to the consummation of our treaty,* as shall be held convenient by your ladiship. I am in extraordinary hast, being ready to goe out of towne; and therefore no more now, but that I am, madam,

Your ladiship's much obliged servant,

WILLM. THORNTON.

Yorke, August 7th, 1651.

(Addressed) For the honorable the Ladie
  Wandesforde, at Hipswell, neere Richmond, these.

Mrs. Gate to Lady Wandesford.

Madam,

If I had knowne that my joyning with my sonne† in passing a fine of Newton and Laistrop, without my husband's concurrence with

---

* See p. 80. The writer refers to the marriage then in contemplation between Mr. Thornton and Alice Wandesford.

† Mr. Thornton.

us, would have beene at all satisfactory to your ladiship, I had done it sooner; and, truly, as soone as I knew your desire in that particular, I did forthwith goe to Hull to the Commissioners, where I did give my consent before them, willingly and cheerfully.* Besides, in case I doe outlive Mr. Gate,† if a further confirmation of this act be necessary, I doe by this paper engage myselfe to doe whatsoever may be conceived further needfull in that matter. My daughters doe present there respects to your ladiship and Mrs. Wandesforde, and so doth she who is,

Madam,

Your friend and reall servant,

Eliza Gate.

Richmond Parke, Novembre 11^{the}, 1651.

(Addressed) For the honorable the Ladie
   Wandesforde, at Hipswell, neere Richmond.

Mr. Thornton to Lady Wandesford.

Madam,

    Since the receipt of your last letter I have been at Hull, and I have seconded those former offers which I have sometimes made to my father Gate, concerning the securing of my mother's joynture to her during her life, viz., I did proffer to give him a bond of a thousand pounds, to assure to her the full right of her aforesaid joynture. But I could not prevaile with him to joyne in the acknowledgment of the fine of Newton and Laistrop, whereupon my mother and I did repaire to the Commissioners for that purpose, and wee have done our parts therein.‡ Now, as concerning Richmond Parke, my father Gate

------

* A fine is a mode of conveying and assuring lands of freehold tenure that has long been in use. It was anciently a determination of a real controversy for the recovery of possession of lands, but afterwards of a feigned action, whereby under the figure of an amicable composition of a fictitious suit, by leave of the king or his justices, the lands in question became, or were acknowledged to be, the right of one of the parties. It is so called because it puts *an end*, not only to the suit thus commenced, but also to all other suits and controversies concerning the same matters. A *feme-covert*, who is a party to a fine, is privately examined by the Commissioners entrusted with the passing of it, whether or not she does it willingly and freely, or by the compulsion of her husband.

† She was buried 11 May, 1655, at Stonegrave. Geffery Gate, at Hull, 19th May, 1665.

‡ See the previous note.

is not once mentioned in either of those conveyances which I sent you, for in the lease my uncle Richard Darley, and my brother Richard, and myselfe are named ; and in the deed one Mr. Jocelin Gate, a kinsman of my father's, my uncle Francis Darley, and Mr. Reed, so that my father Gate hath no new estate by these writings.   Hee hath only an estate for life by virtue of a lease procured from Queene Elizabeth, and as hee is present tennant, his attornment was thought necessary ; which, in case hee should flie from his promise, and refuse to attorne, I doubt not but livery and seisin from the purchasers would enable my uncle Francis Darley and Mr. Reed to passe the reversion, and to make a good estate to mee.   Mr. Jocelin Gate liveth in Kent, and so his concurrence cannot presently be procured.   I shall endeavor to get this paper booke* engrossed as speedily as I can, that it may be signed and sealed.   As for that other paper booke in your hands, if you please to get it engrossed, it may be also signed and sealed, when you give leave that I may come to Hipswell.   As concerning that article for bestowing the thousand pound to be received upon the Irish estate, in a purchase, I am willing to enter into whatsoever covenant you shall please to draw up for my performance in the aforesaid particular.   And as for allowing £300 a piece to yonger children, you may cause that to be inserted in the booke of uses, for I doe cheerfully agree thereto.   Now, that which perhaps your ladiship may most scruple, is my father Gates not having attorned at present, which I thinke by the endeavors of some friends may be procured hereafter, though not presently.   Madam, if what I have now written doe satisfie your ladiship, I shall rejoice ; if otherwise, so farre as I can in my owne person give satisfaction, I shall be willing to doe what you shall require of mee.   Let my extraordinary hast prevaile with you to excuse these scribles, and you will much adde to those manie engagements wherewith you have already obliged

Your reall servant,

WILLM. THORNTON.

Bishop Wilton, November 11th, 1651.

My uncle Darley and my ant present there respects to your ladiship, and to Mrs. Wandesforde.

(Addressed) To the honorable the Ladie
Wandesforde, at Hipswell, neere Richmond.

---

* An old expression for the draft of a legal document.   See page 278.

Mrs. Thornton to Mrs. Gate.

Hon^{RED} Mother,

Haveing this oppertunity afforded me by my uncle Darley's returne, I most chearefully embrace it. That since it hath pleased God to consumate this union betweene Mr. Thornton and myselfe,* I am obleidged to expresse the duty I owe unto you, and shall write the first occasion to give you thankes for your readinesse to complye in such things as weare within the compasse of your ability to performe; and that I may further testifie my gratefull acknowledgement of your large obligations, I willingly subscribe myself, deare mother,

Your obedient daughter,

Alice Thornton.

Hipswell, the 17th of December, 1651.

My mother by these remembreth her cordial love unto you; and allso, I beseech you, give me leave to expresse my true love to both my sisters, desiring theire excuse for not writing at present to them, which I would have donn if I had not bin straitned of time, which allso may plead my pardon for these scribles. I have sent a paire of garters which I desire my sisters doe me the honer to weere.

(Addressed) For her ever hon^{red} mother,
Mrs. Elizabeth Gate, present.

Rev. J. Denton to Mr. and Mrs. Thornton.

Much honred Brother and Sister,

The suddaine and unexpected sad newes of your childe's death† hath very much afflicted me. I doe really sympathize with you in your loss, and though I am not insensible how little I am able to contribute to you by way of comfort, or say anythinge which you are not better able to say to yourselves, yet my affectione will not suffer me to be altogether silent. I must then mingle greefes with you, and acknowledge it is a very great affliction which God hath laid upon you, and a sensibleness of God's hand in it, and a sorrow proportionable to your loss well becomes you; but to

---

* Mr. Thornton was married to Mrs. Thornton 17th Dec., 1657. See page 81. Mrs. Gate was Mr. Thornton's mother, married again to Mr. Gate.

† William, 6th child, born 17th and buried 29th April, 1660. See page 123.

U

grive immoderatly, as those whose hopes (both of themselves and friends) are onely in this life, and soe as either to prejudice the health of the body, or unfitt the minde for God's service, is very unbecoming Christians. Those indeed who know noe better interest, noe wonder if they drowne themselves in sorrow, and give up themselves to intemperance in greife upon any outward loss; but for those who are beeing of better hopes, and cannot loose their happiness until they loose their God (Who yet hath promised " never to leave them nor forsake them "),* to give up themselves to such intemprance of sorrow as to refuse to be comforted, with the consideration of those better things which the gospell both intreasted us in, would argue an undue esteeme of our greatest mercyes, and ingratefull repininge at God's mercyfull and wise dispensations. But I know you are Christian mourners; yet because full submission to the hand of God in this case is a hard lesson, give me leave to minde you as an allay to your sorrow, to consider (which I knowe you doe) Who it is that hath taken away your child, even that God Who gave it to you,† and Who can (and I am confidently perswaded will) make up your loss in kinde, or however Who can (and I doubt not but will) make abundant reparation in spirituall comforts and refreshments, that God Who can be better to you the[n] ten sonns, and Who hath promised to give His a name better than that of sonns and daughters,‡ that God Who hath lent you other sweete children in whome you may take comfort, this God hath taken your deare child (we have good grounds to believe) up to heaven, where he injoyes society with Christ, and the blessed angells, free from that sorrow which you his parents doe now ly under, and after a few dayes of trouble and vanity spent here, you (according to that text you hinted to me) goe to him§ and other deare relations who have taken possession of heaven before you.

O that the Lord would inable you quietly and meekly to submitt to the wise disposeing providence of your Heavenly Father, and command your sorrow into a moderation, that He would make you thankfull for children left, when He might have taken all, that He would loosen your hearts from uncertaine comforts, and make you breath more after communion with Himselfe, Whose pleasure is better than husband, wife,

* Hebrews xiii. 5.
† Job i. 21.
‡ Isaiah lvi. 5.
§ 2 Samuel xii. 23.

children, then life itselfe; that these may be the happy fruites of this
affliction shall be the prayer of

Your verry affectionate and sympathizing brother,

J. DENTON.

May 1, 1660.

I shall, God willing, waite upon you at your returne from Osw[ald-
kirk.] If you had not limmitted me to the time I thinke I should have
beene with you as soone as this letter. My wife, sister, and brother
present their respects to you, and are very much affected with your loss.
My service to Mrs. Norton.

(Addressed) For his much honored
   brother and sister.

MRS. THORNTON TO HER HUSBAND.

DEAREST HEART,

     Not haveing beine acquainted with your determinate resolu-
tion for London* till of late, I forbore to make my application to you in
this way. Nor would I have adventured upon this at present if I could
have spoken to you my thoughts thereon. The bussinesse which calls
you to so hazardus a journey to your person and health I supose must
be either very weighty or urgent, but what motives are, yet [made] knowne
to me either by yourselfe or my brother Denton, who, I can witnesse,
hath endeavoured with many reasons to gaine my consent, under favour
as I humbly conseave, is not of such consequence, or so valid a consideration with me, as the preservation of your life or health, for your
owne, your relations, and children's comforts. Nor doe I presume to
tender you my sence heereof upon any evill designe for yourselfe or
disingenuous malice to Sᵣ Christopher Wandesford, since, if it lay in
my power to doe good, I would lay my life downe for the wellfaire of
the first, and use my uttmost endevours for the other. Albeit, I have
had noe inducements from him, either by the bond of nature, or charity
towards me and mine, yet I trust in the goodnesse of God He will
please to give me to love my ennimies and pray for them that despight-
fully use me.† What then can the true reason be of my diswading you
from this adventure, if you please to consider the truth from whence it

---

* He had gone to London as a witness in Sir Chᵣ Wandesford's suit concern·
ing some boundaries. See page 144.
  † Matthew v. 44.

U 2

proceeds ? I hope still that such is the good will to your poore children, and principally to your little boy, that those affections will move where others are waved.

I must confesse your so offten vissitting London has never beine any delight to my thoughts, whose injoyment of comfort depends most in your presence at home, yet could I with lesse difficulty formerly (when your health and strength would better permitt), give you my consent, for the management of your grand affaires, to be deprived of your scocciety then now, since, through the blessing of God, those are hopefully settled for the future.

Neither can I imagine Sir Christopher Wandesford so irrationall to judge his cause either lost or prejudiced without you, and beleive it, you may buy your service to him this winter att a deare rate, as, for other reasons, as to his procuring the £100 sooner due this Mart^s, and his assistance conscerning Preston's bond. I hope, such is his Christian charity, he will not deny you these at home. However, I still trust solely in the mercys of God for parcells of our dues so well as the whole, and, if He deny us this, He can give us a suply as He hath hitherto don, be men's hearts and actions never so hard.

Now, most deare husband, I beseech you lett not my request seeme strange or be despised in your sight, since I never before desired your forbearance in what might seeme for your advantage. Indeed, I should not have taken upon me this freedom, but am much presed thereto upon the account of my endeared affection (and teares more then common for your wellfaire), as allso beeing bound in duty to God and each other to watch over one annother for good. And I hope that the same God Which hath all along preserved you will still preserve you from evill, and withdraw your mind or actions from tempting of Him to your owne or others harme or discomfort.

I have now put myselfe upon your candid interpretation, who am indeed unworthy to give you any advice, but to present this to your serious consideration that this jorney may proove somewhat fatall to our injoyments (if the Lord in mercy prevent not), which is the humble pettition of her that will not scace to contineue, deare heart,

Your most faithfull and truly affectionate wife, till death,

ALICE THORNTON.

Newton, Octob. 18, 1664.

(Addressed) For my ever dearely hon^{red}
husband Willm Thornton, Esq., these.

Mrs. Thornton to her Husband.

My dearest Heart,

I have receaved both your kind and welcome letters, which assures me of your pleasant journey, and the contineuance of your health, for the which I returne most humble thankes to Almighty God in answering my pettitions at the throne of grace in your behalfe. These lines of your's gives me the greatest comfort and sattisfaction that can be in your absence, and deeplyer ingadgeth (if it can be) to your deare affection. I have endeavoured to start my letters before you, this beeing the third since you went, but you have the advantage of each post to convey your's, which I want, only I hope you will receave them together at London. The man before whom J. King tooke the oath did mistake something for want of a sight of your tab[le ?], therefore John was forced to goe againe to Yorke about the businesse, afterward the affidavit shall be sent to Mr. Jackson. My sister Porting-ton is yet well. I desire to heare what you please to doe with your sorrell nagg, whether he must be turned to grasse or not. And now, my dearest heart, what motive shall I use to thee to make you cairefull of that bodie God has given you; we are so fraile of nature that non can assure themselves health or life one day. I am sorrey to tell you of the death of Colonell Chaitor,* who tooke a sicknesse this last Sater-day night, beeing well and hunting all day, but he departed yesterday, and was buried to day, as Jane Burton brings word, the deepe sence whereof has a little startled my thoughts, but I trust God for you beeing absent so well at present that we shall againe meete joyfully in this world. Our girles and Robin remembers theire duty to you. Robin has a cold, but I hope it will be soone well. My faithfull prayers for your eternall happinesse shall be ever powred out by, deare heart,

Your intirely affectionate and faithfull wife, till death,

ALICE THORNTON.

Octob. 25th, 64.

My service to Tom. Alured,† and all my frends with you.

(Addressed) For Willm Thornton, Esq.,
  at Mr. Robert Pick's house, at
  the Greyhound in Grayes Inne Lane,
  London.

---

* Henry, 2nd son of Sir William Chaytor, Kn^t, of Croft.
† Query of Beverley.

MRS. THORNTON TO HER HUSBAND.

DEAREST HEART,

I have not receaved a letter from you this week, but hopes in God that you are well. In my last I wrote you that my sister Port[ington] was delivered of a sonne, to which she was earnest with me to be a wittness, so I had the favour from my lady Cholmley of her coach to Malton yesterday, when there was another Timothy made.* She is, blessed be God, prittyly recovered. I shall desire you to gett me some pretty fashoned silver cupps for him. Being in exceeding great hast to entertain some of Oswaldkirk neighbours in the house, who came to drinke with me, I rest, deare heart,

Your in truth affectionate wife, till death,

ALICE THORNTON.

My lady Norclife† was at Malton, who was very scivile to me on your behalfe.

No. 18, 64.

(Addressed) For Willm Thornton, Esq.,
    at Mr. Robert Pick's house, att the
    Grayhound in Grayse Inne Lane,
    London, these.

MRS. THORNTON TO HER HUSBAND.

MY DEAREST HEARTE,

I am now very joyfull of this good occasion, to send your horrses‡ to bring me your much desired company, without which I have

---

* Bap. 17 Nov., 1664; bur. 18 April, 1665. See *Addenda*.

† The Honourable Dorothy Fairfax, daughter of Thomas, Lord Viscount Elmley, wife of Sir Thomas Norcliffe, Knight, of Langton.

‡ Journies at this period, and for some time after, were most usually performed on horseback. William Drummond, of St. Johnstone's, co. Perth, merchant, was thus travelling through Doncaster in 1634, during a flood, when "so ryding in the water, the horse foundering, he fell from the horse, and was drowned." (Jackson's *St. George's Church*, Ap. xliv.) In 1649, the Earl of Dumfries, returning from the south, "ridinge on the high rode way, betwixt Lincolne and Doncaster," was "sett uppon" by two robbers, and his own and his servants' horses were taken from them. (*Surtees Soc. Pub.* 40, p. 24.) Thoresby, in his Diary, relates several journies from Leeds to London, and elsewhere, ridden on horseback.

not injoyed much comfort, but I have not failed to give you the trouble of my scribles upon every oportunity I could, and yesterday I sent John King with one to Yorke which was inclosed to another of my nece's Best, least he should be come out of towne, where I did acquaint you, as allso in two of my last, that Mr. Comber did present you his service with desire that you would please to give Mr. Bennet* a vissitt at Southwell, which is within four miles† of Newarke, and to put him in mind of his promise to us in his behalfe by his letters which I now inclose to you, least now that Mr. Bennet haveing gott Bilstrop,‡ as 'tis creadably reported, should leave Mr. Comber in the lirch, or channge with another for a living neare him. 'Tis reported allso by one Mawburne's sonn,§ of Yorke, they say a debauched person, that Mr. Bennet offred his daughter and Stongrave living to him. 'Tis strange if he should be so disingenious to Mr. Comber, there haveing bin former broad signes to him for his daughter which I could wish might be effected, if for both their goods, and as you see cause or not to speake to Mr. Bennet of it; but however that he might not be displaced hence, which I shall entreat you earnestly to prevent, because we may have those put on us we cannot like. Dearest, I beseech God, Which hath hitherto preserved you, still goe along and give us a happie meeting, and I begge your pardon that I send your horrses without comission, which I did in this respect as formerly, and because your's last recceaved was dated 23ᵈ instant, and there was noe letter for me by this last post. Deare heart, fairewell, with my service to Mr. Bennet and all his, ever continuing the dearest love of

Your intirely affectionate wife,

ALICE THORNTON.

No. 29ᵗʰ, 64.

---

* Rev. Gilbert Bennet. See p. 154, note, and p. 215.

† Southwell is about seven or eight miles from Newark. It is a pleasant market-town with a magnificent church, which is both parochial and collegiate, chiefly of Norman architecture. Iu the churchyard are some remains of an archiepiscopal palace and ancient collegiate buildings. It formerly formed part of the see of York, but in later years it has been transferred to the diocese of Lincoln.

‡ Bilsthorpe, a parish in the northern division of Notts., and within the union of Southwell, five miles from Ollerton. The living is in the patrouage of the Savile family of Rufford.

§ Qu. Luke Mawburn, afterwards vicar of Craike?

Mrs. Thornton to her Husband.

My deare Heart,

The content and sattisfaction your two letters bring me in the newes of your good health, with your happie opperation of the waters,* calls for these lines to returne you many thankes for the knowledge thereof, with my humble gratitude and praises to God for the continuance of the same. I trouble you noe further than the acquanting you that we are all well, blessed be the Lord, and shall rejoyce at the safe return to, deare heart,

Your truly affectionate wife,

Alice Thornton.

June 8th, 66.

My neice Danby presents her service to yourself.

(Addressed) These, for my deare and
   hon^{red} husband Willm Thornton,
Esq., at Scarborugh.

Mrs. Thornton to her Husband.

Dearest Heart,

I have receaved three letters from you, since I saw you, and have writt severall to you, and they have had the bad fortune to miscarry, for which I am very sorrey. You may justly taxe me for ingrate that in all this time has not receaved any one; but you may be confident of my prayers, teares, and person hath not boeing idle for your health and restoration, which your last gave me good hopes, by the mercys of God, was in a great measure don; for which I returne my most humble thanks and prayse, begging mercy for us both to bier what time be pleaseth to each comfort. I am glad to heare you have had so good company at Spaw, and shall send you horrses on Thursday. All heare present our dues to you. I pray for a good and comfortable meeting to, deare heart,

Your ever affectionate wife, till death,

Alice Thornton.

June 10th, 1666.

(Addressed) These, for my deare and
   hon^{red} husband Willm Thornton, Esq.,
   at Scarborugh.

* At Scarborough.

MR. THORNTON TO HIS DAUGHTER ALICE.

DEAR NALY,

I thanke thee for thy letter, and as soone as I can come conveniently, I intend (God willing) to see thee. Thy mother and thy brother, I thanke God, are in health. Remember my kind love to your landlord and landlady, and to thy sister, and to Hannah; and tell Kate that she must be carefull of her behaviour, that when I come to Yorke there may no complaints of her. I pray God continue your healths to you all, which is the daily prayer of

thy verie loving father,
WILLM. THORNTON.

Newton, June 14th, 1667.

(Addressed) For Mrs. Alice Thornton, at Mr. Elias Sherwood house in Petergate, these, in Yorke.

(Endorsed) June 14th 1667. My own deer father's letter. The only one whileI was at scool at Yorke that I had from him.

MRS. THORNTON TO MR. THORNTON.*

MY DEAREST ONLY JOY,

You may immagine that I cannot expresse my unutterable greeife and heart-killing affliction for this great and heavy crosse which it hath pleased God to lay uppon me in your vissitation, whereby I am deprived of my sole comfort, both of your scocietty and enjoyment for the present; but humbly desire of my gracious God that Hee will att the length in His good time looke upon your weaknesse, be it in any kind whatever, and remove these sad afflictions from us both, and for the tender bowells of Christ restore you againe to me your disconsolate wife and poore children. I know that afflictions arrises not out of the dust, neither doth Hee afflict willingly, and therefore must lay our mouths in the dust, acknowledging ourselves too much contributing to the drawing this trouble upon us. But I trust in the mercies of our good God that He will forgive all our transgressions, and heale our

---

* No date; but probably written during Mr. Thornton's last illness at Malton in 1668. See pp. 167, 172.

soules, and give us testimony of His love and reconciliation by and in your restoration to me againe. I shall also humbly submitt to the wise dispensations of our Father in heaven, either in my owne life or death, trusting in Him alone for your comfortable recovery. My greife is the more that I am deprived of doeing my duty to you, but I must begge patience in this and all thing ellse, comitting you into the most mercifull hand of our Redeemer, Who never failes them that trust in Him ; begging mercy at the throne of grace for us both ; ever remaning thy deare and disconsolate wife, till death,

ALICE THORNTON.

(Addressed) For my dearest heart.

MRS. THORNTON TO MRS. COMBER.*

SWEETE SISTER,

Since my last to you I have bin so exceedingly imployed in troublesome businesses that it hath detterred me from giveing you the relation of our affairs heere, which, since I am debarred otherwise then by letter, I would willingly have communicated erre this, that we might have had sooner the assistance of your good advice and prayers along with us. I understand by your son (whom God has now made mine in the nearest tie of affinity) that he has acquainted you with the consumation of his marriage with my daughter. We are mutually concerned to begge mercyes and blessings for them in this estate, wherein are many burthens as well as comforts, which is by both of us experienced, and therefore requiring more then ordenary assistance, devine suports, and directions. I hope I may be assured of your prayers and well-wishes, as mine are daily, joyntly and severally, for them, that God may reape His glorie in all condittions by giving them sutable gifts and graces for an holie and sanctified wedlocke, and we enjoie such comforts in and by them as shall seeme best in His devine wisdome. I assure you I have to my uttmost bin his cordiall and faithfull freind, and broake thro' many difficulties 'erre we coulde finish our desires ; which difficulties will, I hope, cause the mercy to be sweeter to us. For my daughter's too young yeares to enter into the world, I confesse they render her more incapable of this estate, and we lesse willing to enter her therein where is required a great deale more of wisdome and understanding to steere our corce then her experience will afford, and could

* Mother of Rev. Dr. Comber, Mrs. Thornton's son-in-law.

have wished a longer stay, if it might have suted with my sonne's desire. But I hope his affection and prudence will paliate such things as time and experience must polish. In the intrime my caire and endeavours, while they are under my roofe, joyned with her true affection, shall not be wanting to render her an acceptable wife to so loving a husband. I hope allso, in God's good time, He will be pleased in them to perpetuate our posterities to our comforts. As for the publishing of our match, we do not judge it convenient till some remote freinds of qualitie be acquainted; and in regard of my so late widdowed condittion,* I deeme rather more prudence yet to conseale it to the world.

Good Sister, as you pleased to leave the transaction of this concerne to my son and selfe, so have we concluded of settlements betwixt us as well, and sattisfactoraly to ourselves and freinds as our judgements could direct. For, considering that my daughter's fortune is certaine, and that which is her due is in reall and personall estate worth £1200, and he could not estate any joynture, it was judged an act of reason and prudence to give her freinds sattisfaction to settle her owne upon her and her children in lieue of an estate for provision for them; and they are to enjoy it during theire joynt lives. But I leave the inlarging of perticulars to my sonne's account, which I have desired him to give more fully. Only shall adde further that as God shall further inable me (who is at present not in soe good a capacity as I hope to be within a little time) I shall be ready to testifie that he shall not be a loser by his affection towards me or mine, nor shall he want the tender love and caire of a parent with me, which I hope you may be confident in, when I have (as it were) imbarked my children and estate in this bottom, in confidence of his pietie and religion. But I am too teadious; I shall, only adde the remembrance of my kinde affection to yourselfe and husband,† ever resting

Your verie loving and affectionate freind and sister,

A. THORNTON.

Easte Newton, Jan. 23rd 68 [9].

(Endorsed, in Mrs. Thornton's hand-
    writing :—
        " My first letter to Mrs. Comber
            affter marriage of my daugh-
            ter to her son, Jan. 23, 1669.")

* Mr. Thornton, her husband, died 17 September, 1668. See page 175.

† Hence it would appear that James Comber was still living, though there is no mention of him in the reply.

Mrs. Comber's Reply to Mrs. Thornton.

Good Madd.

I must crave your pardon for my neglect, in that I have soe long bene sylent. I beseech you imput it not to bee any want of true afectyon or respect to you, to whome I owe more then I shall bee able to pay for your cordiall respect and faste frenship to my sone, whome God hath now made your's, to my greete comfort and sattisfactyon, God having now given him not only a true and cordiall frend, but allsoe a most indulgent parent, who will, I dout not, suply what must of necesity be a wantting in mee at this distance ; I meane in caire and advies, which I ame confydant as it hath nevar beene a wanting heartofore soe much les will it bee now. And I hope the Lord will soe gyde him by His good sperritt that hee shall too the utmost of his power and abillyty make suttable retorns to you. And thogh it is not in his pouer evar to requit you, yet I hop hee will not bee a wanting in anny thing whearin hee may sarve you ethar in a sperrytale or temparall way. And as it hath pleased God to exarcies you, deere madd. whith the sad condityon of widdohood and lose of soe deere loveing and pius a husband (for whoes lose I ame extremely sorry as evar I was for any parson in my life), yeet I hop that in anny thing that my sone can doe to comfort, assist, or sarve you hee will not bee a wanting. And as for the setteling of his wife's estate, to secure it for har and har children, I like it verry well, and I think hee hath sealed too as much as can in reson bee desired or expected. And as for discovaring this consarne, bee it left to your prudence, who I hope will soe discretlye mannage the discovaring of it to har relatyons, that noe offence may bee taken at him, but that as thay have apeered most lovingly and nobly upone all ocatyons for him heartofore, soe, if ocatyone sarve, thay will doe still, for I must confes that is my great fear now that if thoes to whome hee is now related by marriage shold ethar slight or neglect him it wold much discorrage him. God grant it may not soe fall out. I have left him to God's protectyone and his owne coyces,* in which I think him verry happy. God Allmyte bles them both, and make them mutally cumfortable one to the othar, that God may have glory, and wee may have comfort by this consarne, and that hee prove soe afectyonat and good a husband that nethar you, your deere daytar, nor anny of har relatyons may have anny caues to repent it. I shall

* Courses.

not trouble you anny furthar at preesant, but only to subscribe myselfe, Madd.

Your most affectyonet frend and sistar,

MARY CUMBAR.

This 20th ffeb., 68 [69].

Good Madd., let mee bee soe much honnarred as to hear sometimes
a few lynes from your hand, that I may bee informed how things
succeede.

(Addressed) Thees for my Hyly
    Honnarred·frend Madd. Thornton at
    Newtones.

(Endorsed, in Mrs. Thornton's hand-
    writing :—

        My sister Comber first letter to
            me and Naly since theire
            marriage, dated Feb. 20th 68,
            in answer to mine in Jan.
            before.   Re^{vd} this from her
            the 14th of June, 1669.)

REV. THOMAS PURCHAS TO DR. COMBER.*

March ye 6, 81.

S^r,

The extream confidence I have of your worth and candour
makes me presume to give you the trouble of these lines in private,
which are to satissfie you that the repeated professions of affection
which I often made to dear Madam Katherine proceeded from the
bottom of my heart; and could I possibly give larger testimonie of my
love and reality then I have done, none should be more ready actually
to do it; and to convince you that my resolutions of love and service
are as faithfull and as vigorous as ever, and that I am not wholly
sway'd by sæcular interest and advantage, I will be willing (if you please
to release my father from the payment of the £200 he mentions) to give
you all the security I am capable of giving, to add myselfe (after the
estate is setled upon me) £200 for her use and service, after the best
manner you in prudence shall thinke fitt. This, I suppose, will sattissfie

* On a treaty of marriage with Miss Catherine Thornton, which afterwards
took place.

you that my love to her is cordiall, and not gilded over with outward shew and formall appearance; and, did I know of any more effectuall way, I would, with all imaginable readiness, concede to it. S^r, I triumph and congratulate my own fœlicity that I can unburden my thoughts to you at this distance, hopeing that, by your successfull endeavours, things may be brought to a happy conclusion. I cannot, but with my very gratefull acknowledgments, menc'on the kindnesses you have conferrd upon me, and if my power was adæquate to my will, the requitall should soon surmount the acknowledgment. Pray be pleas'd to keep this private from my father, for I am loth to offend him, and 'tis my duty as well as interest to shew becoming respects to him. If it please God that he lives but a very few years, he has promis'd my mother to give me £50 per an. more, but this he conceals from me. I hope you will pardon my presumption, and beleive that my design in this very thing is honest, but shall leave it to your approbation. If you dislike it, pray let it not be communicated to any there. But I am forc'd to conclude, and rest, in haste,

Your gratefull servant,

THO. PURCHAS.

As for the proposalls that my father have sent, if they do not approve of them, yet I hope Mr. Gibson will certainly meet him on Thursday, and my father shall not faile.

(Addressed) For the Reverend Doct^r Comber, at East Newton.

(Endorsed) "Mr. Thomas Purchas, his letter to Dr. Comber, by his man Robert Gent, before the meeting at Sutton, March 2nd (*sic*), 1681-2. Obleiging."

MRS. THORNTON TO HER SON ROBERT THORNTON.

June 12th, 86.

DEARE SON,

That I soe soone trouble you againe with my scribles, haveing answred your's of May 26 on June 3^d, wherein I gave you the best incoragement to goe on in all those good meathods of which I have had an account both from good Mr. Parsons and yourselfe, soe am I now desirous to lett you know that the good carracter which Mr. Parsons contineus to give of you, and your further desings conserning your journey to Oxford,* in order to obteine your Degree att the Commencement, and allso your further progress for Wales, are very sattisfactory and pleasing to myselfe and all your freinds. And by the continuall blessing of the Almighty, Whose unsearchable goodness is to be adored in all His Devine Providences towards you, all these opportunityes may conduct you by right meathods to obteine that great end for which you are designed, both by the Providences of Heaven, my own humble pettitions, and that of your owne good inclinations expressed soe solemnly and seariously in devoting yourselfe to the most holy and sacredest calling to us mortalls. I know you have ever had a great veneration for it, which will be a good stept to a due preparation, and must be don with all possible humility, submittion, and feare, and reverence. To come before the Majesty of Heaven with an uncleane and unsanctified hand and heart, to presume uppon the sacred office without a holy heart and sincere intentions and endeavours of soule and body to serve the Living God, Whose omnypresence is over us, is to tutch consuming fire, and bring a deserved destruction uppon ourselves, being defiled with willfull either uncleaness or polution.

Therefore, deare son, since by this Almighty power and goodnes you are brought into the borders of this sanctuary, I beseech and charge you, in the name of that Etternall God, to enter into it with a cleane hart and holly hands, clenced by the contineall teares of repentance, and purged from your sinns by the sorrowes of contrition for all your offences by past, with great and stricke vowes and faithfull resolutions, a newness of life and conversation, begging heartily of your gracious God a new heart, that, as you will have a new name, soe may

* At page 269 Mrs. Thornton has spoken of her son's debts at *Cambridge*, which is probably a slip of her pen.

Robert Thornton was matriculated at University College, Oxford, 1 June, 1682, aged 19, son of William Thornton of East Newton, co. York, gen. B.A. University, 16 Oct., 1683; elected Fellow of Magdalen College, 1684; M.A. Magd. 28 June, 1686. Died 4 June, 1692. Buried before the place of the second of the nine altars in Durham Cathedral, where is the following, on a stone, placed to his memory by Anne, wife of Dean Comber:—M.S. Hic Jacet Robertus Thornton, A.M., filius et hæres Gulielmi Thornton de Newton in com. Ebor. arm. et Aliciæ uxoris ejus. Socius Collegii B.M. Mag., Oxon., et rector de Bolden; qui obiit Junii iv., A.D. MDCXCII. Pos. A.C. Soror Char. An. MDCXCV. (Communicated by Rev. Dr. Bloxam, Beeding Priory, Hurst-pierpoint.)

it be effectuall to make a new man first of yourselfe. And then, in order to serve this great God in that capacity, that you may be a meanes to bring great glory to God, and many soules by your meanes to be converted to your Heavenly Father. Butt who is suficient for these things? even non of themselves, only he who is washed with the blood of the etternall Son of Righteousnes, and sanctified by His Holy Spiritt, and renud in the inward man, can aproach to this consuming fire; yett in Jesus Christ He has made a way for us to apeare before Him, and in Him all our soules and bodyes and services are accepted. Therefore, deare child of my vowes to Him, be more then ordenary prepared to approach before the Living God, Who has don soe great things for you. And lett your conversation in vertue and conversion from vice be apparent before all men, that you may not irreverently come into His presence, but with such deep humility that is most acceptable in His sight. Soe shall you in mercy be accepted in the bowells of the Lord Jesus to His service, and all your indeavors sanctifi'd and purifi'd. And in thus doing you will not faile of a Crowne of Glory.

I have writ to Mr. Parsons of my consent and desire that you may take this journey into Wales. The Lord prepare you for it, and blesed be His holy name for this happy opportunity. I begg His gracious assistance and preservation of you in order to His Kingdom. But this is to be don affter the solemnency of the Commencement at Oxford, at which time I have desir'd Mr. Parsons to beare you company. And I hope as you have bin advised by him in all good wayes, soe I besech you continue your good meathods, and lett noe vaine company nor conversation defile your soule that is destinated to soe holy an use, and early dedicated to the Lord your God. But lett your stedy fixed resolutions be kept lately made at the Holy Sacrament. And, I besech you, refraine strong liqir. I shall not adde more now, but my humble prayers to God for you, and direction in all these weighty things, and am, deare son,

Your most affectionate mother,

ALICE THORNTON.

Mrs. Thornton to her son Robert Thornton.

(Fragment.) * * *

That you intend sincerly what you have profesed to me and your
best frends, that it is your owne desire and designe to prepare yourself
for that infinitt honor to be admitted a faithful servant at His alter, by
a free resignation to that holy and sacred calling which the world is
not worthy of; yea, blesed are they who are called young to His
service, as Samuel was, and as I designed you, which I hope the Lord
will be pleased to accept of me, the meere handmaid of the Lord, Whoes
vowes was on me when the gospell of Christ and the Church of England
was allmost banished; therefore it is my duty and yours to suport the
Church by whom we have salvation. Lett not your indifferency and
couldness in your choyce to any that either out of design * * *
shall aske you the question, be a menes to dishearten those good resolutions and desires in you, give them or your freinds cause to thinke
you have cast off your first love, or laugh at you for your apostacy.
Mr. Smith is gott to be a scoolemaster and a curate to a good man in
Lincolnshire; he preaches now and is much aproved of. I am glad to
heare soe good an account of him, and my hopes are, that as God has
given you greater opportunitys and posts, soe you will not be behind
him in God's service. I doe now thinke the time will be tedious in
reading these scribles, but I hope you will adde the comfort of your
resolves to me in your next. I am begun to prepare wood for the
building up of my ally,* and doe begg God will give me leave to provide
in His providence to lead it, that I may take some caire to remove
those cloudes hanging over our heads in this family for this act done
by inconsideration or sacraledge. Lett your prayers be devout and
prevalent for a blessing npon my endeavors for you, and be not liffted
up too much in your owne conseitt. Present my cordiall service to
Long and all your freinds, to your master, and to Dr. Jaxe, who is a
very good and wise man. Observe your orders and all good men, and
lett those good parts be sanctified with piety, that you may be a comfort
to my age. And I was beginning to take caire for your suply, but Dr.
Comber tells me he will doe it, because I have all my hay and harvest.
Deare son, lett me heare from you, and lett your behaviour be such to
be an honor to this decayed family. The Lord blesse and preserve you

* The family aisle in Stonegrave church.

x

in health, and prosper your good designes, and lett the will of God be don in your sanctification.   Soe concluds her who is, deare Robin,

Your most affectionate mother,

ALICE THORNTON.

(Addressed.)   These, to Mr. Robert
   Thornton, student in University Coll.,
   in Oxford. By the way of London.
   [Postage] in all, 5d.

MRS. THORNTON TO THE REV. DR. TILLOTSON.*

East Newton, Aprill 20, 1691.

MOST REVEREND SIR,

I received your most obleging lines, which, with your extraordinary kindnes expressed to my son Thornton, are favours soe great that I must not passe them in silence without a return of due gratitude, which I beseech you please accept from my pen, accounting myselfe really very happy by the injoyment of soe good a man and kinde a freind as my good brother Denton, by whose influence I have received much comfort since the losse of my deare and honoured husband, blessing God for this His especiall providence in takeing caire of myselfe and children in him, and raising up soe worthy a freind as yourselfe to give my son your kinde assistance in a matter of soe great importance to his happy settlement, which, as to my owne perticular, would have been more acceptable to me in the north, neere his freinds and estate.†   But the lady, expressing her unwillingness to leave the south, makes me sollicitt my freinds to endeavour his preferment there ; amongst which, worthy Sir, I account you the cheife, not doubting of your assistance in this affaire, which tends soe much to the happy

---

* John Tillotson, D.D., son of Robert Tillotson, a considerable clothier of Sowerby, in the parish of Halifax, Yorkshire.   Both his parents were Nonconformists. Born 1630. Preacher of Lincoln's Inn. Dean of Canterbury, 1672, and afterwards of St. Paul's.   Archbishop of Canterbury, 1691. Died 10 Nov., 1694, ætat. 65.   He was an intimate friend of Mr. Denton, Mrs. Thornton's brother-in-law.

† It seems from this that some negotiations were in progress for young Mr. Thornton's marriage.

settlement of my son, which will further obleige my owne and son's most cordiall gratitude, and shall not cease to beg of God for His blessing uppon all your pieous designes. With my humble service I take my leave, and am,

Reverend Sir,

Your most humble and obleiged freind,

ALICE THORNTON.

(Addressed.) To the Reverend* Dr. John
   Tillotson, Deane of St. Paulls, London.

REV. CHARLES MAN TO REV. ROBERT THORNTON.

Gilling, Feb. 29, 169½.

SIR,

   The hearty respects and goodwill I have for you putts me upon the presumption to trouble you with this scrible. I cannot but rejoyce for your happiness at Durham, that Providence hath ordered both your concern and convenience to ly almost together, having brought you through so many difficultys and dangers, by sea and land, to so happy an harbour, tho' some did not think to see you in that clerical habit. I hope neither yourself, nor any that loves you, will ever think it unbecoming you, or repent it; nor is it below a better person than him that said it to wear. A greater and better, too (I may safely say), was he who wished rather to be a doorkeeper in the house of God†—the meanest office there—than to lord it in unhallowed halls; an office it is which angells would be ready to undertake, men may be proud of; and formerly the heads of familys and the first-born were onely honoured with. May you be daily, more and more, the glory of our Church, the envy of her enemys, and joy of all your friends. God make us worthy of it, and then shall we ever have caus (with St. Paul) to thank God Who hath counted us faithfull, putting us into the ministery.‡ After this, give me leave to add one thing more, which is about your own private concern at Newton. You are the onely hopes of your family; the care and comfort of a tender mother,

---

* From this it appears that the prefix of "Very Reverend" was not then in use in addressing a Dean.

† Psalm lxxxiv. 11.

‡ 1 Tim. i. 12.

x 2

the staff of her age, whose happiness is bound up with yours. Sir, all these, and the wishes of all your reall friends, call aloud upon you, and impatiently desire a speedy performance of those great ends which God and Nature hath design'd you for. I earnestly wish you a good match, which (with submission to your own prudence) I conceive to be a speciall, if not the only way to answer all. Once more I presume, and pray you fail not to shew your affection and care for your dear mother, to comfort and assist her by all means possible; who, by reason of her great weakness of body, and many other incumbrances, is brought into such straits and troubles it's pity a person of her worth should be put to, and the least neglect of your's would be a greif to her above all things. God guide you, and direct all to the best, for God's glory, your own good, your mother's joy, and the establishment of your family. Pardon, I beseech you, this boldness, and accept the reall respects of,

Sir, your faithfull friend and servant,

CHA. MAN.

MRS. THORNTON TO HER SON ROBERT THORNTON.

Easte Newton, May 31st, 92.

MY DEARE AND ONLY SON,

Haveing waited with some impatiency, since your good brother Dean returned home, to have had an accoumpt of your beeing past the danger of your feaver, and proceeding to a hopefull recovery of your health and strength, and not beeing sattisfied in myselfe that I am not capable to do you that part of a poore but affectionate mothr by my attentance and paines about you (and in some measure to beare the burden of your most kinde and deare sister that she undergoes for you in this affliction), I hold it my part to doe what I can and am capable of to serve you in this your distresses and vissittation (from the just and yett gracious hand of God). To that end I have sent this messenger on purpose to give you the assurance that you are never out of my thoughts nor prayers, desiring, if it please Almighty God, Who has soe many millions of times delivrd you and myselfe from death, that I may heare the happy good newes of your recovery.

But yett we must stay and waite His time for it, Who has soe long waited for our repentance. Even when the rod was over our head, and the axe laid to the roots of the tres, have we (I doubt) too long provoked the Devine Majesty to destroy us and cutt us downe. Why cumbreth it the ground ?

Haveing used all wayes and meanes to bring us to Himselfe, and perhaps the great work is not yett don, as it ought to be. Att length He has given us that late severe triall and delivrance, which I hope has had a good effect in me, soe as to take me from the love of the world, and to sett my love intirely upon Himselfe, Who has lov'd me, and given Himselfe for me.

The bennifit of His severe and yett mercyfull dealing towards me in my owne vissitation shall be to sett forth His praise in my future life and conversation, to walke more cairefully, love Him, and feare Him, and serve Him with an intire resignation, Who had soe great pitty for me as to save that life and restore it againe which was lost for a time.

And now, as to your perticular case, who has bin a long time vissited with the hand of God in this sicknes, haveing had many relapses, and has, I feare, much weakned your body and strength, with many other inconveniencys as to your person, and perhaps your spiritt. I dout me it has bin too much pull'd on you for want of a due caire over your-selfe, and goeing out into the ayre too soone, or not ussing the order or meathod of your phisician's advice by way of diet, or anything ellse he cautions you against. If from any of these things you have bin pre-ceded, and indanger your life, I pray God to have mercy on you, and pitty you, by giving you that wisdom, prudence, and Christian caire over your ways, actions, habits, or costoms, which you have don to bring you into this danger and hazard of your life, not taking the good advice of your phisicians and good frends. For you must consider, tho' you do thinke yourselfe a single person, and only one att present, yett Devine Providence has made it apeare by His daily and miraculous ways of preservations and delivrances, His mercys, forbearances, long suffering, and patience towards you, that you are not soe much alone but in your person He has continu'd the hopes of an antient family, as you do injoy the name and blood of your father. Therefore I doe injoyne you, by all the obleigations in the world, as of a son, the only son, the child of my vowes and teares, prayers, and pettitions, and vowes to Heaven, as a Christian, and one who is tied to serve his God in the strictest bond of nature and grace, never to hazard yourselfe by neglect or imprudence, or presumption againe, or indanger your life soe as to provoke your gracious God to cutt of the thread of your life, or to shorten the time He gives you to bestow in repentance, least in soe doing you turne that grace into anger, and make a curse to fall on your owne head first, and then to the ruin of your name and family for ever; which estate to come into, God forbid that any procedeing from your father and myselfe should fall.

And as I desire and beg of you caire of your body to preserve it in health, when God shall please to give you that great blessing, which has not bin soe much prized by you, as I hope you will do with humble gratitud, for the great shaire you have injoyed beyond many others, soe am I more consernd for your precious soule, more deare then this world, beeing the price of your Redeemer's blood, whose wellfaire certainly Hee aymes att in this your vissitation, and has bin so gracious to recover you three times in this late illness; still offering His free grace, and expecting you shall sincerely close with this opportunity He gives of your sincere repentance and reformation. And I hope in the mercys of my gracious Father of Heaven that He will yett be mercifull unto you, and as He hath touched your heart to be sencable of your former errors, as I am informd you are now in your vissitation, (for which I blesse the Lord,) soe doe I humbly begg and crave at the hand of God He will vouchsafe to pardon and forgive all your sinns, and grant you grace to keepe all your vowes and promises to God of reformation; and that He will give you strength to performe these good things He has put into your heart, and make you an instrument of His glory heere and heereafter, to serve Him and love Him, and putt your trust in Him alone Who is able to give you life and health and all things necessary to your salvation. To Him I humbly pray that if it be His good pleasure to spaire you to be a blessing yett to this your family, and a comfort to your poore and desolate mother who has mornd myselfe away for your iniquitys, and now must suffer much more by your calamitys. Butt I referre my soule and body wholely to His devine pleasure Who knows best what to do for us here in all things of this life, and that He would prepare our sufferings heere to His glory and our good, if He smite us heere, that He might spare us to etternity, for "'*tis of the Lord's mercy we are not consumed,*"* for His mercys are as infinit as Himselfe. Therefore I besech you, deare child, and son of my vowes to my God, doe not slight the vissitation of the Lord, but humble yourselfe before Him in soule and body; before Him Who hath wounded me and healed me, and can He not doe the same for you?

* Lamentations iii. 22.

therefore have an awe and reverence for His glorious Majesty, put your whole trust in Him Who has rased you up many times. I have sent a little booke for you to read on when it shall please God to give you any respit of ease, which may be of great use to you, and made by a very holy good Christian and a lernd devine, which booke did me a great deale of good in my extreamity of a sicknes since your deare father died; and I hope shall be for instruction and consolation in this your sicknes. I pray beare the hand of God patiently, for "*it is the Lord, let Him do whatever He pleaseth ;*"* and desire to prepare for the worst, butt hope for and pray for the best, which shall be my owne lesson, for I desire to fitt myselfe for His kingdom in His due time, but allso to be ready to serve Him in my generation as long as He sees fitt for me to be exiled from His heavenly kingdom. I desire you will be thankfull to our good God, Who hath provided soe good a place for you to be with your brother and sister, who I hope will still do this indevor for you, and I hope you will be kind and affectionate to them. Son, I cannot add any more for teares, which I porre out for you, with my humble prayers for you that the Lord Jesus would bless and keep you and save and deliver you from this sicknes and death, if it be His pleasure ; if not, to resigne your soule into His holy hand is the petticion of, deare son,

Your most affectionate and disconsolate mother,

ALICE THORNTON.

(Addressed). These, For my deare son
 Mr. Robert Thornton, att the Dean of
 Durham's, n^r Durham.

* 1 Samuel iii. 18.

APPENDIX.

PART II.

NOTICES OF THE FAMILIES OF WANDES-FORD AND THORNTON.

It is thought necessary, for the proper illustration of this volume, to give some biographical and genealogical notices of the families of Wandesford and Thornton, accompanied with pedigrees. The pedigree of Wandesford, it must be understood, is only the centre of the genealogical tree of that ancient family.

I. INVENTORY OF SIR JOHN WANDISFURTH OF KIRTLYNGTON, Kt.—In primis, xxij quarters whete and rie in the garners and yate house chammer in Kirtlington. Item vij quarters berlie. Item iiij quarters whet and rie in garners and yate house chaumer at Kirtligton. Item iij thuynter noute. In corne grewyng in the feldes xv li. Item xiij stirkes iij li. Item xiiij calfes xxviijs. Hay wᵗin the place and in the feldes grewyng, iiij li. In wode vj li. In coles, tallow, salt, and chesse xls. Item ix faute oxon iiij li. xixs. Item j dublet of tynsell satan xls. Item j gowne velvet x li. Item ij jakettes of velvet iij li.

Res et bona superius specificata remanent in manibus Thomæ Wandisfurth armigeri, bonorum dicti domini Johannis militis defuncti collectoribus invitis et contrariantibus.

Item in manibus Adæ Metecalve de bonis dicti defuncti, xxj swyne xxxs. Item x olde horse and iiij folith iij li. vjs. viijd. One horse, price xxvjs. viijd. Summa vj li. iijs. iiijd.

Bona non appreciata remanentia in manibus dicti Thomæ Wandis-

*furth, de bonis ejusdem defuncti, et per ipsum detenta et occupata præ-
textu cujusdam legati hujusmodi defuncti.* In primis, cccxl shepe, xx
kie, xx oxon, iij saltis of silver parsell gilte, a gilte cope w^t one cover,
one cope chaside di. gilte, one goblet of silver, one peudre box of
silver, xj silver spones, vij feder beddes,—matres.

Item all the hustilmentis of housald and napre beynge in the
housys of the said Sir John at Kirtlington prec'——. Summa ——.

Item iij wanes, iij pluyth, w^t all the gere to thame apertenyng, prec'
——. Summa ——.

*Receptiones per Robertum Chilton de redditibus et fermis quæ debe-
bantur præfato domino Johanni dum vixerit.* Resavyd at Heslerton
iij li. xvs. At Thymmylby xl. vjs. viijd. At Synderby xxviijs. At
Thexton xxxs. At Yorke xxvjs. viijd. Of Here Beste and of an
oyer man vjs. viijd. Of my lord dean of Lincolne v li. Summa xv li.
xiijs (*sic*).

*Debita desperata quæ debentur dicto domino Johanni Wandisfurth
tempore mortis suæ.* My lord dean of Lincolne cc marcs. Sir William
Gascoigne ——. Sir John Rocliff iiij li. William Norton iij li. Sir
Christofer Warde c li. Robert Wivell xxvj li. xs. John Clerk of
Pikall viij li. Thomas Metecalve xxiiij li. Nicoles Girlyngton iiij li.
At Basygham vj li.

Debita in quibus dictus defunctus tenebatar tempore mortis suæ. To
one goldismyth of London iiij li. To one merchand of London for
certan stuf iiij li. xvjs. To William Tunstale x li. To Palmer of one
obligacion iij li. vjs. viijd. To doctor Castell xxs. To Sir John
Cutlere vij li. To Nicoles Midilton c s. To Adam Coplay xxs. To
Bankhouse of Yorke xviijs. viijd. To Mr. Elwald iij li xviijs. To
Orshton, skynner, xxxiijs. iiijd. To Mr. Stokdale vs. vjd. To one
wife in Ripon iij li. To Thomas Waller xlvjs. viijd. To ij listers of
Ripon xxxs. To the house of Saint Leonardis' in Yorke iij li. To
abbot of Funtance iij li. To John Midilton xls. To Adam Metecalve
vj li. xs. To Falbarne wife vjs. viijd. To the kirke of Kirtlington
(*blank*). To the abbot of Funtance for one parcell of launde in Yarnewike (*blank*). To Herre Franke xxiijs. iiijd. To Robert Harlathrope
xxiijs. iiijd. To Roger Aske c s. To Ripon chirch liijs. iiijd. To a
man of Lonnesdale vjs. viijd. To parson of Kirtlington and Sr Thomas
iij li vjs. viijd. To Sissone for one horse, and furringe of one gowne
xxvijs. To John Thexston iijs. iiijd. To Clerkeson (*blank*). To a
peuderer (*blank*). To Stephene Lokismyth (*blank*). To Herre Thuaites

(*blank*). To Herre Rede xs. viijd. To William Walker xiijs. iiijd. To Nevell for farme of Yarnewike for ij yeres x li. To y⁰ house of Saint John of the Mounte (*blank*). For Crakehall fee iijs. vd. To my ladie Malivere for one horse xls. To y⁰ mynisters of Thomas Herdladi's xxs. To y⁰ Mounte of Saint John for y⁰ land feld xvijs vjd. To Sir John Midilton vj li xiijs. iiijd. To William Tunstale lait servant to y⁰ said Sʳ John Wandisfurth, for his wages and liveray, iiij li. xvijs. vjd. To Edmund Malivere xxvjs. viijd. To Ric. Burton ls. ijd. To Ric. Cuthbert xixs. viijd. To William Hakney xxxiijs. iiijd. To William Dikeson xls. To George Cooke, elder, xvijs. To Thomas Morland xxvjs. viijd. To William Cuthbert viijs. ijd. To George xvijs. To Ric. Welles xjs. To Herre Rudstane liiijs. viijd. To Bernerde xvjs. To Miles Bilton xvjs. To William Instance viijs. vjd. To John Hereson viijs. xjd. To Ric. Lond vijs. To Christofer Watson ixs. To Robert Hogerd vs. To Agnes Geffray vjs. To Ellyne xxijd. To Burden ijs. vd. To Sir John Thuaites iiij li. To John Key (*blank*). To Thomas Marshall (*blank*). To Sir William Helmyslay xxs. To Elzabeth xxd. To John Chilton xxviijs. iiijd. To Nicoles Midilton v li., which Robert Chilton is suretie for us be obligacion. Summa (*blank*).

Solutiones factæ per Robertum Chilton certis creditoribus supradicti defuncti, et servientibus ejusdem, ac etiam in aliis expensis per ipsum expositis pro utilitate animæ ejusdem defuncti de bonis per ipsum receptis, ut patet inferius. Paid to Mr. Vause vj li. xiijs. iiijd. To my ladie his wife xxvjs. viijd. To my said lady xiijs. iiijd. To Adam Metcalf vj li. xs. To John Chilton for his wage xxviijs. iiijd. To Sir John Geffrason ijs. vd. To George Kirke xijd. To John Key ijs. I aske alowance of v li which I am bunden to pay, as apperith be obligacion to Nicoles Midilton. In expensis maid be me and of Herre Franke riding to Lincolne and fro and of abidyng wᵗ my horse be the space of ix dais xxvjs. viijd. In expensis in riding agane to Lincolne of me and my servand xs. Expendit y⁰ third tyme yᵗ I rode to Lincolne for y⁰ well and perfurmyshyng of y⁰ last will of Sir John Wandisfurth, be the space of v dais goyng and commyng viijs. viijd. Paid for one commission at for to levay and geder y⁰ goodes of y⁰ said Sir John Wandisfurth iiijs. iiijd. In expensis commyng for the same be the space of ij dais and ij nyghtes iijs. Paid for one sequestracion writing and selyng, and for the costes of Mr Lacestre and myne for the expedicion of y⁰ said sequestracion wᵗ oure servantes vs. Paid for one new commission vjs. For my costes commyng for the same and y^r abidinge be ye space of ij dais iijs. iiijd. In expencis diverse tyme riding to Tanfeld to speke w^t Herre Franke for the entent at the last will of ye said Sir John mythe have bene fulfilled iijs. In expensis maid when I come home w^t the corse to his beriall xxs. Paid for a procurasie writinge and selyng ijs. Yevyn in almuse as I come w^t the corse to his beriall, and oyer tymes, to frears and pure folkes vs. In expensis maid when I lay at Kirtlington for the said cause iijs. iiijd. For writing of this present inventarie and one copie of ye same iijs. iiijd. In expensis maid be me and my sone commyng be the commandment of ye ordenarie to Yorke for ye said cause x tymes xxs. Summa ——.

Solutiones factæ per Thomam Wandisfurth de Kirtlington, arm., de bonis exist. in manibus suis bonorum dicti Johannis Wandisfurth, militis, defuncti, certis viris quibus idem dominus Johannes indebitatus fuit tempore mortis suæ in summis subsequentibus. Paid to William Tunstall servand to ye said Sr John for his hiers and liveras iiij li. xvijs. vjd. To Edmunde Malleverer xxvjs. viijd. To Ric. Burton xxvjs. viijd. To Robert Cutbert xxvjs. viijd. To William Hakney xxxiijs. iiijd. To George Kitson xvijs. To Barnarde xvjs. To Agnes Geffray vjs. (From the original preserved at York.)

II. The Will of Sir George Wandesford of Slenningford.—In the name of God Amen. The xxviijth day of J . . . ., Anno Domini 1597, and in the xxxix . . . : . of the reigne of our sovereigne ladye Elizabeth, by the grace of God quene of England, France and Ireland, defendor of the faith, etc. I George Wandisford, of Slenningford, in the county of Yorke esquire, being determined by God's grace to pass the seas, and to adventure myself in this action or voiage now intended by the right honorable the Earle of Essex, where by reason of the manifold dangers which are allwaies incident to martiall enterprizes, I thinke ytt a parte of Christianitie to prepare myselfe to such success as ytt shall please the Almightie to allott unto me, eyther by liffe or death; and likewise to dispose of soch temporall possessions and goods which ytt hath pleased Him to bestowe uppon me. And consideringe with myselfe that my lovinge brother Wm. Wandisford hath heretofore at my request and for my debte entered into divers recoginizances and bonds of greate somes, the whole burden whereof ys likely to lye uppon my said brother, yf ytt shall please God to call me before my retorne into England ; I doe therfore ordeine and make this my last will and testament in manner and forme followinge (that is to say): First I commend my soule to the mercifull hands of our Lord and Saviour Jesus Christ, and my body to the earth whereof yt is made. Item, whereas by my deede bearinge date the seaven and twenty day of this instant June I have made and constituted my said brother William Wandesford my lawfull attorneye to demande, recover, receive, sue and impleade for all soch debts as are or shalbe any way owinge unto me by any person or persons whatsoever, and to keepe and reteine the same to his owne use towards the dischardge of the said recoginizances and bonds, which authoritie so to him given will become void and frustrate, yet nevertheles willinge that my said brother shall no waies be dampni-fied by the said recoginizances and bonds, I doe ordeine and make my said brother William Wandisford my sole executor to all intents and purposes, wherby the lawe will authorize him to recover and receive all soch debts and duties as are or shalbe any waye due unto me by any person or persons whatsoever.   And further I will that he shall reteine the same to his owne proper use and behoof for ever.   In witnesse whereof I have hereunto sett my hand and seale the day and yeare first above written.   These beinge witnesses, Jo. Bowes, Tho. Smelt, Bryan Thaidy, Edmund Lascells, Jo. White, and Tho. Knight, Stephen Dockwray servant to the said Sir George Wandisford.   Prob. at London, 12 Sep. 1612.   (From the will registered at Richmond.)

III. The Will of Christopher Wandesford of Hipswell, Esq. —Nov. 28, 1598.   Christopher Wandesford of Hipiswell esqr.   To be buried within my porche or quire on the southe side of the parishe churche of Cathericke, nighe unto the place where my firste wief was buried.   To the moste nedie poore of the parishe of Cathericke £5, to be divided amongest them at the discretion of my executors, with th' advise of my worshipfull and lovinge cozen Mr. Ralphe Lawson esqr. my verie good neighbour.   To the poor of parishe of Kirtlington xxs. To my sonne Christofer Wandesforde my signet and bruche of golde, and all my apparell excepte my russett sattan dublett which I doe give and bequeath unto my cosen and servante Christopher Fulthropp.   My will is that my said sonne be advised and councelled in all his causes by my lovinge sister Mrs. Elizabeth Wrenn widowe, my lovinge nephew Mr. Charles Wrenn of Bynchester, and my lovinge nephew Mr. Roger Lassells, parson of Kirtlington.   To my sonne in law Mr. George

Lassells my younge graie amblinge geldinge. To my dau. Ellenor his wief 20 l. and my bedstockes of wallnotte tree, with my bedd of downe, etc., and my beste silver salte. To my goddaughter and grandechilde Elizabeth Lassells there dau. £100, when she is xxi or married. Servante Francis Frere £10, and one of my foure whyes at High Waytwith, in consideracion of his service. Servante William Golightlie 40s. Servante Roger Cottonne 10s. Maid servante Margerie Thursbye my beste milke cowe and one whie calfe. Maide servante Jane Johnson one whye of three yeares owld, goinge at Hipiswell. To Lancelotte Hunte my kytchen boye 30s. to helpe him to an occupacion. To Peter Castell vs. To my servante John Binkes 10s. To my lovinge cosens and servants Roger Futhroppe, Thomas Duffeild and Christopher Fulthroppe eache of them one younge maire of the beste I have at Highe Waitwith. To my servante Francis Calverte one of my fower whyes at Highe Waitwith. To my servantes Roger Browne and Raphe Sadler, 20s. each. To my cosen Mrs. Anne Fulthropp, my said daughter hir servante, ij angells of golde. To my lovinge cosen Mr. Michaell Wandesford of Upsland, £5. To my dau. Mrs. Ellenor Lassells my white graie mare and hir foale called Cloudye browe. To my lovinge sister Mrs. Elizabeth Wrenn, and my lovinge nephewes Charles Wrenn and Roger Lassells a spurriall each. The resedewe— to my said lovinge sister Mrs. Elizabeth Wrenn and my said lovinge nephews Mr. Charles Wrenn and Mr. Roger Lassells—they ex^rs.

Pr. 22 Feb. 1601-2 before Anthony Johnson rector of Richmond, and Henry Thruscross and Richard Bland, clerks, preachers of God's word, at Richmond, by special commission, and adm. to Charles Wrenn gen., salvo jure to the others renouncing (Reg. Test. Ebor., xxviii., 552*b*).

IV. A Suit for a Divorce in the Court of York, William Wandesford, gen., v. Chr. Wandesford, Esq., and Cecily W. alias Metcalfe his alleged wife, 1601-2, March 4, *John Loftehouse of Richmond, tanner, æt. circ.* xxi., saith that Christofer Wandesforde* is accompted heire of Christofer Wandesford late of

---

* The following document is put in as evidence at this trial. By Inq. held at Richmond, Oct. 7, 43rd Eliz., before Walter Strickland, Esq., John Alred, Esq., the queen's escheator in Yorkshire, and Chr. Aiscough, gen., it was found that this Chr. Wandesford was incapable of managing his property.

The result of this suit was that the two were divorced.

Hipswell esquire, his father deceased.   Betwene Lammes and Michaelmas laste paste James Metcalfe and Cicilie his sister intreated this ex^te
and one Henric Greatchead, who dwelte then at Hipswell, where the
said Christofer Wandesford lay, to be a meanes to get the said Christofer
oute at the gates, and to go to the churche with him to marrie the said
Cicilie; and promised this ex^te, if he could bringe that matter to passe,
a hundreth pound.   Whereupon this ex^te perswaded the said Christofor
to go furth of the gates in the nighte tyme; and so he did, together
with the said Cicilie and this ex^te, who all thre went to a place called
Sandbecke bridge where they met the said James Metcalfe and one
Thomas Man, a minister, as it was reported.   All which fyve wente
from thence into Wensadaile and frome thence to Horton in Riblesdaile,
where thay remayned a litle space.   After the premissies, and aboute
one a'clocke in the after noone, aboute the Holie Rood day laste paste,
the said Thomas Man, takinge upon him the office of a mynister, did
marrie the said Christofer and Cicilie in Horton churche, the said
Christofer speakinge after the said Man all the woordes of matrimonie,
savinge that when the said Man asked the said Christofer whether he
would have the said Cicilie to his wyfe or no, he answered, "Nay, I
mighte have a gentlewoman;"   and then this ex^te said she was a
gentlewoman, and then the said Christofer was contente to taike the
said Cicilie to his wyfe at the perswacion of this ex^te, the said Man,
and the same James Metcalfe.   One nighte after the said mariage
the said Christofor and Cicelie beinge at a place called Clapham, certain
Hipswell men cam to searche for the said Christofor; whereupon the
said James Metcalfe conveiged the said Christofor and this ex^te to an
other place aboute a myle frome Clapham, at which place the said
Christofor and this ex^te wente to bed together, the said Cicilie not then
beinge in theire companie; howbeit he saith that in the mornyng the
said Cicilie was in bedd with theime, but what tyme she cam he knoweth
not.

Roger Cottam of York, yeoman, æt. circ. xxi., says that Christofer
Wandesforde gent. is soonne and heire to Christofer Wandesforde late
of Hipswell esquire, deceased, who died possessed of landes and tene-
mentes of the yerelie value of cli. and more, which he the rather
knoweth to be true because he served the said Mr. Wandesforde in his
lyfe tyme.   For twoo yeres together ended aboute twoo yeres agoe
this ex^te dwelte in house with the said Christofer Wandesforde deceased,
duringe which tyme the articulate Christofor his soonne remayned in

the said house and was accompted a lunatyke or madd man, fallinge
for the moste parte once a day into a fitt of frensie or lunacie, in which
fitt he used to teare his clothes frome his backe and burne theime if he
were suffred, and use dyvers other mysdemeaners, whereby it mighte
evidentlie appeare that he was senceles and alltogether destitute of
reason and descrecion.

Michaell Wandesforde of Upsland, gen., æt. circ. l., saith that
Christofer Wandesforde late of Hipswell, esquire, died possessed of
landes of the yerelie value of cc li. or thereaboutes, and that Christofer
Wandesforde articulate is his soonne and heire. The said Christopher
was and is a lunaticke, or madd man, and so was founde by a jurie
impanelled at Richemonde by certain commissioners theire sitting for
that purpose, which he the rather knoweth to be true because he haith
sene the said Christofer behave himselfe lyke a madd man, and was one
of the jurie impanelled.

Henry Greathead alias Bower, of Hipswell, yeoman, æt. circ. xxij.,
says that for the space of fouretene yeares ended at Michaelmas last
past he dwelte at Hipswell, and was for the most parte of that tyme
in companye with the articulate Christofer Wandesford the yonger.
During all that tyme the said Christofer was lunatick. The articulate
Christofer Wandesford now deceased dyed about the syxte of September
last, and beyng deade this ex^te brought the articulate Christofer
Wandesford the yonger his sonn to him saying, "Your father is deade,
loke on him and yow must weepe." "Noe," quoth he, "he is not
deade," and laughed and sayd, "Is he not lying there in his bedd?"
and sayd further, "I will not weepe, whye shoulde I weepe?" by reason
whereof this ex^te was the more assured of his frensye.

John Trotter of Hollins in Dent, yeoman, æt. circ. lxx., says that
Thomas Man for dyvers yeres paste haith bene and yet is a verie poore
man, woorth nothing his debtes paid, having a poore wyfe and aboute
halfe a dozan children* who go a begging for their leving; and, besydes
that, is a haunter of ail howsies, geven to drinking, carding and tabling,
and this ex^te hath sene the said Man so drunke that he could not
governe himselfe, and for thies and other his misbehaviours he was
displaced frome serving the cure at Dent aboute twoo yeres agoe. He
never knew nor hard tell that ever he was minister at Horton in Ribles-

---

* Another witness says that Man had two illegitimate children, for which he
had been excommunicated.

daile, at leaste lawfullye lycenced, and the persons named in this article were none of his parishoners.

William Escam par. Horton, yeoman, æt. circa 56, saith that being borne and broughte upp in the parishe of Horton and dwelling their ever sence, never knew nor hard tell that Thomas Man was ever minister at Horton, nether did he ever serve the cure their savinge at a disorderly mariage solemnized betwene Christofer Wandesford and Cicilie Metcalfe, as thay called theim; nether were the said Christofer and Cicilie ever parishoners of that parishe that this ex^{te} could heare or learne of. Aboute Michaelmes laste paste was a twelvemooncth one James Metcalfe, who was said to be brother to the said Cicilie, and twoo of the Dinesdells cam to this ex^{tes} house accompanied with the said Mr. Christofer Wandesford and Cicilie Metcalfe, as they called theim, and soom others cam all to this ex^{tes} house called Hawber, in Horton parishe, being a vittaylin house, and their lighted and dranke, and soone after wente to Horton churche, and this ex^{te} folowing theim perceved by theim that thay broughte the said Christofer and Cicilie, as thay called theime, to be married together; and the said parties being standing in the bodie of the said churche, and the said Man, as thay tearmed him, being redie to marrie theim, the said Wandesford said, " If I marrie, I will marrie a gentlewoman;" and with that went asyde frome the companye, and one of the companie broughte him again; and when he cam to the companye soom present tould him that he must be maried. Quoth he, " Must I be maried? I know hardly what matrimonie is." And after a while said, " Yow tould me that I should marrie a gentlewoman!" whereunto one of the companie answered saying, "If yow marrie her, she is a gentlewoman;" and then one of the companie whome thay called Lofthous laid his arme over his shoulders untill the woordes of mariage were spokin betwene the said parties by the direction of the said Man the minister, as thay termed him: all which space the said Lofthous mouth was nere Mr. Wandesford's eare; and, as it semed to this ex^{te}, he spoke to him in tymes in his eare, but what he could not heare. The said Christofer semed to this ex^{te} to be of no sound judgement nor discrecion; for, if he had bene, he would not have suffred the said Loftehous to have leaned upon him as he did, nether did this ex^{te} se anie other ever maried having an other man leanyng over his shoulders at the tyme of the said mariage. After the persons afforesaid cam frome the churche thay cam to this ex^{tes} house, being aboute a quarter of a myle a sunder, and being in the

said house by the fyer syde, there was a pece of mutton rosting at the
fier: the which the said Mr. Wandesford laid his hand upon, saying,
"Is this a pigg?"

From the evidence taken on the other side, I give a few extracts
next page.

Cecily Metcalfe was dau. of John Metcalfe.

Ric. Dinsdale went with them from Raydell house to Horton, and
in the waye he had muche talke with Chr. Wandesford, which he
supposed was very sensible, for this respondent, amongest other thinges,
asked him how he lyked the mores whereon they rode, and he answered
that he lyked them well, savynge that theye were somtymes very wyndye
by reason of the hills, and that they lay hye. He further sayth that
after the marrage the weddeners dyned at William Escam, where the
articulate Wandesford seyng a calfe-heade on the table sayd, "Is this a
calfe-head? yt is a verye good one:" which was a calfe-head indede.

Thos. Mann, æt. circ. 48, ex^d says, he married them properly. About
20 years since he was ord^d deacon and priest by the bp. of Carlisle: served
cures at Dent 14 years, at Horton in Westm^d 2 years, at Lowther one
year, at Russendall and Gargrave.

Quest^d. He now lives in Dent. Born in township of Rilston and
went to school at Clytheroe and to Skipton and Pately bridge: then
he taught school at Long Preston 3 years. He taught Mr. Lowther
of Lowther's children 4 years: then served cure at Overton in Westm^d
3 years: after that taught Sedberghe free (school) about a year: then
cure of Gargrave $\frac{1}{2}$ a year: curate of Dent 15 years, ended 2 years
ago. On 26th Sept. last was a twelvemth Wednesday he m^d them: had
20 nobles promised. (From the original depositions in the Court of
York.)

V. The Will of Sir Rowland Wandesford, Knight, his
Majesty's Attorney of the Court of Wards and Liveries,
dated 3 Sep. 1640, written with my own hand. To be buried where it
shall please God to call me, "most earnestlie desiring not to bee un-
bowelled." I forgive the Rt. Hon. Philip Lord Wharton 1000*l.* he
owes me, and in further token of my love to him give him 100*l.* more,
and 40*l.* to his sweet lady to use at her pleasure. To my nephew
Wm Wandesford, esq., 20*l.* for a piece of plate; to my nephew Thos
Norton, esq., 40*l.* To my sister Florence Wandesford 40*l.* Legacies
to 5 servants; residue to s^d Philip Lord Wharton in trust for Phila-

delphia and Elizabeth Wharton my grandchildren, being my daughter's children by the said Lord Wharton; appoint s^d Lord Wharton exor. Supervisor Francis Lord Cottington, to whom 40*l.*, a horse, or a piece of plate. Witnesses, Richd Branthwaite, Arthur Heron, Richard Holmead, Thos Swarland, Richd Waller, and Christopher Goodcom.

Proved 27 Sep., 1653, by s^d Philip Lord Wharton the exor. (From C. P. C. 20, Brent.)

VI. Sept. 28, 1713. Dame ELEANOR WANDESFORD, of the citty of York, widdow. To be buried att the discretion of my executors and of such of my children as shall be with me att the time of my death, in the parish church of Kirklington, near to the place where my dear husband Sir Christopher W. baronet was buried, if I die within one day's journey of it. The agreement I have made with my grandson Lord Viscount Castlecomer touching the payment of 50*l.* per ann. to my son George W., vizt 30*l.* to him, and 20*l.* to his daughter Ann Sharlott W. to be performed. 200*l.* to my son George, and after his death to Osburn and Ann Sharlott W. his children. To my son George a bond for 100*l.* wherein he and his mother in law, Mrs. Mallory, are bound to me. To my grandson Lord Viscount Castlecomer, for life, my wrought bed and damask bed, my gold and silver quilt, and best diamond ring, and my great silver looking glass, to goe to the heires male of the family of my dear husband. The interest of 300*l.* to my daughter Mary W. and my silver dressing plate for her life. To my daughters Lady Pyne and Bossevile 100*l.* Dau. Sweetenham 150*l.* Children of my dau. Bush 40*l.* Grandson Captain George W. brother of my grandson Viscount Castlecomer, 100*l.* Grandson John W. 100*l.* Poor of Lowther 50*l.* Poor of Kirklington 50*l.* To the minister and churchwardens of Hipswell 50*l.*, 1*l.* 1*s.* 6*d.* of the interest thereof to go to the minister for preaching a funerall sermon there yearly, and the rest to the poor. To Mr. Tatham the minister of Kirklington 5*l.* to buy him a mourning gowne. To my nephew, the Lord Viscount Lonsdale, a silver bason of 20*l.* value, to be supervisour. I give 40*l.* to be laid out in a tomb or monumentall stone for my said husband and me. I give the great Herball to my cozen Chr. Norton's daughter now in the Bishoprick of Durham. The rest to my grandson Lord Viscount Castlecomer, and I make my brother Ralph Lowther of Ackworth esq., Revd Mr Pemberton of Bedell, clerk, and my nephew Thomas Comber of East Newton esq. executors in England and Dr Coggin in Dublin, and Robert FitzGerrard of the Castle of Kilkenna esq. in Ireland, and I give them two guineas each for memoriall rings. Proved 23ᵈ Dec. 1714. (*Reg. Test. Ebor.*, lxix., 337.)

VII. Nov. 4, 1725. MARY WANDESFORD of the City of York, spinster. To my brother George W. 20*l.*, and 30*l.* to his son Osborn Wandesford. To my sister Pyne 50*l.* To my sister Swetenham and her two daughters Margaret and Elianor 10*l.* each. To my sister Bosvile 100*l.* To my nephew Captain George Wandesford 10*l.* and to his son Chr. W. 10*l.*, to be laid out in books for him. I give the ovall picture of myselfe to remain at Kirklington to the heir of the family, as I have ordered a golden cup now in the possession of Lord Castlecomer, to whom I do also give all my plate marked M. W. for his use during his life, to remain to my nephew John W., rector of Kirklington. I give my picture of our Blessed Saviour and of the Virgin Mary to Lord Castlecomer, to be kept in the mansion house of Kirklington. I give one pair of diamond ear-rings consisting of many diamonds, and also a necklace containing twenty nine diamonds, to the said John W. To the most reverend father in God the Archbishop of York for the time being, the Honᵇˡᵉ Edward Finch residentiary of York, the Honᵇˡᵉ John Wandesford rector of Kirklington, Wᵐ Woodyear esq. of Crookill and John Bradley residentiary of York, the lands, house and mill which I purchased of Mr. Wainwright in Brumpton upon Swaile, my right to a mortgage upon the estate of Jeremiah Myers late of Allerthorp for 1200*l.*, and 1200*l.* part of my stock in the South Sea Company, for the use of ten poor gentlewomen who were never married, and who shall be of the religion which is taught and practised in the Church of England as by law established, who shall retire from the hurry and noise of the world into a religious house or Protestant retirement which shall be provided for them; and they shall be obliged to continue there for life; and if any person elected into this society by my trustees (whom I do hereby constitute and appoint perpetuall electors) shall either withdraw herselfe from the house or habitation which shall be provided, or shall marry or shall behave herselfe unsuitably to the design and rules of this foundation, the trustees shall have it in their power, and are hereby desired to remove her, and to fill her place with another gentlewoman who may better deserve it. As for the rules and methods of this society I leave wholy to my trustees above mentioned, who are hereby impowered at any time to give such rules and to alter them as from time to time they shall see proper and convenient, and whenever it shall please God that any one of my trustees shall dye, another shall be elected into his room by the surviving trustees. And whereas there is no house as yet provided for the reception and use of the said poor gentlewomen, I do appoint my trustees for the charity to purchase a convenient habitation for them where they may all live together under one roofe, and where they may make a small congregation once at least every day at prayers such as my trustees shall think proper for their case and circumstances. And I do appoint 10*l.* per ann. to a reader who shall be appointed by my trustees and paid by them out of the estate. I give a square picture of my selfe to be hung up and remain in the house bought for the uses above mentioned. I charge upon my estate at Brumpton 20s. every Christmas for the use of the poor of Brumpton, and 20s. more per ann. for teaching such poor children of Kirklington to read, write, and say their catechism, whose parents are not able to pay for their teaching. I leave the nominating of the children to the rector of Kirklington. To the poor of Kirklington, Hipswell, Brumpton upon Swale, and of the parish wherein I shall dye, 5*l.* each to be paid by my nephew John W. whom I make ex^r.

Codicil. It is my desire that all my plate shod be put up together in black trunck and wax'd in the presence of some of my trustees and my ex^r—the black trunk has E. W. upon it and the year of our Lord is in 1692 upon it. To Mrs. Frances Lowther my goddaughter my gold watch and their belonging to it, also a case with many things in it called a setwee. I appoint that 5*l.* be given into the hands of some that goes along with my corps to the burying place, to be distributed to the poor people in the road as they pass along, or put into the hands of the minister or churchwardens to distribute as needfull. I desire that there may be no state nor trouble in my funerall, but 6 of the poorest unmarried women in Kirklington may have white vales from head to foot prepared for them and white gloves, and carry my corps into the church at what place I happen to be buried in. Let the white vales be such cloth as will do them service hereafter. (*Reg. Test. Ebor.* lxxix., iii. *l.*)

VIII. Testamentum Willelmi Thorneton nuper generosi defuncti. In the name of God Amen, the xxviij daye of the moneth of

August in the yere of our Lorde God m^{l}cccclxxxvij, I William of Thorneton of York, gentilman, beyng in gude mynde, makes my testament in this maner.   Furste I give and wyttes my saule to God Almighty and to oure Lady and to all the Seyntes of heven, and my bodye to be beryd in the kyrke of Seynt Cuthbert in Peseholme in Yorke afore the alter of Seynt Katheryn.   Also I gyve and I wyt to the werk of the saide kyrke iijs. iiijd.   Also I gyve and I wit my best garment to be brought to the kyrke w^t my body in the name of my corsepresent. Also I gyve and I wit my newe messe buke to the maner of Newton in Rydale to serve in Seynt Peter chapell to the worlde end.   Also I gyve and I wyt to xiij prestes beyng at myn exequias iiijs. iiijd.   And to the person of the said kyrk xijd.   Also I wyt iiij^{li} wax in iiij serges to byrn aboute my body at my exequias, and jd. for ensens, and for ryngyng iiijd.   Also I gyve and wyt to John Thorneton vjs. viiijd.   Also to Alyson Thorneton vjs. viijd.   Also to Isabell Thorneton iijs. iiijd. Also I gyve and wyt to Johannet my servannt j coverlet, j payre blankettes, and a payre of shetes, and to Bagby kyrk vjs. viijd.   And to ye reparacion of the yle in Steyngrave kyrk vjs. viijd.   And to William Johnson and to William Tylson either of thame xxd.   Also to Thomas Mylson xxd.   Also I gyve and wyt xs. to be distribute to pure people at myn exequias for the wele of my saule.   The residue of my goodes I gyve and wyt to Agnes my wyfe and Robert my son, whome I make myn executores to dispose for my saule as they thynke best.   In wittennesse whereof, to this present testament I have putte my seale. Thies witnesses, etc.   Pr. 17 March 1488-9.   Adm. to exors.   (*Reg. Test. Ebor.* v. 353 *a*.)

IX.   TESTAMENTUM WILLELMI THORNTON, PAROCHIÆ DE STANGRAVE.   In the name of God, Amen.   The xxviijth daye of Maye in the yeare of oure Lord Gode a m^l v^c xxv, I William Thornton of Newton, of goode will and goode remembrance makes this my last will and testament in manner and forme followinge.   First, I bequeith my soull to God Almightie, to oure Blessed Ladie Sancte Marie, and to all the holie company of heaven, and my bodie to be buried in the church of the Blessed Trinitie of Stayngrave.   Item, I give to Robert Thornton my sone one whit geldinge; and to Margerie his wif my gray amblynge mare.   Item, I give to John Thornton my sone iiij kie. Item, I give to Margaret Farfax the doughter of Guye Farfax iij kie and xx gymber hogges.   Item, I give to the churche warkes xs.   Item,

I give to the hie altare ij⁸. Item, I give to Elisabethe Welborne and to Elisabeth Hudson either of theme one quye stirke. Item, I give to Thomas Thornton my brother one cowe with a calf. Item, I give to Sir William Lawson my curate v⁸. Item, I give to every one of Robert Thorntone children, Guye Farfax children, Thomas Metham children, every one of them one gymber hoge; and I make my executours Robert Thornton, Frances Thornton, and Leonarde Wildon, and they to have ther coste borne in that behalf. The residue of my goodes, my dettes paide, my legacies fulfilled, and funerall expenses dischardged, I give to my sex children, that is to saye Anne Farefax, William Thornton, Gregorie Thornton, Edwarde Thornton, Dorothie Thornton, and Margaret Thornton, thes beinge witnesses Georgie Thwyng of Hemylsaye esquier, and Sir William Lawson. 22 Aug. ad. gr. to Robert the exʳ. (*Reg. Test. Ebor.* xiii. 47*b*.)

X. 12 April 1566. FRANCIS THORNTON, of Thornton of the Hill. To good mʳ Sʳ Richard Cholmeley, knyght, one grey colte stagge of two yeares old. To Johan T. my wyf one gold rynge that I wedded her withall. To dau. Margᵗ Chaise one other gold rynge that was her mother's. To Johan T. my doughter one payre of demyssaries that was her mother's. Margerie T. my doughter 40ˢ. etc. Sonne Thomas T. a mylke ewe. To Wᵐ, Thomas, John and Margerie T. my children all suche intrest as I have in my fermes at Thornton of the Hill, Baxbie, and Bransby. I will that Robert Chace and sone T. shall have power to sewe for all my gyftes gyven to me by Mʳ Thomas Dalarever, and wrongfullie by Thomas Ems and Thomas Standevyn [detained]. To Wᵐ and Thoˢ my sonne all my harnes, withe my sweard, buckelers, and wood knyves. The rest to my children—they exors, and my good mʳ Sir Richard Cholmeley kᵗ and my nevie Robert Thornton supervisors. And I desyre my said nevye to be good godfather unto my said sone Thomas T. and his porcion, and to se hym brought upp in vertue. Pro. 11 May 1566. (*Reg. Test. Ebor.* xvii. 458.)

XI. 12ᵗʰ Eliz. 156 [9-70]. ROBERT THORNETON of East Newton esquier. I do give my soull to Allmyghtye God, our Lady Saynt Marye, and to all the celestiall companye of heaven, and my body to be buryed wythin my parishe churche of Stanegrave at th'ende of St Leonerde alter, nyghe wheras my father and other my ancesters do lye and ar buryed. To the churchewardens of the said churche to ymploye and bestowe

for and about the repayringe and amendinge of the said churche vs. To
my true, faithfull and lovinge wyffe, Margerye Thorneton, in full satisfaction of her dowre, thyrdes, and feoffamente—my landes, etc., in
Lasthropp, whiche I dyd lately obtayne and purchasse of Sir Richerd
Cholmeley knyght, late in the holdinge of Guye Fairefax and John
Sleytholme—duringe her lyffe. To my brother Gregorye Thorneton
one annuytye of xxs. of all the reste of my landes in Lastroppe, so that
he be of good demeanour, and beare hymself honestlye to my sonne
and heyre apparent William Thorneton. To my lovinge sonne in lawe
William Wright, and to my lovinge doughter Anne his wyffe xxx li.,
and to ther son Robert Wright x li. To my faithfull and lovinge wyffe
Margerye Thorneton one sylver bowle, all my olde sylver spones, and
my whyte stoned horse. To my lovinge sonne William Thorneton one
standinge goblytt of sylver, a silver bowle, twelve newe silver spones, a
sylver salte, and all my ten kye, threscore of my best yewes, a brewinge
leade, and all other my ymplementes, and householde stuffe within my
house at Est Newton. To Ellenor his wyffe one silver cupp, withe a
cover gylte. To my brother Gregorye Thorneton one mesuage etc. in
Nawton whiche I purchesed of one Peckett. To my syster Methame a
quye of thre yeares of aige, and to my godson yonge Thomas
Methame, my syster sonne, one darke gray filly of fower yeares of aige.
To my servant Robert Blenkynsopp xls. besydes his yearlye waiges.
Servant Symon Richerdson xxs. besydes his waiges. To every of my
women servauntes besydes ther waiges vs. To Henry Hicke xs. and to
Henrye Mede, William Hawkyns, Robert Warrener, xs. each besydes
ther waiges. Thomas Shipperde vjs. viijd. besydes his waiges. To
Nicholas Spawnton a quye and two yewes. To Thomas Thompson vs.
besydes his waiges. To my lovinge cossyn and nephewe William
Fayrefax a blacke filly of fower yeares of aige. To Thomas Ripley
and Thomas Smythe, eyther of them a yewe and a lamb. To Dorothe
Thorneton my sonne William doughter 200 markes to the preferment
of her maraige, if she departe, to go to her nexte brother or syster,
being no heire. To my godsons, John and Robert Butler, Robert
Sympson, Robert Sandwiche, Robert Blensyarde, Robert Rosse,
Charles Newbye, Robert son of Edward Thorneton, Robert Holtby;
Thomas sonne of Francys Thorneton xs. each, and to all other my
godsons vs. each. To my cosinge William sonne of Francys Thorneton
and to his wyffe two yewes. The residue to my sonne and heyre
apparent William Thorneton—he ex[r], and to dispose to the healthe of

my soull, etc. My trustye and right welbeloved brother in lawe Thomas Grymston esquyer, Thomas Thwinge gent. and my cosinge Roger Sympson, supervysors. Wytnesses Robert Layton, Cuthbert Smythe, Christofer Metcalfe, and Roger Sympson. Pr. 24 Apr. 1572. Adm to exor. (*Reg. Test. Ebor*. ix, 493 *a*.)

XII. Sept. 11, 1579. GREGORIE THORNTON, of Brandsbie. To be buried where yt shall please God and my frendes. To Thomas Thornton my sone a yonge amblinge meare. To John Thornton my sone a feley that was of Robert Lamley mare. To Margaret T. my doughter one cowe caulled Whitelockes. To Jennet T. my doughter a cowe caulled Throsh. To Eliz^th T. my doughter a yonge garded cowe, caulled Gavell. To Grace T. my doughter a cortalled quie. To Allyson my wife the lease of my house and of the Downwood for to helpe to bringe upp my children that I hadd withe her, and I desire her to be good mother unto my two doughters that I hadd with my firste wiffe. The rest to my wiffe, and Thomas, John, Margaret, Jennet, Eliz^th and Grace my children. My wiffe ex^x. Pro. 5 June 1580. Admon. to executrix. (*Reg. Test. Ebor*. xxi. 456 *a*.)

XIII. May 5, 1600. WILLIAM THORNTON, of Easte Cambe co. York gent. Poore of Easingewold 6^s 8^d, etc. Wief Barbara my blacke amblinge mare. To my sonne William T. my rapier and dagger with all the rest of my municion and armoure. To my dau. Marie Gibson one bonde wherein my brother in lawe Raphe Westbie, of Ravensfeild, standeth bounde to me for 16^l 13^s 4^d, and 5 marks. To Thomas, Eliz^th and Mary Gibson her children, 5 marks each. To my brother Thomas T. 4*l*. 8^s what he oweth me. To his sonne William 10^s; his dau. Eliz^th 20^s; and his daur^s Mary and Barbara 5^s each. Sister Margerie Willson 20^s. Residue to wife and son W^m, they exors; and they not to be troubled for payment of legacies untill suche tyme as they have received 100^l and 20 marks of Mr Henry Cholmeley which he oweth me. Pro. 30th May 1600. Admon. to executrix, *salvo jure* to son, a minor. (*Reg. Test. Ebor*. xxviii. 127 *a*.)

XIV. Feb. 8, 49th James, 1615; WILLIAM THORNETON of East Newton esquier.—Because my yeares are manie and therefore my dayes of this life can be but fewe; and for that of laite it hath pleased God in His mercie towardes me to visitt me manie tymes with greevious infirmities, thereby the rather to call to mind the necessities of orderinge and disposeinge of my temporall estaite, the better to prevent inconveniences which daiely happen amongest the freindes and kinsfolkes of the dead, I doe therefore make, etc. To be buried within the church of Stainegrave, as nere unto the place where my auncestors have bene formerlie buried as with convenience may be. To my wel-beloved daughter Dorothie Askewith 10*l.*, and to everie of her children two 22ˢ peeces of gold. To my cosen Richmond and his wief and two children which he haith by my grandchild, each a 22ˢ peece of gold. To my cosen William Cheator and his wief, and to their daughter, and the residewe of my daughter Cheator her children, to my brother Wright and sister Wright, and their three sonnes William, Frances, and Nicholas Wright, each a 22ˢ peece of gold. To my cosen William Thwinge 40ˢ. To my cosen Nicholas Bullocke, and my cosen Thomas Bullocke his three children, each a 22ˢ peece of golde. My will is that John Daggitt my servant have the growndes in the Marrishes he now possesseth, for his life, paying the present rent. To my servant James Allanbie the howse and growndes he now holdeth at East Newton, for life, at the present rent. To my servant Robert White, his howse, in like manner. To my servantes Robert Hicke, William Coates, William Tailer, and William Horner 20ˢ each. To my other men and maide servantes, each besides their wage, a quarter's wages. My servant Nicholas Brignell to continew his live stuff at Greenehawe. Richard Castle 20ˢ. To the poore people of the parishe of Stainegrave 20ˢ. Whereas in consideracon of the marriage of my sonne Robert Thornton and his now wief, I did promese to purchase soe much landes (over and besides what I was then seazed of) as should be of the yearelie valewe of c*ˡⁱ*, or to leave him at my death 1500*l.*, and whereas the landes which I laitelie purchased of Sir Richard Cholmeley and Sʳ Henrie Cholmeley knightes, were purchased with monie which I received for some of my aunciont landes which I solde, lyeinge in Sandhutton, Carleton, and Ampleford, and thereby noe parte of the saide agreement and promise was performed; and whereas my said sonne standeth bound with me in greate somes of monie for the porcions and concerninge the tuitions and education of my daughter Cheator her children, as also for that I am desirous with my best meanes to inable him the better to continewe my howse to the pleasure of Almightie God, I give to my said sonne all my leases, plate, goodes, etc. and make him executor, haveinge set downe the reason whie I shold thus respecte him, not of necessitie, but to give satisfaccon to my freindes and those whoe beinge equall in degree with him of kindred or otherwise not farre removed from me, may therewith all hold themselves content, seeinge that some of them have bene, and the freindes of them have heretofore bene advanced by me in marriage with competent and sufficient portions. Supervisors Rowland Wandesforde esq., Robert Wright, Richard Wandesford, and John Wright, gentlemen, my loveinge sonnes in lawe and kinsmen. To each of them two 22ˢ peeces of gold. To the wife of Robert, and to William sonne of the said Richard Wandesforde, each a 22ˢ peece of gold. Witnesses, Henric Aiscought, John Yoward, Michell Sandwith, Nicholas Bullock, Christofer Welburne. Proved 30 June 1617. (*Reg. Test. Ebor.* xxxiv. 572 *b.*)

XV. Dec. 6, 1696. THOMAS PURCHASE, rector of Kirkbywiske. To my eldest son Thomas Purchase my library of books. My estates of Lestropp and Middleham I charge with 1000*l.* to my three younger children, Katherine, Alice, and Benjamin. To them and to my son Wᵐ 40*l.* per annum. To the poor of Kirkbywiske 4*l.* and of Great Langton 20ˢ. My wife exˣ.

Inventory dated 30 Apr. 1697. Of Langton Magna. Sum total 272*l.* 5ˢ. His library bookes in the kitching chamber 100*l.*

29 May 1697. Admon, granted to Catherine Purchase of Langton widow (Benjamin P. of ʼBraithwaite gen. being bondsman) together with tuition of Thomas, Wᵐ, Benjamin, Catherine and Alice Purchase, minors, children of decᵈ. *(Richmond Wills.)*

Benjamin fil. Magr. Thomæ Purchas bap. 11 Feb. 1633-4. Johannes
    fil. do. bp. 12 Apr. 1635. *(Richmond.)*

1682, Dec. 27. Thomas Purchas, M.A. of Langton and Catherine
    daughter of William Thornton esqʳ of East Newton, md. *(Stone-*
    grave.)

1683, Nov. 1 Catherine dau. Mr. Tho. Purchas of Newton bp. *(Stone-*
    grave.)

XVI. 10ᵗʰ March 1696-7. Will of THOMAS COMBER, D.D. Dean of Durham, in good health and of perfect memory.—To be buried either in the cathedral at Durham, or in theʼchoir of Stonegrave, at the discretion of my executrix. Alice, my wife, according to the settlement of the manner of East Newton, dated Aug. 3ᵈ 1692, shall have the whole profits of that estate for life, rentes of farme at Nether-Dunsforth, and free rents out of Rookbargh and Preston in Holderness, as also out of leases of Usburne and Clifton Ings in Yorkeshire, my Havermatts at Billingham, and my farmehold at Ferryhill in co. Durham, for the better maintaining herself and her children by me until 21. To wife, one third of all household goods and personall estate (leases excepted) and she sole executrix and guardian of children. To eldest son William, reversion of mannor of East Newton after his mother's decease, and during her life 60*l.* per an. for his education and maintenance viz., 20*l.* out of farme at Nether Dunsforth, and 40*l.* out of lease at Useburne; also to him reversion of farme at Nether Dunsforth; and, if he shall freely enter into holy orders, all my books, provided he pay to my son Thomas 50*l.* in money, or allow him books value 60*l.* But if William do not enter into orders and Thomas do, then the latter to have all books, paying William 50*l.* in money, or 60*l.* in books. If neither of them be ordained, books to be equally divided between them, giving their sisters books for 10*l.* each. To eldest dau. Alice 30*l.* per ann. out of farme at Ferryhill until 21 or marrige; after, to have the whole; and if I do not otherwise in my lifetime provide for her to the value of 500*l.* more, I give to her 500*l.* out of my farme at Nether Dunsforth. To her also one third of household goods and personall estate (leases excepted). Daughter Mary to have 25*l.* per ann. out of rents of Rookbargh, Preston, Clifton Ings, and Nether Dunsforth, after 21, until marrige; after, to take the whole, and 500*l.* more; also the last third of my household goods and personall estate (leases excepted). To Thomas, 40*l.* per ann. for his education and maintenance, out of the profits of a lease I have taken in his name of the Chapter of Durham of the Havermatts of Billingham, and the rest to be made up out of rents of Useburne. At his mother's death he to pay or secure to his sister Mary 200*l.* charged above upon Useburne, unless I pay it before. If either of my sons dye without issue, before 21, the surviving son shall have the mannor of East Newton clear of all payments after his grandmother's and mother's decease, and shall then also enter upon farme at Nether Dunsforth, paying to his two sisters 100*l.* each. Other arrangements specified. To my niece Mary Puckle 10*l.* per ann. till her marriage, or death of my wife, or till she receive from my executrix or heires 100*l.* I give 10*l.* more to her sister Anne my god-daughter; and 10*l.* each to my dear mother Madam Thornton and my brother Mr. James Comber, to buy mourning. Also to James and Mary, children of my said brother,

and to my sister his wife each one ginney, to buy rings ; and also to Mr.
Man and Mr. Store each a ginney, to buy rings. 20*l.* to the poor of
the city of Durham. To poor of parishes of Stonegrave and Thornton,
in Yorkeshire, and of Westram, in Kent, 10*l.* each parish. Tho.
Comber. Witnesses, John Smith, Robert Lecke, John Rawell, notarie
publique.

12th April 1699. CODICIL. Whereas I have charged my estate
with 500*l.* to my dau. Alice, and with 500*l.* more to my dau. Mary, if
I did not otherwise provide ; I have lodged 460*l.* upon William
Pearson's farme at Ferryhill, and 800*l.* upon Alding-grange, which
make 1260*l.* I give 500*l.* to make up the sum provided to Mary,
and the interest thereof in liew of the 25*l.* per an. menconed for her
maintenance. I give 760*l.* to dau. Alice in liew of the 500*l.* addition
to her portion menconed in will, as also 10*l.* per ann. out of the interest
thereof, to make her maintenance 40*l.* per ann., and residue of interest
to go forward as an increase to her portion. Witnesses, Charles Man
senior, Charles Hutchinson, Joseph Dixon.

23 October, 1700. Alice Comber of Usburn, co. York, widow, and
Robert Kitchin of the same, give bond in 2000*l.* to prove the will of
Thomas Comber, D.D., late Dean of Durham. Seal, Comber impaling
Thornton. Witness Charles Man. 25 October 1700, Received the
original will ; Alice Comber. Witness, Roger Store. Same day A. C.
gives bond to produce the original will of her husband. 27 Nov. 1700,
Probate of will of Thomas Comber S. T. P., Dean of Durham, and
tuition of Alice, William, Mary, and Thomas his children, granted to
Alice their mother. No Inventory. (*Prerogative Act Book. York*).

XVII. April 10, 1705. ALICE THORNTON of East Newton, widow
and relict of William Thornton esq^r, being weake in body. I commend
my soul into the hands of God as into the hands of a faithfull Creator
and Redeemer, humbly beseeching Him yt it may be precious in His
sight (that being washed in the blood of y^t imaculate Lamb that was
slaine to take away the sins of the world, Jesus Christ, our Saviour.)
And whatsoever defilements it may have contracted in this miserable
and naughty world through the lusts of the flesh or the wiles of Satan,
being purged and done away by the operation of the Holy Ghost, Who
sanctifieth me and all the elect people of God, it may be presented
pure and without spott before Him, and may be received into those
heavenly habitations where the souls of them that sleep in the Lord

Jesus enjoy perpetuall rest and felicity. And for my body I commit it to the earth from whence it came, desireing it may be decently buryed (according to the rights and customs of the Church of England) in the north alley belonging to my dear husband's family in the parish church of Stonegrave, as neare to him as can be conveniently (not opening his grave) there to rest in sure and certain hopes of the resurrection to eternall life through our Lord Jesus Christ, in whose faith I was baptized and desire to live and die as a member of His holy Catholick Church in the communion of His Saints, and to be pertaker of the priviledges promised in the Gospel to all that belong to that misticall body, forgiveness of sins, the resurrection of the body, and life everlasting. Amen.

And as for the worldly goods which God gave and God is pleased to take away from mee and me from them, I desire may be disposed of to the discharge of all my just debts, and of what by equity and justice is due from me to others, and as far further as they will extend to severall uses of piety and charity hereafter specified as legacys of my love, and pledges of my respect to God's honour and glory, in manner and forme following.

Imprimis, I doe hereby ratifye and confirme the gifts formerly by me given to the service of God in the parish church of Stonegrave, and doe order that they be inventory'd and registred in ye church book, requiring the minister and churchwardens to look carefully to the same, that they be not spoiled, embezled, misimployed, or put to any profane uses; (viz.) one large pulpit cloth embroidered with silk flowers, silk fringes, and a minster, my owne crest, in sattin; one great cushion of the same cloth with two large silk tassels; one other cushion of the same cloth and work with freinges; one cushion for the reading-deske. Item one large table cloth of the same colour and embroidery with a minster crest in sattin, the same fringe and border of embroidery for the communion table. Item one other table cloth of the same printed purple stufe as the other, for the use also of the communion table; one large purple cushion of the same cloth with silk fring to lay the Holy Bible one. Item one long large damask table cloth with two damask napkins for the service of my God, to be laid upon the Lord's table at the administration of the Sacrament of the Lord's Supper or Holy Communion. Item two curtains, four cushions, two Turky work cushions for the pew belonging to the family of my dear husband abovesaid. Item I give and bequeath the sume of thirty pounds to repair the alley belonging to my dear husband aforesaid, covering the roof with new lead and timber sufficient, which was formerly downe and taken away without my husband's or my consent; also to repaire windows in the said alley stopt up or lessen'd, with glass, as formerly.

Item I give and bequeath the sume of twenty pounds for the rebuilding the chappell at East Newton, which was long since demolished, desiring the heires of Newton and Laystrop to give timber necessary for the same, and that the service of God may be there celebrated according to the order of the Church of England, as now by law established, at morning and evening, and other seasons as often as opertunity shall permitt; but if by reason of certain debts due to me by right cannot be recovered, then my will is that my just debts, funerall expences and legacyes given to perticular persons be first discharged and paid, and then those works of piety and charity in repairing the north alley in the parish church of Stonegrave, and rebuilding the chappell at East Newton above mentioned, and other works of charity hereafter mentioned and by me intended, shall be performed only so far as the money received by my executors out of my estate shall extend, according to the discretion of my executors, hoping that God will except of my good will, and likewise move the harts of some of my successors to performe the work by me intended to be done, if I could have got my right according to the disposition of my dear parents' last wills and testaments, out of their estate and other debts really due to myselfe from others.

Whereas by my deeds of gift made June 11th 1684 to feoffees in trust for the use of my two daughters Alice the widdow and relickt of Thomas Comber, D.D. late deane of Durham, and Katherine the wife of Robert Danby of North Allerton in the county of York, gentleman, [I have given] a considerable part of my household goods to their use dureing their lives, and after their desease to the use of their two daughters, my grandchildren—I confirm the said gifts, only I desire that those given to my daughter Alice Comber may at her decease be devided betwixt her two daughters Alice and Mary; and those given to my daughter Katherine, betwixt her two daughters Katherine and Alice Purchase.

Whereas I have disbursed out of my own estate 300*l*. for the maintenance of my nephew Christ. Danby his wife and children, for the space of 20 years, in tabling and clothing and other necessarys, and being instrumentall to gain him his estate of 3000*l*. per annum, when they had no allowance or subsistance from his father's estate, which 300*l.* the said Christopher and his son Abstrupus Danby has severally faithfully promised to reimburs the said money when God should enable them, which 300*l.* is not yet paid; therefore I desire my executors may use there utmost endeavours that the said 300*l.* may be received, and may be laid out for the uses and intents mentioned in my said will.

To my dear daughter Alice Comber and each of her children, and my daughter Danby and each of her five children twenty shillings a peice, to buy them rings to wear in remembrance of me. To my dear daughter Comber my harpsicall virginalls for her life, and then to her son Thomas Comber and his heires—then to my grandaughter Alice Blackburne—then to my grandaughter Mary Comber. To my daughter Comber the originall picture of my honored father hanging in my chamber, and the best coppy of my father's Book of Advice to his son George Wandesford, during her life (the same entail). To my daughter Comber my weding ring and my gold seal with my father's coat of arms upon it, for her life, and afterwards to her children, according to the disposition of my father's picture and book, to be as heirlooms to the family of East Newton. To my grandson Will. Purchas one of the coppys of my father's Books of Advice to his son George Wandesford, to be preserved for my said grandson's family. To my nephew, Sir Christopher Wandesford's eldest son, my dear and honoured father's pickture in a guilt frame, and his Book of Advice to his son George Wandesford, and after his decease to his eldest son Christopher Wandesford, etc. and to the other descendants of the family at Kirklington, to remaine their as heirlooms for ever. To my grand-nephew Abstrupus Danby, son and only heir to Sr Abstrupus Danby, a coppey of my father's Book of Advice to his sone George Wandesford, and one of his picktures, as heirlooms of that family [of] my dear sister, the Lady Katherine Danby, to be kept in memory of my dear father aforesaid, the Lord Deputy Wandesford. To my grandson Will. Purchase my dear husband's pickture and my owne dureing his life, and after his decease without issue male to his brother Thomas Purchase—brother Benjamin Purchas—my grandchild Alice Purchase—my grandchild Kat. Purchase—my grandchild Alice Blackburne—then to my grandson Thomas Comber. All the rest of the said pictures in the great parlour at East Newton I doe order my ex^{rs} to sell to the best advantage for the performance of my will. To my dear brother Denton one pound to buy him a ring in remembrance of me. To my sister Denton his wife and to his son Mr Robert Denton and his daughter Hellen Denton, each 1*l.*

To the poor of the parish of Stonegrave 5*l.*, to be laid out in a percell of land with other moneys belonging to the parish stock for the relief of the poor of the said parish, if my estate will extend to doe it. To the poor of the parish of Kirklington 5*l.*, to be distributed according to the discression of the minister and churchwardens. To the poor of the parish of Hypswell 5*l.*, to be distributed according to the discretion [of] the minister and churchwardens. I give 5*l.* to be given and distributed at my buriall to the poor in generall [at door] manner of dole, and desire that the expences besides at my funerall may not exceed the sume of 20*l.*, to be laid out at the discretion of my executors. I give to my man servant, over and above his wages then due to him 10s., and to my two maid servants, over and above their wages then due, 10s. each, that shall be with me at the time of my decease.

I give 6*l.* to the church of Stonegrave, to be bestowed in buying a silver pattin for carring the bread at the Holy Sacrament, and also another plate for gathering the offerings there made, a minster to be engraven upon them, with the inscription of my motto [Tout pour l'eglise]: also 20*l.* to be bestowed in one hansome silver flaggon, and also the 8*l.* for a silver chalice and a cover to it for the use of the Communion in Stonegrave church, with the same engravements to be upon them as is abovementioned for the pattin. Item I give and bequeath (to be used in the chappell or within the mansion house at East Newton) one large table cloth of black silk farrenden imbroidered with silk and gold flowers, with a silk fringe black and gold colour laid with black parragon being two yards and halfe a quarter broad, and two yards and three quarters long; also three large cushions of black velvet embroydered with the like gold flowers and silk, and fringed about with silk fringe and four tassels of silk lined with the same, new parragon; also one large dammask table cloth flower-pot work, three yards long and two yards and a halfe wide, marked with the same letters A. T. black; also two large dammask napkins markt with the same letters; and also the wood table that stands under the hall window at the great parlour door. Also I doe present unto my God my new salvo of silver for a pattent to use at the time of the administring the Holy Sacrament of the consecrated bread, and gathering of charity; also a chalice and cover to it, of it, both of silver. Item I give and bequeath my great Bible with the black velvet cover to be kept for the same use appointed

by me as the other ornaments are expressed and used at the Holy
Sacrament in my house or chappell, if there be any.   Also I desire my
said executors to buy a large service booke with guilt leaves and black
leather gilded, of the Common Prayer of the Church of England, to be
constantly kept for the use of the said house and chappell, wherein
prayers ought to be dayly used therein for the service of God : all which
things I desire may be preserved in the mansion house at East Newton
aforesaid for such of my children, or grandchildren, as shall live at the
said house, to be used when they shall receive the Holy Sacrament, and
for no other use or purpose whatsoever.   Item I give unto the chappell
to be rebuilded my great bras pot of bell mettle to be cast into a bell,
and there to remain for ever.

Whereas it has been my desire to have repaired and covered the
alley in the parish church of Stonegrave belonging to my dear husband's
family with sufficient leading and repairing the glass windows now
stopt up, and could not be able as I designed, therefore I desire and
leave it [in] charge with my said daughter Comber to doe the same, if
God inable her to doe it, but if she doe it not, I desire and charge my
grandson Thomas Comber that he will performe and doe the same, for
the honour of God and the satisfaction of his duty to the antient family
of his grandfather Thornton.

I give unto my granchild, Mary Comber, the suite of damask
which is in her mother's keeping for her till she comes to the age of
one and twenty years.   I give unto my grandchild, Alice Purchas, my
great brass pott which is in my own keeping.   I give unto my grandson Thomas Comber all my library of books excep as his mother will
make use of, hopeing God will give him grace to make a pious use of
them, and that he may be educated to be a scholer according to the
desire of his father, a divine of the Church of England as it is now by
law established.   Item I give unto my dear daughter Comber all my
Phisicall books and Recepts, together with my stock of salves and oynt-
ments, desireing her to give unto her sister Katherine Danby what she
may have occasion to use for her selfe or her children.   Item I give to
my dear daughter Comber my weding bodies and crimson stomacher of
flowered sattin, and my fine lawn spreading sheet with three pillowbers,
to dispose of to such of her children as she finds shall be best deserveing
at her decease.   To my granchild Alice Blackburn my fine hollan
Christening sheet with buttons for it, during her life, and at her decease
without issue—to my granchild Mary Comber and her issue—gran-

daughter Alice Purchas and issue—then to Will. Purchas. To my daughter Comber the full halfe of my diaper tabling and napkins which I span myselfe. To my granchild Alice Purchas my fine hollan spreading sheet with two pillowbers to it, and the one halfe of my diaper tabling which I span—in case of her decease without issue to Will. Purchas. To my daughter Katherine Danby my new cloth mourning manty and petecoate of the same black cloth.

To my good brother Mr. John Denton, as a token of my gratitude to him, over and besides what I have given him in this my last will and testament, the sume of five pounds, desireing him to performe the office of a buriall for me, and preach my funerall sermon upon the text, Revelations 14th chapt. and the 13th vers, *Blessed are the dead which die in the Lord*, etc., but if my brother Denton cannot performe the office of buriall for me, then I desire Mr. Charles Man senr to preach a sermon for me upon the aforesaid text; but if [he] cannot preach the said sermon, then my desire is that his son Mr. Man junr may preach the said sermon, and may also have the said sume of five pounds to buy him books withall.

To my granchild Alice Purchas my green emrald jewell of aleven stones and three pearle drops in it set in gold, for her life; if she die without issue—to my granchild Mary Comber and her heires.

To my dear daughter Comber three Books of my owne Meditations and Transactions of my life, and all the residue of my Papers and Books written with my owne hand, and my Recept Books.

Item if any person mentioned in my will be not satisfied with their share of goods or legacies bequeathed to them, the person so dissatisfied shall loose the benifit of the goods and legacies bequeathed.

Item my will and desire is that, if there be assets sufficient, my executors do pay or cause to be paid unto all my son Thornton's creditors, theire widdows or children, what debts they can make out to be justly due from him, myselfe haveing paid as much as laid in my power.

Item in case it shall please God that my executors shall recover any considerable part of my debts, over and besides what shall discharge this my last will and bequest herein mentioned, that then, over and besides what I have given to my daughter Comber and her children, I doe appoint all such moneys which shall be so received shall be laid out in a parcell of land in England, and setled on my daughter Comber during her life, and after her decease to be setled on my granson

Thomas Comber and his heir male—for default of such to his two sisters Alice Blackburn and Mary Comber and their heires—provided that the said land soe to be purchased every hundred pounds per annum shall be charged with two hundred pounds and so more or less proportionably to my grancbild Alice Purchas, and to each of my three younger grandchildren by my daughter Katherine, (viz.) Will. and Benjamin Purchas (*sic*) each of them 200*l.* as an augmentation to their portions out of Laystropp, when 21. I desire, if there be assets, that my goods or debts due to me shall extend so far, to pay to the poor of the three parishes mentioned, and also at my funerall, double the proportion which I have before appointed.

To Mr. Charles Man of Gilling jun^r the summe of two pounds to buy him a ring to wear in remembrance of me.

Lastly. I doe hereby constitute my honoured kinsman Thomas Alured esq. recorder of Beverly, and my respective friend Henry Watkinson chancellor at York, and the Reverend Mr. Charles Man, rector of Gilling, executors of this my last will and testament, desireing they will be pleased to doe that Christian office for me to see that this my last will and testament be performed according to the true intent and meaning thereof; and I doe order and appoint to these my executors all necessary riding charges for the performance of my said last will, and doe alsoe give unto each of them five pounds as a testimony of my gratitude.

In case my personall estate will not amount to pay according to what I have appointed, I order that these summs may be deducted, viz. 5*l.* to the poor of Stonegrave, 15*l.* to the poore of Kirklington, and 5*l.* to the poore of Hipswell, 9*l.* out of 15*l.* given to my executors, and 3*l.* out of 5*l.* for preaching my funerall sermon. Witnesses Al. Dunlop, George Breknbury, Ral. Agar. (*Reg. Ebor.* lxiv., 45.)

Codicil, 10 Apr. 1705. Will confirmed and all former Wills revoked.

A true and perfect Inventory of all the goods, cattell, and chattells of Madam Alice Thornton of East Newton deceased, taken by us whose names are under written, this third day of March 1706-7.

Imprimis her purse and apparell 5*l*.

5 acres of hard corne in the Stamp Cross feild at 1*l*. 15s. per acre, 8*l*. 15s.

One haystack in the chappel garth 3*l*. 10s.

4 cowes 12*l*.

4 whyes comeing three years old, 7*l*. 10s.

3 heifers and a stear comeing two years old, 6*l*. 5s.

4 yearing calves, 5*l*.

One haystack and a peice in Groyne close 5*l*.

18 hogg sheepe 5*l*. 8s. A ram and 4 weathers 2*l*. 10s. 20 ewes 8*l*. Two oxen 10*l*. Hardcorne in the barn, computed to 60 stooks at 20d. per stook 5*l*. Oates computed to 50 stooks at 12d., 2*l*. 10s. Piggs, two 1*l*. 5s. A waggon 4*l*. Two old coops 1*l*. Two pair of harrous, 2 old plows, and a coulter 7s. Two yoakes, 2 teams, 2 shackles and bolts and horse geare, all old, 10s. A sheepe heck 2s. Stoops, rails and stack barrs 5s. An old coach lined with blew Chiney 10*l*. Two old coach horses 8*l*. Armes and buff coate for the L[t] horse, being all very old and broken 1*l*. 5s.

One silver pint, a porringer, 7 spoons and 4 lesser, 2 salts, one wrought cup, two plain ones, one pocket bottle and a sweetemeate spoone, all cont. 50 ounces at 5s. 2d. per ounce, 12*l*. 8s. 4d.

In the Grey Chamber a bedstead and beding, curtains and vallance of purple and all necessary thereto belonging, 7*l*. 3 old chairs, a litle table and a old close stool, a old green skeen, and window curtains and curtaine rodds 17s. 2 old coach cushions upon wood frames 13s. 4d. A lookeing glass 4s.

In the roome within, 2 pair fine sheets and 4 pillow beares, Madam Thornton, marked A. T. with a cross, 2*l*. 10s. An old fustian wastcoat 9d. A dressing table cloth with a lace and a linnen towell 3s. One doz. diaper napkins marked W. T. 18s. A trunke with severall implement things therein 10s. A table cloth for a chamber marked W. T. 3s. 6d. A pair sheets marked W. T. 1*l*. One pair ditto marked A. T. 1*l*. 1s. 6d. One doz. linen napkins marked A. W. with a table cloth the same, 8s. A little callico cloth marked A. T. 1s. A coarse linen sheet 1s. 6d. Dimothy pillow case 1s. 7 damask napkins 10s. Three old truncks and severall boxes 10s. A bedstead and bedding with curtains and vallans thereunto belonging all green, 2 wood chairs and a table, all very old, 2*l.* 2s.

In the Closet within Madam Thornton's chamber, severall implement things, 2*l.*

In her owne Chamber, a bedstead and bedding thereunto belonging with curtains and vallans of green, 2*l.*

8 chairs, a squabb and the hangings of the roome and a little canopy, 3 window curtains all green and old 1*l.* 5s. Severall little cabinetts and boxes 2s. 6d. A standing cabinett, a sweetmeat box and a table 1*l.* 5s. 2 bever skinns 2s. 6d. 2 old blanketts 6s. 8d.

In the Passage—2 sheets and 2 pillow bears 5s. 2 doz. huggaback napkins at 6d. per peice 12s. 2 doz. old diaper napkins at 6d. peice 12s. 3 old diaper table cloths and 3 huggaback table cloths 12s. 6d. 3 diaper towells and 2 side board cloths 3s. 6d. 3 pair old linen sheets and 5 pillow bears 12s. 2 pair coarse linen sheets 8s. One pair of the same coarse 2s. 6d. One pair ditto coarser 6s. A callico casting sheet 4s. 3 huggaback towells 1s. 6d. 2 chests and some trunks and boxes, and 2 tables, all very old, 6s. 8d.

In the Nursery, a bedstead and bedding, and very old curtains, 1*l.* 2 chairs, a table, a stoole, a cradle and a stand 7s. 6d.

In the Great Chamber, some mean offall and trumpery things, 1*l.*

In the Study, a bedstead and bedding and curtains 1*l.*

In the Garretts an old bedstead and table 5s. 5 firr deales 3s. 9d. A bedstead and bedding, a table and a chest, 5s. Some wooll at 2*l.* 10s. A bedstead and bedding, 10s. Some grey old curtains, a table and 2 chaires 6s. 8d. A bedstead, a feather bed, and some old curtains, and a table 1*l.* An old muskett 2s. Old iron and other things at 1s.

In the Kitching, two swills, 4 skeells, 2 little chaires, 6 piggons, a sieve, 4 spitts, the iron rack, a candle case, a broken iron pott and some implement things, 15s. 5 brass panns, two brass candlesticks and a dripping pan 15s. 56 bushells of coales at 8d., 17s. 4d.

In the Pantry 3 doz. 8 pewter plates at 6d. pair, 1*l.* 1s. One doz. and ½ pewter dishes 1*l.* 16s. A bedpan, a flaggon, a pasty pan and 4 old chamber potts 5s. A little tankard, a mustard pott, and 2 salts, 1s.

In the Back Kitchin and Dairy, Larder, a brass kettle, pair iron racks and a churn 14s. Tiffany, and a temse, a churn and 2 tubbs, a table and a cupboard, one doz. milk bowles and a dough tubb 1*l.* A water cart 10s. Severall shelves, a block and a flackett 5s. 3d. A gavelock 1s. Summa totalis 174*l.* 4s. 3d.

APPRAISERS, Fran. Blackburne, Cha. Man senior, George Bowes, John Bowes, Wm Nightingale.

15 Apr. 1707.   Adm. granted to Alice Comber of East Newton widow.

In STONEGRAVE CHURCH are the following Monuments, in the north aisle, formerly dedicated to St. Leonard, which belonged to the house of East Newton.

1. Under a niche in the north wall, the figure of a man in a lay dress of the 14th century, with long flowing robe.   Said to be a Newton.

2. Near it, on a low altar tomb, projecting from the north wall, and partly under it, the effigies of a man and woman, coarsely wrought. The man in a civilian's dress with a shield, charged with a chevron and three sprays of hawthorn, hanging from his left arm.   On the pediment, below, are two shields, one with a similar charge, the other plain.   The same shields, supported also by angels, appear on the roof of the nave, on the north side.

3. Painted on canvas set in a black frame, and hanging against the wall of the aisle, is the following inscription, under a shield of arms thus blazoned :—

Quarterly.   1. (THORNTON.)   Argent, a chevron sable between three hawthorn trees proper.*   2. (NEWTON.)   Argent, on a chevron sable† three garbs or.   3. (HUSSEY.)   Ermine, three bars gules. 4. (. . . .)   Barry of six or and sable, over all a bend compony argent and gules.   5. (LEIGH.)   Argent, a lion rampant gules. 6. (LEIGH.)   Gules, a plate between three crowns argent within a bordure of the last; impaling, quarterly:—1. (WANDESFORD.)   Or, a lion rampant double queued azure.‡   2. (MUSTERS.)   Argent, a bend gules within a bordure engrailed of the latter.   3. (COLVILLE.)   Or, a fess gules, in chief three torteaux.   4. (CONYERS.)   Azure, a maunch ermine.§   5. (FULTHORPE.)   Argent, a cross moline sable.   6. (BLAND.) Argent, on a bend sable three pheons or.

* These trees are sable in the shield.

† In the Thornton pedigree, blazoned by J. C. Brooke, the coat of Newton is given as *argent, on a chevron azure three garbs.*

‡ So in pedigree in Whitaker's *Richmondshire*, ii., 140; but on the monument *sable.*

§ This from the Visitation of 1564.   On the monument it is incorrectly blazoned *sable, a maunch or.*

Crests. 1. (THORNTON.) A lion's head erased purpure, gorged with a crown argent. 2. (WANDESFORD.) A minster proper, with long spire azure.

Motto. Under Thornton, NISI CHRISTUS NEMO. Under Wandesford, TOUT POUR L'EGLISE.

MEMORIÆ SACRUM.

William Thornton Esqr descended from the ancient
and worshipfull family, surnamed De Thornton (Lords of East Newton
from the time of K. Edw. I.) son and heir to Robert Thornton Esqr
By Eliz. daughter of Sr Rich. Darley (of Audby k^t) marryed
Alice (who was the daughter of the Right Honourable Christopher
Wandesford of Kirklington, Lord Deputy of Ireland,
by Alice daughter of Sr Hewit Osbourn of Kiveton k^t) and had
Issue by his said wife, three sons, William, ROBERT, and Christopher,
And four daughters, ALICE, Elizabeth, CATHERINE and Joyce,
And having lived most religiously 45 years, dyed Septemb.
17 MDclxviii lamented by all, especially by his affectionate and sorrowfull widow, who hath dedicated this to his dear and pious memory.

---

4. On the floor, near the tower:

> Here lye The Bo
> dys of Thomas Th
> ornton gent y^e
> Third son of Ro
> Bert Thornton
> of East Newton
> Esq. who dyed
> Aug. 16th An. Dom. 1685.
> And also of John
> Thornton Gent.
> Fourth son of The
> Said Robert Tho
> Rnton who dyed
> May 22th A.D. 1669.

5. On a small marble tablet in the Nine Altars of DURHAM CATHE-
DRAL:

M . S .

Hic jacet

ROBERTUS THORNTON

A. M. FIL : & hær : GUL : THORNTON

de NEWTON in Com : EBOR : Arm :

& ALIC : ux. ejus, Socius Coll : D :

MAGD : OXON, & Rector de BOLDO^N

Qui obijt Iunij iv°

AN : DOM : MDCXCII°

Pos. A. C. soror char : An :

MDCXCV°·

Anne Wandesford, to whom her gr.-father Hansby left 1000 marks when 21 or married. Mar. at Kirklington March 4, 1621-2. Bur. at Richmond 23 Dec., 1683. "My Aunt Norton."	=	Mauger Norton, esq., of Clowbeck and St. Nicholas, near Richmond, æt. 72 in 1666. Bur. at Richmond Dec. 12, 1673.	Michael Wandesford, bap. at Bishop Burton Oct. 2, 1597. St. John's, Camb., B.A. 1617, M.A. 1621. Rector of Kirklington; Prebendary of the first stall at Ripon, 28 Feb., 1624-5, to 1637; made Dean of Limerick 11 May, 1635, and exchanged it for that of Derry in the same year. Died 1637 (Cotton's Fasti Hibern.). Married, and had an only daughter, who d. young. His widow mar. . . . . . Humberton.	John Wandesford, bap. at Bishop Burton 16 Dec., 1593. His gr.-father Hansby leaves him and his brothers Michael and William 100 marks each. At one of the Inns of Court; sometime Consul at Aleppo. Died s. p.* * A John Wandesford of Kirklington, gen., occurs as one of the sureties in £50 for Wm. Elsley, gen., who at the special assizes at York in Jan., 1663, was bound over to keep the peace. (*Surt. Soc. Pub.*, 40, p. 82 *n.*)

Edmund Norton (see p. 55). Adm'on gr. at York 4 June, 1649, to his brother William. Bur. at St. Michael le Belfrey, York, Nov. 19, 1648.	William Norton (see pp. 163-4). Æt. 38, Visit. Ebor., 1665.	Christopher, æt. 34, Visit. Ebor., 1665.	John, died at St. Nicholas 1646 (p. 53).	Gillian, bp. at Richmond Jan. 6, 1632-3. Died there 9 Apr., 1649 (p. 55).	Mary, bp. at Richmond 12 July, 1635. Mar. 20 Aug., 1651, Sir John Yorke of Gowthwaite, to whom she administers 15 July, 1663. "My lady York."

1576.   July 10.   Michael Wandesford and Margery Bulmer m'd.   (Kirklington.)   The Bulmers lived at Upsland.

1589.   Sept. 27.   Ann, dau. of Michael Wandesford, bur.   (Kirklington.)

1601-2.   Michael W. of Upsland, gen., a witness at York, æt. 50.

1608.   Oct. 15.   George, son of Mr. Wm. W. of Kirklington, bap.   (Kirklington.)

1619.   Sept. 10.   Administration of Michael W. of Redeham or Redholme to Margery his widow. (Richmond Registry.)

1672.   May 3rd.   Adm'on of Chr. W. of Kirklington, esq., to Mauger Norton of Richmond, esq., his principal creditor.   (Richmond Wills.)

Pedigree of the Family of Wandesford.

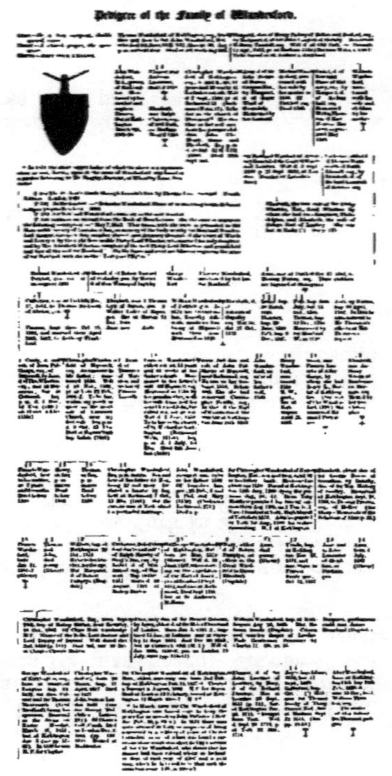

Thomas Comber of East Newton, esq., eldest surviving son, bap.=Anne, dau. of Andrew Wilson, vicar of Easingwold, and widow of Elias
at Stonegrave Dec. 4, 1688; bur. there May 15, 1765. | Micklethwaite, rector of Gilling; bur. at Stonegrave June 19, 1754.

Thomas Comber, LL.D. of Jesus Coll., Camb., rector of Buckworth and=Mary, dau. Willm Brooke, M.D., of Field Head in Dodworth, near   Other issue.
Morbourne.   Bap. at Stonegrave June 16, 1722; bur. there 20 Apr., | Barnsley, co. York, by Alice, d. and c. of Wm. Mawhood, alder-
1778, æt. 56. | man of Doncaster, his cousin.

Thomas Comber, eldest son, of Jesus Coll., Camb., rector of Oswaldkirk, bap. at Stonegrave=Elizabeth, dau. John Coote,   Other
Mar. 6, 1765; mar. 30 May, 1792.   Vicar of Creech St. Michael, co. Somerset, 1793. | esq., of Hampstead.   issue.

Henry George Wandesford Comber, only son.   Vicar of Creech St. Michael; rector of=Hester, dau. Rev. Thomas Cautley,   Other
Oswaldkirk 1813; born at the former place 2 May, 1798; mar. 11 July, 1820. | issue.

Henry Wandesford Comber, born at York 24 April, 1821.   Other issue.

Pedigrees of this family are entered in the Yorkshire Visitations of 1563, 1584, 1612, and 1665.   Mr. Comber also possesses a pedigree, drawn
evidently from family evidences by his distinguished ancestor, Dean Comber: also a fine illuminated roll; but not to be relied upon in the early descents.

Pedigree of the Family of Thornton of East Newton.

APPENDIX.

PART III.

ADDENDA ET CORRIGENDA.

P. 8, note, line 4. For *Arabella* read *Arbella*.

P. 13, line 26. Neston. " When the state of the tides in the river Dee would not allow the passengers to and from Ireland to embark or land at the city of Chester, they used the landing place at New Quay, and those of Park Gate and Neston, lower down the river Dee."—*Lancashire and Cheshire, Past and Present*. Baines and Fairbairn, 1857. Vol. iii., p. 23.

P. 19, *et seq.* The Marquess of Ormonde possesses a large collection of historical papers, letters, etc., relating to the affairs of Ireland, during the Lord-Lieutenancy of his ancestor, James, 1st Duke of Ormonde; from which a vast amount of information might be derived. Letters to and from Christopher Wandesford, Sir George Radcliffe, Wentworth, etc., occur. (*See* " 2nd Report of the Royal Commission on Historical MSS.," 1871, p. 209; 3rd ditto, 1872, p. 425, *et seq.*; 4th ditto, 1874, p. 539, *et seq.*) We observe that in the index Lord Deputy Wandesford is incorrectly called *Sir* Christopher, and that he is confused with his son who was made a baronet.

P. 22, n., line 4. For 1503 read 1593.

P. 23, line 5. Cut pigeons.—MEDICAL SCIENCE IN SPAIN.—A correspondent, writing from Madrid, gives an account of a few of his patients, and the course of treatment to which they had been subjected prior to having consulted him. He says that one of the prescribers of the nastinesses enumerated is an ex-court physician, and that another fills a professorial chair.

Case 5. Pablo Isnari, aged 30, plasterer, had had six months' doctoring for heart disease, following rheumatism. The last prescription was a newly killed pigeon, split open down the middle and applied over the left chest [the region of the heart] for nine days, and to go to work.—(From the *British Medical Journal*, No. 716, p. 377.)

P. 32. " On the 18th of July, 1643, Sir William Brereton appeared with his army in front of the city of Chester, and the next morning made a desperate attempt to carry the city by assault. In this, however, he signally failed, the works being much too strong to be carried without the help of cannon, and the garrison, which included all the principal royalists of the county, being alike numerous and brave. The loss of the parliamentary forces in this attack was very great; whilst that of the garrison was quite insignificant, consisting of only one man killed and another wounded."—Baines and Fairbairn, 1857, vol. ii., p. 487.

P. 37.   (Compare this with the note on p. 37.)

Edward Fleetwood, rector of Wigan, was fourth son of Thomas Fleetwood of Heskin, co. Lanc. (2nd son of William Fleetwood and Helen, dau. of Robert Standish, of Standish) by his first wife, Bridget, dau. of Mr. Robert Spring, of . . . in Suffolk.   The rector was uncle of Sir William Fleetwood, of Cranford, co. Middlesex, Receiver of the Court of Wards and Liveries, the father of Sir Miles Fleetwood, kt., who held the same office in the year 1630.

Edward Fleetwood was instituted to the rectory of Wigan, Feb. 8, 1570–1; " on the resignation of William Blackelache, on the presentation of Queen Eliz., by reason of the minority of Thomas Langton, the patron."

He was dead 12 October, 1604, when Gerard Massie occurs as rector.—*Lanc. MSS.*, vol. xxii., p. 54.   F. R. R.

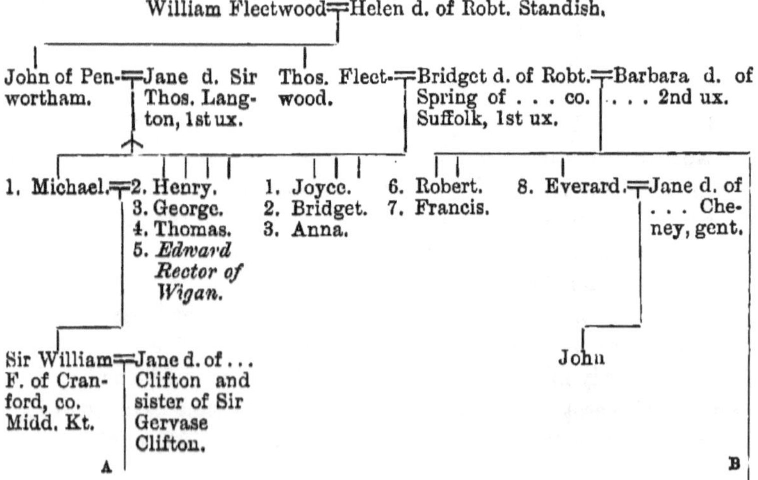

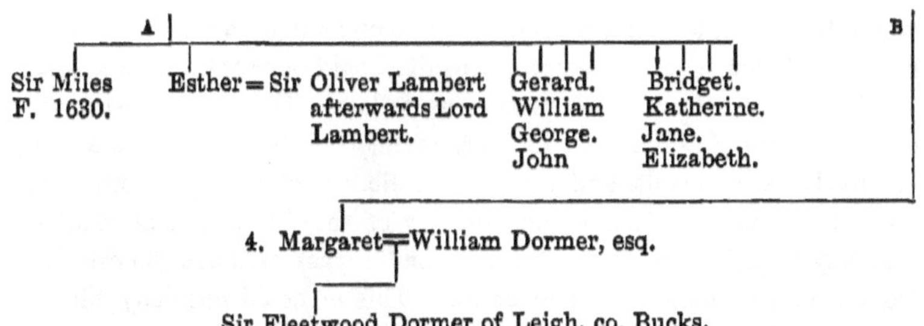

Pp. 44–47. Captain Innis and Jeremy Smithson—Mrs. Thornton, in another book* alludes to these men in " The great deliverance I had from a rape by Captaine Innis, a Scott, who did sweare to ravish me from my deare mother's ground, when I had gon to Lowes [if that is the word] with her maides ; but that his owne servant that I cured of a wound did discover it to me, and I was saved. Blessed be my God for evermore, Amen." Also, " My great deliverance from beeing stolen away out of my mother's pasture which was laid waite for me by Mr. Jeremy Smithson, when I was at Hipswell, and I would not indure his suite by his freinds. He had laid waite to have catched me from my mother's pasture when I went to Lowes : but by a poore man's meanes, Tho. Binks, he did pray me not to go out of the house, for that man had sworne to lay wait to have catched me by some others, and to have forc'd me to mary me or distroy me ; but the Lord have mercy on me, and delivered me out of the devil's temptations. I will glorify the name of God for evermore. Amen."

P. 56. The following curious account of the condemnation of Charles I. is taken from some MS. of Mrs. Thornton, now lost, which is printed as a note to the life of Dean Comber :—

" Not long after the death of the said King, being in company with my said uncle and some others, condoling his fate, and condemning the barbarous and bloody fact, he told me there happened to be a cabal, or meeting of several persons at his house, the day before the said tragedy

---

* This is a small memorandum book three and a half by two and a half inches in size, and consisting of about 196 pages, which has the appearance of having been Mrs. Thornton's original " Booke of Remembrances of all the remarkable deliverances of myselfe, husband, and children wth their births and other remarks as conserning myselfe and family begining from the year 1625." From this she has afterwards transcribed, literally or substantially, the several occurrences, etc., into the three larger books from which the text of this volume has been copied.

was acted, about the execution of it, as he understood afterwards, to his great grief, that such an odious consult should be within his walls, the particulars of whose relation were as follow: That Mr. Rushworth, author of the ' Collections in Parliament,' came to him some days before the said consult, and desired the liberty of a large room in his house for that day; to give him the key of the door, that he and his company might meet privately, pass and repass without molestation, trouble, entertainment, or attendance. This he could not deny him in respect of their mutual friendship, and some past civilities; yet the care that was taken for such a convenience, and so much caution to transact it so secretly, made him not a little wonder, and so curious as to observe them. The company came in the morning, not together, but one after another, and were above a dozen. He saw several disguised faces, particularly he knew the Lord Baltimore and Mr. William Lilly, the almanack maker, to be among them, and others suspected by him to be papists and fanatics, which strange mixture did much surprize him. Towards evening he took notice that Mr. Rushworth and another gentleman went out, and staid two hours before he returned, and then presently after the company broke up and departed.

"That a few days after Mr. Rushworth, meeting him, gave him thanks for his late civility, and casting off some words by way of enquiry about the meeting there at that time, he freely told him that the persons there met were the ' Close Committee,' to consult about the king's execution; that he and another were ordered to wait on his majesty, and use all their art and arguments to persuade him to recede something from his former rigour and resolute stiffness, insisting so much upon his own innocence, and charging the guilt of all the blood shed in the late wars upon the parliament, and to own himself, at least in some measure, to have been the cause thereof, and justify their proceedings; which, if he would do, all of them from whom they came promised to serve him to the utmost of their power, set him on his throne again, and make him a glorious king; but that he obstinately refused the offer as most unreasonable and unjust, and that he could not do it without manifest wrong to his honour, his cause, and his conscience, and thereby should offend God, disoblige his friends, and gratify his adversaries, and force all the world to condemn him as a wicked bloody tyrant, and a self-condemned miscreant unworthy to live; and, if he could not have his life, but upon such base compliance, he was content to die.   So when they could, as he says, do no good on him, being resolved to persist in his wilful way, they bid him prepare himself, for the next day he should be executed, at which he said, ' God's will be done,' and they left him, and what the result was is too well known.

(Signed)   " ALICE THORNTON."

P. 58, n., line 2.   For *Thomas* read *William* Siddall.

P. 58, n., line 7.   Read *Abraham* Hemmingway.   Philip Nesbitt was buried at St. Martin's, Micklegate, 15th October, 1663.   His widow, Susan, 19th April, 1683.

Page 61.   Among the names of those who compounded for their estates (in 1655) appears that of William Wandesford, of London, draper, for 100*l*.

Page 63, n., line 5.   For 1667 read 1668.   Colonel Darcy, of the Manor, was buried 29th April, 1668, in the chancel of St. Olave's. His lady was buried there 17th April, 1667.

P. 65, n.   For *Seeby* read *Skeeby*.

P. 81.   The marriage is thus recorded in the parish register of Stonegrave.

" William Thorneton, of East Newton, in this parish, esqr., & Alice, ye daughter of Christopher Wandesford, of Kirtlinton, esq., were maried together at Hipswell upon the 15th day of December, 1651, by Michaell Siddall, clerk, in the presence of Maior Norton of St. Nicolas, neere Richmond, esq., John Dodsworth of Thornton Watlas, esq., Francis Darley of Awdby, gent., Ralph Ianson of Thorp, Robt. Webster of Nunington, Robert Loftus of Waitwith, & divers others."

The births and deaths of all Mr. and Mrs. Thornton's children are recorded in the Stonegrave Register, probably by Mr. Denton.

Pp. 93-9.   Catherine Thornton is twice named Alice by the Diarist erroneously.

P. 97, n., line 7.   For *vicar* of Oswaldkirk read *rector*.   Mr. Denton, moreover, was never rector of Stonegrave, but he seems to have acted there as curate to Dr. Comber.   I give some notices of his life, etc.

John Denton of Manningham.   Of Clare Hall, Cambridge.   Adm. sizar and pupil to Mr. David Clarkson, 4th May, 1646.   Ejected in 1662 from the living of Oswaldkirk.   Lived at East Newton and officiated at Stonegrave when Dean Comber was rector. Installed prebendary of Husthwaite at York, 1st Dec., 1694. He and Tillotson were great friends at College and afterwards, and it was at Oswaldkirk that Tillotson preached his first sermon.—*See* Birch's *Life of Tillotson*, p. 11.

1654. John Denton, par. Oswaldkirk, clerk, and Elizabeth, dau. of Robert Thornton, of East Newton, esq., m^d 8th May, at East Newton, by James Colwhone, of Haram, clerk.—Stonegrave Register.

1668-9, Feb. 14. Elizabeth, wife of John Denton, of Newton, gent., bur. After this Mr. Denton married again.

1671-2, 29th Feb. Eliz., dau. John Denton, of Newton, gent., bap. Bur. 30th June, 1673.

1673-4, 10th Feb. Thos., s. John Denton, of Newton, gent., bap. Bur. 26th Nov., 1674.

1675-6, Jan. 11. Robert, s. John Denton, clerk, bap.

1677, Nov. 22. Hellen, dau. John Denton of Newton, clerk, bap. (1705, Nov. 13. Wm Cocke de Kendall, gen. and Helen Denton, rev. viri dom. Denton de Newton, par. Stonegrave filia, nupt).—*Spenni-thorne.*

1708-9, Jan. 16. The Reverend Mr. John Denton of East Newton was buryed in the north ile. He dyed January 14th, in the eighty-third year of his age.

Dec. 12, 1705. John Denton of East Newton. I have heretofore settled by deed all my lands in Manningham upon my eldest son John and his heirs. I stand seized of a fee farme rent of 64*l.* 17*s.* out of the mannor of Temple Hurst, of which a moiety belongs to me, I give it to Elizabeth my wife for her life, and then to my deare son, Robert and his heirs, paying out of it to my daughter Hellen 250*l.* To my son Robert all my bookes, except such books of practicall divinity as my said deare wife shall chuse. The residue to my wife. She executrix.—*Reg. Test. Ebor.*, lxv., 207.

1715, Dec. 19. Mrs. Elizabeth Denton the widow of the Reverend Mr. John Denton of East Newton was bury'd. She dy'd the 17th of December.—*Stonegrave.*

1747, April 4. The Reverend Mr. Robert Denton, rector of this church, bur.—*Ditto.*

He was ordained deacon by the Archbishop of York, 24th Sept. 1699, being A.B. of Catherine Hall, Cambridge; and priest 26th May, 1700. On 27th May, 1700 he was instituted to the rectory of

Stonegrave, vacant by the death of Dean Comber, at the presentation of the King, and was inducted by John Denton, clerk (his father).

The monuments of Mr. Denton and his father were destroyed during the restoration of Stonegrave church.

Extracts from the Stonegrave Offertory Book.

Mr. Denton began in 1690 in a 4to volume, which has been continued by his successors in the living, an account of his yearly receipts and disbursements of the offertory, etc.

In 1690 and 1691 his receipts amounted to 9*l.* 15*s.* 4*d.*

In 1691 the Communion was celebrated four times, viz., on Good Friday, Easter Day, Whit Sunday, and October 11 (Old Michaelmas), the collections amounting to 2*l.* 15*s.* 11*d.*

Received Dec. 2nd, 1690, of Dr. Comber, the money remaining in his hand belonging to the said poor, 3*l.* 7*s.* 8½*d.*

1690. I did by Dr. Comber's and Mr. Bows's advice pay six pence per week to John Sympson from Nov. 2, for five-and-thirty weeks, 17*s.* 6*d.*

The money was all given away among the poor, generally after each collection.

1692, June 13. Received from Madam Comber, which she gave for the poor of Stonegrave parish when her brother Mr. Robert Thornton dyed, 2*l.*

1692. Paid for physick which Tho. Playford had when sick, 5*s.* 7*d.*

—— For wollen winding sheet for Robert Sympson, 3*s.*

1691-2, Feb. 18, by my Lady Preston's order,* to Ralph Tayler's wife lying-in child-bed, 5*s.*

1693. Sum for the year, 10*l.* 5*s.* 2½*d.*

1692-3, March 5, the poor complaining for want, it being severe weather and corn dear, and no work to be had, I gave 8*s.*

—— March 17, given Elizabeth Hick towards repairing her house, 5*s.*

1693, April 28. Charges of Tho. Playford's funerall. Winding sheet of flannel, 2*s.* 6*d.*; bread, 4*s.*; ale, 3*s.* 3*d.*; grave-making, 6*d.*

Given for the parish to one who had his house burnt, 1*s.*

Mem. Alexander Dawson was by covenant when he took Tho. Playford's young girle, to receive from the parish 2*s.* 6*d.* yearly at Christmas for four years.

* Of Nunnington.

1694-5, Jan. 30.　Given to the poor, there having been a long storm, 8s. 6d.

——, June 12. To Tho. Lawson, when he was to go with his wife to work on Wolds, 2s. 3d.

1696, April 10.　Rec^d of the Right Honble Lady Preston, 2l. 10s. There were Communions on Easter Day, Whit Sunday, Michaelmas, and Christmas, at Stonegrave *and* Newton, twice on each day.

1696.　Given to a poor woman of Ampleford, whose house was faln.　She had a letter of request which she desir'd might be published in the church.　I thought fit to give her 3s.

1697.　Mem. What was collected at the Communion at Newton (at Easter) which was 6s. 6d., was at Madam Thornton's desire given to Alice Boys and her daughter.

Rec^d by Mr. Worsley's order of the overseer of Ness 12s. 6d., which was a fine laid upon one of Ness for killing of hares.

To G. Lawson, charges of carrying his son to Whitby to bind out, 2s.　To help him in building his house, 10s.

1698, June 5.　Pad 8s. the king's duty for the buryall of two of Rich. Harwood's children, he by reason of his great charg not being able to pay it.

1698-9, Jan. 1. Mr. Dunlop received the Communion at Stonegrave, and gave 1s. 6d., which was then distributed to J. Sympson and A. Boys.

1700.　Rec^d of Lady Preston 1l. 5s.

—— Collected at the Communion at Newton and Stonegrave on Good Friday and Easter Day, 2l. 4s. 9d.

—— June 16.　Rec^d by the hands of Mr. Jackson a legacy given to the poor of Stonegrave parish by Mrs. Susanna Grahm by her last will, paid by order of the Lord Dartmouth her ex^r, 5l.

1700-1, Feb. 23.　Rec^d from the ex^{rs} of my Lord Falconbridg, 10s.

—— Sept.　Rec^d of Madam Comber, a legacy given to the poor of Stonegrave, by Dr. Comber, late Dean of Durham and rector of Stonegrave, 10l.

1701.　Given to Th. Lawson at severall times, being sick and lame, 5s. 6d.　For a plaister for him, 1s.　To Mr. Lakin for physick for him, 4s. 6d.

1702, July 9.　Rec^d of Mrs. Susanna Jackson for the poor, given by her father Mr. Jackson at his death, 5l.*

---

* 1668, Sept. 13.　Susanna, dau. Mr. Thos. Jackson, of Nunnington, bap.

1702, Feb. 8. Collected at a private Communion at Mr. Jackson's, 7*s.* 1*d.*

—— March 17. Collected at a private Communion at Madam Thornton's, 6*s.* 6*d.* At another private Communion there, 9*s.* 6*d.*

—— May 31. Rec^d of Mr. Anthony Hunter a legacy given by Mrs. Barbary Whitfeild at her death, to the poor of Stonegrave parish, 5*l.**

—— Oct. 23. Collected at a private Communion in Mrs. Thornton's house, 13*s.* 6*d.*

—— Rec^d of Madam Comber after her son William's death, to be distributed to the poor of Stonegrave parish, 1*l.* 10*s.*†

1703. Madam Comber gave towards the purchase of the fee farm rent of 18*s.* per ann., the stock falling short, 2*l.*

—— April 24. Given R. Thomson towards the buying a horse, his old one being dead, 7*s.* 6*d.*

1669, Oct. 17. Mary, dau. Thos. J., gen., bap., bur. 14th Nov.

1670-1, Jan 20. Mary, d. Thos. J., of Nunnington, gen., bap., bur. 13 July, 1672.

1672. Richard, s. do., born 23rd, bap. 28th July, bur. Dec. 24, 1701. Mr. Richard J., of Nⁿ.

1674-5, Jan. 10. Thos., s. do., bap.

1678-9, Feb. 13. Mrs. Mary Jackson, wife of Thos. J., of Nunnington, gent., bur.

1702, July 8. Mr. Thomas Jackson of Nunnington bur. (all from Stonegrave).

On a marble monument in the nave of Stonegrave church, close to the door :

In this ile lyeth the body of Tho* Jackson of Nunnington in this parish, gent., with Mary his wife. He departed this life 7th July, 1702, aged 71. Mary his wife dyed 12th Feb^{ry} 1678, aged 42. They had issue eleven children, five sons and six daughters, Richard, Thomas, Reynold, Elizabeth, and three Marys, which all dyed young; Ann dyed 19th Jan^{ry} 1697, aged 27 ; Richard dyed 22^d Decr 1701, aged 29 ; Thomas dyed 6th July, 1737, aged 63, after being Town Clerk of London thirteen years, and was interred in the City at St. Lawrence Jury Church by his wife and son Thomas. He left an only daughter Dorothy, who was married to John Shaftoe, Esq., of Whitworth, in the Bishoprick of Durham.

Arms.

---

* 1702, May 31. M'ris Barbary Whitfield, of the Marishes in Thornton parish, bur. (Stonegrave).

† 1684, Dec. 4. William, the son of Tho* Comber, rector of Stonegrave, baptized. His Godfathers, Sr Edward Blacket, baronet, George Hicks, D.D., Dean of Worcester, his grandmother (*i.e.*, Mrs. Thornton) his Godmother.

1702-3, March 8. Mr. William Comber, of East Newton, bur. (Stonegrave.)

1702.　P^d the king's duty upon the buriall of Anne Lawson, 4*s.* P^d Isabell Lawson for the nursing of G. Lawson's child, the mother being dead, 1*l.* 4*s.*

—— June 3.　P^d Mr. West for the fee farm rent, 21*l.* 12*s.*　P^d Lawyer Barker for his opinion of the title, and drawing and ingrossing the deeds of purchase, 2*l.* 10*s.*　P^d Mr. Agar for writing a copy of the said deeds in the town book, 5*s.**

1704, Oct. 8.　Collected at Communion at Newton, 1*l.* 3*s.* 6*d.* ; of this M^d Thornton gave a guinea.

1705, Dec. 17.　Rec^d more of M^d Comber towards the purchase of the fee farm rent, 1*l.*

—— Oct. 13.　P^d towards the curing the sore heads of Tho. Lawson's 2 youngest children, 2*s.* 6*d.*

Given to John Westow towards binding his son an apprentice, 7*s.* 6*d.*

1707, Dec. 1.　Rec^d of Mr. Carleton, my Lord Preston's share of the fee farm rent for 2 years, 1*l.*

P. 125, n.　Lady Wharton was probably the daughter and heiress of Sir Rowland Wandesford.　See pedigree.

P. 142.　Mr. Luccock was probably William Lowcock, rector of Nunnington, instituted 5th April, 1658, buried 31 May, 1678; who may have been son of William Lowcock, and baptized at Old Malton, 5th February, 1616-17.

---

* The deed alluded to is as follows, as abstracted from the parish book :—

By indenture dated July 1, 1703, Lewis West, of the City of Yorke, esq., conveys to John Denton, of East Newton, clerk, Robert Denton, rector of Stonegrave, clerk, George Bowes, of East Newton, yeo.; John Hicks and Thos. Swann of Stonegrave, yeomen ; and Thos. Sunley of Westness, in consideration of the summe of 21*l.* 12s., a yearly fee farme rent of 18s. out of certain lands, etc., in Nunnington for the use of the poor of the parish of Stongrave.

Mr. West and Mr. Barker were well known York lawyers.　Mr. Agar was master of the endowed school at Nunnington.

1719, May 21, Mr. Ralph Agar of Nunnington, and Mrs. Mary Dixon of East Newton, spinster, by licence.　1720, July 14, Thos. s. Mr. Ralph A. of Nunnington, bap.　1720, Sept. 25, Edward s. ditto, bap.　1724, June 29, Ralph s. ditto, bap.　1726-7, Feb. 27, Richard s. ditto, bap.　1728-9, March 24, John s. ditto, bap.　1732, May 9, Mr. Ralph Agar of Nunnington bur. Uriah his son, bap. at the same time that his father was bury'd.　1734, June 23, John Agar, a child, son of Mr. Ralph Agar of Newton, schoolmaster, deceased, bur.　1756, Jan. 4, Mrs. Agar, relict of Mr. Ralph A. of Newton, bur. in church near her husband (Stonegrave).

P. 142, n., last line.   For *neice* read *niece*.

P. 143.   Mrs. Thornton's devoting her son from his birth, like Samuel, may be illustrated by the will of Rev. Stephen Arlush, 26 June, 1681 :—

·1681, June 26th.   Stephen Arlush, of Knedlington, an unworthy minister of the Gospel—the tuition of my son Nathaniel, till of age, to my brothers-in-law, my brother Elcock and my brother Taylor.   " It is my desire that my son be educated in the study of Divinity, to which I have dedicated him from his birth, if it please God to encline his minde to it, and to endow him with grace and guift fit for that imployment, which I heartily wish and hope for, though it be a profession now in contempt with many, yet I doe and alwaies have esteemed it to be of greate necessity, excellency," etc.

P. 154, n., line 5.   For 1699 read 1669.

In a letter from Dr. Comber to Abstrupus Danby, 7th March, 1676, we find him making the following allusion to his family : " As to my family, I can demonstrate my ancestors to have been gentlemen bearing arms of many descents, and I am allyed to some of the best familyes in Sussex; my neer relation, Dr. Comber, Master of Trinity Colledge, loosing £1,000 per an. for his loyalty to the late king; and it is well known that there is a gentleman of my name who hath been high sheriffe of Sussex, and is able to purchase all the estates the Danbys have left in England, to whom I am (by his own confession) so nearly allyed that I am in a faire possibilityes to be his heir as you are to get possession of Thorpe," etc.

P. 157.   Mr. Norcliffe states that Timothy Portington of New Malton, apothecary, was aged 38 in 1665.   Had a license to erect a pue in the church of St. Michael, 23rd March, 1658-9.   In 1671 he gave £1 to the repair of the old church at Malton.   Was a witness to Sir Hugh Cholmley's will, of Whitby, 28 Oct., 1688.   Married first, at St. Michael's, Malton, 11th June, 1654, Mary, daughter of Thomas Pye, and she was buried 18th Nov., 1654.   His second wife was Mary, daughter of Robert Ruddock, of Eddlethorpe grange ; she was buried at St. Michael's 12th Feb., 1661-2.   Her brother, Edward Ruddock, settled that estate on his niece and her issue female, 13th Nov., 1697, and dying 11th Oct. 1708, aged 57, was buried at Westow.   Mr. Portington's 3rd wife was Frances, dau. of Robert Thornton ; her marriage licence dated 3rd July, 1663 ; was buried at St. Michael's 11th March, 1704-5, having had a son baptized by the name of Timothy 17th Nov., 1664, and buried 18th April, 1665. In "1697, June . . . Mr Timothy Portington went to London to be cut for the stone, and dyed there June 26, and was buried at London." By his second wife before-named, Mr. Portington had a daughter and heir, Elizabeth Portington, baptized 8th Nov., 1661; married 30th Nov., 1680, to John Pierson, esq., of Raistrope. Mrs. Pierson lived at York, and died there. As a widow she was buried at St. Michael's, Malton, 23rd Nov., 1723. Their children, whose names follow, were all baptized at St. Michael's, Malton, viz., John Pierson of Rotherham, 1739; baptized 12th May, 1696. Edward Pierson of Raisthorpe, 1739; baptized 26th June, 1698; buried at Kirby Grindalyth, 9th Dec., 1752, having married at Wharram Percy, 26th June, 1740, Dorothy Greame. Portington Ruddock Pierson, baptized 31st Jan., 1694-5; was buried 8th July, 1695. Timothy Pierson, baptized 18th, and buried 30th June, 1697. Mary, living unmarried, 1737. Sarah, living 1723, married at Wharram Percy, 18th May, 1723, to John Pierson, esq., of Mowthorpe, who died s. p. 2nd May, 1737, aged 56. Elizabeth, baptized 9th Dec., 1692, living 1737 as wife of Nathaniel Wilson of York. Frances, baptized 16th July, 1700, lived at York till her marriage at Wharram Percy on 12th May, 1730, to Francis Pierson, esq., of Beverley and Mowthorpe, a major in the army, by whom she had, besides a daughter Margaret, Francis Pierson, Major of the 95th Regiment (*Gent. Mag.*, 1781, p. 42), who was killed at St. Helier's, Jersey, 6 Jan., 1781, part of whose epaulette is preserved at Langton Hall, Malton.

27th Nov., 1695. Timothy Portington, of New Malton, gen., Brother Henry P., 3[l] yearly for life. Sister Rachel 20[s]. Francis and Timothy P., sons of my brother Henry P., 20[s]. Poore of Elloughton 20[s]. Poore widdowes in New Malton, 30[s], etc. Brother in law Mr. Edward Ruddock, brother in law Mr. John Denton, Mr. William Mason, Sir W[m] Strickland, William Palmes, esq., and Christ[r] Percehay, esq., 20[s] each for a ring. To my wife a silver cup, which was me sonne Timothye's. Granddaughters Mary, Sara, and Eliz. Peirson, 100[l] each, Residue to dau. Eliz. P. She ex[x]. (*York Registry.*)

P. 163, last line but three. *Murderer* should probably be read *murderers.*

P. 173, line 20, n., Mr. Sinclair. Probably the Rev. Enoch Sinclair, sometime schoolmaster of Hedon, vicar of Owthorne 17th March, 1680-1; murdered, an aged man, 1706; discovered, 18th April, 1721; buried 23rd April, 1721. (See Poulson's *Holderness*, ii.)

Most likely he was a son of Mr. Enoch Sinclair, buried 15th Nov., 1678, at St. Leonard's, Malton, by his wife Anne . . . who was buried at the same place 14th April, 1666. George Sinclair, who was buried at St. Michael's, 11th April, 1694, married first, Drusilla . . . by whom a daughter, Isabella, baptized 13th April, 1673: secondly, Elizabeth . . . . buried at St. Leonard's, 18th Jan., 1680-1, by whom Bethiah, baptized 24th September, 1676; Elizabeth, baptized 22nd Feb., 1679-80. Samuel Sinclair, rector of Huggate, 1644-54, had a son named Benjamin. Mrs. Anne S., the widow or daughter of the former, married 20th July, 1654, Rev. James Browne, rector of Burnby.

P. 175. Cousin William Ascough. Qu. the same who died at York and buried at Thirkleby, 20th Nov., 1675.

P. 175, line 24. For 16*th* read 18*th*.

P. 175. Cousin Bullocke. Margaret Thornton, great aunt of Mr. William Thornton, who died 17th Sept., 1668, was wife of Lancelot Bullock of Holme. (Flower's *Visitation*.)

P. 175. Cousins Ralph and John Crathorne were Mrs. Thornton's nephews, æt. 24 and 26 at this time.

Cousin Edward Lassels does not appear in any pedigree known to me, but may be the " Mr. Edward Lassels buried at Belfrey, York, 22nd August, 1675."

P. 178. The lines beginning, " Leave me, O love," etc., are by Sir Philip Sidney. " Farewell, ye gilded follies," etc., are by Sir Henry Wotton. In the last line but seven, last word, an *s* has been omitted.

P. 183. Admon. to the effects of Christopher Wandesford of Dublin was granted at York, 6th August, 1642, to William Wandesford of London, merchant tailor, to the use of Chr., John, and Alice his children, together with their tuition.

P. 185, n., line 13. For *Raley* read *Raby*.

    ,,   ,,   12. For *Arabella* read *Arbella*.

    ,, It should be stated that the abstract of the will of Lord Deputy Wandesford, given in the note, was kindly furnished by the Rev. C. B. Norcliffe, who informs the editor that at one time, some years ago, he went to Dublin on purpose to make a search for this will, and that he had almost as much difficulty in finding it as Mrs. Thornton appears to have had.

Page 211. " Have a false quarter in them," etc. It is worth

noticing how very violent the dislike of the Scotch has always been in Yorkshire and the northern counties generally.

P. 216. Mr. Tullye's. 1682-3, Jan. 25, Mr. Humphrey Tully of Westnesse, gent., buried. (*Stonegrave*). The name is connected with Carlisle and other places in the north of England.

P. 219. n. Mr. Callis was ordained deacon by Thomas, Bishop of Durham, 1st March, 1639; priest 31st May, 1640; instituted *per com. Oliveri* 21st March, 1651; subscribed 15th August, 1662. He does not appear to have been buried at South Dalton. His wife Elizabeth was buried there 30th Oct., 1659. His successor was instituted 15th Nov., 1671.

P. 221, n. Mr. Thomas Comber of Newton-le-Willows, Lancashire, a descendant of the Dean, possesses an Armoury of the Nobility and Gentry of England, in Dean Comber's handwriting, which is probably the MS. referred to. It is evidently the production of an amateur who had more zeal than knowledge.

P. 231. Mr. Charles Man. Charles Man, A.B., Sidney Sussex College, Cambridge, ordained deacon by the Archbishop of York 25th Sept., 1664, and priest 3rd March, 1669-70. On 26th May, 1668, he was instituted to the rectory of Scawton, on the death of John Barnet, at the presentation of Viscount Emley; which he ceded when on January 18th, 1675-6, he was instituted to the rectory of Gilling at the presentation of Charles Lord Fairfax, Viscount Emley.

March 22nd, 1709-10. Charles Man, rector of Gilling. All to my dear son, and he sole ex^r, paying to my sister, Ann Man, 6*l*. per ann. for life, in testimony of my kindness to her, and care for her. I give the money in such a purse as I told my son of, to the poor, to be distributed according to his direction. Pr. 2nd May, 1710, and adm. to Charles Man, clerk, his son and ex^r. (*Reg. York.*)

1679, July 24th. Phillis uxor Caroli Man, rectoris ecclesiæ de Gilling sep.,—1710, sepultus Carolus Man, hujus parochiæ rector per annos triginta quatuor, anno ætatis 68, Martii 28°. (*Gilling Register.*)

1694, 23rd Dec. Charles Man, A.B., of Sidney Sussex College, ordained priest by Archbishop of York.

In the large catalogue of books printed for sale by John Hildyard of York in 1751 occur the following articles :—

6713. MSS. by the late Rev. Mr. Charles Mann, late rector of Gilling, 9 vols., 2*l*. 2s.

6714. Miscellaneous, and notes on several books, MSS. by the same author; wrote 1700, 2s.

6715. Fifteen MSS. by the last author's father, 1s.

P. 253. "My cousin Allan Ascough." Allan Ascough of Skewsby was aged 69, 11 Aug., 1666. (Visitation of Yorkshire, 1665. Surtees Society, p. 342.) He was third cousin to Mrs. Thornton's father, his great-grandfather William Ayscough of Cowling having married Jane, daughter and co-heir of John Fulthorpe, esq., of Hipswell, and Frances Wandesford, another daughter and co-heir, whom in his will he calls Anne. The families were related in another way as well.

P. 321, line 5, *dele* the words *next page*.

COPY.

(*Spelling modernized.*)

To all nobles and gentles, these present letters reading, hearing, or seeing, William Flower, *alias* Norroy Principal Herald and King of Arms of the north, east, and west parts of this realm of England, from the river of Trent northwards, sendeth due and humble commendations and greeting. Equity willeth and reason ordaineth, that men virtuous and of noble courage be by their merits and good renown rewarded; not only their persons in this mortal life, so brief and transitory, but also after them those that shall be of their bodies descended, to be in all places of honor, with others renowned, accepted, and taken by certain ensigns and demonstrances of honor and noblesse, that is to say, blazon, helm and timber, to the end that by their examples others may enforce themselves to use their days in feats of arms and works virtuous to get the renown of ancient noblesse in their lives and posterities. And whereas Robert Thornton, of East Newton, esquire, of long time hath borne arms, and, not being certain of his crest, hath required me, the said Norroy King of Arms, to assign unto him his said crest unto these his old ancient arms, as of long time hath been accustomed. In consideration whereof I, the said Norroy King of Arms, by virtue, authority, and power annexed, assigned, given and granted to me, and to my office of Norroy King of Arms, by express words under the most noble great seal, have given unto the said Robert Thornton, esquire, and to his posterity, a crest due to be borne; that is to say, on a torse argent and sable, a lion's head razed purple, about his neck a crown argent, as more plainly appeareth depicted in this margin.   To have and to hold the said crest to the said Robert Thornton, esquire, and to his posterity, to use and enjoy for evermore.   In witness whereof I, the said Norroy King of Arms, as aforesaid, have signed these presents with my hand, and set thereunto the seal of my arms, with the seal of my office of Norroy King of Arms.   Dated at East Newton aforesaid, the fourth day of October, in the fifth year of the reign of our Sovereign Lady Elizabeth, by the grace of God Queen of England, France, and Ireland, Defender of the Faith, and in the year of our Lord God a thousand five hundred threescore and three.

(Signed)   MOY WILLIAM FLOWER,
alias Norroy Roy d'Armes.
Allowed, ratified, and confirmed by me,
Richard St. George, Norroy King of
Arms, in the Visitation taken by me in
Anno. 1612.

Seen and allowed, 12th Sept.,
    1665, by me,
        WILLIAM DUGDALE,
            Norroy King of Arms.

From the original in the possession of John Thornton, esq., 7 Onslow Gardens, London.   Cf. Tonge's *Visitation of Yorkshire*, Appendix xl., xli.

INDEX OF PERSONS.

INDEX OF PLACES.

A

Ackworth, 322.
Alding Grange, 332.
Aldby, 152 *n*, 343.
Allerthorp, 323.
Ampleford, 85 *n*, 329, 352.
Antwerp, 275 *n*.
Appleton-le-Street, 152 *n*, 265 *n*.
Arden, 236 *n*.
Armin, 47 *n*.
Aske, 65 *n*, 125.
Awdby, 349.

B

Bagby, 325.
Basygham, 313.
Baths, The, 15.
Batley, 274 *n*.
Bedale, 3 *n*, 38 *n*, 40, 43, 105, 108 *n*, 117 *n*, 189 *n*, 224, 322.
Beeding Priory, 303 *n*.
Beeford, 228 *n*.
Beverley, 84 *n*, 293 *n*, 339, 356.
Bilsthorpe, 295.
Billingham, 331.
Bishop-Wilton, 63 *n*, 288.
Bolden, 303 *n*, 344.
Bossall, 152 *n*.
Braithwaite, 330.
Brandsby, 148 *n*, 149 *n*, 213, 328.
Bristol, 13, 15.
Brompton-upon-Swale, 65 *n*, 323, 324.
Brough, 116 *n*.
Bucks Co., 347.
Burnby, 357.
Burne-Park, 80, 84 *n*, 181, 182, 280.
Burneston, 117 *n*.
Burton-Constable, 68 *n*.
Buttercrambe, 63 *n*, 82 *n*, 84 *n*, 85, 114 *n*, 214.
Bynchester, 316.

C

Callis, 100.
Cambridge, 22 *n*, 105, 161, 162, 163, 191, 219, 269, 303, 349, 350, 358.
Cambridgeshire, 100.
Carleton, 329.
Carlisle, 358.
Castlecomer, 114 *n*, 183 *n*, 185 *n*, 186.
Catterick, 43 *n*, 58, 67, 91, 92, 95, 96, 116, 117, 185 *n*, 316.
Catherine Hall, Camb., 350.
Cave, 41.
Cheshire, 345.
Cheshunt, 108 *n*.
Chester, 31, 32, 33, 36, 37, 74, 105, 187, 281, 345, 346.
Chester, Co., 27 *n*, 32 *n*, 345.
Chevet, 54 *n*.
Chopwell, 55.
Christ Church, Dublin, 25, 39 *n*.
Christ's College, Camb., 105, 161 *n*.
Clapham, 318.
Clare Hall, Camb., 349.
Clifton Ings, 331.
Clints, 40 *n*.
Clitheroe, 37 *n*.
Clowbeck, 2 *n*, 5 *n*.
Clytheroe, 321.
Colburne, 63 *n*.
Copgrove, 94 *n*.
Cottingham, 80, 214 *n*.
Cowling, 359.
Craike, 295 *n*.
Crakehall, 314.
Cranford, 346.
Crathorne, 84 *n*, 214, 98 *n*.
Crookhill, 323.
Cuerdale, 38 *n*.

D

Dales, The, 61 *n*.
Dalton, South, 219 *n*, 358.

B B